NO LOVE LOST

Rachel Ingalls was born in Boston in 1940. She dropped out of school and spent time in Germany before studying at Radcliffe College. She moved to Britain in 1965 where she lived for the rest of her life. Over half a century Ingalls wrote eleven celebrated story collections and novellas, all published by Faber. Her debut, *Theft* (1970), won the Authors' Club Best First Novel Award. In 1986 – to her surprise – her 1982 novella, *Mrs Caliban*, was named by the British Book Marketing Council as one of the greatest American novels since World War II alongside titles by Toni Morrison, Philip Roth, John Updike and Thomas Pynchon. Ingalls died in 2019 in London.

Patricia Lockwood is the author of four books. Her novel *No One Is Talking About This* (2021) was an international bestseller, finalist for the Booker Prize and the Women's Prize for Fiction and was translated into twenty languages. Her memoir *Priestdaddy* (2017) won the Thurber Prize for American Humour and was named one of the *Guardian*'s 100 best books of the twenty-first century. Lockwood is also the author of two poetry collections, *Motherland Fatherland Homelandsexuals* (2014) and *Balloon Pop Outlaw Black* (2012). Her writing has appeared in the *New York Times*, the *New Yorker* and the *London Review of Books*, where she is a contributing editor. She lives in Savannah, Georgia.

Praise for *Mrs Caliban*:

'Perfect.' **Max Porter**

'Disturbing but seductive.' **Margaret Atwood**

'Still outpaces, out-weirds and out-romances anything today.' **Marlon James**

'A broadcast from a stranger and more dazzling dimension.' **Patricia Lockwood**

'So curiously right, so romantically obverse, that it creates its own terrible, brilliant reality.' **Sarah Hall**

'A feminist masterpiece: tender, erotic, singular.' **Carmen Maria Machado**

'So deft and austere in its prose, so drolly casual in its fantasy . . . An impeccable parable, beautifully written.' **John Updike**

'Astonishing . . . *Mrs Caliban* has the melancholy, bittersweet air of a romance that has come to no significant resolution.' **Joyce Carol Oates**

'Ingalls's great gift for language and time keeps you hooked on the end of her line and she reels in the story like an expert fly fisherman.' **Melvyn Bragg**

'Genius . . . Like *Revolutionary Road* written by Franz Kafka . . . Exquisite.' *The Times*

by the same author

THEFT
THE MAN WHO WAS LEFT BEHIND AND OTHER STORIES
MRS CALIBAN
BINSTEAD'S SAFARI
THREE OF A KIND
THE PEARLKILLERS
THE END OF TRAGEDY
FOUR STORIES
DAYS LIKE TODAY
TIMES LIKE THESE
BLACK DIAMOND

Rachel Ingalls

NO LOVE LOST

Selected Novellas

with a foreword by

PATRICIA LOCKWOOD

faber

This selection first published in 2023
by Faber & Faber Ltd
Bloomsbury House, 74–77 Great Russell Street,
London, WC1B 3DA
This paperback edition first published in 2023

Typeset by Typo•glyphix, Burton-on-Trent, DE14 3HE
Printed and bound by CPI Group (UK) Ltd, Croydon, CR0 4YY

All rights reserved
© Rachel Ingalls, 1970, 1974, 1985, 1986, 1987, 2002, 2023
Foreword © Patricia Lockwood, 2023

The right of Rachel Ingalls to be identified as author
of this work has been asserted in accordance with Section 77
of the Copyright, Designs and Patents Act 1988

This book is a work of fiction. Any references to historical events, real people, or real places are used fictitiously. Other names, characters, places, and events are products of the author's imagination, and any resemblance to actual events or places or persons, living or dead, is entirely coincidental.

A CIP record for this book
is available from the British Library

ISBN 978–0–571–37658–2

Printed and bound in the UK on FSC paper in line with our continuing commitment to ethical business practices, sustainability and the environment.
For further information see faber.co.uk/environmental-policy

2 4 6 8 10 9 7 5 3 1

Contents

Foreword
by Patricia Lockwood

In the past, in order to read Rachel Ingalls, you had to be a collector. My particular prize was a copy of *The Pearlkillers* purchased in Key West with the promotional materials still inside. I spotted it on a high shelf as a woman's voice came incongruously in my ear, 'And then my co-worker said, "Say, did you and your husband ever try *roleplay*?"' That was her kind of line, I thought, tossed off by a background character at a dinner party that is about to turn strange, as I flipped over the postcard to read, 'We thought you might want to share your thoughts on Rachel Ingalls' magical novellas with a friend.' This struck me as funny. Who would be there to receive it, I wondered, if I finally filled it out and mailed it?

If you know Rachel Ingalls, you probably know her for *Mrs Caliban*, in which a grief-stricken, unhappily married woman named Dorothy falls in love with a six-foot-seven-inch frogman recently escaped from the Institute for Oceanographic Research. He has been so heavily experimented upon that just about the first thing he does is pop a boner for her, though maybe this is testament to her desirability – we want to believe it is, that she is God's ripest avocado for him. Or perhaps you know her for *Binstead's Safari*, recently re-released by New Directions, in which an unfulfilled housewife named Millie goes on safari with her anthropologist husband and finds herself blooming, in love and being invoked in songs about the lion god and his lion bride. On the strength of these two novels, there has been a manful attempt to expand her audience to readers of cryptid pornography, which hasn't been entirely successful. (*Binstead's Safari* also includes group sex in a balloon, another possible untapped market.) But none of our efforts have been entirely successful, have they? A dozen abject introductions have been written – read her, we beg, rescue her, as if she is one of her own inert female figures. I am here to say, however, that we are dealing with a freak, who never needed us at all, who does not need us now. We are the unimaginative husbands, and she left us long ago for someone bigger, better, glorious.

The eight stories collected here, varying between thirty-three and eighty-eight pages, are evidence of a call in the night. No one wants novellas, or suggests that you write one, or lights up when you tell them you have an idea for a 117-page story. They are things, outcast forms like the creatures who call to her women through windows, creeping, caught between two worlds. In an interview with the *New York Times* in 1986 – one of the years of her revivification, when the British Book Marketing Council named *Mrs Caliban* one of the twenty best American post-war novels – she gave a quote that has been invoked in almost every consideration of her writing since, regarding its 'odd, unsaleable length'. She said, too, that she only ever once got royalties; one imagines her getting a cheque for a cool $49, one for every page.

She was born in Cambridge, Massachusetts, in 1940. Her father was an eminent scholar of Sanskrit at Harvard – this is a little funny, in one of her stories it would be funny – and her mother kept house, which in one of her stories would be treated as a matter of seriousness, even possible peril. She dropped out of high school when she was seventeen and spent two years in Germany, first living with a family and then auditing classes at various universities, then returned to the US and graduated from Radcliffe in 1964. Her 2019 obituary in *The Times* contains a correction that she 'did not graduate cum laude', which would also be funny in one of her stories. That very same year, in the grip of an idea, she did something . . . quite extraordinary, really, but we will come back to that later.

A Rachel Ingalls story unspools something like one of Isak Dinesen's fireside tales, mixed with a B-movie. It happens in some country in between England and America, the speech a little stilted, fallen out of its time. Even if the streets are familiar, we see them through the eyes of someone in the witness protection programme. Or else the characters are on a journey – after long years of a death-in-life marriage, they walk under green trees or among white ruins, now on one continent, now on another. And every so often someone says something like, 'Say, did you and your husband ever try *roleplay*?'

Not quite like this, not exactly like that. The seductions are like Angela Carter's, if she wrote in very plain language and did not know who Croesus was. The mood, particularly in the travel stories, is like Daphne du Maurier's – a story like 'I See a Long Journey' could be set against 'Don't Look Now'; those like 'Inheritance' and 'Friends in the Country' could lie side by side with 'Monte Verità'. The humour is something like Muriel Spark, as is her willingness to suddenly set her characters on fire. 'If she were writing Lorrie Moore's stories,' I wrote in my notebook, 'all the husbands would die.' But I think she does not sound like other people because she is playing an entirely different game.

Better not to know too much about them, maybe. And best not to check how long they are before you begin, so that their real feeling can steal upon you gradually, like the feeling of not being able to run in a dream. In a favourite story of mine, 'Friends in the Country', Lisa and her uninspiring lover, Jim (no one in Ingalls' universe is ever a boyfriend, really), arrive at a country house, and it becomes clear over the course of the night, after a dinner of thick tarry wine and a stew of what might contain ears, that they will not be allowed to leave. Why? Well, there's the fog, and the fact that it's the toads' breeding season, and then of course, Henry Kissinger is supposed to show up tomorrow. 'Norman Mailer was here last weekend,' one of the other guests tells them. 'He talked for hours about glands.' Alone in their guest bedroom, Jim and Lisa question whether they know these people at all. 'I mean, maybe we took the wrong road. Are you sure they're the right people? That sign we passed: the one that had a name on it – that isn't their name, is it?'

Or maybe you do know them – maybe, as in 'Inheritance', they are the family you've never met. After her divorce and the death of her grandmother, Carla travels to meet her decayed, cobwebbed great-aunts Gisela, Gerda and Ursula. There is something off about them – they seem obsessed with lineage, and they just keep repeating 'We are German' as a sort of code, like American political candidates. The family's holdings are vast, they tell her, and the family flaw is . . . well. She'll see for herself, soon enough. In a matter of days, Carla finds herself caught up in an affair with Carl, a man obscurely connected to her aunts and who, it appears to Carla, 'could be driven to frenzy by the idea of large stretches of saleable land'. He takes her to visit the family estate in South America, where everyone looks curiously alike, servants and masters, and where the whole place seems to have been holding its breath for her. The pace of 'Inheritance' is almost too perfect – again we are in a dream, stalked by something inhumanly patient. The story is slowly sewn on Carla's body like a wedding dress, and though we are given enough information to know what's coming, still it leaps upon us in the end.

Perhaps the supernatural quality in her work is this inhuman patience. She will lie in wait forever for us, for the characters; she has all the 'odd, unsaleable length' in the world. In 'Something to Write Home About', a more conventionally plotted story with a more delicate touch, John and Amy Larsen are on a tour of the Greek isles. The year is 1965 (one of the tourists they encounter is reading *Fanny Hill*), and they've been married for eighteen months; she recently graduated with a degree in English. This happens, and that happens; they go here, and they go there, and all seems in order except that Amy cannot stop compulsively buying postcards, filling them out, mailing them. At one point, as she writes, her hair drawn over her face so that passing soldiers stare at her, John squeezes her shoulders and assures her, 'It isn't inherited, Amy.' But Amy, compelled to share in the unspooling of the story, keeps writing. Share your thoughts on Rachel Ingalls' magical novellas with a friend!

Here and there she pinches time together or performs some other artful fold. 'No Love Lost' compresses a whole imagined wartime – the conflicts leading up to it, the clash itself, the stripped and brazen ingenuity that follows – into seventy pages, while still ultimately revolving around a two-person dance of domesticity at the centre. Mostly, though, she trusts in the power of pure sequence. The radio always on in the background is the greed for a baser (and more basic) narrative, splashes of gore, *Twilight Zone* music, here and there a snatch of opera. What plays behind everything are the twists, the turns, the possibilities that your husband might die in that car crash, might be cheating on you with your best friend, the family curse might be on you. And we will believe what happens because it is what comes next.

The most powerful force here is *whim*. A novella like *Mrs Caliban* might have been planned from page to page; here is the monster, here the romance, here the grand reveal. But the movement of other stories is tricksy and offhand and discovered, as if you are encountering the same surprises she did as you go. This movement requires strange lengths; it requires you to walk on, stumble, be misled – even, for certain intervals, to be lulled almost into sleep. This is a little boring, isn't it, you ask, thirty pages into 'Theft', as the day of the beginning darkens into night, and then all at once it becomes the least boring story in the history of the world. This happens again and again. You are lured on, past the point where you could find your way back, and finally you are not even convinced the whim is hers – the same voice is calling you both. Go on a little further, says the voice. Come this way.

The whim called her on. It called her to London in the summer of 1964, to celebrate Shakespeare's quadricentennial; she wished 'to see and hear his plays as close to the source as possible' – the source, one assumes, being Shakespeare's actual mouth. Upon reaching her destination, she decided to move there. That is not a sane decision, it has the logic of poetry. 'I was dead on my feet for years,' Millie tells her husband, Stan, in *Binstead's Safari*. 'I didn't wake up till London.'

'How did London wake you up?'

'Well, I've been talking my head off about it to anyone who'd listen. *Romeo and Juliet*. Covent Garden. Et cetera.'

The great pleasure of a reading life is to be in another mind as it works. You are with Shakespeare as he has those ideas, comes on those turns, uses words for the first time, invents the name Miranda. But to give yourself physically to him as a gift, on the occasion of his 400th birthday, is a split-second decision of the body. She was swept up, off her feet. Et cetera.

One thing that recurs again and again in her stories is that someone suddenly becomes wonderful. In *Binstead's Safari*, it is Millie, drowned in domesticity, who 'fended off an induced crack-up for many years'. But after her illumination in London, on safari, she flares out like a match. 'Strength had come back into her, and just as suddenly as this: the sun rose and everything was different. It hadn't ever been this way before, not during the years of her marriage, nor before that, when she'd lived at home with her family. Only now. Nothing threatened her. She had found her life.'

In 'Blessed Art Thou', it is Ambrose, a monk who gets pregnant after a mystical encounter with the angel Gabriel. He turns sulky and beautiful and very, very funny. '"You weren't chosen," he sneered. "I was. And", he said defiantly, "his skin was like honey."' The other monks gather in a circle of worship around him: one dresses his hair every day, the others offer to bring him pickles, smoked mackerel, watermelon. One day he undoes his robe in front of them and reveals 'the full, cup-shaped breasts of which he was now immensely proud. There was a silence until he started to pull the robe together again.

"Wait," Dominic said, and William begged, "Not yet. I haven't finished looking."'

Ambrose is like her other heroines to whom love comes as a late transforming light. This arriving love – which the heroines never had in their teens or twenties – turns them almost into children again, wide-eyed, noticing everything. Their bodies, which had previously gone to waste, are now put to proper use. When Gabriel appears to Ambrose, he 'seemed to be shedding light from his nakedness into all parts of the room.' It is the same place, but now he can really see it. In *Mrs Caliban*, the day-to-day life Dorothy lives with Larry is not so different – it is still a domestic, quiet, fundamentally suburban life, their midnight trips to the beach notwithstanding. They make spaghetti and salads, listen to the radio, move between the same rooms of the same house. But now it is the right life because he is there.

There is a physical readiness in her people that is startling; let the right one show up, and they will walk out of their lives on the instant; they will leave children, houses, whole continents without ever looking back. Even if the love can never be consummated, they will go on in a kind of violent willingness, years and years, to the end of the line. In 'I See a Long Journey', a woman on a trip with her husband makes a pilgrimage to a child goddess, not really believing, of course, and ends up confessing to her. 'She began, "I don't know what to do. Year after year. My life is useless. I have everything, nothing to want. Kind husband, wonderful children. I feel ashamed to be ungrateful, but it never was what . . . it never seemed like mine. It's as if I'd never had my own self. But there's one thing: a man. He's the only one who isn't corrupted, the only one I can rely on. I think about him all the time. I can't stop. I can't stand the idea that we'll never be together. He's only a servant. And I don't know what to do. I love him so much." She ended on a sob and was silent.'

A man. The word shines in her writing the way the word 'shop' does: a place to walk into, spin around till your skirt flares and at last get everything you want. The stories are so hetero-sexual that they almost become gay. In 'In the Act', the 'right one' is not the gigolo that Helen's husband Edgar reluctantly builds her – after she discovers the sex doll he has been building in the attic, makes off with it and stows it in a locker at the bus station. 'Auto', as she calls him, is not what she wants at all, not even after he has been reprogrammed to teach her Italian and flower painting and intermediate cordon bleu. What she wants might be the common thief, named *Ron*, who shows up with Edgar's original invention Dolly, hoping she can be repaired. Helen tells her husband frankly that Ron is 'more the kind of thing I had in mind.'

"What?"

"To wind up and go to bed with. That man there."'

'Theft', her first published work, won the Author's Club First Novel Prize in 1970; one imagines the jury looking around at each other, shrugging, and saying, 'I guess that's what this is.' She lets herself go physically in 'Theft' in a way that she never really does again. There is a capacity for ecstasy – wide, rushing, roaring – that is later diverted into a subterranean current, only breaching occasionally in a phrase, a sentence. In 'Theft', a man named Seth is locked in a curiously archaic prison for the crime of stealing a loaf of bread. His cellmate is his brother-in-law, Jake, who seems to be a political prisoner, and the one guarding them is a near-mythical Greek figure named Homer. 'Later on Homer came in. He gave me the pot and some water and came back again a spell later and stayed to talk. He told us all kinds of stories from all over the world and had us both laughing [. . .] There was just one time where I suddenly felt bad, when Homer was in the middle of a story and I wondered if they were all his or whether he'd collected some of them from the men he'd been in charge of and if maybe some of those men had been put to death.' Before the men are led to their own execution, Homer gives Seth a handful of leaves to chew. This is an old trick and a good one, as reliable as a high fever. Seth's intoxication will lift us into the air with him, it will make the story a story, and it will give us the first of her great lovers: tall, blue, unsuitable.

'I was looking at the sky. I saw it and I knew it as no man ever saw it before, looking into the heart of it, as no other man will ever know it.

I'd never noticed before just how it is, how it is a face that looks back and looks with love, and is arms that open for you. How sweet and calm it is. How blue. How it is lovely beyond belief and goes flying away into farther than can be known. And it goes on like that, on and on. Forever and ever. Without end.' A figure, a form and arms open for you. Let yourself be loved by the strange thing, and lie down with its voice in your ear.

This is instructive. Are you living the right life? Is it strange, is it rich, is it surprising? I think of a lesser-known story (not included here) first published in *The End of Tragedy*. In 'An Artist's Life', we are introduced to Axel, who has always dreamed of being an artist but feels 'that in putting the paint on the canvas he had been responsible for adding to the ugliness in the world'. Instead, he lives a small part of his friend Eino's life, who shrugs and paints what he wants without worrying that the French will always do it better. But Axel, though he hears the call, lacks the courage to live inside his 'dismal, misshapen daubs'.

One night, consumptive, dissipated, disgraced, he dreams of standing at the entrance to a room where people are talking and laughing and of a host who beckons Axel to sit next to him at the head of the table. 'His host then took up a decanter and poured out wine into a glass, which he handed to Axel. But Axel saw that the decanter had been emptied; he was the only one at the table who had any wine. He thought it would be rude to let the others go without anything. So he handed the glass back, in order that some of the wine could be given to the rest of the company. His host smiled, accepted the glass again, and, instead of doing what Axel had expected, turned to the sideboard nearby and set the glass there, where it remained throughout the course of the dinner.'

This is a characteristic Ingalls scene: the room echoes, the people are faceless, everything is *almost* normal, and yet somehow it has the power to follow you into your sleep. In the morning, Axel coughs blood. Tossing with fever, nearing the end, he 'remembered his dream about the host who had offered him the glass of wine. And suddenly he realized the meaning of it: the host was God and he had given Axel the full glass that he was meant to drink. It couldn't be distributed among any of the other guests because it was intended for him alone. It had been the life he was supposed to live. And when he had refused it, it had to go unused by anyone.'

Life. This is the other word that shines in her: another one where you can walk inside, turn around – drop out of high school, move to England to marry Shakespeare – take what you want if you dare. 'And he knew that – as he had once hoped – his life had indeed been picked out, from the beginning, to be the life of an artist, which wasn't like the life of other men. An artist's life was his work.'

I will not say that her life was her work. I will say that *my* life is my work, and part of it has been to read her – to be in the mind as it twists and turns, to follow the call as she heard it. A measure of fame came to her late, and she enjoyed it, but I doubt she would have wanted it sooner. Before it arrived, she was most often called 'neglected', as if she were a housewife in curlers and pearls. A better word might have been evasive. There is a sense in which she escaped us, to keep doing exactly what she wanted: listening to that radio, buying alligator pears with the grocery money, falling asleep in long green arms in the middle of the afternoon. Et cetera. Consider her called to be loved by the strange form of the novella, six feet seven inches tall, in frogskin, with a voice you would know anywhere.

Blessed Art Thou

Brother Anselm had come into the chapel early. He seemed to want to confess. Brother Francis had gone to the confessional and waited, but nothing had happened. When he'd come out to look, Anselm was in the covered archway, pacing to and fro; he was making vestigial, instantly repressed explanatory gestures in the air and occasionally he'd turn his head towards the square of green grass beyond the stone pillars, though he didn't appear to be taking it in.

Francis became interested. It was rare to see such signs of distress in a brother; ever since the new permissiveness, most people had become too good at dissembling. His friend, Frederick, who ran the place, had clamped down so hard on all unusual behaviour that from being a recently liberated enclosed order they had become practically suffocated by stricture. And this reaction against licence had actually forced them into a departure from tradition. Francis realized that. He would never have said so to Frederick. Their monastery was definitely a one-man show. It always had been and remained so even now, when Frederick was only the acting head. At times Francis thought of himself as the First Mate and of Brother Adrian as the Second Mate. Frederick stood indisputably at the helm.

Francis and Frederick had been through so much together that they were like old soldiers; each had sustained the other through more than one crisis of faith. They could speak their doubts and not have the words taken the wrong way. They knew their faults and still liked each other. Neither one of them was so sure that they liked Brother Adrian very much, though they certainly knew his faults, too. Brother Adrian was short, meaty, red-faced and opinionated. He was sometimes right, but, right or wrong, always at loggerheads with Frederick, who was a tall, elegant, ironic man often prone to outbursts of ferocious rudeness, bad temper and bigotry. Brother Francis was the peacemaker. He recognized the important fact that both men had faith. He knew in his heart that that would overcome all obstacles.

But there was no doubt that for the past four years life had been monotonous in the order: dull and without flavour. He had even heard young Brother William say to his friend, Elmo, that violence was not necessarily to be deprecated, as sometimes it 'cleared the air', a sentiment for which he had been reprimanded. And when the rebuke had been administered, the boy had made everyone gasp by asking, 'Is Brother Francis going to be censured for eavesdropping?' That was the last scandal they had had – two months ago. All wounded feelings had now healed. William had even admitted that he had been more or less shouting at the time. And life had returned to the uneventful rules and routines. So, it was intriguing to see Anselm displaying such uncustomary agitation.

Francis watched for a while without showing himself. He was pretty sure that Anselm wouldn't go away until he'd made some kind of decision. He began to feel more and more curious as he watched.

He was patient. He knew that Anselm was a serious young man who liked to think things over for a long time before committing himself to an opinion. His faith was divided; his approach to God was intellectual and therefore in constant danger of attack by itself. He was twenty-seven, had dark hair and dark eyes, and was nice-looking but nervy. He sometimes talked too fast. When he had the feeling that he wasn't getting through to people, or that his ideas would escape if he didn't put them into words – it was like a panic, he'd said to Francis: there was always a right moment, and you could miss it.

The order was fortunate in having so many young men. Elmo and William were in their early twenties, James and Duncan in their thirties. Just at the time when the young ones had rushed from the open doors of other monasteries, theirs had received recruits. Frederick had said sourly that there would always be some who found relief in seeking out suffering for a while. But their young ones had stayed. They hadn't all had an easy time. Francis had felt so sorry for them that in his own recurrent crises of faith they had nearly caused him to despair. There had been one terrible, long night when he'd been roaring drunk, saying it was a crime to inflict mental torture on the young; Frederick had had to hold his head while he was sick.

*

Anselm stalked past the stone columns, the green wedges of grass showing between. 'Father,' he muttered, 'I have . . . that is to say, you aren't going to believe this, but . . .'

At last he came to a stop and sat down with his back against one of the pillars. He longed for a cigarette, but he'd given them up six years before. He shut his eyes, opened them again on the picture of stone archways, grey skies and grass, and sighed.

It had been just like this, but a wonderful day, not overcast like today: a time taken out of a milder season – springlike, marvellously full of sunshine, the sky blue as if enamelled, the air warm. And he was on the other side of the building, just like this, when he wasn't supposed to be – he'd just skipped his duties and routines and thought somebody could go ahead and report him: he didn't care. And nobody had reported him, either, which was also strange, but of course it was nothing compared to what was to come, because – he was looking out, like this, into the warm, grassy courtyard and when he'd lifted his face to the bright air there had been a loud, rapid fluttering sound, a heavy thump, and there in front of him on the expanse of green was a handsome young man, stark naked and smiling. Behind him, quivering and drawing themselves inward, were two large wings made of what appeared to be golden feathers. As Anselm watched, they pleated together and disappeared, leaving – so he was later to discover – no bodily trace on their owner. The young man looked right at him. He was still smiling. He took a step forward and held his arms out.

Anselm knew straight away that this was the friend he'd been hoping for all his life. He had made a mistake to think that he could look deep into his own spirit and find a new and better self; the elusive other self was already inhabiting someone else. Only by loving another person did you find that part of yourself.

He moved forward, opening his own arms, falling into the waiting embrace. The young man kissed him on the cheek, on the neck, on the mouth; hugged him, stroked and patted him lightly, and started to undo his clothes. Anselm was fairly certain that there was no one around at the moment, but there might be one other person who, like him, had decided not to do what he'd been ordered to that day; so he told the young man, breathlessly, that they'd better go to his cell. He pulled him quickly across the sunny grass, into the dark stone archways and corridors, to his tiny room. He closed the door.

The young man removed the rest of Anselm's clothes and fell on the bed with him. He seemed to be shedding light from his nakedness into all parts of the room. Anselm could hardly breathe. Her knew what was happening but he couldn't quite connect it with anything else. He supposed it was really only the kind of thing he'd been warned about all his childhood: they tried to do it to you in washrooms, everyone had told him. And the Church frowned on it. Of course he'd somehow suspected it must be fun, otherwise people wouldn't be so much against it, but all the same, he wasn't prepared for this: to be touched all over, lovingly and thoroughly, in every kind of way, as he'd always – though he knew it was wicked – dreamed it would be like to make love. He was very nervous, but he was overjoyed.

He kept his head enough to ask the man's name afterwards. 'Gabriel,' his friend told him. Anselm fell asleep in his arms. When he woke, Gabriel had gone.

Anselm got up and dressed, walked back to the courtyard and looked around. He thought he could detect some indentations in the grass that might have been made by the pressure of the angel's feet as he'd taken off.

He expected Gabriel to meet him at the same hour the next day. He rushed to the place long before it was time and waited, his eyes devouring every inch of his surroundings in an excess of anticipation. But Gabriel didn't return.

Anselm waited the next day too, and was again disappointed. He began to feel desperate. He couldn't eat. He didn't think he was going to be able to live through the next day. But he still believed that Gabriel would come back.

Three different people criticized him for neglecting his duties. Although usually he was so overly diligent that he'd have been thrown into consternation by any expression of disapprobation, now he really didn't mind. Waiting for Gabriel was more important. He actually told the most persistent of his critics to shut up and mind his own business.

By the end of the week he knew that it was over. Gabriel wasn't going to come back. It had been a single visitation: not to be repeated.

He realized that he had never before known what it was to suffer. The pain of trying to accept the loss of love was too much for him. He felt himself beginning to break up, to become confused; he couldn't remember things, he couldn't keep his attention on anyone. He had to talk to somebody.

The only person he could think of was Brother Francis, who was usually understanding and kind, and got along with everyone.

He should go to Brother Francis and confess. He knew that; he was ready to do it. Not until he was outside the chapel did it strike him that it wasn't going to be that easy to begin. He worked himself into such a state that by the time he finally entered, his head was down and his arms hanging. He shuffled towards the confessional.

Francis nipped in at the other end.

Anselm stared into the darkness and sighed. He said, 'I don't know how to put it.'

'It's all right, Anselm,' Francis told him. 'Just make a beginning somewhere. Have you sinned?'

'And how.'

'I beg your pardon?'

'All over,' Anselm babbled, 'kissing and touching – it was wonderful, lovely. It was so delightful, and I know it's a sin, but it's the only truly magical thing that's ever happened to me – right out of this world. I'm not sorry about it. All I can think of is how much I want it to happen again. But every time I go there and wait for him, I know it's the end; he isn't comimg back. And I can't stand it. I just don't know what to do now. It's so lonely. It's killing me, Francis. What am I going to do?'

'Anselm, you know we're supposed to give up all – all – all that sort of thing.'

'I didn't have to give it up – I never had it. No, never before. And maybe they're right about the other kind; I don't know. But this was wonderful. The feeling of joy – and it didn't leave me afterwards. It grew. I felt transformed. I knew I should confess it, but it was like a secret he'd trusted me with. And after all, he takes precedence, doesn't he?'

Brother Francis forgot the rules. 'This is appalling,' he said.

'The only really sublime, magnificent thing that's ever happened to me. An angel – an angel from heaven, coming down to earth. But now he's gone, I feel so sad. I miss him. I can't tell you how much I – all day long, all the time, all . . .' Anselm started to cry.

Francis knew that he shouldn't say anything more without consulting someone, but he couldn't remain silent while his fellow man suffered. 'It's all right,' he said. He got up from his seat, went around to haul Anselm out into the light, and made him sit down in one of the pews. Anselm leaned forward, his head against his hands and his hands gripping the edge of the pew in front of him. Francis patted him on the back and repeated that it was all right. 'Who did you say this other young man was?' he asked.

'Gabriel.'

'I can't recall a Brother Gabriel in the order.'

'He's an angel. I told you. He came – he just landed, and folded up his wings.'

'Wings?'

'I still remember the joyfulness, but how can anything be the same again? It was amazing the way he appeared, out of nowhere. And now ordinary life isn't any good. It feels unliveable.'

'Wings?' Francis said again.

'Golden wings. The real thing.' Anselm's voice sounded choked and tearful. He slumped forward on to the floor. He seemed to have fainted. Francis pulled him up. He told him to go back to his cell and lie down, and that he'd send Duncan to him.

'I don't need a doctor,' Anselm said, but he went back to his cell obediently, lay down and fell asleep.

*

Francis was worried. He went to see Frederick. 'I think something's wrong with Anselm,' he said, and told him the story.

'Should you be telling me this?' Frederick asked.

'Consider it a confession. I don't know what to do.'

'That's simple. We find the joker and throw him out.'

'Who?'

'The gardener's boy? Damn it, you can't tell about anyone any more. He looked perfectly harmless to me. A little drip that could barely put one foot in front of the other.'

'Exactly. Definitely not the type. Not like the last one.'

'Yes, well. A heavy drinker, but marvellous with the bulbs. I suppose we'd better just wait till Anselm pulls himself together.'

'He said it was an angel. With wings. Golden wings.'

'I see. Have you asked Duncan to take a look at him?'

'He won't see Duncan.'

Anselm went back to his ordinary life. He didn't speak to anyone else about his visitation, but somehow word ran around the monastery that he had seen an angel in a vision. People began to come to his cell to ask him about it. He told them all the same thing: 'I don't want to talk about it.' But the higher powers became alarmed by this evidence of interest.

They called Anselm before them. He sat in a chair facing Frederick, Francis and Adrian.

Frederick said, 'All right, Anselm. Tell us about it.'

'It's just what I said to Francis,' Anselm mumbled. 'I don't think it should be anyone else's business. I'm trying to get used to it.'

'I'm sorry, Anselm,' Francis said. 'This is only because the others have been talking.'

'Oh, it isn't you. I don't blame you.'

'Who do you blame, then?' Brother Adrian said.

'Who do you? Why am I here?'

'Delusion.'

'You think it was an optical illusion?'

'Delusion. Delusions of grandeur. *I did it with angels.*'

'Only one.'

'Or', Frederick said, 'could it have been a man? Someone in the order, for example?'

'No.'

'These things sometimes occur, regrettable though they may be.'

'Who regrets it?'

'Who was it, Anselm?'

'I've told you. And you don't believe it. All right, never mind. May I go now?'

'Let's be more specific about what actually happened.'

'I do not propose to discuss what went on between us.'

'You don't have to. I can imagine it well enough. That wasn't what I had in mind. What I'm trying to ascertain is whether at any stage during this alleged encounter the wings got in the way.'

'I've said already: they'd disappeared.'

'Where to?'

'Inside.'

'Inside? How?'

'Well, I'm not sure. When I saw it happen, he was facing me. I guess they must be like those fold-up umbrellas you can get: you know, sort of collapsible. When you don't need them, you can –'

'Anselm, this joke has gone far enough. Come on, now. What's going on? You're feeling the need of drama and eventfulness here?'

'A lack of attention?' Adrian added. 'But you didn't join our order for that, did you?'

'I joined it because I love God. And now, at last, I've got the proof that He loves me back. He sent His angel to me and showed me. You say you can imagine, but you can't. You just can't. It was a pleasure beyond anything.'

'Oh, Christ,' Frederick muttered.

'And he was beautiful.'

'A figment of the –'

'I felt like a tree,' Anselm said wildly. 'A barren tree that's come into flower for the first time.'

'That's rather vague,' Francis said. 'What happened?'

'Well, after he took off my clothes, we sort of fell on to the bed and –'

'Please,' said Frederick. 'Spare us the details.'

'Francis asked what happened.'

'This is so sordid,' Adrian murmured.

Anselm exploded. 'How dare you?' he yelled. 'How dare you say that about any of God's creatures, much less an angel? We are not sordid. We're good. God made us and God loves us the way we are, even if we don't always do everything right.' He burst into tears. 'I can't go on,' he sobbed.

Francis made a move to rise and go to him, but Frederick held up his hand. Anselm fought for control. He began to calm down.

'I think you should have a talk with Brother Duncan,' Frederick told him.

'I'm all right now. I just got upset.'

Adrian said, 'You can claim you saw this, and you can claim you saw that, but the fact remains that nobody else saw –'

Anselm turned his head. 'You weren't chosen,' he sneered. 'I was. And', he said defiantly, 'his skin was like honey.'

'That's enough of that,' Frederick said. 'I'm ending this interview now. Anselm, if you won't agree to talk to Brother Duncan, you'll have to consider yourself confined to quarters until further notice.'

*

The incarnation was intended to be a punishment, but it also showed that they were afraid he might get out. Why would he want to do that? He lay on his bed – on the same bed where it had all taken place, and where he could remember if he shut his eyes or even lowered the lids a little – and tried to figure out why they were so worried. From their point of view, of course, he'd just been seeing things. Most closed communities were stiff with people who hadn't been able to stand the strain; even if they didn't crack, it was uncommon to find more than half of them without some kind of fissure. But they stayed, naturally. The world outside was so much worse. He himself, as they knew, had sought out the order as a refuge – a solution. And now it was where the best thing of his life had happened to him. It didn't make sense that he should want to leave, yet they were afraid. He started to feel apprehensive about their fear.

At the other end of the building from his cell, the senior brothers argued. 'You're making him a martyr,' Francis said. 'That's just what so many of the young ones want: the glory and romance of the persecuted believer.'

'He isn't all that young,' Frederick said. 'Nearly twenty-seven. That stuff's for the teenagers.'

'Haven't you noticed how the rest of them are taking his side against you?'

'Against us.'

'Except Adrian. That's a surprise. I never thought he'd agree with you on anything. I think he's just set against the poetry of it. He doesn't think other men, especially young ones, should have such fancy ideas.'

'Francis, it's the question of the morality that's so repulsive.'

'Yes, I'm not very fond of morals myself.'

'The lust, Francis. The gross flagrancy of the sexual intercourse. The immorality in any case, but in this case much more so. The perversion, for heaven's sake.'

'Perhaps.'

'Definitely.'

'I hope you and Adrian will take into account my firm conviction that it's necessary for people to be able to have their dreams.

For the young, it's essential. And in a place like this, there's almost no other way to express the more flamboyant aspects of their nature. Do you understand?'

'I guess so. But it's the others I'm concerned about.'

'The others think it's too harsh to shut him away for a harmless fantasy. He didn't need to talk about it, after all.'

'Oh, talking about it was the point. You don't think all that big, lush story of kisses and touching would have been half as good without other people's reactions, do you?'

'He's always been a good boy, and conscientious. A bit serious and moody, a bit frightened of other people. But spiritually sound, Frederick. His heart's in the right place, I think.'

'It wasn't his heart he was boasting about.'

'He wasn't boasting. He was in distress.'

'Boasting. Adrian was right about that. "I was chosen," he said. And so on.'

'I just think, to be so severe – it might not be the right way to handle it.'

'One more week. Then we'll have another talk with him.'

*

Anselm let himself dream. He lowered his eyelids and remembered. He was happy, even though he didn't think it was very healthy to be cooped up the way he was. He did exercises in the cramped space, but they didn't seem to help much. He had pains in his chest. He lost interest in his theological texts. He yearned for things he'd left long ago – for instance, he'd have liked to see a really exciting movie full of car chases. It took him a long while to recover from his night's sleep. He didn't seem to wake up so quickly or so fully as usual, and the morning meal of lumpy porridge and tough old wheatmeal bread made him feel nauseated.

At last the brother who brought the food came to say that the sentence was up. The man's name was Dominic and he'd been dying of curiosity all the time he'd been coming to the cell. He had tried to sound Anselm out but had got no response, so when anyone asked him about his prisoner, he'd invent something. He made up anything he thought might be interesting, though nothing malicious; he said that one evening a bright light had seemed to be coming from under the door – brighter than could be accounted for by the ordinary lighting system available to the brothers; that kind of thing. By the time he unlocked the door and left it ajar, there was a fairly large corpus of mythological incident circulating through the monastery. He waited by the door, smiled widely and said, 'No more restrictions.'

Anselm stood up. He nodded.

Dominic said, 'Good heavens, they must really trust your sanity. I've never known them to allow anyone else in solitary to keep a razor.'

Anselm went back to the cloister, where he strolled up and down to stretch his legs. He also needed to think. He paced back and forth in front of his favourite tree, a pear tree, which had come into bud while he'd been shut indoors, and would soon be in flower. Things were no longer simple; or, if they were, then they were so simple that nobody else was going to be able to agree with him.

He went to eat lunch with the others. He sat down late. The brothers had already joined in silent prayer. When the talk began again, heads turned towards him. The bread was passed around. Brother Adrian said loudly, 'You need a haircut, Anselm. See Brother Marcus after lunch. Did you hear me?'

Anselm ignored him. He looked down the table to where the doctor sat, and said, 'Brother Duncan, if it won't be disturbing you, I'd like to talk to you after the meal.'

'Did you hear me?' Adrian bellowed.

A silence fell over the company. Anselm murmured, 'How could anyone at this table fail to hear you, Brother Adrian? You're shouting so loudly. I'm perfectly capable of dealing with my hair, just as you must be of looking after what's left of yours.'

The roar of laughter from his companions turned Adrian red. He tried to stand up. The two brothers at his side held on to him.

Francis said, 'Argumentation is detrimental to the digestion, brothers. We all know that. Let's have some ideas and opinions on the new wines, all right?'

'They haven't settled down yet,' Brother Robert said. 'It's unfair to judge them at this stage.'

Everyone waited for Brother Robert to say more. He had a flair for the possibilities of a wine. He was a prematurely dried-up, pernickety little man, not the sort of person anyone would take to be an expert on a matter concerning the senses. He could drink huge amounts and, since the effect was to make him progressively quieter, he never seemed to be drunk – unlike Brother Adrian, who pontificated loudly and slurred very early on during the wine-tasting examinations and thought everything tasted pretty good.

'But just as a guess, Robert?' Francis asked. 'Good or bad?'

'Oh, the red is probably going to be ordinary enough. Drinkable, that's all. But the white could conceivably turn out to be something rather special for a California wine. Don't quote me. That's just off the top of my tonsure, ha-ha.'

Two of the brothers groaned. Brother William, one of the youngest, said, 'I thought the order hadn't had tonsures since Father Clement's time. I thought those were all just natural.'

'Go back to sleep,' his friend James told him.

'I wasn't asleep. I was thinking about something I wanted to ask Anselm, but now I've forgotten.'

Anselm glanced in William's direction. William twisted

around in his seat and stared back. He looked baffled. He said, 'I just can't remember.'

Brother Adrian thundered down the table at Robert that the red wine this year was going to be full-bodied and rich as a ruby, not like the usual cat's piss the white wine drinkers were addicted to.

Most of the table joined in the quarrel. Since the entire monastery was divided into lovers of white wine and lovers of red, the subject was normally a guarantee for heated debate.

Anselm didn't take part. He chewed his food slowly, watched by the doctor from the other side of the table.

*

'Well, Anselm, what can I do for you?' Duncan asked. 'Feeling nervous again? Depressed? Having dreams?'

'I've always had dreams, Doctor. Haven't you?'

'Of course. The thing to remember about dreams is that you shouldn't let them run away with you.'

'I heard from somebody once that your great dream was to be a missionary doctor, like Albert Schweitzer. Is that true?'

'That's right, yes. What good memories people have around here. We all have our fantasies when we're young.'

'You're still not too old to do it.'

Duncan pointed to his heart. He said, 'I'm too old here.'

'So, if it was offered to you, you wouldn't accept?'

'Probably not. How did we get on to this? I was supposed to be asking you about your health.'

'I'm not sure that what I've got is really a matter of health.'

'You look different. Were you eating all right, the past few weeks?'

'Feel my cheek, Doctor,' Anselm said.

Duncan put out his hand and touched the side of Anselm's

face. 'What's wrong?' he said. 'It doesn't feel like a temperature to me.'

'No beard,' Anselm explained. 'My beard has disappeared. It's just gone.'

Duncan hitched his chair closer. He took Anselm's face between his hands and turned it, first one way, then another. 'That's certainly what it looks like,' he said.

'And other things,' Anselm continued, 'have disappeared.'

'Oh?'

'And I'm getting fat. And I'd like you to take a look at my chest.' He stood up, turned his back, unsnapped the front of his robe and took out a towel he'd kept folded there. Then he turned around, holding the robe open so that the doctor could see: two round, exuberantly forward-pointing breasts, each about the size of a pomegranate.

Brother Duncan stood up. His mouth opened. He held out his hands as if to touch the breasts. Anselm picked up the towel and closed his robe. He sat down in the chair again.

The doctor continued to stare. At last he said, 'What the hell? Who are you?'

'I'm Anselm. You know very well. I've been in solitary confinement for a long time, so you know I couldn't have been switched. Maybe you heard something about the reason why they put me there?'

Duncan sat down. Once more he examined Anselm's face. 'I can't understand it,' he said.

'It isn't hard to understand, only hard to believe. I'm pregnant, that's all.'

'Right. Get your clothes off. All of them. This time I'm going to give you a complete examination.'

'Not on your life. I don't see why I should be subjected to any such thing without another woman present.'

'I'm a doctor.'

'Does that make you better than anyone else?'

'This is my job, Anselm.'

'But how much do you know about women?'

'I had a thorough medical education.'

'Exactly. That means: not much.'

'For Christ's sake, what do you think I'm going to do to you? I just want to look.'

'I bet. You can give me a urine test and find out that way.'

'Anselm, you don't seem to be taking this very seriously.'

'I'm taking it the only way that makes sense. I was chosen, and I accept it, and I'm glad. It's only everybody else who finds trouble in taking it. First of all they said I was crazy and seeing things. What are they going to say now?'

'Well, if it's true, how long do you think you can keep it secret? There's going to come a time when it'll start to show.'

'It shows already, without the towel.'

'Well, everybody's got to know pretty soon, then. Unless you're planning to leave here.'

'No, I couldn't leave. Doctor, you know that's what's happened, don't you? You know it's a sacred thing. And you're bound by your oath to preserve life. You're also pledged to keep my confidence.'

'I can keep quiet. But in your condition, you'll give yourself away. Don't you think it would be better if I examined you now, and after that we could both go to Brother Frederick and have a chat?'

Anselm yawned. He said, 'I suppose so. But I'm relying on you. If they shut me up again, I won't be able to get the exercise I need. It wouldn't be healthy. If you really need to, I guess you can do an examination. But I'm warning you: try anything dirty, and I'll knock your teeth out.'

'This is what holiness has done for you, is it? Talking to me like that.'

'I've been put in a position of trust. My body is a sepulchre. It shouldn't be tampered with.'

'Relax. I'm not going to tamper. I'm going to palpate.'

'That sounds worse.'

'Anselm –'

'Oh, all right,' Anselm said. He began to pull furiously at his clothes to get them off. He found that tears were running from his eyes. He cried easily now and got irritated, and felt sleepy during the daytime. 'And my back hurts,' he said.

*

'There's no doubt about it,' Brother Duncan said. 'Anselm is expecting a child. Physically, he is now in every respect a woman.'

Anselm leaned back in Frederick's easy-chair. He had positioned the pillow so that it would give support at the small of his back. The pregnant belly loomed out in silhouette. His hair was brushed back and seemed much longer; the style made his face look like a woman's.

It took a while for Frederick, Francis and Adrian to digest the news. In the end, Frederick had to bring out the brandy. Anselm alone refused.

'Oh dear,' Brother Francis said, 'oh dear, oh dear.'

Brother Frederick looked the doctor in the eye and told him, 'It just isn't possible.'

'Who knows? Darwin wasn't wrong about everything. Eels are sexually ambivalent, and snails are both male and female at the same time; but maybe they weren't always that way. Maybe they became like that after some other way for a long time. Do you see what I mean? Maybe Anselm is only the first. He's evolved, so that –'

'No,' Anselm interrupted. 'I was chosen.'

'Perhaps mind over matter,' Francis said tentatively. 'If the desire was so strong. I'm not saying that it's psychosomatic, but . . . I don't know.'

'Yes,' Anselm said. 'I know what you mean. Love conquers all. I know that's true now. I've had the proof. In fact, I am the proof.'

Brother Adrian looked at Anselm with revulsion. He declared, 'It isn't in the realm of nature.'

'Nature covers a lot of territory. And it's changing all the time.'

'You know what I think we should do, Anselm? I think we should bring back the old practices and burn you at the stake.'

'Oh dear,' Francis said. 'Calm down, Adrian, please.'

'If it's a question of the survival of the Church?'

'But this is Anselm. We've known him for five years. He's a good boy.'

'He must have been a plant. By evil forces. Who knows what really went on? We have no idea.'

'I told you,' Anselm said.

'That's what I mean. The depths of sexual depravity.'

'It doesn't have anything to do with morality. It's all a question of love. I was given the love and it transformed me. And now that it turns out I've been given something else, that's going to be a wonderful reminder of –'

'Stop,' Frederick said. 'This is ludicrous.'

'Monstrous,' Adrian said. 'This progeny, whatever you want to call it, has got to be a monster. You're a living blasphemy, Anselm.'

'Don't say that.' Anselm took out a handkerchief and dabbed at his eyes.

'He's a medical anomaly, that's all,' Duncan said.

'This is not a miracle,' Adrian insisted. 'It's an abnormality. Brother Anselm is a freak, not a phenomenon.'

'Oh, you nasty man,' Anselm said, sniffing into his handkerchief.

'Yes, Adrian, really,' Francis said. 'Have a little compassion. In his state – after all, we don't want to upset the baby.'

'Baby? I wouldn't be surprised if it turns out to be a toad.'

'Gabriel,' Anselm whispered. He hid his face in the crook of his elbow. Francis patted his back and gripped his shoulder.

Frederick rose from his chair. He said, 'Well, Anselm, we'll just have to wait and see what you produce. In the meantime, I hope I don't have to tell you that no word of this is to leak out of this building. And while you remain here, you're to conduct yourself with modesty and decorum. That will be all for the moment. You may return to your cell. Perhaps you'd accompany him, Doctor? Him, her, whatever you want to call yourself.'

Anselm stood. 'God forgive you,' he said. He turned towards the door. Duncan took his arm. Brother Adrian shouted after them that Anselm would burn in hell for ever and ever.

Anselm let himself be led quietly to his cell. He lay down on his back and closed his eyes. He knew that he should try to think of some plan, some way of protecting himself. There were malicious and unscrupulous men around him, who despised him and who would have him at their mercy when the baby was born. He couldn't decide whether telling the outside world would help him or put him into greater danger.

He thought about the baby and smiled. He was feeling good in spite of the backaches. He fell asleep smiling.

*

Frederick went to Francis for comfort. He said, 'Francis, this thing will be the end of me. I don't know what to do. I can't tell anyone outside. On the other hand – I mean, it couldn't be. It couldn't be. You don't believe it, do you?'

'Well, the trouble is, we all know that he was a man when he arrived here.'

Frederick paced the room, smacked his hands together and pulled at his hair. He kept repeating that it wasn't possible.

'But it's happened,' Francis said.

'OK, OK. What I meant was: it isn't possible that it could be another divine birth. In which case, in which – you aren't helping, Francis.'

'In which case, it's an ordinary human birth.'

'Yes. A phantom pregnancy brought on by Anselm's overwhelming neurotic craving to become the object of his devotion: the Virgin Mary.'

'And when he gives birth?'

'It's all going to be gristle and leftover pieces of stuff.'

'Frederick, sit down for heaven's sake. You heard what Duncan said. It's going to be a child like any other child.'

'Then he was screwing somebody in my monastery, damn it all.'

'As a man or as a woman?'

'Oh, Christ,' Frederick said. 'Years clawing my way up the ladder, being polite to creeps and crazies, and playing along with the whole business: you do me a favour, I'll do you a favour. And then I got my own team and whipped it into shape. I worked like hell on this place, you know that. Not that they'd actually let me have it for my own – no, I'm only the deputy; that makes it less trouble for them. And now this happens.'

'But no matter what's caused it, it's a joyful thing.'

'Not for the man in charge, Francis. No, siree. What the hell am I going to do?'

'All these emotions – it's wearing me down. Try to relax and be happy. Don't work yourself up like this.'

'Easy for you to say. You aren't going to have to carry the can.'

'Neither are you. Nobody's going to blame you for this. Especially if you call in Duncan to explain the situation.'

'He doesn't have an explanation.'

'That's just it. What you do is what everyone else is going to do: wait and see.'

'No. We believe in God, the Virgin Birth, Christ the Redeemer, the teachings of Mother Church and the life everlasting. And that's damn well it. None of this newfangled nonsense. And don't start quoting Vatican Two at me – I'm sick to death of it.'

'But you wouldn't do anything to harm Anselm, would you?'

'How are we to know that this isn't some kind of unholy thing? That's what Adrian believes.'

'The man's a fool, you know that. He's jealous of Anselm and he's frightened of his own feelings. Forget what he believes. Let's say for the moment that we're dealing with an ordinary mother and child. It would be very wrong to do anything to harm them.'

'I wasn't thinking of harming anyone. Don't look at me like that.'

'You tell me what you were thinking about, then.'

'I don't know. There doesn't seem to be any way out. Why did this have to happen to me?'

'It didn't. It happened to Anselm.'

'But it affects us all. No man is an island.'

'And no woman, either.'

Frederick jumped up again, kicked the table, and said, 'Damn it, damn it, you can't keep them out of anything.'

*

Anselm walked back and forth for exercise. He passed his favourite tree, the flowering pear. He had stood for a quarter of an hour in front of it the night before, astonished at how its pale petals held the light so that he was able to see the whole tree blooming in the darkness.

In the daytime the tree seemed smaller than it had at night. He wondered why that should be. Maybe it had appeared large in isolation and because of being surrounded by black: a trick of the light and of the eye perceiving it. Or maybe the night showed the truth and the daytime tree was deceptively small.

He dropped all his duties and lived a life of ease. Most of the brothers felt that he had a certain amount of justification for it, though not necessarily because he had been touched by God. Everyone knew now that he had turned or been turned into a woman, and that was enough to excuse a lot. That in itself was a breach of discipline. It was breaking the rules like nobody's business.

A few people agreed with Brother Adrian and sat with him for hours at a stretch, discussing just what evil, unnatural, or evilly unnatural, or unnaturally evil cause could be behind the whole thing. But most of the young ones were on Anselm's side. And in his own wing of the building he became a focal point for afternoon meetings. He had a little club of admirers. They were zealously noted by Adrian and his followers, who reported the members to Frederick. But when Frederick suggested stamping out the coterie, Francis persuaded him that that would just make everything worse. They were to wait.

'There's a right time for everything, you know,' Frederick said. 'Remember the Bible. Sometimes it's a mistake to wait.'

'Not this time,' Francis told him. 'And that isn't what that passage is about, anyway. Calm down, Frederick.'

Anselm's friends brought him quantities of pillows, many of them silk and satin, to help support his back. He lay reclined on them like an oriental princess, smiling sweetly at the other brothers as they confided their troubles to him.

They drank coffee or tea or wine. Sometimes they'd flirt with him. Brother Elmo was especially obstreperous. You could still see the pierce-mark where he'd worn the earring in his left ear;

he'd received the call, so he said, on a trip. 'A trip to where?' Brother William had asked. 'A trip to outer space, man. A trip on speed. Get in focus, Billy.'

Elmo was delighted with Anselm's transfiguration. It proved, he claimed, that he'd been right all along: anything could happen in life, and everything did, only most people were so unaware, so lacking in powers of observation, that they didn't notice. He stared possessively at Anselm and asked, 'So when are you going to let us have some fun with you, babe? It better be soon, before you get too big.'

'Don't be naughty,' Anselm said. He made a motion of hitting at Elmo with a small peacock-feather fan that had come wrapped up with one of the pillows.

'Come on, Anselm. We're your friends, aren't we? Who else are you going to play around with if it isn't your friends?'

'It's not a joke.'

'At least let us see your tits.'

Anselm fanned himself lazily.

'We'll bring you some extra food. You're eating for two now, remember.'

'I do have these terrible strong desires for certain tastes: dill pickles, cheesecake, raspberry ice cream, walnut and pecan mousse, smoked mackerel and watermelons.'

'We'll get them for you.'

'Promise?'

All the brothers nodded vehemently. Anselm undid his robe and exposed the full, cup-shaped breasts of which he was now immensely proud. There was a silence until he started to pull the robe together again.

'Wait,' Dominic said, and William begged, 'Not yet. I haven't finished looking.'

'Crazy, man,' Elmo said.

'Weird,' said Dominic.

'Cute. They look just like a girl.'

'Weird.'

'Can I touch one of them, Anselm?'

'Certainly not.'

'Why not? I just want to feel.'

'That's all meant for the baby, you know.'

'How did you work it?' William asked. 'How did you get them to grow? Did you wake up in the morning and find them like that?'

'No, it happened gradually. They got a little bigger every day.'

'Did it hurt?'

'Not hurt, exactly. Everything felt very tender and sore all over my chest. And so forth.' He snapped up the front of his robe again.

Brother James, at the back of the group, said he thought he had an explanation. 'Maybe –' he said, 'it's got something to do with radioactive fall-out from the atom bombs.'

'Or Mount St Helen's,' Dominic added.

'It was the angel,' Anselm said. 'I told them in the first place. It was Gabriel.'

*

'They're sitting around drinking wine in there,' Frederick said. 'Next thing you know, there'll be luxury and viciousness all over the place. Everybody knows about the stimulating properties of alcohol.'

'We should,' Francis said. 'We make a living out of it. They're just talking.'

'It makes me jumpy.'

'How can you stop them being interested? It's an absolutely extraordinary thing.'

'It's unnatural.'

'It's what happened to Our Blessed Lady.'

'I don't want to get into that argument. Anyway, when it happened to Mary, it wasn't a sin. It was pure. This is terrible.'

'You've been listening to Brother Adrian.'

'He talks a lot of sense sometimes, in spite of being a little over-emphatic.'

'Crass. He's a crass man, and frightened. And now he's infected you. Did you drink up all the whisky? That's right, he always has that cffect on you.'

'Unnatural,' Frederick insisted.

'How can it be unnatural if it's happened?'

'It shouldn't have happened.'

'What do you call conception through the ear-hole? That's supposed to be the way the Holy Ghost got in, isn't it?'

'We have to regard these events in a philosophic light, as representing symbolic manifestations of spiritual truths.'

'What?'

'And Brother Anselm just isn't in that league. Also, the whole thing is against the teachings of Mother Church.'

'Nonsense. A miracle is a miracle is a miracle.'

'Is that what you really think this is?'

'I don't know what it is. Truly.'

'Brother Duncan says he thinks Anselm was androg . . . an andr . . . whatever the word is.'

'Hermaphrodite?'

'And he lived all one way for years, even though the other half was there all the time, lurking under the surface, just waiting to show itself – which it finally did, all at once.'

'Complete with child?'

'No. That came later. First of all he hid it and had carnal relations with somebody in here, and when he found out he was pregnant, then he came to you.'

'Neat.'

‘The whole rigmarole is having a profoundly unsettling effect on the order.’

‘Especially on you.’

‘On me too, of course. I don’t deny it. But look at Adrian. And in the other direction – what about Marcus?’

Brother Marcus had become a regular visitor to Anselm’s room. He had been so completely won over that it was now his greatest pride to be responsible for making Anselm look as attractive as possible. He delighted in finding new arrangements in which to set Anselm’s luxuriant dark hair, which was growing so quickly that it was already down to his shoulders. ‘Let’s put it up today,’ Marcus would suggest, or, ‘How about side-swept for a change?’ He came every morning and evening, his sausage-like fingers deft among the glossy masses of hair. He had managed to acquire a set of pins and ornaments for keeping the hair in place and twining it into piled-up shapes. And while he worked, a light of happiness shone from his face. He had changed. He’d always looked as strong and coarse as a picture of a Victorian butcher, but now he displayed moods of elephantinely delicate playfulness and good humour.

‘God Almighty,’ Brother Adrian said under his breath as Anselm moved up to the table with his slow, billowing gait and his elaborately perched hair-do, ‘it’s like sitting down to dinner with the Whore of Babylon.’

‘You should be so lucky,’ Brother Robert told him. ‘What I hear is: he doesn’t sell it and he doesn’t give it away for free. Admiration from afar is his line.’

‘Maybe he’s saving himself for another bout with the supernatural.’

‘If it’s true,’ Brother James said, ‘no amount of repentance is going to make up for the way you’re talking about him now.’

‘It isn’t true,’ Adrian told him. ‘And it’s a blasphemy even to think it might be.’

*

Before Frederick's era, the monastery had been run by Father Clement. He had been a rather absent-minded, scholarly person, until Vatican Two. And then he threw over the traces with a vengeance. As Frederick had said at the time, no one could have suspected such an intense urge towards chaos in the man. All at once Father Clement espoused every cause and crackpot movement that had been hitting the headlines for the past three decades while he'd been supposed to be tilling the vineyards and praising the Lord. He went from Flower Power to Hard Rock in three weeks. He became interested in Scientology. And he allowed anybody in: Hell's Angels, ballet dancers, health food freaks and gigolos.

That was the trouble with tolerance: you could get too much of it. Too much – and people stampeded over you. The time came when Father Clement welcomed a set of what were to anyone's eyes ordinary winos so far gone in the abuse of alcohol that they were already brain-damaged. There was a scandal. The papers got hold of it. It was deplorable; atrocious. Father Clement was now, so everyone believed, in Hawaii, teaching Shakespeare to the Japanese. And the monastery was still awaiting a replacement, although in the meantime Brother Frederick was in command. It meant a great deal to Frederick that his interregnum should be peaceable and well-ordered. A promotion to the top was more than merely possible.

He had thought that he'd begin by weeding out the more sinister or cranky newcomers, but by the time he took over, the men were leaving so quickly they were practically tripping over each other trying to get to the door. They were like the rats leaving a sinking ship. And then, miraculously, the new influx arrived, even younger: a fresh generation of believers; however, their belief wasn't of the old quality, their education up to the same level. Some of them had had hardly any religious instruction at all. 'Beggars can't be choosers,' Brother Robert had said over his wine one evening. 'God', Frederick had answered grandly, 'does not need to beg.' Robert had given him a pitying look and shaken his head, and almost immediately been proven right: a bad flu rampaged through the order, turning the place into a geriatric ward. The old monks began to die off. Those who didn't die had to be cleaned, fed and manoeuvred on to bedpans. Frederick realized that he wasn't going to be able to kick many young men out. The solution would be to keep them there and change them into better monks. And, all in all, having had inferior material to work with, he hadn't done too badly. He was proud of his record.

Sometimes he thought about the ones his own age who had left – who had voluntarily jettisoned the calling to which they had been dedicated, reneged on their vocations. He thought of them as deserters or, at times, escapees. They thought of him, too. A lot of them regularly sent postcards and letters back from the outside. When he was feeling particularly glum and grouchy, he'd remember the messages:

I never knew what living was like till I left the order.
What are you trying to prove?
Come on in, the water's fine.
Freddie, you're a jerk to stay.

Often the more strait-laced they had been, the more fatuous their greetings were. The Classicists had gone, to become pragmatists. The Romantics stayed.

Brother Francis used to say that there was no need to keep anyone who didn't have faith. As far as the vineyards went, they could hire workers. The order was dedicated to God – there was no necessity, and should be none, to accept anyone below standard. But Robert told him, 'We just cannot afford to turn down men who come to us for our novelty-value. We have to assume that there's a genuine desire underlying the frivolous impulse.' And it was true that now you could see he'd been as acute about that as about the grapes. They'd had many vintage years for wine lately; not so many for men. They needed the numbers.

Most of Anselm's admirers were entirely untutored; they'd had no religious training in childhood. Many of them had come to their faith, as he had, under the pressure of some dramatic event or crisis. Elmo, who had served with the Oakland Fire Department, had preserved the lives of people who later tried to murder each other; and he had failed to rescue the innocent. He'd had a breakdown after a particularly ferocious tenement conflagration in which the only member of a large and quarrelsome family that he hadn't been able to save was the baby: it lay at the top of the house, its lungs scorched by smoke, while the demented relatives down below shrieked with frustration and beat him nearly to death, calling him a son of a bitch and a bastard. He had been furious, ashamed, and found that whenever he remembered the helpless baby up at the top of the fiery house, he wanted to cry. It took him six months to work out his thoughts and feelings. In the end, it came down to a simple formula: if there was nothing, he couldn't stand it; but if there was something, then in some way – even though no one knew exactly how – the baby was all right.

William's conversion had come through someone else: his young wife, who had fallen from an open stairway on a pier and hit one of the boats near their own. She had injured her spine so badly that at first the doctors thought she'd die in a few hours. It took her weeks, and during that time she was in agony. William had stayed with her right up to the end, when she suddenly received a revelation of God and said that the pain had vanished completely. She was dying then; they had a few final days together and William caught her belief as if it had been a germ in the hospital. But he didn't want to be cured of it afterwards. He was happy with the monastic life – that is, he was happy until the strange business about Anselm took over.

Dominic's was another case of hospitalization, though he had been the chief actor in the drama: he had been struck by lightning, thrown forty feet into a neighbouring field, and was in the hospital for four weeks recovering. Then he was at home for three months, just thinking about it. Twelve cows in the same field had been killed by the bolt. He had an idea that he'd been given a warning of some kind because his life wasn't the model of righteousness it was designed to be. A cow was a very big animal; twelve of them had died, yet he had been spared. That seemed to be a sign. He made preparations to try to save his soul.

James was different. He'd gone to Italy on a holiday after college. 'I was such a hick,' he said. 'I didn't know anything. Some friends asked me to the opera, and that's how it began. I stayed longer than I'd intended to. Then another friend took me to see the mosaics in Ravenna. And that's how I became a Christian. I had no idea of the way of life. That all came later. I'm probably the only example you'll ever meet of the redemptive power of art. Nature, and human nature, is so much more impressive.'

'And how about you, Anselm?' the brothers asked.

Anselm had started out in the order by keeping the books, as he had done in the world outside. He had entered just in time to take over from a Brother Timothy, who died, as everyone had expected, the next day. In view of the fact that the auditing was just about to come up, Anselm's arrival was seen as providential.

He had been trained as an accountant, had jobs in various small firms and then begun to work in large corporations, finally settling in a well-paid and interesting job at a bank. He was ready to branch out in his career and aim for the heights, when one day he saw a newsreel about surfboarding. The next morning he quit work and went down to the beach.

He had decided to become an expert. Only the experts could ride the big waves out in the islands: the ones like the one in the movie, which had shown a huge wall of green glass quivering forward, and – tracing a thin white line across the middle of it – a tiny dot: the surfer. He wanted to be good enough to go through the really dangerous waves – the ones that curled over on themselves, forming a tube, so that you could ride down the centre as if going through a tunnel; but, because your feet would be lashed to the board in case it bounced up, threw you, and came back to hit you on the head at a hundred miles an hour, you'd be in danger of losing your foot: if a sharp piece of coral caught you as you were going by, that was it – the foot would be sliced off. At least that would be better, the other surfers told him, than getting killed by your board.

He got night work in factories and as a watchman in warehouses. He finally found a job in a vast complex of storage buildings where he worked with two men who agreed with him to spell each other so that two of them could always get six hours' unbroken sleep every night. And then he found the right day, when all the waves were perfect. And the right wave – just like the one in the newsreel – which he knew would never end; he'd be able to ride it for ever all around the world from ocean to ocean.

And then all at once, unexpectedly, he was in the water. Something had slammed him hard on his head, shoulders and back and he was under the surface, not knowing which way was up. He must have taken a breath instinctively and saved his life that way. But soon he started to thrash around in terror. He needed air. He fought wildly – luckily without success, since the water itself buoyed him to the surface against his efforts. He was saved. And from those moments of remembered fear, his wish for a faith was born. Looking back, he figured out that – unlikely as it seemed – he must have been struck by some kind of fish jumping from the sea; a board or any other hard object would have broken every bone in his body. But the agent of the accident was a minor question. The truly puzzling mystery was his survival.

He simply couldn't understand how he had escaped death if something else hadn't been helping him. What could it have been? What was more powerful than a great force of nature like the sea?

'That was how it started,' he said. 'I tried to think it out. But now I know thought is useless when it comes to the important things.'

*

The front of Anselm's robe was studded and stuck with the trinkets and tokens he'd been given by other monks. Some of the gifts looked like votary offerings. He never asked where they came from. For years the cells and cloisters of the monastery had been bare of ornament; now from nowhere shiny buttons and pins appeared, so that they could be presented to Anselm.

'The creature is positively bedizened,' Brother Adrian snarled. 'Decorated like a Christmas tree.' He got drunk for two days and couldn't be roused.

'You see', Frederick told Francis, 'the effect it's having.'

'Just on Adrian. He was nearly this bad over the legal rights on the new vineyard eight years ago. Remember? That's the way he is. He wouldn't be tolerated for a minute in the outside world.'

'Don't kid yourself – he'd be one of the ones running it. And in his clearer moments, he's actually extremely capable.'

'But not likeable. Even talent has its limits.'

Francis heaved an enormous sigh. He threw up his hands to heaven and for a few seconds scrabbled at the air before sighing again and returning to normal. 'I got three postcards today,' he said. 'Brother Aloysius has become a Buddhist. He says he doesn't hold anything against us.'

'That's nice of him.'

'Ungrateful old swine. I hope they have as much trouble with him as we did.'

They turned to the right by the chapel and saw Anselm in the distance.

'What do you think?' Francis said.

'Oh, it's a mess. Just the kind of slipshod entanglement a boy like Anselm would be apt to get himself into.'

'Not a miracle?'

'Are there such things?'

'You know very well there are. But maybe you have to wait for somebody else to tell you that's what they are.'

'Your nasty moments are always so refreshing, Francis. One doesn't expect them.'

'I put it badly. What I meant was that it's like seeing a new movie or a new play. Some people say it's all right, one or two that it's wonderful, and a lot say it's worthless. Or the other way around. In time, everyone knows what to think. When something is completely new, it's got to be fitted into its place. It has to be assimilated. And every age has its miracles.'

*

Anselm looked through the papers. He came across a story about a Chinese boy who could read through his ears instead of his eyes; they'd blindfold him, hold a book up to his right ear, and let him read it. (The left ear appeared to be illiterate.)

He turned to a page near the back. A column next to the gardening news reported the uncanny ability of a five-year-old girl to turn tennis balls inside-out by the power of thought. And in the same issue there was a short item that told of a man who had died from just drinking water. He'd drunk thirty-five pints. According to friends of his, he'd said that he was 'trying to clean out his system'.

He started to order books from the public library. He got them through Brother Duncan, whose attitude towards him was becoming irritatingly proprietorial. The books were all about babies and the habits that could be discerned in them as soon as they were born. The romping movements, Anselm read, were for exercise; the grabbing and clinging instinct apparently went way back to the time when the human young would have to be able to get a grip on the mother's fur.

'Fur?' Elmo said. 'Have you been holding out on us? We thought you only had the usual accessories.'

'Shh,' Anselm told him. He continued to read from the book. The brothers were fascinated. Everyone wanted to help bring up the baby.

Eventually they talked about what sort of a child it would be, why it had been 'sent', and how they should educate it. Or perhaps it would be enough just to love it.

Other monks, at the far side of the cloister, also talked. Two of them on the way to Matins hurried across the courtyard together. One said, 'She came among us in a disguised form. That's why we didn't recognize her.' The other said, 'No, it's just the reverse. He's in a disguised form now.' It was like a quarrel about whether a dog was white with black spots or black with white spots. And, in any case, they weren't supposed to be discussing it.

*

Deep in thought, Anselm strolled along the pillared porches. In the distance he could see William standing still and looking intently, forlornly, at him.

Anselm moved closer. William began to edge nearer. He was in love with Anselm. He had picked a blossoming branch as an emblem of his love and wanted to offer it, but didn't quite dare.

Anselm rocked gracefully towards him, the swell of his skirt bearing him forward as if by sail or by balloon. He reached the spot where William stood transfixed by the sight of him. Anselm gave him a soft glance; the long lashes over his dark eyes were longer than ever. 'Hello, William,' he said.

'I wanted to give you this,' William told him. He held out the branch.

Anselm recognized the flowers as part of his favourite tree. He blinked languidly.

'For the baby,' William whispered.

Anselm took the branch. 'Thank you, William,' he said. 'How sweet of you.'

William dropped to his knees. He caught the edge of Anselm's robe in his hands and buried his face in it.

Anselm bent down slowly, touched William's head as if in blessing, and passed on.

William remained on his knees and began to pray.

*

'You've seen how Brother William is taking it?' Adrian demanded.

'A simple heart,' Frederick said.

'Rife for corruption.'

'Ripe.'

'This place could become a hotbed of debauchery overnight.'

'Really, Adrian, I think that's overstating the case.'

'All I want to know is what you're going to do about it.'

'You leave that to me.'

'No, Frederick. We've all waited long enough. If I don't see some action, I'm reporting it.'

'Be careful, Adrian. If you go too far, you'll be confined to quarters. I don't want any heroics out of you.'

'Me?' Brother Adrian cried. His tone was one of wounded innocence, his face nearly purple. Frederick knew that this mood of his was even harder to deal with than his rages.

*

Anselm waited for Francis outside the chapel until an older monk, Brother Theodore, had left. Then he came forward.

'Francis, may I ask you a question?'

'Certainly.' He hadn't heard Anselm's approach and was startled by the way he looked – so obviously pregnant, so like a young woman of the ancient world as it was pictured by the great Renaissance painters; and so pretty.

'This isn't a confession,' Anselm said.

'That's all right. Sit down.'

They sat in the pews, Anselm sliding in sideways and near a corner, to rest his back. 'What I want to know,' he said, 'is if you think that after the birth I should continue to lead a single life.'

'I hadn't thought that far, as a matter of fact.'

'Because there's somebody who loves me. And I feel that we'd be very well matched and everything. And a child needs a father.'

'Yes,' Francis said. 'But supposing – I mean, perhaps it would end up having two of them. It might be possible that after the birth, you'd go back to the way you were.'

'It might. Anything could happen. In that case, I'd have to find a mother for my child instead, wouldn't I?'

'Not necessarily. You could raise it alone. After the first few weeks, it's the father that's important: a figure of authority. A loving authority.'

'That doesn't matter. Authority is what you are or where you stand, not whether you're male or female. It's politically determined.'

'Authorities are male.'

'Only because things are organized like that.'

'But if you're trying to come to a decision, that makes a difference, doesn't it?'

'I guess. And I've become so fond of this person.'

'Brother William?'

'Sweet William. Before the Annunciation, I used to think he was a bit of an oaf. Now he seems so nice – true-hearted and full of life.'

'If you reverted to your former state, you might return to your first opinion of him. It might go with the alteration. So maybe you'd better wait.'

Anselm ran a hand through his hair, rumpling the sleekly regimented locks. 'I'd thought all the problems were solved,' he said, 'everything taken care of.'

'It's causing a lot of complications around you, you know.'

'Oh, that. That's just people's attitudes.'

'I worry about it.'

'Good. You can worry about it for me. I'm not going to.'

'Anselm, I do worry. Not everyone is kind. And it isn't everyone who can take the detached view.'

'Well, do you have an answer?'

'You haven't been to Mass in a very great while.'

'No.'

'It's for your sake, not mine or ours.'

'Don't let it bother you, Francis. I'm in God's hands.'

'We're all in God's hands. I just thought – well, I don't know. Your prayers are important, too. It isn't enough just to exist and not take part.'

'But every minute I live is given to God. He sent His angel. He –'

'The Mass, Anselm.'

'For me, that's secondhand now.'

'That's a very arrogant and wrong-headed thing to say.'

'Why? It's true.'

'Oh dear,' Brother Francis said.

*

'I don't want any X-rays.'

Brother Duncan said, 'It isn't an X-ray. It's a scan for finding out if the baby's going to be a girl or a boy.'

'Scan – what does that mean?'

'It's –'

'You can hear the heartbeat. Isn't that all right? And you can feel it kicking now. We'll find out what sex it is when it's born.'

'It would be nice to know now.'

'Nice for who?'

'Aren't you curious?'

'Doctor, I want you to promise me something. This child has got to be born alive and well, whether it's normal or not.'

'Who says it isn't going to be normal?'

'I want you to promise. The decision is not yours. Do you understand?'

'I've taken the Hippocratic oath, Anselm.'

'And we all know how much that's worth.'

'Who's been filling your mind with these fears?'

'They come naturally. It's an anxious time. Look at all my badges and buttons. I'm superstitious about everything now. I've got to be able to trust you. I know you don't believe what happened, but I've got to have your help.'

'I definitely believe you changed sex. There's no doubt about that.'

'I'm asking you as a doctor, and also as a Christian. The temptation is going to be great. They're leaning on you, aren't they?'

'There's a certain amount of pressure, of course. That's my problem. I can handle it.'

'Since I've been pregnant, I've begun to understand a lot of things about doctors and women – telling them what to do, regulating them, applying a system. I used to think there were so many more male doctors than female ones just because it's such a highly paid job, but now I'm not sure. Now I'm coming to believe it's all to do with power – that men look at all other creatures as things on which to practise their power, that they think freedom means being able to carry out that practice; and they don't like it if anyone is really free just to be the way they are.'

'Anselm, you're going to find that you're increasingly prey to all kinds of fears, but – believe me, they have no foundation. I'm a doctor; I know.'

'You may be a doctor, Duncan, but compared to me, you're an ignoramus.'

'Thanks a bunch.'

'My knowledge comes directly from God.'

'So you've said.'

'Where do you think this child came from?'

'I'm not asking that question. I'm interested in facts as they are.'

'But they're so changeable. Facts can change in an instant. That's what happened to me. It's like peacetime and wartime, like happiness and sorrow. You never know when the change is going to come.'

'But not like male and female.'

'How do you know?'

'Do you think you're the only person this so-called visitation ever happened to? Except the first instance, I mean.'

'I've wondered about that, too. All I can say is that if there were others, they kept quiet about it. Or it was hushed up. Or no one believed it. That would be the most likely explanation. Not many people here believe me, either.'

'You don't think you're the only one?'

'I do. But that may only be because everything that happens to people seems to be special to them. It seems unique.'

'I've never heard or read of anything like it. The occasional hysterical woman, yes – nothing like this.'

'That's the trouble. Right from the start it was medically exciting. You still think it's the prize-winning case-history. But they're giving you orders above me, aren't they?'

'Nobody wants anything but your own good, Anselm.'

'And if they didn't, what could I do about it? It's giving me the creeps. Look at the way I am. How could I defend myself? They're all running themselves in circles about scandal and reputation and theology. This matters more. If you're any kind of a doctor, there must have been a time when you thought so too.'

'I wanted to become a doctor,' Duncan said, 'because I wanted to know about the human soul, life and death, where people went to when they died, why they were the way they were. I studied in the laboratories, in mortuaries. I had parts of people on the table in front of me like pieces of a Sunday chicken. We had all kinds of things – insides – to look at. When I was a student, I had a collection of innards in jars. A whole shelf full. I even had a foetus in a bottle. I studied it. I also used to wonder about it a lot – whether it was a miscarriage, or whether the mother wanted to get rid of it; a lot of them do, you know. A lot of them wouldn't give you two cents for the Hippocratic oath. It seemed to me at that time, even more important than the question of where we went was the question of where we came from. The embryo I owned was a person. They were all, all the pieces in jars . . . Then I got to thinking about how the whole of that side of life was entrusted to women. And that was where my understanding broke down. They're so patently unworthy. Strange as your case is, Anselm, the one thing about it that makes sense to me is that, if it's true, it should have been a man who was chosen this time. If that's what happened.'

'That's what happened. But that isn't the part I think is important. I'm the same. I'm the same person now that I was then. I've got a different body, that's all. Do you think we're what our bodies are?'

'We live inside them. We inhabit them. We're influenced by them, very. The state of a person's health can change his personality.'

'It can't change him into something he had no capacity for from the beginning. Or can it?'

'You think you were a woman all along?'

'I think I was chosen, and because the female body is the one made for carrying and feeding children, I was given that. Do you think I'm going to change back afterwards?'

'What?'

'As soon as I stop breast-feeding, do you think I'll go back to being a man?'

'Oh my God, Anselm.'

'It's like a joke, isn't it?'

'It simply never occurred to me.'

'I hadn't thought that far myself. I was just happy. But now I'm beginning to get a little anxious. I don't want anything to go wrong.'

'Nothing will go wrong. Relax. You're very healthy.'

Anselm stood up. It took him several movements now. He felt as ungainly as a camel getting to its feet.

He went for a walk in the courtyard and then down past the potato gardens. He stopped a few times to think. He leaned against one of the stone walls in the garden and partly closed his eyes. He remembered the way it had been at the beginning: Gabriel alighting on the green square of grass. Once again, like warmth from a flame or a breath from the air, the remembered touch ran tickling over his skin.

He knew that the central event was all right and assured. His worries were all about the peripheral effects. Whether man or woman, he was living in the world as it was at a particular time. And in most parts of the country, despite the revolution in morals, changed attitudes towards sexual freedom, the high incidence of divorce and the promulgation of certain doctrines by the women's movements – still, in general, illegitimacy was disapproved of. Because he was single, things were going to be made difficult for him. And if he remained single, they'd be made difficult for the child too. There were hundreds of ways in which a child could be hurt, shocked, shamed or cruelly teased by other children at school. Schools were full of quarrels and fights and name-calling.

On his way back to his cell he went near the chapel, where the brothers were singing Compline. The baby began to move boisterously. Whenever there was music, it kicked hard. Anselm thought maybe it picked up the vibrations and was trying to dance.

He passed by, going to the right and down the hallway that led to his corridor. A burst of laughter came from behind one of the closed doors; shouted opinions followed. There seemed to be at least three, perhaps four voices. Anselm heard himself named and turned back.

'What I think –' one of the voices said.

Another one interrupted: 'She's asking for it.'

'Miracle, my arse.' The voice could have been the first man again, or a different one. Through the closed door it was hard to tell. One of them said something in a low murmur that Anselm didn't catch. The others cackled like witches. He could guess, from the remark that had gone before, what kind of comment it had been. After that, there was a loud crash and a despairing cry: 'Jesus fucking Christ, you've done it again.'

'Not so loud.'

'Second one you've broken.'

'Shut up.'

'Let's have some more blood of the lamb, Brother Eustace.'

'Let's go pay Sister Anselm a call.'

'One more drink.'

'I don't want to get mixed up in anything like that. He's got a lot of friends now.'

'I wouldn't give a plug nickel for his friends. My friends are bigger than anybody's friends.'

'I don't give a damn. I don't give . . . I don't give a whatever, not about anything.'

'It might be true.'

'Oh, come on.'

'I'm not saying it is, but you just tell me how you can explain it.'

'It's a rip-off, of course.'

'What kind of a rip-off can do that?'

'What I think is, we shouldn't take it for granted.'

'Take what for granted? What are you talking about now?'

'Anything, anything. You should never take nothing for granted. Eyesight, now – a wonderful thing, a marvel. It can be lost in a second. That's true, you know. I have a brother-in-law; but never mind. What I'm saying is, you shouldn't count on it. Course, in the end we lose everything: sight, hearing, so on.'

'Jesus, don't get so gloomy. You're spoiling the fun. How could we lose everything?'

'Getting old.'

'That isn't so bad. I know a lot of pretty old people. Well, not a lot. Some.'

'And then we die.'

A different voice said, 'But we live again in Christ.'

'Well,' the first man answered, 'it's a nice thought.'

Anselm felt dizzy. He made his way to his room, lay down on the bed and closed his eyes. He thought he'd like to pray lying down, since it was so uncomfortable getting on to his knees and having to bend forward.

He put his hands together. 'Holy Mary,' he began, and stopped. He couldn't think of anything more to say.

Surely, he thought, William would understand. If he remained the way he was, a woman, they could stay together as a family. And if he changed back, they could split up, or even keep on going like that, too.

He didn't join the others for supper. Dominic brought him a bowl of soup, some bread and butter and an apple.

'Aren't you feeling well, Anselm?' he asked.

'Sure. I'm all right. Just tired.'

'You take care of yourself. We've all got bets riding on you.'

'What's the verdict?'

'Oh, everybody thinks it's going to be a boy. If it's a girl, about three people are going to clean up. They'd be millionaires. Everybody else would be out in the cold. You want a boy too, of course, don't you?'

'Naturally. That's the way it's supposed to be.' He drank his soup and felt better. Brother Ignatius and Brother Sebastian in the kitchen were working overtime now, making sure that nothing sat too heavily on his stomach.

He started to feel still better late in the night when he thought about the birth. He was afraid of the pain but he was certain that the event was going to be of such cataclysmic importance and excitement that the pain would have to become secondary. And it would all be worth it, anyway. Now that he could feel the baby pushing and bumping, he was beginning to know it. It kept him company. He talked to it. He told it stories – things he made up, as well as the more traditional fairytales he remembered from his own childhood.

Once upon a time, he said to himself, *there were three bears: a mamma bear, a pappa bear and a baby bear.* There was a king who had three daughters, a woodcutter with three sons. *Once upon a time there were three little pigs and they all lived in the forest, where there was a big, bad wolf.* Everything went in threes and everything was told as if it had happened only that week, or it could just as easily have been centuries ago. *Once upon a time,* he thought, *there was the Father, the Son and the Holy Ghost.*

*

'Brother Adrian', Francis said, 'is in trouble. I think he's going out of his mind, Frederick.'

'No more than usual. And he's always got emotional troubles. You know Adrian – that's the way he is. He runs on it: it's like a fuel. Francis, I want to ask you to help me with something.'

'I don't know how much good advice I've got left for today.'

'I don't need advice. What I'm going to need is your vote. I want to get William transferred.'

'That would be hard on Anselm, just as his time is drawing so near.'

'Francis, they're planning to get married.'

'Not yet. I think they're going to wait till after the birth. To find out if Anselm reverts.'

'Judas Priest, there's no end to the ramifications. This whole thing has degenerated into a farce. It's preposterous.'

'It's a mystery, Frederick. That's what it was from the beginning, and that's never changed. The rest is what we make out of it.'

'No.'

'We interpret and we explain. But the central fact is the only truth, and it's inexplicable.'

'It was a sign and I failed to act on it. I didn't even see it till the business about William. Francis, I've missed the boat – I should have gone to a higher authority right at the beginning, and I didn't. Now it's too late. I didn't recognize this as the great trial of my life – of all our lives. No, I don't believe it's a miracle, damn it. But I do believe it's here to test us. And I've been found wanting.'

'Don't be silly.'

'In my own eyes, first of all. But what are the others going to say?'

'They wouldn't have acted any differently.'

'Who knows? You never know these things till they happen. You say to yourself, "If. If." But that's no guide. Brother William has got to go.'

'If we sent Brother Adrian away instead –'

'He's only an outside irritation. Brother William is about to become intimately involved.'

'Do you dislike Anselm?'

'Of course not. I resent the confusion he's caused, that's all. He causes it, I have to deal with it. If you can't help me with William, it's Anselm who'll have to go. Either way, they've got to be kept apart.'

'I just don't see why.'

Frederick settled himself deeply into his chair. There were three ways he could appeal to Francis's fears, hopes and sense of right. He prepared to use them all in the order of their power to tempt and persuade. He said, 'Very well. We'll go through it again till you do.'

*

'That's right,' Brother James told Anselm. 'He wasn't at supper and he wasn't at breakfast. They drove him away in the early evening.'

Elmo and Dominic corroborated the story. Elmo said he'd

heard from Brother Anthony that the car had left from the kitchen entrance. Brother Ignatius had seen it.

Anselm held tightly to the crumpled paper he'd been handed by Marcus when he'd come to do his hair that morning. The note was from William, who said that he was being moved to another place, that he would remain true and never forget him, that Anselm and the baby would be in his thoughts and prayers, and that William loved him.

'It was Adrian,' Elmo declared.

Anselm said, 'It was Frederick.'

'Brother Adrian's been bucking all month to get at least one of us out. But don't worry. You've still got friends.'

'Adrian wouldn't have the authority. Somebody had to take the responsibility for this. The only one it could have been is the man at the top.'

'It's incredible how everything always ends up political,' Dominic said.

'It's because the structure is political,' Elmo told him. 'Anything extra you put in it is going to assume that shape.'

'He won't see me,' Anselm said. 'I've asked for an appointment and he won't give me one. I can only talk to Francis.'

'Are you coming to eat?' James asked.

'I'm banned. I'm lucky I haven't been confined to my room.'

'We'll do something about it,' James said. 'This is beyond the limit.'

Anselm nodded feebly. He held the letter to his heart and turned his head away.

*

When he woke, Brother Sebastian was bringing in a cup of soup and some crackers. 'They're having a big fight,' he whispered. As soon as he'd put down the tray, he started to hop with impatience, gesturing towards the door. 'Brother Eustace and Adrian against the others. When I left, they were all screaming like monkeys. I'll be back later, Anselm. I want to see what happens.'

Anselm waved his hand graciously. He started on the soup and flipped through a new magazine that had arrived in the morning mail. On the cover was a picture of a really darling baby, just the kind he wanted.

*

In the dining-room no single voice could be heard above the total uproar. All the brothers were yelling and pelting each other with food. A few of them were throwing bowls and bottles, too. Francis was socked hard in the side of the head while trying to make peace between one man holding a broken glass and another one brandishing a knife. He lost his hearing for a moment and had to sit down. He put his hands over his ears and let the tumult rage around him. Frederick, who had played right half-back at the seminary, fought his way to the door. He punched and jabbed a great many brothers on his way out and left the room feeling satisfied and invigorated.

*

Anselm read through the letters to the editor in his magazine. He liked finding out about how new mothers felt and what problems they had to contend with.

The first letter was from a woman who wanted to know how she could overcome her fear that friends who came to the house were going to pass on their microbes and bacteria to her baby. The editor advised her to relax and stop worrying. Anselm thought she had a point: these things were, after all, invisible. The second writer asked why sanitary towels weren't state-subsidized, as she was finding them increasingly expensive and it wasn't her fault that she had to have them – all women of child-bearing age needed them; they couldn't help it. The editor said that as a matter of fact, in poorer countries where people weren't so well-nourished, the women didn't wear any special clothing against menstruation and only ever saw a couple of drops of blood in a month; so, if you were healthy enough to menstruate heavily, that probably meant you were rich enough to afford the kotex and tampax.

The third, and last, letter was from a woman who claimed that according to her experience, unmarried mothers in the hospital she'd been in were treated with a coldness, hostility and neglect that could be dangerous for the child and certainly contributed to the mother's sense of loneliness and inferiority. Many of the nurses, she said, came from strongly religious backgrounds, and she thought it was a shame that people who were supposed to believe in peace and love-thy-neighbour should be so unfeeling, snobbish and narrow-minded.

Of course, Anselm thought, it would be true. No matter what the woman herself thought, the doctors and nurses would regard the pregnancy as an unfortunate, unplanned and unwanted accident, maybe even thinking they would be doing the mother a favour to let the child die.

He slapped the pages of the magazine together and threw it aside. He had always imagined that women enjoyed a special kind of freedom because nothing was ever going to be expected of them, but now he saw that they were just as trapped as men. He had to find a husband, and as soon as possible. It didn't matter now whether it was someone he was genuinely fond of, like William, or a man he didn't care about at all. Anybody would do, and for the baby's sake any deception would be justified. He shouldn't have second thoughts about explaining anything, or mentioning possible future transformations. Whatever the nurses were like in the hospital Duncan had chosen, he was certain their prejudices would be the same as those of other nurses. And even before he got that far, there was his life in the monastery to consider. Brother Adrian had forced Frederick to remove William: there was no telling what might happen next.

Well, he thought, he was going to have to start being like other people – to set things up and make them come true, to hustle and manipulate. He'd have to try to get rid of his enemies. If he were alone, he wouldn't care; but for the baby's sake, he had to.

Frederick could hurt him officially. But Adrian was more dangerous: violent and unpredictable. And he made Frederick nervous enough to feel compelled to act.

Anselm got up and went for a walk through the cloisters. He heard a commotion coming from the dining-room. The monks sounded like howling spectators at a football game. He kept going, down corridors and across courtyards.

He came to his favourite tree. It was a different shape because it was in leaf now. It seemed also to look older. First it was in bud, then all blossom, then covered in leaves, then came the fruit. And next year, all over again; like the stages of a woman's life.

Soon after lunch Brother Adrian went berserk and had to be taken away in a straitjacket. Before the jacket, they had used a rope.

Anselm had seen him rushing from the direction of the dining-room and coming towards him very fast, oblivious to everything around him until all at once he realized that Anselm was only a few yards away. He stopped dead, his pudgy, engorged face stiff with angers and grievances he'd been recalling.

Anselm sauntered negligently towards him, smiling kindly. Brother Adrian didn't know what to do. He looked wary, then embarrassed, and then almost afraid.

Anselm came right up close, looking into Adrian's face, and with one of his pretty, long-lashed dark eyes, winked.

The reaction was beyond anything he'd have considered possible: Adrian shrieked obscenities and fell writhing to his knees. He tried to pull at Anselm's robe, but Anselm swished decorously away. Adrian crawled after him, screaming that he was going to tear off the garment and show the stinking sin beneath; he scrabbled along the stone floor, he gibbered and finally laughed with fury. But Anselm walked ahead, whisking his skirts to the side in order to avoid the clawing hands. And when he came to the next turning, he scooted around the corner as fast as he could, and went back to his room.

*

'Did you provoke him, Anselm?' Francis asked. They were standing outside Frederick's office.

Anselm looked tranquil and he was smiling. 'Brother Adrian provokes himself,' he answered. 'That's his misfortune. It appears to be an exaggerated sense of aggression against others, but actually the main conflict is within.'

'He cracked completely.'

'It may mean that when he comes out, he'll have solved the original trouble.'

'He might not ever come out of it.'

Anselm would have liked to say: *It was him or me.* He asked, 'Do you think he was a bad man?'

'Was?'

'We're not sure what he is now. He's just collapsed.'

'Not bad, no.'

'And me? Do you think I'm bad, or morally reprehensible, or something like that?'

'Of course not. But I do think it's bad that you haven't been to confession or to Mass, or anything, in so long.'

'I've told you: there's no need. I'm in the care of a higher power.'

'It's been months.'

'Since the Annunciation, yes.'

'Was it a higher power that struck down Brother Adrian?'

Anselm laughed. 'I love these verbal tennis games,' he said. 'They're just like theology. This is the way they decide how many angels can dance on the head of a pin, and get the exact number, too. Disquisitions and inquisitions. Nobody's interested in the truth. Look at me, Francis. This is the truth.'

'Anselm, I think you're going about things the wrong way.'

'If you were in my place, would you be scared?'

'I don't know what I'd be.'

'You were always the understanding one. You have a sense of humanity. But against Frederick's ambitions and neuroses, you're impotent.'

'I wish you wouldn't talk like this.'

'Francis, who was there to speak up for me against Adrian? I needed protection against him. Did you or Frederick give me that? No. You stand there and ask me if I provoked him.'

Thudding and scraping sounds came from beyond the door. It sounded as if Frederick had begun to move the furniture.

'Don't feel bad about it,' Anselm added. 'I still like you, Francis. I just don't like the situation.'

The door opened suddenly. Frederick glared out at them. 'All right, Anselm,' he snapped. 'Come on in.'

'Should I –?' Francis offered.

'You go back to the chapel.' Frederick held the door for Anselm and then swung it away fast so that it slammed. He hurled himself solidly into the best chair. 'Sit down,' he ordered.

Anselm settled himself gingerly on the side of the sofa, with plenty of pillows behind him.

'Anselm, you do realize we can't keep you here?'

'Oh? Isn't the mother of God good enough for your order?'

'It's a question of morality.'

'It always is.'

'Men and women under the same roof. Besides, there's no proof that there was divine intervention.'

'You could say that every woman is the mother of God.'

'You could. I wouldn't. And in your case it isn't even proven how far the womanhood extends.'

'Was the divine aspect proven the first time? I thought they just took her word for it. She told her old husband and he believed it, or said he did.'

'There's a certain amount of feeling in the community that your story is put at a great disadvantage by the absence of, ah, a halo.'

Anselm glanced up, looking at a reproduction of the madonna and child which hadn't been on display the last time he'd been in the room, or at any other time he could remember. It was undoubtedly the cause of the noise he and Francis had heard from outside: it must have taken a long time to get it out from where it had been hidden. The heads of mother and child were each encircled by a band of light like the orbit of a moon around a planet.

'The halo', Anselm said, 'is a symbolic representation of an inner warmth or glow. Fire around the head is supposed to indicate enlightenment of the mind. It isn't peculiar to the Christian tradition.'

'Nevertheless, it is strongly felt that the presence of a halo would be a desirable adjunct to anyone entertaining aspirations to a holy state. It would add authenticity to your claims. Such as they are.'

He had never believed it. Frederick wouldn't countenance anything that wasn't in the books.

'If you doubt me all along the line,' Anselm said, 'what do you think the explanation is?'

'I wouldn't presume to advance a theory as to that. All I know is that the Church is against it.'

'How do you know that?'

For a moment Anselm thought that Frederick would actually break loose and say: *Because the Church is against women.* It seemed to be what he thought; but instead he answered, 'Because it doesn't make sense.'

'What does?'

'It doesn't fit in with scriptural, social, or indeed biological precedence.'

'You think it should have happened to you?'

'Heaven forbid. You don't even seem to understand that in other people's eyes this is a hideous and freakish thing to have occurred.'

'I know that. Oh, yes. Or funny. But not for all of them. A few have been good about it. I expect it's those few that scare you.'

'Scared? The Church has weathered a great many storms over the past centuries.'

'And caused some.'

'It isn't scared.'

'I give up,' Anselm said. 'You won't even think about it, will you? You just push it away. All right – you don't want me here; where do I go? I'll have to live on something, and I won't be able to work when the baby comes.'

'Brother Duncan has given me the name of a reputable nursing home.'

'The arrangement was that I was to go into a place where they'd have all the latest equipment. Either that, or stay here and have an old-fashioned home delivery. Duncan didn't want to risk that.'

'Well, the arrangements have been changed. Brother Duncan now agrees with us that the discretion of the private clinic outweighs the conviviality of a public ward. The medical attention will be in all respects identical.'

Anselm clasped his hands lightly over his bulging front. He knew now what they were going to do to him. First it was

William, and then the business with Adrian must have given them a better idea: to put Anselm in a home for the insane. He was sure that that was what they had in mind.

'All right,' he said. He fished around awkwardly for support and lumbered to his feet. Frederick made no move to help. *I hope your nose rots away,* Anselm thought, *and your fingers drop off one by one. I hope you die in pain. I hope it feels like your death lasts longer than your life ever did.*

'Goodbye, Frederick,' he said. 'I hope you think about me sometimes.'

'Of course, Anselm. I don't reproach you.'

'I hope you think about what you've done.'

'I have the welfare of the order at heart, you know that.'

'Horseshit.'

'If that's the way you're going to behave, perhaps you'd better leave now.'

'I'm trying to.' Anselm reached for the doorknob and opened the door. He said, 'And now you can go wash your hands.'

*

He pounded on Duncan's door with his fist and opened it himself. The doctor was sitting at his desk, papers in one hand and a ball-point pen in the other. Anselm closed the door behind him.

'Are those my committal documents?'

'How's that?'

'Don't smile at me, Judas. The whole damn gang of you.'

'Anselm, we're doing our best for you.'

'Going to put me in the loony bin, and my baby too.'

'The child will have the best care imaginable.'

'The best care imaginable is me.'

'An unmarried mother cannot be said to be a person of high moral standards.'

'Then I think you'd better marry me.'

'I thought you didn't like me. Or, so you said.'

'There isn't any choice. You're the last one on the list. William was the one I wanted. And after that, Francis is at least a good man. But he doesn't have any strength left. You're the only one around who can protect me.'

'I see. And why should I?'

'What did he give you, Duncan?'

'I don't know what you mean.'

'Oh yes, you do.'

'It doesn't matter.'

'Then it won't make any difference if you tell me. What was the bribe?'

'They promised me I could go to Africa. Have my own hospital. A crew of novices working under me – everything. All my dreams.'

'That's a lot more than it's worth, unless my story's true. And if it is, then there isn't any price high enough, is there? Do you think they'll keep their word?'

'Now that I think about it, no.'

'Of course not. They've strung you along for so many years now, they know they can do it for ever. All the part of you that could have been your life has become your fantasy world. And your real life has become theirs. It's been going on for years, till you don't have a life of your own any more. You do what they tell you.'

Duncan dropped the pen and papers. 'Go away,' he said.

'And they're telling you: *Get rid of Anselm.* You know what that means. If you have to kill me, they won't care. How much does being a doctor mean to you?'

'It's the way I came to God.'

'And when did you stop believing?'

'Right at the beginning,' Duncan said. 'During the long cold spell when all the old men stayed in their beds.' He looked away and sighed. 'That was before your time. I realized they'd be better in a nursing home, but I also saw how they were degenerating from day to day; how the decay of the body was becoming the decay of the mind. It was a natural progression. And the next stage was for both to come to a stop.'

'Why did you stay?'

'Because it broke me. I used to think I was too good to stay outside. I found out I wasn't good enough to go back. I didn't think it was worthwhile trying to save anybody from anything.'

'Are you going to marry me?'

Duncan's gaze ranged over the shelves where his medical reference books stood, and the filing boxes that held all the case histories of the monastery for the past twelve years. He looked at his framed certificates hanging on the wall, at the small crucifix propped against the one-volume Webster's dictionary; and at Anselm.

'All right,' he said. 'Get ready to leave tonight. I'll come to your door at eleven.'

*

They drove all night, Duncan behind the wheel. Anselm fell asleep and woke to hear the doctor talking to himself.

'Silly', Duncan muttered, 'to worry about them being able to stop me getting to Africa. I see the light now. The case of my career. Lucky I've taken a lot of notes.'

They were driving along a straight desert road at a speed of nearly ninety miles an hour.

'Slow down,' Anselm ordered. When Duncan didn't seem to hear, he shouted, 'Slow down, I said. We're going too fast.'

The doctor eased his foot from the pedal. 'I was thinking about something else,' he said.

'Think about the road.'

Anselm went back to sleep and woke once more to find that they were driving very fast again. It kept happening all through the night. Towards morning he was exhausted and beginning to feel cramping pains. They came to a place in the road where he could see slopes of green meadows ahead and a stream beyond.

'Stop the car,' he said.

'We've got to get as far away as possible.'

'I've got to go to the bathroom. Now.'

Duncan pulled over to the side.

They were in the middle of an empty landscape. It was just before daybreak; everything lay quiet in the grey light.

Anselm got out. He nearly fell. The pains were growing worse. He staggered across the field towards the stream. He was frightened. He thought he might be dying or that the baby could have been hurt, or that he had started to bleed. And he remembered how Duncan had said that as a student he used to have a foetus in a bottle and had studied it.

It would be better, he thought, to drown himself in the river straight away.

'Come back,' Duncan called after him, but Anselm struggled forward against the surging pain that threw him from side to side.

He was coming to the bank of the stream just as Duncan caught up with him and grabbed him by the elbow. Anselm beat back with his free hand, screaming.

'It's all right, Anselm – I'm a doctor,' Duncan shouted at him.

'Let me go –'

'Cut it out. Stop that, or I'll give you an injection.'

'Bastard!' Anselm shrieked. He kicked and twisted. The doctor let go, dropped to the ground and took a tight grip on Anselm's knees. Anselm fought. He dragged himself forward with the doctor hanging on. The dawn began to break around them. He tried with all his strength to gain the bank. He screamed for help until at last, impelled on the tide of his urgency, he reached the water's edge.

The sky opened. Brightness rained down on him. And he was carried along quickly, borne up and up and forward in the sweeping rush of the power he'd been searching for all his life: the wave that goes on for ever.

In the Act

As long as Helen was attending her adult education classes twice a week, everything worked out fine: Edgar could have a completely quiet house for his work, or his thinking, or whatever it was. But when the lease on the school's building ran out, all the courses would end – the flower arranging, the intermediate French and beginning Italian, the judo, oil painting and transcendental meditation.

She told Edgar well in advance. He nodded. She repeated the information, just in case. He said, 'Mm.' Over the next two weeks she mentioned the school closure at least three times. And, after she and her classmates had had their farewell party, she told him all about that, adding, 'So, I'll be at home next week. And the week after that. And so on.'

'Home?' Edgar said. 'What about your adult education things?'

She went over the whole history one more time. At last he was listening. He looked straight at her and said, 'Oh. That means you'll have to find something else to occupy yourself with on those afternoons.'

'I suppose so. I might stay home and paint here.'

'I'll be busy up in the lab.'

'I could make a kind of studio down in the cellar.'

'I'll be working. I need absolute peace and quiet.'

'Well, painting isn't very loud.'

'Helen,' he said, 'I'd like to have the house to myself.'

She never got angry with him any more; that is, she'd discovered that it did no good: he'd just look at her coldly as if she were exhibiting distressing habits usually encountered only among the lower species. Raising her voice – when she'd been driven to it – produced the same reaction from him. She'd learned to be argumentative in a fudgy, forgiving drone she'd found effective with the children: enough of that sound and the boredom level rose to a point where people would agree to anything. Edgar had a matching special tone for private quarrels: knowing, didactic, often sarcastic or hectoring. Whenever he used it outside the house, it made him disliked. It was a good voice for winning arguments by making other people hysterical. His hearing seemed to block off when it started.

She said, 'If you'd like the house to yourself, you can have it. Maybe you wouldn't mind fixing some supper for us while you're here. That way, I'd have something to look forward to, soon as I get in from walking around the block five thousand times.'

'There's no need for that.'

'OK, you can take me out. Twice a week. That'll be nice. We could see a lot of new movies in just a month.'

'You're being unreasonable.'

'Of course I am. I'm a woman,' she said. 'You've already explained that to me.'

'Let's not get into that.'

'Why not? If I'm not even allowed to paint downstairs somewhere for two afternoons a week? I never come up to the attic, do I?'

'You're always tapping on the door, asking me if I want a cup of coffee.'

'Only that once.'

'It was a crucial moment.'

'Well, now you've got your thermos bottle and everything, you're all set up there.'

'You came up other times.'

'That big noise – explosion, whatever it was: of course I did. I was worried. You could burn the house down.'

'I think this is time number fourteen for telling you that the experiments are not dangerous.'

'Fourteen? I'm sure that must be right. You keep track of things like that so well. Each time I conceived, it was a positive miracle of timing. I can remember you crossing off the days on the calendar.'

'You're trying to sidetrack me.'

'I'm trying to get you to allow me to stay in my own house.'

'I really do need complete freedom to work. It simply isn't the same when somebody else is in the house. Even if you didn't try to interrupt me again.'

'The only other time I knocked on the door was when there was all the screaming.'

'I told you,' Edgar said. 'I got the volume too high.'

'It sounded like real people.'

'It was a tape.'

'For heaven's sake, Edgar – where can I go?'

'See some friends? Look around a museum or two. Find another one of those adult education places.'

All at once she felt hurt. She didn't want to argue any more, even if there was a hope of winning. She was ready to walk out and tramp up and down the streets like a child running away. She said, 'I'll try,' and went into the living-room. She walked around the corner, into the alcove where the desk was. She sat down in the plump, floral-patterned chair, put her knees up and curled into a ball. She heard his feet going up the stairs, then up the next flight to the attic. He wouldn't be wondering whether he'd made her miserable. He'd be getting out the keys to unlock the attic door, which he kept locked all the time, and if he was inside, bolted too. He'd be sighing with pleasure at the prospect of getting back to his experiment. Of course he was right: she'd have to find something to do with her time. But just for a few minutes, she'd stay in the flowered chair, with her arm over her eyes.

*

The next morning, she was angry. He read through his newspaper conscientiously, withdrawing his attention from it for only a few seconds to tell her that she hadn't cut all the segments entirely free in his grapefruit – he'd hit exactly four that were still attached. She knew, he said, how that kind of thing annoyed him.

She read her letters. Her two sons were at boarding school. Edgar approved. She herself would never have suggested sending, or allowing, the boys to go away: in fact, the suggestion had come from them. They had suddenly clamoured for the expensive snobberies of the East Coast; they needed, they wanted, they couldn't live without education at the last of the all-male establishments. Helen's attendance at adult education classes dated from the time of their emigration.

Both of the boys had written to her. Usually she was delighted by whatever they had to say. This morning their news seemed to be nothing but boastful accounts of how they had won some sports event or beaten another boy at something, shown him who was who: and so forth. She was probably lucky they were far away. That would have been two more grapefruits she wouldn't be able to get right.

When she passed the letters over to Edgar, he was soberly pleased with the boys' victories. He wasn't too bad as a father. He wasn't actually too bad anyway, except that sometimes he irritated her to distraction. She still couldn't believe he was asking her to get out of the house every Tuesday and Thursday, so he'd have the whole place to himself.

'What's wrong with the coffee pot?' he added.

She snapped back out of her thoughts. 'I was wondering about adult education classes,' she told him.

'Fine. More of that flower arranging, or maybe a new language.'

'Yes, maybe. Who would I talk to in a new language?'

'Well, the teacher. Anybody else who speaks it.' He went back to the paper. Soon afterwards he took his last sip of coffee, looked around for his briefcase, and left the house for the pathology laboratories where he had his job. They did a lot of work for the police as well as for hospitals and private clinics. His speciality was haemoglobin.

With the dusting and vacuuming she worked off some of her vexation. Then she sat down with a cup of coffee. She phoned about the plumber's bill, the bracelet link that was supposed to be done but still wasn't, the garage. Nothing was ready. She was about to call up her friend, Gina, to complain about life in general, when she had a better idea: she'd go up to the attic.

She had a key. Long before the day when there was the explosion or the one when she'd heard the screams, she had wanted to see inside his laboratory. The loud noise had at first scared her off from the idea of trespassing, and then reinforced her initial desire: to go in and take a look around – make sure everything was all right up there. The screams too, at first frightening, had made her eager to see, to know; for a few moments she had been convinced that there were real people up there. Not that Edgar would be carrying out any experiment that would cause pain to someone, but – she didn't really know what she thought about it all.

The way he locked the door before he came downstairs; the way he locked up as soon as he entered the lab and shut the door behind him, shooting the bolt across: it made her nervous. If there was nothing inside that could harm her, it was an insult to keep her out. On the other hand, if there was something dangerous up there, did she dare go in and find out about it?

The key was one of the extras from the Mexican bowl that had been shoved over to the end of a workbench in the cellar. The bowl was filled with old keys. Helen had looked through the whole collection when they had moved in; she'd assumed that they came from other houses or even from workplaces long vanished. There were about fifty keys, some large, long and rusted, like the sort of thing that might be needed for a garden gate or a toolshed. After the screams, when her frustration and curiosity about the lab had reached a sudden peak, she'd remembered the bowl of keys. Some could be discounted straight away, but about a dozen were possible.

The one that fitted was an ordinary brass key. She'd unlocked the door, pushed it open slowly, peeked in and locked up again. She hadn't stepped over the threshold. Now, standing in the middle of her living-room rug, she wondered why she hadn't gone in and had a thorough look at everything. She seemed to recall that what was in the room had been fairly uninteresting: tables, benches, racks of test tubes, a microscope, a couple of bunsen burners, two sinks, a bookcase against the wall. Never mind: this time she'd go through the place carefully.

She got the key and started up the stairs, moving fast. She had the door open before there was time to think about it.

The room looked slightly different from when she'd last seen it, and more crowded. There were more bottles, jars and test tubes. Standing racks had been added at the far end, where the empty steamer trunks used to be. She also remembered a rather nice sofa; more like a *chaise longue*. Edgar had occasionally stayed up in the lab overnight, working while she'd watched the late movie downstairs, or read a detective story. She'd always thought the sofa was too good to leave up in the attic, but Edgar had insisted that he needed it. Now she couldn't see it. But, as she moved forward, she noticed with surprise that a bathtub had been added to the collection of sinks and troughs; it was an old, high-standing type. She couldn't imagine how Edgar had managed to get it in there. He'd have had to hire people. *Out of the van and to the front door*, she was thinking; *up the stairs*. She began to worry about the weight. Even though the house was well-built and strong, and most of the heavy equipment stood around the sides, it wasn't a good idea to fill up a place with too many heavy objects. Edgar had undoubtedly gone into the question of beam-stress and calculated the risks; he'd have found out all about the subject. Of course, every once in a while, he was wrong.

She looked into the first alcove: empty. She turned into the second, bigger one. There was the sofa. And there was a bundle of something thrown on top of it, wrapped in a sheet. She was about to pass by when she saw a hand protruding from one of the bottom folds of the sheet.

She let out a gurgled little shriek that scared her. She looked away and then back again. Propped against the edge of the sofa's armrest was a leg, from the knee down. Next to it lay an open shoebox containing fingers. She began to feel that her breathing wasn't right. She wanted to get out, but there was still the question of what was under the sheet. She had to know that. If she ran out without looking, she'd never summon the courage to use the key again.

She counted to ten, wiped her hands down the sides of her skirt and told herself that whatever the thing was, it couldn't be worse than what they were liable to show you nowadays on television, even in the news programmes. She reached out and pulled down the edge of the sheet.

It was pretty bad: a head with the face laid bare. The muscles, tendons and other bits across the face were mainly red or pink, a few of them darker than she'd imagined things like that were supposed to be. But they weren't wet; there was no blood. She bent her knees and looked more closely. From inside the still open skull she caught the glint of metal. There were lots of small wheels and bolts and tubes inside, like the interior of a watch or a radio.

She straightened up, rearranged the sheet and gently put out a hand towards the half leg. She felt the skin below the place where the joint should have been attached to some knuckly part of a knee.

A chill ran over her scalp. The skin, though unwarmed, was creamy, smooth, soft and silky, uncannily delicious to the touch. She pulled back her hand. For about five minutes she stood just staring at the wall. Then, she understood. The body wasn't real. Naturally, it couldn't be real: a dead body would have to be refrigerated. Therefore, that thing there on the sofa in pieces was not a corpse Edgar had taken from the pathology morgue; it was a body he had built himself out of other materials. Why on earth he'd want to do such a thing was beyond her.

She left everything in place, closed the door behind her and locked it with her key. Later in the day the answer came to her: her husband must be pioneering research on victims of road accidents. She had read an article several years before, about a medical school that simulated injuries by strapping life-sized replicas of people into cars; after smashing them up, they studied the damaged parts. The project had been funded by an insurance company. No doubt Edgar was working on something similar, although greatly in advance of anything she'd heard about. That skin, for example, was fantastic. And all the intricate bands of muscle and everything – the thing was very complicated. She still didn't understand what the clockwork mechanism in the head would be for, but maybe that would have something to do with a remote-control guidance system. The whole business was explainable. She stopped feeling scared. Nevertheless, she was thankful that the eyelids had been closed.

Edgar worked hard up in the attic for several days. She thought she'd give him a week and then go up and check on the progress he'd made. In the meantime, she looked into the possibilities of new adult education schools. She had lunch with Gina, who was worried about her daughter's weight problem and who poured out a long story to her about psychologists, behaviourists, weight-watchers and doctors. Helen listened sympathetically; she was glad to have such a convoluted narrative to concentrate on – there was no room for temptation to talk about what was troubling her: Edgar and the activity he was engaged in up in the attic.

Two days later, Mr Murdock from the old oil painting classes asked her to tea with Pat and Babs. The three of them cheered her up. Mr Murdock had already left the new classes they'd joined; the other two were going to, but for the moment they were sticking it out in order to be able to report back all the latest stories about the odious Miss Bindale. Miss Bindale was driving everyone away: she might end by causing the teacher to resign, too. It was a shame, they all said: one person could spoil everything. Mr Murdock recommended a language school he'd gone to for French. The place wasn't so much fun as their adult education school – it was more serious, the classes were mostly for businessmen and unless you applied for the weekend, everything was in the evening. Pat said, 'It'd be a really good way to meet men. If you don't want the address, I'll keep it myself.'

'You'll never get anywhere if it's a language,' Babs told her. 'Car maintenance, that's the one. There aren't any other women at all.'

'Or karate,' Helen said.

'I wouldn't try it. You pick the wrong type there – they'll throw you against the wall and say it was an accident because they forgot to leave out some basic move. No thanks.'

Pat said that a friend of hers, named Shirley, had gone to a couple of other adult education places and had given her the addresses; four different ones. 'I liked the first one, so I never tried the others, but I can send you the addresses. I'll take a good look around, see where I put that piece of paper.'

Edgar spent the whole of the weekend up in the lab: Saturday night and Sunday too. He came down for meals. On Friday he'd brought her flowers, given her a talk about why the work was going to be necessary; when, where and how he'd expect his meals during the period; and how he appreciated her cooperation. She said, 'Yes, dear,' to everything, put his red roses in a vase, took it into the living-room and told him they looked lovely. She preferred daffodils, chrysanthemums, tulips, daisies, stocks, sweet peas, asters: almost anything. And if they had to be roses, any colour other than red.

He stayed in the bedroom Friday night, making sure that she didn't feel neglected. He wanted her to be satisfied with the arrangements. She was not only satisfied; she was surprised.

She carried out her appointed cooking tasks with grim cheerfulness. She could hardly wait until Monday, when he'd be out of the house and she could go look at what he'd been doing.

On Sunday she knew that he'd achieved some kind of break-through in the work. He was transformed, radiant. He looked tired, but serene. Whatever it was, was finished. However, he didn't say anything about coming downstairs. He stayed up in the attic that night.

The next morning she waited a while after he'd gone. She was going to give him enough time to get all the way to work, and more: in case he'd forgotten something and had to come back for it. She wanted to be able to look at everything and not feel rushed. Whatever he'd completed was still up in the attic – all he'd taken with him was his briefcase.

She did the dishes, made the bed, checked her watch. She looked out of the window, although she didn't need to: it was one of those unnecessary things people do when they're anxious about something. She got the key.

The attic workroom looked the same, as far as she could see. She stepped in, closing the door lightly, so that it touched the jamb but didn't click into the frame. She walked forward. Her eyes jumped from place to place.

She peered into the first alcove: nothing. She hurried to the second; there was the sofa. And on it lay a young and beautiful woman: the creamy skin was as it had been before. The face had been fitted with its outer coating; everything there was in place: the lilac-tinted eyelids with long, dark lashes, the cupid's-bow mouth, the small, pert nose.

The face lay in the centre of a cloudlike nest of twirly blonde ringlets. A blue ribbon peeped out from a bunch of them at the back. The dress she wore was pink and cut like some sort of ballerina costume: the bodice like a bathing-suit top, the skirt standing out with layers of net and lace and stiffening. Her feet and legs were bare. The toe-nails, like the nails on the fingers, had been painted red.

Helen reached out towards the left leg. She ran her hand over it, stopped, and then quickly pulled back. The skin was warm. She moved along the side of the sofa, to where she could be near the head. 'Wake up,' she ordered. There was no response. Naturally: this wasn't a person – it was some kind of doll. It was so lifelike that it was almost impossible to believe that; nevertheless, her husband had built it.

As she stood there, trying to imagine why Edgar should have made a doll so detailed in that particular way, with painted nails and a blue satin bow and everything, she began to wonder how lifelike the rest of the body was. That was an important question.

If she hadn't seen the thing in its partly assembled state the week before, she wouldn't have known this was a replica, a machine. But having seen it complete, there was – all at once – no doubt in her mind that her husband had invented it for his own private purposes: otherwise, why make it so definitely non-utilitarian?

She thought she'd better know what she was up against. She examined the doll thoroughly, taking off the pink dress first, and then the black lace bra and underpants. She started to lose her sense of danger. She was getting mad. Who else, other than

Edgar himself, could have chosen the pink dress and black underwear? He couldn't walk into a dress shop in her company without becoming flustered, yet she could picture him standing at a counter somewhere and asking for the clothes, saying in his argument-winning voice, 'Black lace, please, with a ribbon right about here.' He'd known the right size, too – but of course he'd known that. The doll had been built to specification: his specifications. *Oh,* Helen thought, *the swine.*

And the thing was so real-looking. She was sitting on the edge of the sofa and fiddling around with the doll's head, investigating the way the hair grew, when she felt her finger push down on what must have been a button behind the left ear.

The doll's eyelids rose, revealing a pair of enormous blue eyes. The lips parted in a dazzling smile, the torso began to breathe.

'Oh,' Helen said. 'Oh, dear.'

'Oh, dear,' the doll repeated gently. 'What can the matter be?'

Helen thought she might be going crazy. She asked – automatically and politely – 'Who are you?'

'I'm fine,' the doll told her. 'How are you?'

'Not how. Who?'

The doll smiled lovingly and relapsed into an expression of joyful delight. The eyelids blinked every once in a while. Helen watched. The action had evidently been programmed to be slightly irregular, to avoid an impression of the mechanical. Still, there was something hypnotic about it. The lips were silent. The voice too must be on a computer: the doll would only answer if you spoke to it. The voice-tape scanner didn't seem to be quite perfect yet, either.

She was trying to push the button again, to turn off the eyelids, when she hit a nearby second button instead and sent the machine into overdrive. The lids drooped, the arms went up and out, the knees flew apart, the hips began to gyrate in an unmistakable manner, and the lips spoke.

Helen shot to her feet, stumbled back a few steps and crashed against the wall. She folded her arms and stayed where she was, staring with mesmerized intensity while the doll went through the cycle it had begun. Probably there were many other things it could do – this would be merely one of the variations. Out of the rosebud mouth came a mixture of babytalk and obscenity, of crude slang and sentimentality.

She gripped the sides of her arms and waited sternly until the exercise appeared to be over, though the doll was still begging in sweetly tremulous whispers for more. She stepped forward and slapped it across the face. 'Darling,' it murmured. She scrabbled among the golden curls, grabbed the ear and pushed every button she could see. There were five, all very small. They looked like pinheads. There were also two tiny switches she decided to leave alone. She'd seen enough. She was quivering with rage, shame and the need for revenge.

When she thought about wearing herself out doing the shopping and cooking and scrubbing, she prickled all over with a sense of grievance. She'd been slaving away for years, just so he could run up to the attic every evening and keep his secrets. And the boys were turning into the same kind as their father: what they wanted too was someone menial to provide services for them. And then they could spend their lives playing.

She saw herself as a lone, victimized woman beleaguered by selfish men. Her anger gave her a courage she wouldn't otherwise have had.

She ran out and across the hall to the other side of the attic – the side that wasn't locked. There were the trunks and suitcases, including the nice big one with wheels. There too was the chest full of spare blankets and quilts. She pulled out two of the blankets and took them into the lab. Then she carried the suitcase downstairs to the front hall.

She went up to the attic again, dressed the doll in its clothes, rolled it into the blankets and dragged them across the floor and down the stairs. She unzipped the suitcase, dumped the doll inside, folded the legs and arms and began to pack it tight, zipping the outside as she stuffed the pink skirt away.

She went up to the attic one more time, to put the blankets back and to shut the door of the lab.

She got her coat and handbag. The suitcase was easy to manage until she had to lift it into the back of the car. That wasn't so easy. Edgar was the one with the big car. Still, she could do it. All she'd have to worry about would be steps. The doll seemed to weigh exactly the same as a real woman of equivalent height and size.

There were three choices: the airport, the bus depot and the train station. The train station was large and nearer than the airport. She'd try it first.

Everything went well. She found a parking space straight away and was able to wheel the suitcase across the road, on to the sidewalk and through the doors, up an escalator and across several waiting rooms, to the locker halls. There was a whole bank of extra-large lockers; she heaved the case into one of them, put in enough money to release the key, and went to get some more coins. She ended up having to buy a paperback book, but the woman at the cash register agreed to let her have two big handfuls of change. She fed the money meticulously into the slot. The suitcase would be paid up for over two weeks.

*

Ron was getting out of his car when he saw the woman slam her car door and start to wheel the suitcase across the parking lot. She looked possible: the case seemed heavy.

He followed, walking casually. He had a repertoire of walks calculated to throw off suspicion. He hadn't had to learn any of them – they came naturally, like all his other athletic talents. That was what he was always telling Sid down at the gym: *I got natural talent. I don't need nobody teaching me nothing.* He still couldn't understand how Sid had knocked him out in the third round. He hadn't given up the idea that something had been slipped into his Coke. Sometimes there was a lot of heavy betting going on, even when you were just sparring.

She looked like a nice, respectable woman; pretty, took care of herself. The kind that said no. Her clothes cost something, which was a good sign; so was the trouble she had getting the wheels of the case up on to the kerb. Of course, she could be getting on a train.

He followed her all the way around the corner to the lockers. He watched, standing against the wall and pretending to look at his paper. When she was through, he followed her far enough to see that she was coming back. She put a lot of money in the locker: good – the case would be there a while. But he'd probably better get it quick, before somebody else did.

She left the building. That might mean she was going for a second suitcase that she hadn't been able to handle in the same load. He looked around, folded his paper, held it to cover what he was doing, and stepped up to the locker. He took a metal slide out of his pocket and stuck it into the keyhole. It was a cinch.

Some people could never have looked unsuspicious while wheeling away stolen luggage, but you had to believe in yourself: that was the main thing. Ron did his best. He didn't hurry. He got the bag into the back seat of his car and started off. Her car, he noticed, was already gone.

Normally he'd have stopped just around the block somewhere, to go through the contents; but the traffic was building up. He decided to drive straight on home. He was beginning to get curious about what was inside. The suitcase was really heavy. The moment he'd pulled it from the locker he'd thought: *Great – gold bars; silver candlesticks.* A lot of people had those lockers.

She hadn't looked like that type, but how could you ever tell? She could be helping a pal, or a husband. A guy he knew had found some cash once – a whole overnight bag full of the stuff. And all of it counterfeit, it turned out; he'd done time for that.

He got the bag out of the car, into the apartment block where he lived, up three floors in the elevator, down the hall to his bedroom. He broke the locks as soon as he'd thrown his jacket over the back of the easy chair. He unzipped both sides.

A powerful odour of mothballs was released into the room as the lid sprang open, disclosing a blonde woman in a pink dress. She was huddled up like a baby rabbit and he was sure she was dead. He'd be suspected, of course. He'd have to ditch the case someplace, fast. He put his hand on her arm to squash her in again. The arm was warm. He jumped away. He closed the curtains and turned on the lights.

He couldn't put her back. She might be alive now, but soon she'd suffocate. It was a good thing he'd found her in time. When he thought of that respectable type who'd shut her in the locker, he was amazed.

He got the plastic sheet he'd used to cover his Norton Atlas before one of his friends had borrowed the machine and smashed it to pieces. He spread the sheet over the bed and lifted the woman on top of it. He thought she looked fabulous, just like a dream. She seemed to be unharmed except for a mild discoloration on her left cheek, which might have been sustained in the packing. There was no blood that he could see. He thought he'd better do a complete check, to make sure she was all right. He took off her clothes. The dress was a bit weird, but she had some pretty classy underwear. Under the underwear was OK, too. He thought he might have some fun with her, while he was at it. He'd saved her life, after all: she owed him.

He was beginning to wonder what was going on – despite the warmth, she didn't actually seem to be breathing – when, accidentally, as he was running his hand through her hair, the side of his thumb hit two tiny, hard knobs of some kind and his problems were over.

The woman sighed and stretched out her arms. Her hands came softly around his back. Her eyes opened, her mouth smiled. She said, 'Ooh, you're so nice.'

*

Helen was curled up in her favourite living-room chair when Edgar came in from work. She was reading the paperback she'd had to buy at the station; a nurse novel called *Summer of Passion*. She heard the car, the slam of the door, his feet crunching on the gravel of the driveway, the door being opened and shut. He called out, 'Hi,' going up the stairs. She answered, and read to the end of the paragraph: *at last Tracy knew that she had found the man of her desires and that this summer of passion would live in her heart forever.* Helen yawned. She put the phone bill between the pages of the book and stood up. Edgar was taking his time. Maybe he was running around the attic in circles, every time coming back to the empty sofa and not believing it. She didn't feel sorry. She felt mean-hearted, even cruel, and absolutely satisfied. Let him be on the receiving end of things for a while. It might do him some good.

The attic door slammed. He'd figured out she had to be the one to blame. He came thundering down the stairs and across the front hall. She put the book down on the coffee table. Edgar dashed into the room, breathing loudly. His hair was sticking up, as if he'd been running his hands through it. 'Where is she?' he demanded.

'Who?'

'My experiment. You know what I'm talking about.'

'Oh? It's a she, is it?'

'Where is she?' he shouted. 'You get her back here, or you're going to wish you'd never been born.' He took a step forward.

'Oh no, you don't,' she said. 'You lay a finger on me, and you'll never see her again.'

'What have you done with her?'

'That's my business. If you want her back, we're going to have to talk it over.'

He looked defiant, but he gave in. She took up her stance by the red roses, he struck a pose in front of the Chinese lamp with the decorations that spelled out Good Fortune and Long Life. He said, 'You don't know what you've done. It's a masterpiece. It's as if you'd stolen the Mona Lisa. The eyes – my God, how I worked to get the eyes right. It's a miracle.'

A woman, she thought, *can get the eyes and everything else right without any trouble: her creative power is inherent. Men can never create; they only copy. That's why they're always so jealous.*

'What's her name, by the way?' she asked.

He looked embarrassed, finally. 'Dolly,' he said.

'Brilliant. I suppose you're going to tell me this is love.'

'Helen, in case you still haven't grasped it after all these years – my main interest in life is science. Progress. Going forward into the future.'

'OK. You just let me know how long it's going to take you to come up with the companion-piece.'

'What?'

This was her moment. She thought she might begin to rise from the floor with the rush of excitement, the wonderful elation: dizzying, intoxicating, triumphant. This was power. There was even a phrase for it: drunk with power. No wonder people wouldn't give it up once they got hold of it. It was as if she'd been grabbed by something out of the sky, and pulled up; she was going higher and higher. Nothing could hurt her. She was invulnerable.

'I want,' she said, 'what you had – something nice on the side. A male escort: presentable, amusing, and a real stud.'

'No way.'

'Then I guess it's goodbye, Dolly.'

'If you don't tell me –'

'Don't you dare touch me,' she shrieked. 'It's all right for you to play around in my own home, while I'm down here doing the housework, isn't it?'

'I don't think you understand.'

'I don't?'

'It's just a doll.'

'Pubic hair and nipples everywhere you look – that's some doll. And what about that twitch and switch business she does? That's a couple of giant steps ahead of the ones that just wet their pants and cry mama.'

'It may turn out to have important medical uses. Ah . . . therapeutic.'

'Good. That's just what I'm in need of.'

'Helen,' he said, 'let's forget all about this.'

'OK. It isn't that important to me. I can find a real man anywhere. But if you want your Dolly back, you can make me a perfect one. That's only fair. One for you and one for me.'

'I don't know why you're so steamed up.'

'I'm not that crazy about adultery, that's all. Especially if I'm the one who's being acted against.'

'There's no question of adultery. In any case – well, in any case there's no moral lapse unless it's done with another person.'

'No kidding? I thought the moral lapse was there even if you only did it in the mind.'

'Let me explain it to you.'

'Fine,' she told him. 'Just as long as you keep working at my gigolo. And if there aren't any lapses, we're both in the clear, aren't we?'

*

The instant Dolly opened her eyes, Ron fell in love with her. Everything was different. Everything was solved. He'd never thought it would happen to him. He hadn't believed in it: Love. It was going to come as a big surprise to his friends down at the gym – they'd all agreed long ago that life was a lot better without women. They'd just have to get used to her. She was part of his life now. The fact that she was a doll he regarded as an advantage. You didn't need to feed her or buy her drinks or stop the car so she could keep looking for a rest room every five minutes. She was unchanging. The extraordinary skin she possessed cleaned and preserved itself without trouble; the mark on her cheek faded even before the smell of mothballs had worn off. A fresh, spring-like fragrance seemed to breathe from her body. His friends would have to accept her as they'd have had to if he'd gotten married. That was what things were going to be like – like having a wife, except that not being human, of course, she was nicer.

That first day, he figured out how to use all the push-buttons. He knew her name because she told him: she got right up close to his face, winked, gave a little giggle and whispered, 'Dolly wants to play.' She was so good at answering his questions that it took him some time to realize she was repeating, and that if he asked a particular question, she'd always give the same response, or one of several set replies. A similar repetitiveness characterized some of her physical reactions, but he didn't mind that. And when you thought about it, her conversation wasn't much more limited than most women's. She sometimes said something that didn't fit, that was all – never anything really stupid. And if she came up with the wrong wording, that wasn't her fault. It almost never happened. Her answers were so good and she was so understanding about everything, that he believed she knew what he was getting at; even if she was a doll, even if she wasn't real in any way. To him she was real. When he looked into her beautiful eyes, he was convinced that she loved him. He was happy. He was also sure that there were no others like her. There could be only one Dolly.

He told her everything. All about himself, what he wanted out of life, what his dreams of success used to be, how he'd grown up: all the things he used to think. He didn't know what he thought any more and he didn't have any dreams left. He cried in her arms. She stroked his hair and called him darling. She said, 'Hush, darling. It's all right.' He believed her. He talked to her for hours. He knew that if she could, she'd speak as freely as he did.

*

Edgar applied for emergency leave from his job. It knocked out the holiday they'd been planning to take with the boys in the summer vacation, but he needed the time. He worked all day and most of the night. Helen brought up his meals on a tray. She tried to make comments once. He screamed at her. He shouted threats, oaths and accusations, ending up with a warning that if she didn't shut up about absolutely everything, he wouldn't be responsible. She smiled. She said in her gooey, peacemaker's voice, 'What a pompous twerp you've turned into, Edgar.' It was all out in the open now.

And he no longer felt guilty about his infidelities, mental or physical. It served her right. He wished that he'd been more adventurous, all the way back to the beginning, when they'd married: he wished he'd led a double life – a triple one. It was galling to be so hard at work, wasting the strength of his body and brain on the creation of a thing intended to give her pleasure. He could do it, of course; he had mastered the technique and the principles. But it was infuriating. It seemed to him now that there hadn't been a single moment when she'd been anything but a hindrance to him. She nagged, she had terrible moods, she wasn't such a wonderful cook, every once in a while she made a truly embarrassing scene – like the one at Christmas with his uncle – and she could wear really dumpy clothes that he didn't like. She'd keep wearing them after he'd expressly told her he didn't like them. And he didn't think she'd brought the boys up that well, either. They got away from her just in time.

He had needed Dolly in order to keep on living with his wife. If he couldn't have Dolly back, there was no point in going on. Now that there was no longer any secrecy, there was probably no more hope for his marriage. Still, as long as he could recover Dolly, there was hope for him.

When he thought about Dolly, he was ready to go through any trial, do any amount of work. He missed her. He missed the laugh in her voice and the look in her eyes when she said, 'Let's have a good time. Let's have a ball.'

He lost his concentration for a moment. The scalpel slipped. The voicebox let out a horrible cry. He waited to see if Helen would come charging up the stairs to crouch by the banisters and listen. Nothing happened. Now that she knew, she wasn't worried. She'd wait and be silent.

*

At the beginning Ron was satisfied with keeping Dolly in his bedroom. But as he began to depend on her, he felt the desire to take her out. He'd found the buttons to make her walk and respond to his request for her to sit down or get up. A mild pressure on her arm would help her to change pace, turn a corner. Naturally the pink dress wasn't right for outdoor wear. He bought her a T-shirt and a skirt. She looked great in them. But the shoes were a problem: you had to try them on. He didn't want to spend money on the wrong size. He asked his friend, Charlie, in a general way, what to do if you didn't know your size and couldn't put the shoes on to find out: if you were buying a present, say. Charlie told him to try L. L. Bean. 'All you need to do,' he told Ron, 'is send them a tracing of your foot.'

He had a lot of fun making the tracings with Dolly. He sent away for a pair of flat shoes. When they arrived, he walked her around the room in them for a long time, examining the skin on her feet at intervals. He didn't know what would happen if her skin got badly broken or damaged. He had no idea where he could take her to be fixed. He asked if the shoes felt OK; she said everything was just fine and she loved him – he was wonderful.

He sent away for a pair of high heels and some rubber boots as well as socks, a parka, a shirt and a sweater, a pair of corduroy trousers and a blue and white flannel nightgown with ruffles around the neck. He also went out and bought some fingernail polish. Her nails appeared to be indestructible, but the polish was chipping. The girl behind the counter gave him a little lecture about the necessity of removing the old polish before putting on a second coat. She sold him quite a lot of cosmetic equipment. He thought, since he was there, he might buy eye make-up and lipstick, too. 'Does it come with instructions?' he asked. The salesgirl sold him a book with pictures and an expensive box full of tiny brushes.

He got hold of an airport case that contained a roll of traveller's cheques and five silk suits. He won on the races and after that, at the tables. Dolly was bringing him luck.

He took her out. People turned to look at her because she was so beautiful, not because they thought something was wrong. He felt like a million dollars walking down the street with her. It was too bad that he couldn't get her to eat or drink, because then he'd be able to take her into a restaurant or a bar. But just walking along, arm in arm, was nice. One afternoon he bumped into Charlie, who took a look at Dolly and nearly fell over. 'Jeez, Ron,' he said, 'what a doll.'

Dolly wrinkled up her nose and giggled. She squirmed a little with excitement. Her eyes got bigger.

'Jeez,' Charlie said again. 'You going to introduce me?'

'Charlie, this is Dolly,' Ron said. 'Say hi, honey.'

'Hi, honey,' Dolly said. She put her hand in Charlie's.

Charlie said, 'Oh, boy. You been holding out on us, pal. Hi there, Dolly. I don't know why my old buddy Ron here didn't tell me about you before.'

'We got to be going,' Ron said.

'Oh, come on. You don't have to go, do you, Dolly?'

'Yes,' Ron said. 'Say goodbye, sugarpie.'

Dolly twiddled her fingers at Charlie. She gave him a breathy, hicupping laugh and then whispered, 'Goodbye, sugarpie.'

'Oh, boy,' Charlie said again.

Ron pulled her away fast. She clip-clopped beside him quickly in her high heels, her hips swaying, her large eyes roving happily.

It hadn't gone too badly, but he didn't trust her for extended conversation. He figured they'd better put in some practice first.

He took on a job delivering goods for a friend. Everything was packed up in boxes. Maybe the boxes contained stuff he shouldn't know about. Normally he wouldn't care, but now he kept thinking about Dolly: what would happen to her if he got caught? She'd be found by somebody else, who'd take her away and keep her, just the way he had.

He stopped checking out the airport lockers. He began to look through the papers for legitimate work. Down at the gym they thought he was crazy – at least, they did at first. Word had gone around about Dolly; everybody asked about her. When was Ron going to bring her in to meet the gang?

He coached her for a while and then took her down to the gym. They all loved her. And they thought she was real. They said they could understand how Ron would want to settle down to something steady, if he had a girl like that. An older man named Bud actually clapped him on the shoulder and said something about wedding bells.

Ron wondered if maybe he could get away with introducing her to his sister and her family. He didn't see why not. He phoned Kathleen. She said sure.

'Only thing is,' he explained, 'she's on this very strict diet, so she won't eat anything. I thought I'd better tell you.'

'Well, I can fix her a salad.'

'No, it's sort of everything. She's allergic.'

Kathleen told him not to worry. He put Dolly into the car, together with a change of clothes and her rubber boots. He drove carefully, thinking all the time that if they crashed, or if she were to cut herself in some other way, he wouldn't know what to do, where to take her. He didn't even know what was inside her; if she got hurt seriously, whatever was in there might all leak out.

Kathleen decided, as soon as she saw Dolly: she didn't like her. Her husband, Ben, thought Dolly was great. The children liked her too, but they didn't understand why she wouldn't pat their dog, when it was evidently so interested in her and kept sniffing around her. Ron grabbed the dog and kept it by him. Later in the afternoon while they were walking along the path by the creek, the dog ran ahead and almost made Dolly trip over. At that moment Ron thought it couldn't work: his friends at the gym were going to accept her, real or not, but his family never would.

Before he drove off he sat Dolly in the car, walked back to where Kathleen was standing, and asked, 'Well? Do you like her?'

'Sure. She's fine,' Kathleen said. 'A little dumb, maybe.'

'But nice. She's got a heart of gold.'

'I guess it's just – if people are really silly all the time, it's too much like being with the kids. I start to get aggravated.'

All the way back to town he felt angry. It wasn't right that he should have to hide Dolly away like a secret vice. She should be seen and admired.

The next day he took her on an expedition into town: through the parks, into the big stores, around one of the museums. The weather was good, which was lucky. He didn't know how she'd react to rain or whether she'd be steady on her feet over wet sidewalks. Of course, he didn't know how a prolonged exposure to sunlight was going to affect her, either, but she seemed all right. Her feet, too, looked all right.

He took her by public transport, since that was part of the idea. They rode on the subway, then they changed to a bus. He had his arm around her as usual, when one of the other passengers got up from the seat behind them, knocking Ron's arm and the back of Dolly's head as he went by. Ron clutched her more tightly; inadvertently he hit several of the control buttons.

Dolly's arms raised themselves above her head, her eyelids flickered, her legs shot apart, her hips began to swing forward and back. 'Ooh,' she said, 'you're so good.'

He tried to find the switch. He panicked and turned it on higher by mistake.

She went faster, gasping, 'Ooh, you feel so nice, ooh do it to me.'

He fumbled at her hairline while people around them said, 'Come on, Mister, give us a break,' and, 'That's some girlfriend you've got – can't you do it at home?'

He found the switch just as she was telling him – and the whole bus – the thing she loved best about him.

The driver put on the brakes and said, 'OK, Mac, get that tramp out of my bus.'

Ron refused. If he got out with Dolly before he'd planned to, he'd never be able to walk her to where they could get a cab or find another bus. 'She can't help it,' he said. 'She's sick.'

The driver came back to insist; he had a big beer-belly. Ron got ready to punch him right in the middle of it and then drive the bus away himself. Dolly slumped against him, her face by his collarbone, her eyes closed. 'It just comes over her sometimes,' he said. That wasn't enough of an explanation, apparently. He added, 'She had a real bad time when she was a kid.'

The bus went quiet. Everyone thought over the implications of what Ron had said. The driver went back to the wheel. The bus started up again. Still no one spoke. The silence was beginning to be painful. Ron didn't know why he'd chosen that particular thing to say, even though it had worked – it had shut everybody up fine. But it left him feeling almost as strange as everyone else seemed to. By the end of the ride he'd begun to have a clear idea of the appalling childhood Dolly must have lived through. And he promised himself to take even better care of her than before, in order to make up for her sad life.

When his stop came, he carried her out in his arms. She appeared to be asleep. A few of the other passengers made hushed exclamations and murmurs of interest as he left.

He had to admit that there was always going to be a risk if he took her out in public. Driving alone with her in the car wouldn't be such a problem. He wanted to take her to the beach: to camp in the dunes and make love on the sands at night. He thought her skin would be proof against the abrasions of sand, the burning of the sun, the action of salt water. But he wasn't sure. The more he thought about her possible fragility, the more he worried. If he were hurt, even severely, he could be put together again: but could she?

*

Helen did the shopping, cooked the meals and began a thorough cleaning of everything in the house: the curtains, the chair covers, the rugs. She wouldn't have a spare moment to use for thought. She wanted to maintain her sense of outrage at a high level, where it could help to keep her active. She had no intention of breaking down into misery. She vacuumed and ironed and dusted. She washed and scrubbed. Once, just for a moment, her anger subsided and she felt wounded.

Edgar had done all that, she thought – he'd been driven to it, because she wasn't enough for him. She obviously hadn't been good enough in bed, either, otherwise he wouldn't have needed such a blatant type as compensation for her deficiencies. Her only success had been the children. She should really give up.

She caught herself just in time. She fought hard against despair, whipping her indignation up again. If things were bad, you should never crumple. Do something about it – no matter what. She stoked her fury until she thought she could do anything, even break up her marriage, if she had to. She was too mad to care whether she wrecked her home or not. *Let him suffer for a change,* she thought.

She could sue him: win a divorce case hands down. You could cite anybody nowadays. There had been a story in the papers recently about a man whose wife, without his knowledge, and – if he'd known – against his will, had had herself impregnated by a machine in a sperm-bank clinic. The husband had accused as co-respondent, and therefore father of the child, the technician who'd switched on the apparatus. The fact that the operator of the machine was a woman had made no difference in law. And soon you'd be able to say it was the machine itself. Helen could name this Dolly as the other woman. Why not? When she produced the doll in court and switched on the buttons that sent her into her act, they'd hand the betrayed wife everything on a plate: house, children, her car, his car, the bank accounts – it would be a long list. If she thought about it, she might rather have just him. So, she wasn't going to think about it too hard. She kept on doing the housework.

Up in the attic Edgar worked quickly – frenetically, in fact – although to him it seemed slow. When the replica was ready, he brought it downstairs to the living-room and sat it on a chair. He called out, 'Helen,' as she was coming around the corner from the hall. She'd heard him on the stairs.

'Well, it's ready,' he told her.

She looked past him at the male doll sitting in the armchair. Edgar had dressed it in one of his suits.

'Oh, honestly, Edgar,' she said.

'What?' He sounded close to collapse. He probably hadn't slept for days.

She said, 'He looks like a floorwalker.'

'There's nothing wrong with him. It's astounding, given the short time –'

'He looks so namby-pamby. I bet you didn't even put any hair on his chest.'

'As a matter of fact –'

'You didn't?'

'The hair is extremely difficult to do, you know. I wasn't aware that all women found it such a necessary item. I understand a lot of them hold just the opposite view.'

'And the skin. It's too smooth and soft-looking. It's like a woman's.'

'Well, that's the kind I can make. Damn it, it's an exceptionally lifelike specimen. It ought to give complete satisfaction.'

'It better,' she said. She glared at the doll. She didn't like him at all. She moved forward to examine him more closely.

'And now,' Edgar announced, 'I want Dolly.'

'Not till I've tried him out. What's this? The eyes, Edgar.'

'They're perfect. What's wrong with them?'

'They're blue. I wanted them brown.'

'Blue is the colour I know how to do.'

'And he's so pale. He almost looks unhealthy.'

'I thought of building him so he'd strangle you in bed.'

She smiled a long, slow smile she'd been practising. It let him know that she realized she was in control of the situation. She asked him if he wanted to check into a hotel somewhere, or maybe he'd stay up in the attic: because she and her new friend planned to be busy in the bedroom for a while.

'Don't overdo it,' he told her. 'It's possible to injure yourself that way, you know.'

'You let me worry about that.' She asked for full instructions about the push-button system. She got the doll to rise from the chair and walk up the stairs with her. Edgar went out and got drunk for two days.

She tried out the doll at all the activities he was capable of. She still didn't like him. He didn't look right, he could be uncomfortable without constant monitoring, and his conversation was narrow in the extreme. His sexual prowess was without subtlety, charm, surprise, or even much variety. She didn't believe that her husband had tried to shortchange her; he simply hadn't had the ingenuity to programme a better model.

As soon as Edgar sobered up, he knocked at the door. He was full of demands. She didn't listen. She said, 'Who was the nerd you modelled this thing on?'

'I didn't. He's a kind of conglomerate.'

'Conglomerate certainly isn't as good as whoever it was you picked to make the girl from.'

'I didn't pick anyone. Dolly isn't a copy. She's an ideal.'

'Oh, my. Well, this one is definitely not my ideal.'

'Tough. You made a bargain with me.'

'And you gave me a dud.'

'I don't believe it.'

'He's so boring to talk to, you could go into rigor mortis halfway through a sentence.'

'I didn't think you wanted him to be able to discuss the novels of Proust.'

'But that could be arranged, couldn't it? You could feed some books into him?'

'Sure.'

'And he isn't such a high-stepper in the sack.'

'Come on, Helen. Anything more and you'll rupture yourself.'

'Reprogramming is what he needs. I can tell you exactly what I want added.'

'You can go jump in the lake.'

'And I want him to teach me Italian. And flower painting and intermediate *cordon bleu.*'

'No demonstration stuff. I can do a language if you get me the tapes, but they'll have to be changed when you graduate to the next stage. There isn't that much room inside for extra speech.'

He was no longer angry or contemptuous. He looked exhausted. He made all the changes she'd asked for on the doll and added a tape of Italian lessons. She tried everything out. The renovated model was a great improvement. She felt worse than ever.

'Where is she?' Edgar pleaded, looking beaten, unhappy, hopeless.

Helen gave him the key to the locker.

*

Ron stopped taking Dolly to the gym when the boys began to pester him with too many questions. They pressed up around her in a circle, trying to find out what she thought of everything; that got him nervous and mixed her up. And then they started on him. What they most wanted to know was: where did she come from?

He had no answer to that, but no ideas about it, either. Lots of things – some of the most important things in life – remained completely mysterious. That didn't matter. It made more sense just to be happy you had them instead of asking questions about them all the time.

But one day while they were making love, instead of waiting for the end of the cycle she was on, Dolly went into a totally different one. Ron guessed that he must have given her some verbal instruction or physical signal. She started to do things he hadn't realized she knew about. He'd never done them himself, only heard about them. He did his best to keep up. She laughed with pleasure and said, 'Does Edgar love his Dolly?'

'Who's Edgar?' he asked.

'Edgar's Dolly's honeybunch, isn't he? Dolly's so happy with her great big gorgeous Edgar, especially with his great big gorgeous –'

'I ain't Edgar,' Ron yelled at her. He did something calculated to startle and possibly hurt her. She told him he was wonderful, the best she'd ever had: her very own Edgar.

It wasn't her fault. She didn't know any better. But it just about killed him.

He began to feel jealous. He hadn't wanted to think about how she was made – he'd assumed that she'd been made by machines. But now he had it figured out: she'd been custom-made for one person – a man named Edgar. It still didn't occur to him that this Edgar could have built her himself. He didn't think of things as being made by people. He thought of them as being bought in stores. She would have come from some very fancy place like the big stores where rich people bought diamond necklaces and matching sets of alligator-skin luggage, and so on. You could have all that stuff custom-made.

Someone else had thought her up. She'd been another man's invention. And Ron hadn't been the first to love her; he was sure about that. A sadness began to grow in him. The fact that she couldn't hold a real conversation still didn't bother him, nor that the things she said were always the same. What caused him pain was to hear her calling him by another man's name. He began to think he could live with that too if only in some other phrase she'd occasionally call him by his own name, too.

The sadness began to overshadow his love to such an extent that he thought he'd have to do something about it. He got the suitcase out from the back of the closet and went over the inside. There was a piece of white cardboard tucked into one of the shirt-racks in the underside of the top lid. Someone had written a name and address on the card, together with a promise to reward the finder for the return of the case. The name matched the initials on the outside. The first letter of each was E; E for Edgar, maybe. People were so dumb, Ron thought. He'd never put a name or address on anything he was carrying around. Somebody could decide to come after you and clean up.

He put the card in his wallet but he still hadn't really made up his mind.

The next morning everything was decided for him while he was making breakfast in the kitchen. He'd cracked a couple of eggs into the frying pan and was walking over to the garbage pail with the shells. One of them jumped out of his hand. He scooped it up again and threw it out with the others. He meant to wipe a rag over the part of the floor where it had landed but the eggs started to sizzle in the pan. He stepped back to the stove. And at that moment, Dolly came into the room. Before he had a chance to warn her, she was all over the place – skidding and sliding and landing with a thump.

He picked her up and sat her down on top of the folding stool. He asked, 'Are you OK, honey?' She smiled and said she was fine. But he could see, in the middle of her right arm, a dent. He touched the centre of the injured place lightly with the tips of his fingers, then he pushed the flat of his hand firmly over the higher edge of the indentation; he hoped that the pressure would bring the hollow back up to its normal level. But nothing changed. The thing he was afraid of had happened.

'Dolly's hurt,' she said. 'Dolly needs a four-five-four repair.'

'What's that?'

'Dolly needs a four-five-four repair on her arm.'

'Uh-huh,' he said. He didn't know what to do. All through the day he watched her, to see if the dent got bigger. It didn't; it stayed the same, but at regular intervals she reminded him that she needed to have the arm seen to.

He knew that it was dangerous to keep putting off the moment of action. He should find out what she'd need to have done if something worse went wrong. He could only do that by getting hold of whoever knew how to fix her; and then by trickery, threats, bribes, blackmail or violence, making sure he got the person to help him. If he could find somebody to teach him how to carry out all her repair work himself, that was what he'd like best.

*

When Edgar began his drive back to the house, Helen was sitting on the living-room sofa at the opposite end from the male doll, who was teaching her how to conjugate the verb *to be* in Italian. While she was answering the questions put to her, she stared up at the wall, near the ceiling. She was already tired of him. The renovations had been minimal, she decided. Edgar wasn't able to programme a better man, more intelligent, attractive. Perhaps no alterations would make any difference; maybe she just wanted him to be real, even if he was boring. Edgar evidently felt the other way: what he'd loved most about Dolly was that she was perfect, unreal, like a dream. The element of fantasy stimulated him.

For Helen, on the contrary, the excitement was over. Even the erotic thrill was gone. Owning the doll was probably going to be like driving a car – you'd begin by playing with it for fun and thinking it was a marvellous toy: but you'd end up putting it to practical use on chores like the shopping. From now on she'd be using the doll only as a routine measure for alleviating frustration. As soon as Edgar got Dolly back, there'd be plenty of opportunity for feeling frustrated and neglected.

She remembered what Edgar had said about the possible therapeutic value of such a doll. It could be true. There might be lots of people who'd favour the companionship of a non-human partner once a week. Or three times a day. No emotions, no strings attached. She thought about her sons: the schoolboy market. There were many categories that came to mind – the recently divorced, the husbands of women who were pregnant or new mothers, the wives of men who were ill, absent, unable, unfaithful, uninterested. And there would be no danger of venereal disease. There were great possibilities. If the idea could be turned into a commercial venture, it might make millions. They could advertise: *Ladies, are you lonely?* She might lend the doll to Gina and see what she thought.

'Dove?' the doll said.

'Qui,' she answered.

The front door opened and banged shut as Edgar's footsteps pounded through the hall. He was running. He burst into the living-room and roared, 'Where is she? I want the truth this time. And I mean it.'

'The doll?' Helen said. 'I gave you the key.'

'Oh, yes. But when he got there, the cupboard was bare. There's nothing inside that locker. It's empty.'

'It can't be. It's got two more days to go. Edgar, that was the right key and I put the suitcase in there myself. They aren't allowed to open those lockers before the money runs out. I put in so many –'

'But she isn't there.'

'She's got to be. You must have tried the wrong locker. Or maybe the wrong part of the row. All those things look alike.'

'I looked everywhere. I saw the right locker. It was the right one, but there wasn't any suitcase in it. If there was ever anything in it, it's gone now.'

'Well, if it's gone,' she said, 'it's been stolen.'

'It can't be stolen. No.'

'That's the only explanation I can think of. That's where I put her, so she should still be there. I guess it happens sometimes that they get people forcing the locks, or whatever they do.'

'How could you be so careless? To put her in a public place, where anybody could get at her.'

'I didn't want to try to hide her in the house. I thought you'd find her.'

'But how am I going to get her back?'

'I don't know.'

'You'd better know. If I can't find her, Helen – it's the end.'

'You could make another one, any time.'

'Impossible.' He shook his head slowly and sat down in a chair. He still had his coat on.

Helen said, 'I guess we could share Auto.'

'Otto?'

'His name,' she said, looking at the doll. 'Automatico. Auto for short.'

'Buon giorno,' the doll murmured, making a slight bow from the waist.

Edgar said, 'Hi,' in a loud, unpleasant tone.

'Come sta?' the doll asked.

'That's all right, Auto,' Helen said. 'You can be quiet now. We've got some things to talk about.'

'Bene, signora.'

Edgar stared at the doll and snorted. 'That's really what you wanted? The guy's a pain in the ass.'

'He's getting to be very boring. He's about as interesting as a vibrator.'

'I did just what you said.'

'But I'm getting sort of sick of him. I always know what's coming next.'

'I could programme him for random selection – that's the best I can do.'

'Maybe what I needed was you.'

'It's a little late.'

'It was a little late even before you started work on that thing. It began way back, with the computer – didn't it? Remember? When you stopped coming to the table. You'd make me bring in your meals and leave them. You can get a divorce for it nowadays: you cite the computer.'

'I could cite Auto here.'

'Not if you made him. I don't know what they'd call that – complicity or connivance, or something.'

'I think I'll go out for a walk.'

'What's your opinion of putting a doll like this on the market? It could become the new executive toy.'

'Certainly not.'

'Why not? We could make a fortune selling them. You think we should give them away?'

'Why stop with selling? You could run a rental service. Go into the call girl business: charge for every time.'

'That's no good. If we didn't agree to sell them, they'd get stolen. People are going to want their own. Would it make a difference to let them out in the world – could somebody copy the way you do them?'

'Not yet. It's my invention. But if there's money in it, you can bet there'd be people after the process. Life wouldn't be worth living. We might not even be safe. That's one of the reasons I decided from the beginning, that if I had any success with the project, I'd keep it to myself.'

'You said the dolls could have a therapeutic value.'

'Yes, well . . . you had me cornered. The therapy was for me. Just as you suspected. I only wanted to make one.'

'But all those techniques and materials – the skin, the vocal cords – everything: they could be used in hospitals, couldn't they?'

'No. It's all artificial.'

'But it responds to touch and sound. If the dolls can do that, so could separate parts. You could fix almost any physical injury.'

'Theoretically.'

'It's possible?'

'In theory.'

'Then you've got to. I didn't think that far, before. If it's really possible, it's our duty.'

'Jesus God, Helen. You take the cake. You just do.'

'Me? Who had the idea for this in the first place?'

'Not as a business.'

'Oh, I see. That's what makes the difference, is it?'

Out in the hall the phone rang. Helen turned her head, but didn't move. Edgar said, 'Aren't you going to get it?'

'I want to finish what we're talking about.'

He stood up and went into the hall. She called after him, 'Why don't you take your coat off?' He picked up the receiver and barked into it, 'Hello?'

A muffled voice came over the wire, saying, 'I got something belongs to you.'

'Oh?'

'A suitcase.'

'Yes,' Edgar said quickly. 'Where is it?'

'Something was inside it. Something kind of blonde, with blue eyes.'

'Where is she?'

'I'll do a deal,' the voice said. 'OK?'

'We can talk about that. Bring her here and we'll discuss it.'

'Oh, no. I'm not bringing her anyplace.'

'You don't understand. It's a very delicate mechanism. She shouldn't have been away so long. She could be damaged.'

'She looks fine.'

'She could be damaged and it wouldn't show. Internal injuries. I've got to have a look at her. She's supposed to have regular inspections.'

There was silence at the other end. Edgar was covered in sweat. He couldn't think up any more reasons to tell the man why Dolly should come back. He said, 'What's your name?'

'Ron,' the voice told him.

'Well, Ron, you'd better believe me. If it goes beyond a certain stage, I can't fix anything. I've been worried out of my mind. She's got to come back to the lab.'

'Are you the guy that, um . . .'

'I'm the designer.'

'Uh-huh. OK.'

'Now.'

'Right. I'll be over.' He hung up.

Edgar banged down the phone, threw off his coat and started up the stairs. Helen came out of the living-room behind him. 'Where are you going?' she said.

'He's got her.'

'Who? What have you done with your coat?'

'A man that called up. Ron. He's bringing her over here now.'

'Are you going out?'

'Of course not. Dolly's coming here.'

'Well, come back and sit down,' Helen said. She picked up his coat and hung it in the hall closet.

'I'm the one who knows about her,' he muttered. 'He can't do anything without me.'

Helen pushed him into the living-room and sat him down in a chair. She took Auto out, around the corner. She steered him to the downstairs guest room where Edgar's grandmother had once stayed after her leg operation. She stood him up in the closet and closed the door on him.

She waited with Edgar for ten minutes. As soon as they heard the car outside they both ran to the windows. They saw Ron get out of the car. He was wearing blue jeans and a red T-shirt. Helen said, 'Well, he's a bit of a slob, but that's more the kind of thing I had in mind.'

'What?'

'To wind up and go to bed with. That man there.'

'Mm,' Edgar said. He was wondering if he'd be strong enough to tackle a man like that, who looked as if he could knock people down. He began to think about what must have happened all the time Dolly was away. A man like that wouldn't have let her alone, once he'd seen her. Of course not. Edgar was ready to kill him, despite the difference in size.

Ron got Dolly out of the car. He handled her carefully. He walked her up the front steps. He rang the doorbell.

Edgar jerked the door open. The four of them stood looking at each other. Edgar said, 'Hello, Dolly.'

'Hello there, Edgar-poo,' Dolly answered.

'How are you?'

'Dolly's just fine when Edgar's here.'

Helen leaned close to Ron. She said, 'I'm Helen.'

'Ron,' he said. 'Hi.'

'Why don't we all step into the house?' She led the way. She put the three others into the living-room, brought in some coffee and sandwiches, and said she'd take Dolly into the next room.

'She stays here,' Ron declared.

'She makes me nervous. I'm just going to put her in the guest room. You can come see.'

Ron went with her. Helen opened the door to show him the empty room. She smiled at him. 'See?' she told him. He laid Dolly down on top of the bed. He looked all around the room and stepped back. Helen closed the door.

Ron followed her back to the living-room, where Edgar had changed from coffee to whiskey. Edgar said, 'Want a drink?'

Ron nodded. He knew he had the upper hand, drunk or sober. Even over the phone Edgar had sounded like a drip. Maybe he'd put Dolly together, but she was Ron's by right of conquest. Possession was nine-tenths of the law: that was what they said. Let Edgar what's-his-name try to take her back. Ron had a good left as well as a good right: he'd show this Edgar. And the woman was giving him the eye; he might be able to get her to back him up. Now that it occurred to him to notice, he knew who she was, too. She was the woman who'd put the suitcase into the locker.

Edgar began to talk, to plead, to describe the vague glimmerings of the dream he'd had: when Dolly had first come to him as a mere idea. He began to sound so desperate, he'd been so choked up at the sight of Dolly, that Ron pretended to soften. It didn't do any good to scare people too much while you were still trying to line them up; they could go and do something crazy. He said, 'Look, Ed, I guess I can see how it is. You feel the same as me. But I can't let her go. You understand? I never thought I'd say it, but we're going to have to do some kind of a deal about sharing.'

'Share Dolly? Not for anything.'

'That's the way it's got to be. Or – you can make up your mind to go on without her. I'll just put her in the car and drive her out of your life again. It could be a long time till I needed to bring her back to you. You built her to last, didn't you?'

'I? Yes. I'm the important one. I'm the creator. You two – what are you? I created them.'

'You create, maybe,' Helen said, 'but you don't appreciate.'

'That's right,' Ron told him. 'You couldn't ever love Dolly like I do.'

'I invented her, man. She's all mine – she's all me.'

Helen said, 'If you could hear what you sound like, Edgar.'

'I sound like a man who's been treated badly. Helen, you used to understand me.'

'Oh? That must have been nice for you. And did you understand me?' She stood up, went to the liquor cabinet and said, 'You still haven't brought in the Cinzano. I'll get it.' She marched from the room.

Edgar said to Ron, 'It's true. You're the one who needs me.'

'Right. That's why I'm willing to talk about it. You don't have to bother with this. You can make yourself another one. Can't you?'

'No.'

'Sure. You make one, you can make two.'

'I made a second one. It was no good.'

'What was wrong with her?'

'It was a male replica. For my wife.'

'Yeah?'

'It was her price for telling me where she put Dolly.'

'No shit. And she didn't like it?'

'It isn't real enough, apparently. She says she's bored with it.'

'Maybe you're only good at them when it's a woman.'

'No – I know what the trouble is. It's that I put all my best work, all my ideas and hopes, into that one effort. Dolly was the only time I could do it. I'm like a man who falls in love just once and can't feel the same about any other woman.'

Ron didn't believe it. He thought Edgar wouldn't want to give anything to other people: that was the reason why he'd fail.

Edgar made himself a fresh drink. Helen, having found her bottle of vermouth, carried it to the guest room and parked it on the dresser while she took off Dolly's clothes, got Auto out of the closet and then stripped him too. She put him on top of Dolly, arranged both dolls in appropriate positions, and pushed the buttons behind their ears.

She took the bottle into the living-room. She poured herself a drink.

Ron said, 'OK. I get it. But you've got to see it my way, too. We do a deal, right?'

'I might go back on it,' Edgar said.

'And then I'd come after you. And I've got a lot of friends, Ed. They don't all have real good manners, either. You think about that.'

Helen drank three large gulps of her drink. She could hear the dolls. After a few seconds, the others heard too.

'What's that?' Edgar said.

'What's going on out there?' Ron asked. 'Who else is in this house? You trying to pull something on me?'

'Let's go see,' Helen suggested. She bounced towards the door and danced into the hallway. The raucous noise of the dolls drew the two men after her.

She smiled as she flung open the door to show Auto and Dolly engaged on what must have been round two of the full ten-patterned cycle: he whispering, 'I could really go for you, you know,' and she panting, 'Oh, you gorgeous hunk of man,' as he began to repeat, *'Bellissima,'* with increasingly frenzied enthusiasm.

Edgar and Ron called out curses. They rushed past Helen and grabbed Auto. They tore him away from his exertions. They got him down on the ground and began to kick him. Then they hit out at each other. Helen took the opportunity to batter Dolly with the bottle she still held. Vermouth sloshed over the bed, on to the fighting men. Edgar slapped her across the face. The dolls, against all odds, continued to try to fornicate with anything and anyone they encountered, still mouthing expressions of rapturous delight, still whispering endearment and flattery; whereas Helen, Ron and Edgar roared out obscenities: they picked up any weapons they could find, laying about with pokers, shovels, baseball bats. Pieces of the dolls flew across the room. Springs twanged against the walls and ceiling. Reels of tape unwound themselves among the wreckage. And the battle went on; until at last – their faces contorted by hatred – husband, wife and stranger stood bruised, bloody, half-clothed and sweating among the rubble of what they had been fighting over: out of breath in the silent room, unable to speak. There was nothing to say. They stared as if they didn't recognize each other, or the room they were standing in, or any other part of the world which, until just a few moments before, had been theirs.

Friends in the Country

It took them an hour to leave the house. Jim kept asking Lisa where things were and why she hadn't bought such and such; if she'd intended to buy that thing there, then she should have warned him beforehand. 'Otherwise,' he told her, 'we duplicate everything and it's a waste of money. Look, now we've got two flashlights.'

She let the shopping bag drop down on the floor with a crash. 'Right. That's one for you and one for me,' she said. 'And then we won't have to argue about it when we split up.'

His face went set in an expression she recognized. He'd skipped two intermediate phases and jumped to the stage where, instead of being hurt, he started to enjoy the battle and would go for more provocation, hoping that they'd begin to get personal. 'In that case,' he said, 'I hosie the blue one.'

She laughed. She leaned against the wall, laughing, until he had to join in. He said, 'We can keep the black one in the car, I guess. It might come in useful.'

'You think we should phone them?'

He shook his head. He didn't know anything about this Elaine – she was Nancy's friend – but he was pretty sure her cousin wouldn't want to begin eating before eight on a Friday night, especially not if she lived out of town. 'And they shouldn't, anyway,' he added. 'Eight thirty would be the right time.'

'But some people do. If you're working nine to five, and if you –'

'Then they ought to know better.'

There were further delays as he wondered whether to take a bottle of wine, and then how good it had to be if he did. Lisa heard him rooting around in the kitchen as she stared closely into the bathroom mirror. She smeared a thin film of Vaseline on the tips of her eyelashes, put her glasses on, took them off and leaned forward. Her nose touched the glass. Jim began to yell for her to hurry up. Her grandfather used to do the same thing: she could remember him shouting up the stairs for her grandmother; and then if there was still no result, he'd go out and sit in the car and honk the horn. Jim hadn't learned that extra step yet, but he might think of it at any minute. They'd been living together for only a few months. She was still a little worried that one day he might get into the car and drive off without her.

They were out of the house, in the car, and halfway down the street when she remembered that she'd left the bathroom light on. She didn't say anything about it. They moved on towards the intersection. Jim was feeling good, now that they'd started: the passable bottle of wine being shaken around in the back seat, the new flashlight in the glove compartment. He looked to the left and into the mirror.

She tried not to breathe. She always hated the moment of decision – when you had to hurl your car and yourself out into the unending torrent of the beltway. Jim loved it. They dashed into the stream.

The rush hour was already beginning, although the sky was still light. Pink clouds had begun to streak the fading blue of the air. When they got off the freeway and on to the turnpike, the street lamps had been switched on. They drove down a country road flanked by frame houses.

'What did that map say?' he asked.

'Left by the church, right at the school playing field.'

They were supposed to go through three small towns before they came to the driveway of the house but – backtracking from the map – they got lost somewhere around the second one and approached the place from behind. At any rate, that was what they thought.

They sat in the car with the light on and pored over the map. Outside it didn't seem to be much darker, because a fog had begun to mist over the landscape. He blamed her for misdirecting him, while she repeated that it wasn't her fault: not if he'd worked it out so carefully beforehand; she couldn't see all those itsy-bitsy names in the dark, and anyway she'd said for him to go exactly the way he'd instructed her.

'Well,' he said, 'this should do it. Can you remember left – right – left?'

'Sure,' she answered. And so could he; that was just the kind of thing he'd told her back at the house.

He started the car again and turned out the light. They both said, 'Oh,' and, 'Look,' at the same time. While they'd been going over the map, the fog had thickened to a soupy, grey-blue atmosphere that filled the sky and almost obscured the trees at the side of the road. Jim drove slowly. When the road branched, he said, 'Which way?'

'Left – right – left.'

They passed three other cars, all coming from the opposite direction. As the third one went by them, he said, 'At least it doesn't lead to nowhere.'

'Unless it's to somewhere else.'

'Meaning what?'

'I don't know,' she said. 'It just came to me.'

'Wonderful. You should be working for the government. Which way now?'

'To the right.'

'And there's a street sign up ahead. At last.'

When they got near enough to the sign to make out what it said, they saw that it didn't have any writing on it at all. It was white, with a red triangle painted on it, and inside the triangle was a large, black shape.

'That's great,' she said. 'What's it supposed to mean – black hole ahead?'

'Look, there's another one. The whole damn road's full of them. What's the black thing? Come on, you can see that.'

Lisa opened her window. The signs were as closely spaced as trees or ornamental bushes planted along a street to enhance its beauty and give shade during the summer.

She leaned her head out and looked at the black object inside the red triangle.

'It's like a kind of frog,' she said, pulled her head back in and shut the window. She'd just realized that she hadn't brought her glasses with her; not that it really mattered for a single dinner party, but she always liked to have them with her in case she had to change her eye make up under a bad light, or something like that.

'I remember now,' he told her. 'It's OK. I've just never seen it before. It's one of those special signs for the country.'

'What?'

'They signpost all the roads they've got to cross to get to their breeding grounds or spawning places, or something. People run over so many of them when it's the season. They're dying out.'

'Frogs?'

'No, not frogs. Toads.'

'I hope it isn't their breeding season now. That's all we need.'

'Which way at the crossroads?'

'Left.'

In fifteen minutes they came to a white-painted wooden arrow set low in the ground. It said 'Harper' and led them on to a narrow track. The headlights threw up shadowy patterns of tree branches. Leaves brushed and slapped against the sides of the car.

'This better be it,' he said.

'Otherwise we break open the wine and get plastered.'

They lurched along the last curve of the drive and out into a wide, gravelled space, beyond which stood a building that looked like a medievalized Victorian castle. Lisa giggled. She said, 'So this is where your friends live.'

Jim reached into the back seat for the wine and said he hoped so, because otherwise it was going to be a long ride to anywhere else.

*

The door was opened by someone they couldn't see. Jim stepped forward into darkness and tripped. Lisa rushed after him. There was a long creak and the heavy door groaned, then slammed behind them.

'Are you all right?' she asked. She fell on top of him.

'Look out,' he said. 'The wine.' It took a while for them to untangle themselves. They rose to their feet like survivors of a shipwreck who suddenly find themselves in the shallows.

They could see. They could see that the hallway they stood in was weakly lit by a few candles, burning high up on two separate stands that resembled iron hat racks; each one expanded into a trident formation at the top. The candles were spitted on the points.

Lisa turned to Jim, and saw that a man was standing in back of him. She gave a squeak of surprise, nearly blundering against a second man, who was stationed behind her. Both men were tall, dressed in some kind of formal evening wear that included tails; the rest of the outfit looked as if it might have been found in an ancient theatrical wardrobe trunk. 'Your coat, sir,' the one next to Jim said. He held out his arms.

By the time their coats had been removed and the bottle plucked from Jim's hands, they were ready for anything.

One of the men led them down a corridor. Like the hallway, it was dark. The floor sounded as if it might be tile. The air was cold and smelled unpleasant. Lisa reached for Jim's hand.

The tall man in the lead threw open a double door. Light came rushing out in a flow of brilliance. In front of them lay a bright, inviting room: glass-topped tables, gilded mirrors, chrome and leather armchairs in black and white, semi-circular couches. There were eight other people in the room. They'd been laughing when the door had opened on them. Now they were turned towards Jim and Lisa as if the room had become a stage set and they were the cast of a play.

'Your guests, madam,' the first butler said. He snapped the doors shut behind him.

A woman who had been standing by the mantelpiece came forward. She had on a long, blackish velvet gown and what at first appeared to be a head-dress, but which – seen closer – was actually her own dark hair piled up high; lines of pearls were strung out and perched in wavy configurations along the ridges and peaks of the structure.

Jim let go of Lisa's hand. She could feel how embarrassed he was. He'd be fighting the urge to jam his hands into his pockets.

'Um,' he began, 'Elaine –'

'We thought you'd never get here,' the woman said. 'I'm Isabelle.'

She took his hand lightly in hers and let it go again almost immediately. Then she repeated the action as Jim made the introductions. Lisa realized that although the woman was certainly middle-aged and not particularly slim, she was beautiful. But something was wrong with the impression she gave. She had enough natural magnificence to carry her opera-diva get-up without appearing ridiculous; and yet she seemed out of date. And the touch of her hand had been odd.

Isabelle introduced them around the room. Dora and Steve,

the couple nearest to them, were grey-haired. Steve wore a grey flannel suit that might once have been office regulation but at the moment looked fairly shapeless. Dora sported a baggy tweed jacket and skirt. Both husband and wife were pudgily plump, and they wore glasses: his, an old-fashioned pair of horn-rims; hers, an extraordinary bat-wing design in neon blue, with rhinestones scintillating at the tips. It came out in subsequent conversation that the two were schoolteachers and that they were interested in the occult.

Isabelle gave no hint as to the marital status of the next four people introduced: who was paired with whom, and in what way. There were two women and two men. The women were both young: Carrol, a plain girl with long, straight orange hair and a knobbly, pale face; Jeanette, pretty and brunette, who had shiny brown eyes and a good figure. She was an airline stewardess.

'And Dr Benjamin,' Isabelle said.

The doctor bowed and said, 'Oh, how do you do.' He was a small, stooped man, just beginning to go white at the temples. He reminded Lisa a little of the father of a girl she'd been to school with.

'And Neill. You probably recognize him.' The young man Isabelle indicated gave Jim and Lisa each an effortless, charming smile, just specially for them. He said, 'A lot of people don't watch TV.'

'I'm afraid we don't,' Jim said. 'We get home tired, and then we eat.' And then they jumped into bed, or else they did that before eating, or sometimes before and after too, but they hadn't watched much television for months.

'Are you in plays and things?' Lisa asked.

'I'm in a mega-soap called *Beyond Love.* The cast calls it *Beyond Hope,* or sometimes *Beyond Belief.* It really is.'

'What's it about?'

'The short version, or the twenty-three episode breakdown?'

'We all adore it,' Isabelle said. 'We miss it dreadfully now that the electricity's going haywire again. We were hoping to watch it over the weekend.'

'Just as well you can't,' Neill said.

'Not another shooting? They aren't writing you out of the script, are they?'

'I think this is the one where I lose an arm. My illegitimate father whips me from the house, not knowing that – you did say the short version, didn't you?'

Isabelle said she didn't believe any of it and he'd better behave. 'And finally,' she told Lisa and Jim, as she swayed ahead of them over the satiny rug, 'my husband, Broderick.' She left her hand open, her arm leading them to look at the man: swarthy, barrel-chested, bald and smiling. He looked like a man of power, an executive of some kind, who relaxed while others did the work he'd set up for them. He was leaning against the mantelpiece. The introductions had brought Jim and Lisa full circle in the room.

'A quick drink,' Isabelle suggested, pouncing gracefully upon two full glasses next to a silver tray. She handed them over, saying, 'Our very own mixture, guaranteed harmless, but it does have some alcohol in it. If you'd rather have fruit juice –'

Lisa was already sipping at her drink. The glass was like an oversized Martini glass but the cocktail wasn't strong, or didn't seem to be. It tasted rather delicate: herblike, yet pleasant. 'This is fine,' she said.

'Sure,' Jim added. She knew he wouldn't like it but would be agreeing in order to be polite.

'Now, we're going to move to the dining-room soon, so if any of you ladies need a sweater or a shawl, there's a pile over there. Or bring your own from your rooms.' She said to Jim, 'It's such a nuisance – we have to keep most of the rooms a little under-heated. Something to do with the boiler.'

'Not the boiler,' Broderick said.

'Well, pipes, or whatever it is. Poor Broderick – he's suffered miseries over it.'

'On the contrary. I just kicked out those two jokers who were trying to fleece us for their so-called work, and that's why we're up the creek now. Can't get anybody else for another three weeks. Maybe it'll get better tomorrow. It ought to be a lot warmer at this time of year.'

'It wasn't bad in town,' Jim said. 'I guess you must be in a kind of hollow. We hit a lot of fog. That's why we were late.'

'Yes, it's notorious around here,' Isabelle said. 'The locals call it Foggy Valley.'

One of the mournful butlers opened the double doors again and announced that dinner was served. Jim and Lisa tilted their glasses back. On the way out with the others, Lisa lifted a shawl from a chair near the doorway. All the other women had picked up something before her.

*

Carrol sat on Jim's right, Jeanette at the left. He preferred Jeanette, who was cheerful, healthy-looking and pretty, but somehow he was drawn into talk with Carrol.

The room was intensely, clammily, cold. He started to drink a lot of wine in order to warm himself up. Lisa, across from him, was drinking too – much more than usual.

Carrol kept passing one of her pale, bony hands over her face, as if trying to push away cobwebs. She said that she'd felt very restless and nervous ever since giving up smoking. 'I tried walking,' she said. 'They tell you to do that, but then I'd get back into the house and I'd want to start eating or smoking. So, I knit. But you can't take it everywhere. It sort of breaks up the conversation. And I'm not very good at it, even after all this time. I have to concentrate on the counting.' She blinked several times, as if about to cry.

From his other side Jeanette said, 'I guess we're all looking for different things. Except – I bet really they're not so different in the long run. In my case it was the planes. I'd get on and begin the routine, get everything working right, count the meals, look at the chart, see the passengers going in, and suddenly I'd just know: this one is going to crash.'

'What did you do?' Jim asked.

'I got off. They were very nice about it when I explained. They didn't fire me. But they said I had to take therapy.'

'And?'

'And I did. It was fine. It was a six-week course and it really made me feel a lot better. So, I went back to work again and everything was OK for another year. I thought I had it licked. And then it started up again, just like before. That's where I am now.'

'What are you doing for it this time?'

'I'm here,' Jeanette said.

Jim took another sip of the thick, brownish-red wine. It tasted dusty and bitter, although it seemed to be fairly potent, too. The bouquet reminded him of some plant or flower he couldn't place. He took another swallow. His feet were beginning to feel cold. 'You mean, here to relax?' he said.

'I'm here to consult Isabelle and Broderick.'

'Oh. And is that helping?'

'Of course. They're wonderful.'

'They've helped me too,' Carrol said. 'No end.'

The two cadaverous butlers managed the refilling of the wine glasses and the serving of the meal, the main course of which was a stew that they ladled out of an enormous green casserole.

Lisa looked longingly at the food as it started to be passed around. She wished that she'd taken two shawls with her instead of one. It wasn't just the cold, either, or the general darkness of the room; there was a distinctly disagreeable, dank smell emanating from the corners, from the floor under the lovely old rug. Perhaps there was some reason, connected with the low temperature, for the odour: mould, or that kind of thing. She'd suspected at first that it might be coming from the wine, which she'd nearly choked on: it was like taking a mouthful of plasma. Neill had asked for, and been given, two more cocktails. She was thinking that she should have done that herself, when he handed both glasses straight to her without asking if she wanted them.

She'd been seated between him and Dr Benjamin. She turned her attention to the doctor first. 'Are you a medical doctor?' she asked.

He said no and told her what he was, which she didn't understand. 'Algae,' he explained. 'Pond life, biology.' Then he made an encompassing gesture with his right hand and arm, adding, 'But it's all connected, you know. The animal kingdom, the vegetable kingdom, fish, flowers, rocks, trees. Fascinating. We're only part of it.'

'Oh,' she said with delight, 'yes.' She'd caught his enthusiasm and all of a sudden she was drunk. She said to Neill, 'I think I got a better deal on the cocktails. It's just hit me. What's in them?'

'I should have warned you – they're pretty strong. The ingredients are a closely guarded secret, but the rumour is that they're dill, parsley and vodka, with a squeeze of lemon and a touch of aniseed. But mostly vodka.'

'Nice. Better than the wine.'

'The wine is an acquired taste. You'll get to love it.'

One of the butlers put a heaped plate of the stew in front of her. A rich, spicy aroma steamed up into her face. She looked towards Isabelle, who had lifted her fork, and dug in.

The food was nearly as strange as the wine. The meat had a

tang like game. 'What is it?' she asked, after she'd chewed the first mouthful.

'Chicken livers, I think,' the doctor said. 'Delicious.'

Lisa continued to eat. Surely they didn't make chickens that big. And anyway, the pieces of meat were so chewy and tough, you could almost imagine they were parts of a bat.

'I've never tasted any chicken livers like this,' she said.

'Oh, it's all health food,' Dr Benjamin assured her. 'The flavours are much stronger and more natural. Our jaded palates aren't used to them.'

'Except the wine,' Neill said. 'It isn't one of those health wines.'

'Quite superb,' the doctor agreed, raising his glass. The two men smiled at each other across Lisa. She bit down on another piece of her meal and hit a horny substance that resisted. It was too slippery to get back on to her fork again. She chewed rapidly, then gave up, reached in, quickly took it out of her mouth and put it on the side of her plate. It was a large, rubbery black triangle of cartilage. Her glance darted to the side. The doctor had noticed.

'Wonderful stuff,' he pronounced. 'Terrific for the spleen.'

'If you can get it that far,' she said.

'It's good for the teeth and gums to have to chew.'

'That's true,' Neill said. 'I've got caps. Anything happens to them, it's my salary in danger. But I've never hit a bone in this house. You can relax.' He began to talk about the degree to which a television actor was dependent on his face, how you began to look at yourself completely dispassionately, as if seeing a mask from the outside. And then you stuck the emotions on afterwards. To do it the other way – beginning with the emotion and building towards the outward expression – was so exhausting that you could kill yourself like that, or go crazy. 'You can go crazy in any case. I started to flip about three years ago. That's why I'm here.'

'I thought actors were supposed to like pretending and showing off.'

'It was the series. Auto-suggestion. I got to the point where I'd think the things they were making up in the story were actually happening to me. Those characters in the soaps – they really go through it, you know. I was like living that crap. It broke up my life. Broke up my marriage.'

'You got divorced?' she asked. 'Separated?'

'It started with a coldness. Then there was an estrangement.'

He stopped speaking. The mention of cold had made her conscious once more of the chilling damp. It seemed to be pulling the room down into ever darker and deeper layers of rawness.

'Then,' he said, 'she took the children and left, and got the divorce.'

'That's awful,' Lisa said. She looked at him with sympathy, but he smiled back, saying, 'It turned out to be all for the best. It's how I found this place. I'd never have known how far gone I was. I wouldn't have tried to get help. Maybe an analyst, maybe not. But now I'm fine.'

'How?'

'Broderick and Isabelle.'

'Are they doctors?'

'He's a healer. She's a medium. They don't advertise it or anything. They aren't in it for the money, like the fakes.'

Just for the power, Lisa thought. She was surprised that a couple who looked as capable as Broderick and Isabelle should be mixed up in the occult. That, she thought, was for people like Dora and Steve.

'I take it you're not a believer,' he said.

'Oh, I believe in faith-healing. That's half of medicine. Well, not half. Forty-five per cent.'

'You'll come to see the rest, too,' Dr Benjamin told her complacently. She felt angry suddenly. She didn't know what she was doing at this stupid dinner, with these weird people, in a freezing room and eating such revolting food. Even the liquor was peculiar. She tried to catch Jim's eye, but he was stuck with Carrol.

The dessert arrived: a minty sherbet that hadn't set right. The constituents were already separating, and the areas not beginning to melt were oozing and slimy. Lisa took one bite and left the rest. The after-taste was peppery. Jim finally looked at her from across the table. He gave her a defeated smile. She almost made a face back.

'Coffee in the living-room?' Isabelle asked the table. She stood up. Everyone followed. Lisa went straight to Jim. She whispered that she hoped they'd be cutting the evening short, right after the coffee. He nodded and whispered back, 'You bet.'

'They're some kind of psychic health freaks,' she said.

'They cure people of psychosomatic things. Fears and stuff.'

'I've got a fear of horrible food.'

'Jesus, yes. Even the rolls and butter.'

'I didn't see them.'

'It was sort of like trying to eat my jacket.'

They wanted to stay together but Broderick moved them to chairs where they'd be near the people they hadn't sat with at dinner. Lisa was expected to talk to Dora; the heat of the room felt so good that she didn't mind. She attempted to look interested, while Dora spoke about the difficulty of finding a really good nursery. For several minutes Lisa thought they were talking about children.

She was handed a cup of coffee and lifted it to her lips. It was black, scalding, acrid, and didn't taste like coffee. It was like trying to drink a cup of boiling urine. She set it back on its saucer and looked across the room. Isabelle's neat hands were still busied with the silver pot and the cups. Carrol was actually drinking the stuff; so were Neill and Jeanette and Dr Benjamin. Dora's husband, Steve, was positively slurping his with enjoyment.

She watched Jim take his first swallow. His nostrils flared, his eyes screwed tight for a moment.

'And that's the most important thing, isn't it?' Dora said.

'What?'

'The soil.'

'Of course. Basic,' Lisa said. She knew nothing about gardening. When her sister had been out in the back yard helping their mother to do the weeding, she'd stayed indoors to draw and cut up pieces of coloured paper. She said, 'Do you teach botany at your school?'

'Biology.'

'Like the doctor.'

'He's a specialist. Most of his work is done through the microscope.'

'I guess a lot of his job must be finding out how to get rid of all the chemical pollution around.'

'It's a crime,' Dora said. 'Is that your field?'

'I work for a museum,' Lisa told her. 'I help to plan the exhibition catalogues and everything.'

'How interesting.'

It wasn't actually very interesting so far, because she was right at the bottom, just picking up after the other people who did the real work. But some day it was going to be fine: she'd travel, and do her own designs, and be in charge. The only trouble would be trying to fit everything in so that it worked out with Jim.

She could see that Dora was about to go back to biology when Jim stood up at the far end of the room. Lisa said, 'Excuse me just a minute.' She got up and joined him.

He was talking to Isabelle, who had made him sit down again, beside her on the couch; she was saying, 'But you can't.' She looked up at Lisa. 'You can't possibly just run off. You're staying for the weekend.'

Lisa sat next to Jim. She said, 'Just for dinner, I thought?' She took him by the arm and dug her fingers in.

'It's very nice of you,' he said, 'but we must have gotten the signals wrong. We don't even have a toothbrush between us.'

'Oh, we can lend you everything.'

'And Aunt Alice tomorrow,' Lisa said, 'and Mrs Havelock at church on Sunday.' She'd used the same made-up names for the past year: ever since the evening when she'd flung a string of them at Jim and he'd repeated them, getting every one wrong. Now they had a private pantheon: Aunt Alice, Mrs Havelock, Cousin George, the builders, the plumber, the twins, Grandmother and Uncle Bob, Norma and Freddie, and the Atkinsons.

'I'm afraid it's too late in any case,' Isabelle said. 'The fog here gets very bad at night around this time of the year. I don't think you'd be able to see your hand in front of your face.'

'It's true,' Jeanette said. 'I took a look before we sat down. It's really socked in out there.'

'If it's anything urgent,' Isabelle suggested, 'why don't you phone, and stay over, and then you can leave in the morning. All right? We'd rather have you stay on, though. And we were counting on the numbers for tomorrow night.'

Jim turned to look at Lisa. If the fog was worse than when they'd arrived, there was probably nothing they could do. He said, 'I guess –'

'If we start off early in the morning,' Lisa said. 'It's nice of you to ask us.'

'I'll show you the way right now,' Isabelle told them.

*

Lisa stared at the huge bed. It was the biggest one she'd ever seen and it was covered in a spread that looked like a tapestry. The room too was large; it seemed about the size of a double basketball court. Everything in it was gloomy. All the colours were dark and muddy. The main lighting came from above: a tiny triple-bulbed lamp pronged into the ceiling above the bed and worked from a switch by the door. There was also a little lamp on a table at the far side of the room.

'This old place,' Isabelle said. 'I'm afraid the bathrooms are down the hall. Do bear with us. We try to make up in hospitality. Broderick simply loves it here – his family's been in the district just forever. But I must say, I can never wait for the holidays. Then we go abroad to Italy. When the children come back from school.'

'How many children do you have?' Lisa asked.

'Three boys. I don't know why I keep calling them children. They're already taller than their father – hulking great brutes.'

Isabelle led them down the corridor to a bathroom that was nearly as big as the bedroom. There was a giant tub on claw feet, a toilet with a chain, and a shower partly hidden by a stained plastic curtain. The place was tiled halfway up to the high ceiling. In the corner opposite the toilet the tiles were breaking apart or disintegrating as if the cement had begun to crumble away.

Isabelle said, 'I'll just go see about getting you some towels. We'll meet downstairs. All right?' She left them standing side by side in front of the bathtub.

Lisa whispered, 'Some friends you've got.'

'It's pretty weird.'

'It's unbelievable. What was that stuff we were eating?'

'Jesus, I don't know. I kept trying to guess. I got something on my fork I thought was an ear, and then a hard piece that looked like part of a kneecap. It all tasted like . . . I don't know what.'

'They're crazy, aren't they?'

'I doubt it. Pretentious, maybe. Dora and Steve are the crazy types: dull and normal on the surface, but really looking for leaders to show them their occult destiny.'

'She's got a thing about soil. God, I wish we didn't have to stay over.'

'At least it's warm up here,' he said. 'And they're right – it's like pea soup outside.'

'First thing in the morning, we leave. Right?'

'Definitely. I get the strangest feeling when I'm talking to Broderick, you know. And Isabelle, too.'

'I know what you mean.'

'I mean really. As if there's something wrong. As if they're the wrong people, or there's been a mistake.'

'I've just thought of something. Wouldn't it be funny if you didn't know them at all?'

'Well, I don't. They're friends of Elaine's parents. Or of her mother's cousin. Something like that.'

'I mean, maybe we took the wrong road. Are you sure they're the right people? That sign we passed: the one that had a name on it – that isn't their name, is it? Or the name of Elaine's friends, either.'

'Well . . . I don't know what we could do about it now, anyway.'

'It really would be funny, wouldn't it?'

'And embarrassing. It would be just about the most embarrassing thing I can imagine.'

'Oh, not that bad. Not after that fabulous meal they just gave us. And the coffee; how do you suppose they cooked that up?'

'Maybe they had those two butlers out in the pantry just spitting into a trough for a couple of days.'

Lisa pulled the shower curtain to one side. 'Look at this,' she said, holding it wide to inspect the stains, which were brown and might almost have been taken for bloodstains. 'The whole house.' She pulled it farther. As she drew it away, she could see the corner of the shower. A mass of dead brown leaves lay heaped on the tiles. 'See that?' she asked.

'Smells bad, too,' Jim said.

They both stared down. Lisa leaned forward. Suddenly the leaves began to move, the clump started to split into segments.

Her voice was driven, growling, deep into her throat. She clapped her hands to her head and danced backward over the floor, hitting the opposite wall. Then she was out of the door and down the hallway. Jim dashed after her. He'd just caught up with her when they bumped into Isabelle.

Isabelle said, 'Good heavens. What's happened?'

'Toads,' Lisa groaned. 'A whole gang of them. Hundreds.'

'Oh dear, not again.'

'Again?'

'At this time of year. But there's nothing to worry about. They're harmless.'

'They carry viruses,' Lisa babbled. 'Subcutaneous viruses that cause warts and cancers.'

'Old wives' tales,' Isabelle laughed. 'You just sit down and relax, and I'll deal with it.' She continued along the corridor and down the stairs.

Jim put his arm around Lisa. She was shivering. She said, 'I can't stay here. Jesus. Right in the house. Thousands of them. Please, Jim, let's just get into the car and go. If we're fogged in, we can stop and go to sleep in the back seat.'

'We can't now,' he said.

'Please. I'm grossing out.'

'Just one night,' he told her. 'I'll be with you. It isn't as if they're in the bed.'

'Oh, God. Don't.' She started to cry. He hugged and kissed her. He felt badly for not having been able to resist the temptation to frighten her. It was so much fun to get the reaction.

'Come on,' he said. 'I'll try to find you a drink.'

'Oh boy,' she sniffed. 'Some more of that wonderful coffee.'

'They've got to have a real bottle of something, somewhere. If everything else fails, I'll ask for the one we brought with us.'

He led her back to the brightly lit living-room. Broderick stepped forward with a glass in his hand. 'Say you forgive us, please,' he begged. 'And take just one sip of this.'

Lisa accepted the glass. She raised it to her lips. She wanted to get out of the house and go home, and never remember the place again. She let a very small amount of the liquid slide into her mouth. It was delicious. She took a big gulp.

'Nice?' Broderick said.

'Terrific.'

'Great. We'll get you another.' He pulled her over to the couch where Neill was sitting. Neill began to talk about making a TV film in Italy one summer a few years ago: Broderick and Isabelle had been there at the time. And Broderick talked about a statisticians' conference he'd been attending.

Everyone began to drink a great deal. Lisa felt wonderful. She heard Jim and Carrol and Jeanette laughing together across the room and saw Dora and Steve sitting on either side of Isabelle, the doctor standing behind them. She had another one of the drinks, which Broderick told her were coffee liqueur plus several other things. She laughed with pleasure as she drank. She wanted to hear more about Italy and the museums and churches she'd only ever seen pictured in books. It would be so nice, she said, to go there and see the real thing in the real country.

But why didn't she? Broderick thought she certainly should: go to Italy as soon as possible; come with them that summer and stay at the villa. 'Oh, wouldn't that be nice,' she told him; 'wouldn't it be just like a dream? But Jim's job. And mine, too . . .'

There was a break. She came back, as if out of a cloud, to find herself in a different, smaller room, and lying on a couch with Neill. She knew she was pretty drunk and she had no idea if they'd made love or not. She didn't think so. They both still had all their clothes on. Her head was heavy and hurting.

As she moved, he kissed her. She sat up. He reached towards her. She could see under his shirt a red patch composed of flaking sores. It looked as though the skin had been eaten away. 'What's wrong with your chest?' she said.

'Make-up allergy. Badge of the trade. Come on back.'

'I think I'd better be going. I'm pretty plastered.'

'So's everybody.'

'But I'd better go.' She got up. He let her find her way out alone. She stumbled through hallways in near darkness, thinking that any minute she'd fall over or be sick. She came to the staircase and pulled herself up, leaning on the rail.

The bedroom was empty and autumnally moist. There was a smell, all around, of rotting leaves. A pair of pyjamas and a nightgown had been draped over the foot of the bed. The sheet was turned down. She got undressed and climbed in.

The light was still on. She was thinking about having to get up again to turn it out, when Jim lumbered in. He threw himself on top of the bed, saying, 'Christ, what a night. Where did you get to? I looked everywhere.'

'I don't know,' she said. 'I feel terrible.' She closed her eyes. When she opened them again, he was already sleeping. The light was still on. She turned her head and fell asleep herself.

When she woke again, the room was in darkness and stiflingly hot. The odour in the air had changed to one of burning. 'Jim?' she said. She started to throw the covers back. He wasn't anywhere near. She felt around in the dark. It was so pitch-black that it was like being trapped in a hole under the ground. What she needed was a flashlight; they'd brought one with them – the black one – but it was still in the car. 'Jim?' she said again. She sat up and clasped her knees. She was about to peel off the borrowed nightgown she was wearing, when he touched her hands.

'I can't sleep,' she said. 'It's so hot.'

His hands moved from her fingers down to her shins, to the hem of the nightdress and underneath it, up the inside of her legs, and rested on her thighs. She held his arms above the elbows. He sighed.

She said, 'Let me get out of this thing,' and was reaching down and back for the nightgown hem when a second pair of hands slid gently up to the nape of her neck, and a third pair came forward and down over her breasts. Close to her right ear a fourth person laughed. She yelped. Her arms jerked up convulsively.

They were all on top of her at once. She whirled and writhed in the sheets and yelled as hard as she could for Jim, but they had their hands everywhere on her and suddenly she was lifted, thrown down again, and one of them – or maybe more than one – sat on her head. She couldn't do anything then; the first one had never let go of her legs.

She couldn't breathe. Two of them began to laugh again. She heard the nightdress being ripped up, and then, from a distance, the doorknob turning. Shapes bounded away from her across the bed. Light was in her eyes from the hall. And Jim was standing in the doorway. He switched on the ceiling lights.

She fell out of the bed, on to the rug, where she knelt, shuddering and holding her sides. She whined about the men: how many of them there were and what they'd been trying to do to her. The words weren't coming out right.

'What's wrong?' Jim demanded. He put down a glass he'd been carrying.

'Where were you?' she croaked.

'I went to get some water. What's wrong?'

'Men in here – four, six maybe, a whole crowd of them.'

'When?'

'Just before you came in.'

'They left before that?'

'The light scared them.'

'Are you OK?'

'I guess so,' she said.

He made her drink half the glass he'd brought back. 'Which way did they go?' he asked.

'They're still here. Unless they ran past you when you opened the door.'

'No,' he said. He looked around. 'There isn't anyone,' he told her. 'Look. Nobody here. Just us.'

'They're under the bed.'

'Come on.'

'Take a look,' she ordered. Her teeth started to chatter. She wrapped herself in the torn pieces of the nightgown.

He got down on his knees and peered sideways under the bed. 'Nothing,' he said.

She joined him and took a long look herself.

'See? Nobody,' he said. 'Nothing. Not very clean, but no other people.'

'They were here.'

'Look at your nightgown,' he told her. 'How much did you have to drink, anyway?'

'Not enough for all that.'

'We could both use some sleep.'

'I'm not staying in this room unless the light's on. I mean it. If you want the light out, I'm sleeping in the hall: I'm running out of the house. I won't stay here.'

'Take it easy. You want the light on, we'll keep it on.'

'And the door locked.'

'I thought they were still in here.'

'The door,' she shouted.

He went to the door, which had a key-hole but no key. He pretended to be twisting something near the right place, and returned to the bed. He got in under the covers and put his arms around her.

'I can't wait to get home,' she said. 'Tomorrow. As early as possible.'

'Um. But we might stay just a little.'

'No.'

'Broderick was telling me about this business deal he's got lined up. It sounds really good. We could travel, everything.'

'Jim, we don't even know them. And this whole house is completely crazy. And all this occult crap, and – Jesus, nearly getting raped the minute you walk down the hall.'

'I think we all had a lot to drink.'

'Not that much.'

'I didn't mean you. If there was anybody, maybe they thought this was the wrong room. Maybe it's part of that occult stuff they were talking about at dinner.'

'Oh?'

'That would explain it, wouldn't it?'

'If you call that an explanation.'

'There are even people who spend every weekend that way.'

'Sure.'

'They do.'

'Not in this part of the world.'

*

Broderick sat at the head of the breakfast table. He'd finished eating, but drank coffee as he read the papers. He was still in his pyjamas and dressing gown. At the other end of the table Isabelle poured tea. She wore a floor-length housecoat that had a stand-up collar. Her hair was pulled high in a coiled knot.

They were in a different room from the one in which the last night's dinner had been laid. The windows looked directly on to a garden, although nothing was discernible of it other than the shadow of a branch next to the panes. Everything else was white with fog.

'Tea or coffee,' Isabelle said, 'or anything you like. Just

tell Baldwin or Ronald if you don't see what you want on the sideboard.'

The other young members of the party weren't yet down. Dr Benjamin was seated on Isabelle's left. He dipped pieces of bread into an egg cup. Dora and Steve sat side by side; he was eating off her plate, she was buttering a piece of toast. 'I just love marmalade,' she said.

'Is it always like this?' Lisa asked, looking towards the windows.

'It's a little worse than usual today,' Broderick said, 'but it should break up by lunchtime. We'll just have to keep you occupied till then. Do you swim? We've got a marvellous swimming pool. Really. Art Nouveau tiles all over. This place used to belong to – who was it? A real dinosaur. But the pool is great. And it's got three different temperatures.'

'I don't have a bathing suit,' Lisa said.

'We've got lots of extra suits.'

Lisa and Jim each ate an enormous breakfast. She looked at him swiftly as they rushed to the sideboard for third helpings. They almost started to laugh. The food was entirely normal, and the coffee too.

The morning passed pleasantly. Broderick showed them over most of the house. Some of the rooms were light and modern, others old-looking and apparently mouldering. 'We used to rent parts of it out,' he told them. 'For a long time that whole side over there was used as a retreat by a religious organization that Isabelle's Aunt Theda was involved with. If we sold it, I guess somebody'd turn the place into a school. They all want me to sell. But I couldn't bear it. My parents bought this house when I was seven. I remember moving in.'

There was a billiards room, a game room with ping-pong tables in it, a library. The pool was indeed magnificent. Jim and Lisa put on the suits they were offered. Broderick and Jeanette joined them. Neill sat in a canvas chair where it was dry; he said the chlorine made his skin allergy itch. And Carrol, who had sat down next to him, pulled out her knitting and shook her head. She was waiting, she said, for her consultation with Broderick.

Broderick swam for about ten minutes, got out of the pool and went up to Carrol. 'Right,' he said. She packed up the knitting without a word and left with him. Neill challenged the rest of them to a ping-pong match.

It was surprising, Lisa thought, how much she was enjoying herself. But after the ping-pong they passed through a hallway that had a window, and she rushed forward to look out. The world was still white, but it was as bright as electric light. The sun was going to burn off the fog quickly.

'We can start soon,' she said to Jim.

'Well, not right away. We could stay for lunch.'

'As soon as possible.'

'It wouldn't be very polite.'

'What happened last night wasn't very polite, either.'

'Let's not start on that again.'

'OK. Let's just get out fast.'

'This thing Broderick talked about – it sounds really good. It could make a big difference to us.'

'Jim, for God's sake,' she said.

'Just cool it, Lisa. There's no hurry.' He pushed forward ahead of her and turned to the right. She leaned back against a green stone statue that held a bowl meant for flowers. She wondered if she had the strength of will to get into the car herself and just drive away on her own.

He had the keys. It was his car. And he was the invited guest, even if this wasn't the right house. All the embarrassment would be his to deal with after she'd gone. She couldn't really do that to him.

Jeanette met her at a turn in the corridor. 'Are you staying for the session?' she asked.

'I don't think so. We'll be leaving pretty soon. We've got to get back to town.'

'That's too bad. The sessions really help.'

'In what way?'

'Well . . . just talking. Broderick says that fear – fear itself is a disease. Do you believe that?'

'To a certain extent. Sure.'

'It helps to talk about it.'

'It helps if the thing you're afraid of goes away. If you can make that happen by talking, I guess that's good.'

'Of course you can. Because it's in the mind.'

'The things I'm afraid of,' Lisa said, 'are definitely not in the mind. They're in the world.'

'But if they haven't happened yet –'

'A little anticipation keeps us all alive. Right?'

'It keeps us frightened.'

'Frightened people are careful. And careful people live longer.'

'Sometimes it isn't worth it,' Jeanette said.

They reached the breakfast room. Steve and Dora were still at the table. Sunlight streamed in through the windows.

*

She ran upstairs, got her purse and raced down again. She felt wonderful: the sun was out and at last they could leave.

Broderick met her at the foot of the stairs. 'Where to, and so fast?' he said. He smiled jovially but his eyes gloated at her.

'We've really got to get back now,' she said.

'But Jim said you were staying through lunch.'

'I'm afraid not.'

'It's all fixed. He said he'd phone whoever it was you had to meet.'

'It isn't that simple. Where is he?'

'Out in the garden somewhere, I think. Want me to help you look?'

'No, thanks,' she said. 'It's all right.'

She stepped out the side door on to a brick terrace. Stairs led down to a garden of white-flowering bushes. Beyond them stood a statue of a woman, one signalling arm raised out of her marble drapery. Neill was sitting on a bench at her side.

Lisa asked, 'Have you seen Jim?'

'No.'

'Who's this?'

'One of those goddesses. Artemis, maybe. Bow and arrow – is that right? I didn't pay much attention in school. Most of the time I was bored stiff. Couldn't wait to get out and see the world.'

'I loved it,' she said.

'Sit down.'

'I just came out to find Jim. We're leaving.'

'I thought you were staying till Monday. I hoped you were. Don't go.'

'We really have to,' she told him, walking away.

He got up and fell into step beside her. He said, 'Tonight and tomorrow are the best times. People come from all around. It's when we hold the séances.'

'Oh, God,' she said. In the distance Jim was walking towards them. He raised a hand. 'There he is. I'll just have a couple of words with him.' She hurried ahead.

*

'We're staying,' he said.

'Jim, I can't stand another minute in this place.'

'Every time I turn around, you look like you're having a great time with that Farley Granger clone.'

'Last night I was nearly raped by four men while you were getting a drink of water.'

'Last night you were completely pie-eyed and suffering from massive wish-fulfilment.'

'Oh Jesus, how can you be so stupid? How –'

'We're leaving right after dinner, but if it's too late, then we'll go in the morning. Whatever happens, we're definitely staying till the late evening, because Henry Kissinger's invited.'

'Who?'

'Ex-Secretary of State, Kissinger, a name you may have seen in the papers?'

'What are you talking about?'

'He's coming here for dinner tonight.'

'Why?'

'Christ. Because he was asked, of course.'

'Well. Well, so what?'

'Look, Lisa: I see nothing wrong about name-dropping, and if I get a chance to sit at the same table with a name like Kissinger, a part of American history, I'm sure as hell not going to miss it. Are you? Isabelle says he tells wonderful stories. Come on, Lisa, are you with me or what?'

'Give me the keys,' she said.

'Keys?'

'I'll drive back, and you can get a ride with Henry Kissinger or somebody else.'

'Of course not. It would be unforgivably rude.'

'I don't believe he's coming.'

'He is.'

'I'll make a scene.'

'Hah.'

'I'll say I recognize him from photographs as the Nazi commandant of a concentration camp. I'll –'

'Lisa,' he said, 'you just shut up and be nice. It's been a little strange, but you're going to have to take it. I've got an important deal on with Broderick and if you mess things up, believe me you're going to be sorry, because I won't stand for it.'

He'd never spoken to her like that. She felt her whole body, and especially her face, go rigid with fury and desperation. She wheeled around and ran off across the lawn.

She reached the front drive and slowed down. It wasn't yet noon, the sun was bright; she could walk through all the country roads until afternoon, and by that time she'd hit the highway and find help. She'd phone the police or the Automobile Association, or a friend from town, to come get her.

She settled into a regular stride. It wasn't going to be easy in her party shoes, though they weren't too high and so far felt comfortable. Her lips moved but she wasn't actually muttering. She was thinking about all the times he'd been in the wrong and unfair to her – how this was really the limit and it would serve him right.

She ploughed through a muddy field of deep grass and came out on to the driveway. It took her a lot longer than she'd expected to reach the road. Everything looked different in the daytime. In fact, it all looked beautiful. If the house hadn't been such a perfect replica of Haunted House Gothic, the setting could equally well have accommodated a fairytale palace. Everywhere she looked there was a superabundance of blossoming hedges, gnarled trees, mossy banks and starry flowers. She began to feel stronger as she went on, despite the shoes: a long walk over stony and uneven ground wasn't going to do them any good – she could tell that already. They'd be ruined afterwards for anything but rainy days.

She hummed a little. She reached the road and stopped, looking from left to right and rubbing her hands. She realized suddenly that she'd been scratching at her hands for a long while, trying to get rid of an itch in the folds between her fingers. She'd made all the itchy spaces bright pink. Red spots like the beginnings of a rash had come up between two of the fingers on her left hand. Nerves, she thought; or possibly a reaction to the peculiar food from the night before.

She turned to the left. For five minutes she walked without seeing a car or a person. Then ahead, coming towards her from around the next corner, she saw two men: rough-looking, bearded and wearing dungarees. She felt apprehensive straight away. She wanted to turn around and go back. Should she look at them, or past them; say hello, or what? What could she do to make them walk on and not take any notice of her?

One was short, the other tall. They didn't look right at her as they went by, but they were fooling. Almost as soon as she'd passed they were back again, one on each side of her, walking in her direction and near enough, if they wanted to, to grab her arms.

'Looking for something, girlie?' the short one said.

'No thanks, I'm fine,' she answered in a small, tight, terrified voice that made her even more frightened.

'Well, we'll just walk along with you a-ways,' the big one said. 'Keep you from getting lonely. Just in case something was to happen to a nice little girl like you.'

She looked up quickly. They were both grinning. Would they just terrorize her, or did they mean to act? Maybe they'd kill her afterwards, so she couldn't identify them. Maybe they meant to kill her anyway, just for fun. She'd never be able to run fast enough. It was probably better to give in as soon as possible and die quickly. If she were strong, at least she'd be able to hurt them back somehow.

The little one was beginning to jostle her. They were ready to start; pretty soon his friend would be doing it too. She stepped back and to the side, saying, 'Well, if nobody's going to leave me alone today, I might as well go back to my friends. They were right behind me.' She began to walk back, in the direction of the house.

They turned and came with her.

'Now isn't that a shame?' the tall one said. 'She doesn't like our company.'

'That really hurts my feelings,' the short one told him.

She was itchy and sore all over now. It was difficult to keep walking.

'You think she meant to be mean like that?' the small one asked. 'You think she's one of those stuck-up bitches that takes it out on you?'

'I think maybe that's just what she is,' the big one said. 'I met plenty like her. I know her type.'

Her pulse was drumming in her throat and the hairs rising on her arms. Surely it wouldn't happen. It couldn't happen, because she was having such a hard time simply continuing to breathe that long before they started to drag her across the road, she'd have a heart attack. She hoped she'd have one – that everything would just stop all of a sudden and be no more.

She took her eyes from the surface of the road and looked towards the turning. In front of her, emerging from a thicket of bushes to the left, were two people who waved. 'There they are,' she called out, and sprinted ahead. She could run after all. But she stopped when she was a few yards away. It hadn't occurred to her that she might really know the couple. Now she recognized them: it was Dora and Steve.

'Friends of yours?' Steve said.

'I never saw them before.' She turned and looked back. The two men were gone.

'I didn't think they looked very trustworthy,' Dora said. 'This is a lonely road. You'd better come on back with us.'

'So, you're a friend of nature, too?' Steve asked. He had a note-book and ballpoint pen in his hand, field-glasses hanging from a strap around his neck. 'This is wonderful country for it. Best in the world. That's the other reason we keep coming here.'

'I can't stay,' Lisa told him. 'We were only coming for supper last night, that's all. I've got to get back. For private reasons. And now Jim won't even let me go by myself. But that's silly. It isn't fair. I was trying to walk it.'

'In those shoes?' Dora said. 'Oh, dear.'

'You have a car here, don't you? Could you drive me? Just to a bus stop or a train station?' She scratched violently at her hands.

'You've got that chlorine reaction, too,' Dora said. 'I've got an ointment I can lend you.'

'I just want to get home,' Lisa wailed.

'But you wouldn't want to miss the party. You know who's going to be here tonight, don't you?'

'This is important. It's a family matter. Couldn't you?'

'All right,' Steve said. 'Of course. Right after lunch. Just let us finish the notes first, otherwise we'll have to start all over again. That's soon enough, isn't it – say, just before three? I'd make it earlier, but this is a working weekend as well as pleasure. We're compiling a book – did I tell you?'

'Oh?'

'Toads.'

'Dear little things,' Dora said. 'And fascinating.'

'You could stay indoors and do all the research you need,' Lisa said. 'They're in the house, too.'

'What do you mean?'

'In the upstairs bathroom, in the shower. There was a whole nest, a big pile of them. Last night.'

'Don't tell me they got out?' Steve said.

'It must be another batch,' Dora told him. 'Ours were fine this morning. I guess you're lucky they didn't nip your toes when you were stepping in there. They're carnivorous, you know.' She laughed in hearty barks that ended in a whoop of amusement.

Lisa said, 'Thanks for telling me.'

They came in sight of the house. Dora said she'd go get that tube of medicine, and added that she couldn't believe Lisa was really going to run off and miss the opportunity of meeting Henry Kissinger. They walked around the terrace to the far side, passing as they went a line of large, brand-new and expensive cars parked against the balustrade. Steve said the cars belonged to patients.

'You'd be surprised,' he told Lisa, 'how many people consult Broderick and Isabelle. In all walks of life, too: movie stars, politicians, big businessmen – you name it.'

'Kissinger?'

'I think he's just an ordinary guest.'

'Norman Mailer was here last weekend,' Dora said. 'He talked for hours about glands.'

'Hormones,' her husband corrected.

'And Henry Fonda before that.'

'He's dead,' Lisa said.

'Well, maybe it was the other one.'

'Which other one? The son?'

'Gary Cooper. Or was it John Wayne?'

'I think we're getting all these names a little mixed up,' Steve explained. He winked at Lisa.

'Anyway,' Dora said, 'he was very nice.'

*

They had a cold lunch of food that once again, like the breakfast, was good: salads with chicken, ham and beef; fruit and ice cream afterwards. The coffee looked all right too, but Lisa didn't want to try it.

Jim wouldn't look at her. She heard a long account from Dr Benjamin about tree frogs in Africa. He examined her hands and told her there was nothing to worry about: all the redness was simply a result of friction. As she listened, she could see Carrol, only four seats away, scratching and rubbing herself, touching her face all the time.

She said to the doctor, 'Steve and Dora are giving me a ride back to town at three, but I'm in kind of a hurry. I'd like to get away sooner than that. Did you come by car?'

'I came with them,' he told her. 'And I think Broderick picked the two girls up on his way out from town. Why don't you ask him? I'm sure he'd run you in.'

'I'd hate to bother him,' she said. 'We'll see.'

She went upstairs to wait till three. She paced all around the bed, looking carefully at the dark edging of the heavy, brocaded spread. She sat down on top of it, inspected the material and then slowly prepared to curl up. She lowered her head, but she kept her shoes on. She slept for a few minutes, waking up in a rush as soon as she heard someone walking down the hall.

Jim opened the door, shut it behind him and came over to her. He said, 'What's wrong with you?'

'I want to go home. Please, Jim. Remember the food last night?'

'It was fine just now.'

'And the cold, and the smell. Those animals in the shower. And I mean it about what happened when you left. You don't believe me, but you don't believe anything from me any more.'

'I'm not staying here for an accusation session.'

'Just let me have the car keys, for God's sake. What difference is it going to make to you?'

'If you walk out of here, if you're rude, if you make a scene – it makes me look bad.'

'No, it doesn't. I act on my own.'

'You're here with me.'

'I tried to leave. I was going to walk. Look at my shoes. Two guys on the road tried to grab me.'

'Uh-huh. Guys trying to grab you every time you turn around.'

'Just let me get out, Jim. Please.'

'We're leaving Monday morning.'

'Monday? This is only Saturday.'

'We've been invited for the weekend.'

'Well, if this is even the right house, it was only supposed to be supper on Friday. I don't have a change of underpants or anything. Neither do you.'

'Isabelle says she can let you have whatever you like.'

'What I'd like is to get back to town.'

They argued back and forth in a normal tone at first, then in whispers, and nearly shouting. He wanted to know how she could be so parochial as to leave just when Henry Kissinger was about to arrive: wasn't she interested in world politics, in history?

She said, 'You don't believe he's really coming here, do you? To eat mud soup and old tyres? Him and Norman Mailer and John Wayne and all the rest of them? They just want to get us to stay here, that's all.'

'Why?'

'I don't know. They just do.'

'You mean, they're telling us lies?'

'Of course they are.'

'But why would they do that?'

'Because they want us to stay.'

'It doesn't make sense.'

'Does any of it? Look at me.' She held out her hands. The skin was patched with pink lumps. 'Look at my hands,' she told him.

'What have you done to them?'

'I haven't done anything. They're itching because of something in this house.'

'Oh, Lisa. I don't know what's gotten into you. Try to calm down.'

She stood up. 'Right,' she said. 'Steve and Dora can give me a ride. And now I know how much I'd be able to count on you.' She snatched up her purse and looked at her wristwatch. It said four thirty. 'God, I'm late. Oh, God.'

'That settles it.'

'Yes. I'll see if they'll still do it. And if they won't, you'll have to.'

'Nope.'

'And if you don't, we're through.'

'That's up to you. You're going to feel pretty foolish when you look back and see how unreasonable you're being.'

'And I'm calling the police.'

He stood up and threw her back on to the bed. 'Everything you want,' he hissed at her. 'Always for you and never for the both of us, never for me. Who's going to have to build up a career and pay off the mortgage and all the rest of it, hm? You won't cook for my friends, you won't do this or that –'

'And what about you?' she screeched. 'Leave me there with a list of all the errands I've got to run for you: I've got a job too, you know. You're a grown man. You can wash your own goddamn socks once in a while.'

'You aren't going to give me that Women's Lib stuff, are you?'

'Just this once – just get me out of here and I'll do anything. You can come straight back, if you like. Please.'

'Don't cry like that. Somebody could hear you.'

'Please.'

'All right,' he said.

She sprang towards the door. He followed slowly. They went down the stairs together, Lisa running ahead.

Isabelle was standing at the foot of the staircase. She was dressed in another long, dark robe and her hair was even more elaborately arranged than on the night before. This time the string of pearls that twined through the pile of stacked braids included a single jewel; it hung from the centre parting on to her forehead. It looked like a ruby, surrounded by tiny pearls. 'And where are you two off to?' she asked.

Lisa said, 'I'm sorry, Isabelle – I really am. It's been so lovely here, but we left town thinking it was just for supper last night. I had three people I was supposed to see today, and now I've got to go – I've really got to. The others are going to be furious. I'll have to patch that up somehow, but my mother –' her voice quivered. 'My mother's operation comes first. I've just got to get back. We should have said straight away. Jim –' she turned to him; he could do some worrying for a change, after putting her through all this: 'Jim thought you'd be upset if we refused your hospitality. I was sure you'd understand. He can stay, of course. But my mother can't wait, I'm afraid. Not even for Mr Kissinger.'

'That's another disappointment. He just called. He can't make it tonight. Maybe tomorrow, he said. Such a shame. We look forward to his visits so much.'

'Tomorrow?' Jim repeated. He sounded hopeful.

'Not for me,' Lisa insisted.

Broderick had appeared at the end of the corridor, the other guests grouped behind him. He began to lead them all down the carpet towards the staircase and the light. 'What's this?' he said.

'Lisa wants to leave us,' Isabelle told him.

'I don't want to. I've got to, that's all. My mother's having a serious operation.'

'When?' Broderick asked.

'On Friday afternoon they told me it was going to be tonight, possibly tomorrow morning. I've got to get back.'

'I can drive you,' Broderick offered.

'Thanks, but Jim's going to.'

'I know the roads around here. And I'm used to the fog. Have you seen what it's like?'

'We waited for you,' Steve complained. Dora, beside him, asked, 'Where were you? You said three.'

'I couldn't find you,' Lisa said. She suddenly didn't believe that they had waited, or that Henry Kissinger had ever been on the guest list, or that she was going to be allowed out of the house, which was definitely the wrong house. She put her hand on Jim's arm. Her fingers, her whole arm, trembled.

'Why don't you phone the hospital?' Isabelle suggested. She picked up the receiver from the telephone on the table next to her.

They were going to try to fake her out, Lisa thought. But she could phone a taxi, or even the police, if she wanted to. Or – a better idea – a friend: Broderick was undoubtedly on good terms with all the lawyers, doctors and policemen in the neighbourhood, as well as any local politicians who lived nearby. 'That's a good idea,' she said. She let go of Jim's arm and came down the last few stairs.

Isabelle put her ear to the receiver. She said, 'Well, wouldn't you know it? It does this sometimes in a thick fog. It's gone completely dead.'

Me, too, Lisa thought. She turned to Jim and said, 'I mean it. Now.'

He spread his hands towards Isabelle. 'I'm really sorry,' he said.

'Another time,' she told him. She shook his hand and smiled. She shook Lisa's hand too, holding the friendly look and the smile.

Broderick called after them, 'Come on back if the fog catches up with you. They can be dangerous. People can actually choke to death in them.'

*

All the air outdoors was smoky. They got into the car. Lisa said nothing, although she felt safe already. If they had to, she wouldn't mind sleeping in the back seat. At least they'd be away from the house. Jim turned the key. He drove the car across the gravel. Lisa waved at the dimly lighted doorway.

They moved down the drive, along the woodland road and out on to the highway, where almost immediately they hit the real fog. Jim went very slowly. The fog came towards them in long strips like white veiling that kept tearing in pieces or bunching up around them.

'What was all that about your mother?' he said.

'I had to think of something they couldn't explain away. It would have looked bad if they hadn't been sympathetic.'

'Isabelle was very nice about it.'

'She was mad as hell.'

'She was not. She was kind and understanding.'

'And she has Kissinger for dinner just all the time – oh, yes. And what a surprise: the phone doesn't work.'

'What are you getting at?'

'Those weirdo people holding occult meetings together.'

'They're wonderful people. They're studying phenomena that can't be explained yet by any of the scientific principles we know of so far. How do you think anyone ever gets to know things, anyway? There's always a time when it sounds crazy and crack-pot – when it's all being tried out experimentally. As soon as a thing's accepted, then it's considered normal.'

'You think that house is normal?'

'Well, the heating's kind of erratic and the pipes don't work so well, and what do you expect? It's a big old place down in the country. It'd cost a fortune to fix it up.'

'It wouldn't cost a fortune to give us tuna salad to eat, instead of whatever that horrible stuff was. It wouldn't –'

'Wait,' he said. All the windows had suddenly gone stark white. The effect was blinding until he turned off the lights. He slowed the car to a crawl. 'If it gets any worse, you'll have to walk in front, to show me where the edge of the road is.'

'No. We can just stop here and sleep in the car. Pull off the road.'

'You heard what Broderick said about the fog.'

'I don't believe it.'

'Well, I do.'

'I'm not going back there, Jim,' she said.

'Jesus Christ,' he shouted, 'what's wrong with you?' He stopped the car and switched off the ignition. 'I think you're crazy,' he said. 'I really do. Just like your whole damn family.'

'OK. You can think what you like, as long as we never have to go back to that place.'

'This is the end of us, you know. I can't go on with you after this.'

'If we just get home, we'll be all right.'

'You screwed up everything with them. I don't know how anybody could have behaved the way you did. Completely hysterical, and lying your head off. It was obvious.'

'But does that mean I've got to die for it?'

'Die? Nobody's going to die.'

'And why do we have to split up? Why do they mean more to you than I do? You didn't even know them before yesterday.'

'I guess maybe I didn't know you very well, either.'

'Oh, shove that.'

'Uh-huh. Nice.'

'You know me. And you know how I feel about you.'

'Maybe not.' He opened his window a crack. They could see the white fog creep in like smoke. He tried the lights again. This time the glare wasn't thrown back, but the lights didn't seem to penetrate more than a few feet into the shifting areas of blankness.

She said, 'When you got up for that drink of water last night, where did you go?'

'Down the hall to the bathroom.'

'You were with somebody else, weren't you?'

'No,' he said. 'But it's a good idea.'

The whiteness became all-enveloping. The temperature began to drop inside the car. The sound of rain seemed to be coming from somewhere, though they couldn't see any.

'I don't understand,' she said, 'how you could have let us get into all that.'

'It was too foggy to drive back. It was like this.'

'And this morning, when I asked you for the keys?'

'This morning you were already crazy; people grabbing you left and right. If this doesn't clear soon –'

'We sit it out.'

'I suppose so.' He was about to cut the lights, when something dark thudded against the windshield and was gone again.

'A bat,' Lisa called out.

'No. It didn't look . . . I think it was rounder. Maybe a bird. I guess the light attracted it.'

There was another sound as two more of the things struck Lisa's side window. She undid her safety belt and moved nearer to Jim.

He was watching the glass in front of him. Several more of the dark shapes hit. They sounded like rubber balls being thrown against the car, all over the metal parts suddenly: on the roof, too. He leaned forward. 'Frogs,' he said. They were everywhere, bouncing up and down, lying still, or slithering across the glass.

'Not frogs,' Lisa moaned. 'Toads.'

'Jesus, will you look at them – there must be hundreds.'

'Thousands,' she said. 'Oh, my God.'

He turned off the lights. It didn't have any effect. The toads continued to bombard the car.

'Maybe if we start moving again,' he said.

'We can't. They're jamming themselves into the exhaust. Can't you hear them?'

'I could really step on it and blow the muffler off.' He switched the engine on again, turned the lights high.

Now the toads were all over. They blocked the view from the windows. They were also a great deal bigger than before. When one of them landed, it sounded like a soccer ball.

He started to drive. The exhaust pipe roared, the car inched forward. He tried to use the windshield wipers, but the toads hung on until the blades stuck in one position. There were swarms of the animals, uncountable. Clusters of them lay squashed or flattened on the windows. And the big ones crashed down on top of them. A dark liquid began to run over the panes.

'Could they break the glass?' she asked.

'I don't know. It's safety glass. They might be able to bang into it hard enough, if they all jumped together.'

'They're carnivorous,' she said.

Something to Write Home About

The big tourist boat was about to dock and most of the passengers were standing up on deck to watch. John and Amy Larsen sat inside on a bench in the lounge where the evening before they had listened to music and drunk wine.

"I don't have any more postcards," she said, and rummaged through her purse. From the outside pocket of it she took out three postcards, already written on and stamped. All were addressed to the same name and place, and at the top left-hand corner of each she had conscientiously put down the day, and the month, May, and year, 1965, as though the cards were intended to be saved for posterity.

"Don't worry about it," her husband said. "We can buy some more as soon as we get off."

They had been married for eighteen months, although they did not look married. To look at, they might even have been related by blood rather than by law. They looked like students, and John Larsen was one; his wife had graduated the year before. She had majored in English, he was in his last year at business school.

Standing near them was another American couple, who were on their honeymoon. They came from New York, and, in contrast to the Larsens, looked well-dressed, sophisticated, and as though they were either not married at all or had been married for several years and were taking a break from the children and a life of suburban cocktail parties. Their name was Whitlow. And they were on their honeymoon, all right. When the boat had put them ashore at Crete for the day, the Whitlows had had a quarrel of some kind and John and Amy had found Mrs. Whitlow alone, standing as though posed, with the sun on her shiny hair, and her tropically flowered sleeveless dress looking brand new, like a magazine ad for winter holidays in the Caribbean. She had walked forward towards them, peered this way and that into the other sightseers among the reconstructed ruins of King Minos' palace, and recognized them.

"Lost your husband?" John had asked.

"Well," she had said, "he went off in a huff, but I think maybe he's lost now. I've been wandering all over the place."

That night they had laughed about it as they drank with the Larsens. Another couple named Fischer, a New Jersey businessman and his wife, had joined them. The Fischers were already grandparents, but were throwing themselves into the spirit of things with more zest than the younger couples. They had all begun to talk about the places they had visited or would have liked to see. The Whitlows had been to Nauplia.

"Oh, we were there, too," Amy had said. "That's where we couldn't get any artichokes."

"We sat down on the terrace of the hotel restaurant, you know, facing the harbor——" John had said.

"That's where we were, too," Whitlow had told them.

"And two tourist buses drove up and parked. We started to order dinner and the waiter handed us the menu and said, 'With group?' "

"With group?" Amy had repeated, in the voice the waiter had used.

"So we said no, not with group, and started to order."

"And there were artichokes on the menu, which I just love."

"We were okay till we hit the artichokes, and then it turned out that they were all for group, forty-seven darn orders of artichokes. That just about finished the place for us."

"Did you notice what a funny kind of butter they had there?" Amy had asked. "It was white. It tasted just like Crisco."

"I told you, it was some kind of margarine," John had put in.

"Not tasting like that. I'm sure it was Crisco."

"Did you go to the island?" Mrs. Whitlow had asked.

"Yes, we had tea there."

"So did we, but we made a mistake about the boat. Tell them about the boat, Hank."

"Well, when Sally and I got there, we saw this beautiful boat tied up at the landing-stage."

"A yacht, really, but a small one——"

"And later we wanted to get out to the island, but the boat was gone. We went and looked at the sign, and it had the times of sailing on it."

"So then——"

"Do you want to tell it?"

"Oh, go ahead."

"So then later in the day we saw it there again and barrelled down to the jetty to get on board. My God, it was somebody's private yacht. Nobody on board but the English mate. The real boat was a rowboat."

"Then we got into the rowboat and this girl who was staying on the island climbed in too, and dropped a paperback she'd been carrying, and Hank handed it back to her——"

"*Fanny Hill.* No kidding. Sort of broke her up. She'd been reading it with the cover held back."

"The rooms out there were gorgeous, weren't they? If we'd known you could stay on it, we'd have booked in there."

"That boat was a beauty," Whitlow had said. "Some big wheel owned it and chartered her out for the season. The mate said it was built in Holland."

"Never mind," Sally Whitlow had said. "One day we'll have one."

"Diamond-studded," her husband had agreed, and they had shaken hands on it.

"Did you get to Delphi?" John had asked them. The Whitlows had been all through the Peloponnese and driven up to Delphi from Athens. They had really wanted to go all the way up into Macedonia too, but there was only so much time. This was the fifth and last week of their honeymoon. The Larsens had missed Delphi, which they regretted, but they had hired a car and driven through some of the Peloponnesian cities. The Fischers had seen Athens, taken a day's excursion to Hydra and Aegina, and that had been all.

The boat they were on had stopped at Mykonos, with a side trip to Delos, and at Crete. Mrs. Fischer had liked Mykonos best.

"Well, I know it's supposed to be a photographer's paradise," John had said, "but that whitewash and bougainvillea and arts and crafts just leave me cold. I think you either like Mykonos or Delos."

"And you liked Delos," Mrs. Fischer had said, smiling at him.

"Yes, maybe the best of all. What I'd really like to do is go back there and stay a couple of days."

"But there isn't any hotel."

"Yes, there is. At that tourist pavilion, they've got about four rooms they can rent out. I asked them about it. Friends of ours stayed there last year."

"They loved it," Amy had said.

"They said that at ten o'clock the caique from Mykonos pulled in with all the sightseers who spent a few hours scrambling over everything and climbing up the hill, and when the boat pulled out again the island was covered in shoeprints and sneaker marks. Then it took about an hour, and when you looked after that, all you could see on the ground were lizard prints."

"And the starlight is bright enough to see by even when the moon isn't out," Amy had said.

John had touched her hair and told her that they would go back there some day.

But now the boat was docking at Rhodes, and they had their luggage ready, because they were leaving the group in order to be able to spend two days on the island. Then they would fly back to Athens, and from there would take a plane home. The tour leaders had allowed them to reclaim a small part of their tickets. They had even given the Larsens the name of a good, cheap hotel they could recommend. But the Larsens would be joining the group again for lunch at the luxury hotel and might go along on the guided tour of the city in the afternoon, since that had all been paid for and couldn't be refunded. Only the morning would be different. In the morning the other passengers were going to take buses to Lindos and then visit the monastery of Philerimos. The Larsens were to visit both places the following day when they would be able to take their time. Amy had liked the cruise, but John was beginning to tire of constantly being hustled along from one thing to the next.

The boat was almost at a standstill.

"There's that creep again," Sally Whitlow said to her husband.

One of the passengers, who had started off the tour standing with the German-speaking guide and had changed to standing with the English-speaking guide because of Mrs. Whitlow, shuffled into the lounge. His eyes were always on her, and he had been attempting to strike up a friendship with both the Whitlows all during the voyage. Mrs. Whitlow turned her head sharply away. Her husband glared at the man, who tried to start a conversation about what a nice day it was. Whitlow didn't answer. The man sat down. The boat struck against something.

"Feels like we've landed," John said.

Mrs. Whitlow stood up and walked out. Her husband followed. The German-speaking man stood up and began to walk behind them. Whitlow turned around and shoved him in the chest.

"You stay right here," he said, and turned his back and walked off.

The Larsens went up on deck, carrying their bags. The Whitlows were leaning against the rail, and Sally Whitlow was saying, "It just makes me nervous, that's all. You could knock him down ten times and he'd come up like a rubber ball. There's just something missing. Really, somebody ought to lock him up, you know."

"Oh, I think he's harmless enough," Whitlow said.

"For God's sake, Hank. He's out of his mind. He ought to be in an institution."

The Larsens passed along the deck under the strong sunlight, and joined the line that had already formed.

"I don't like her," Amy said.

"She's all right. She didn't realize, that's all."

"Just the same, I don't like her."

"Be fair, Amy. How could she know?"

She watched the men working with the cables and preparing the way for the passengers to step ashore. Her husband looked at her: short in her skirt that was too long, and her long-sleeved blouse that she wore sloppy Joe art-major style outside the skirt. She had a small-nosed, intense face like a terrier, and her ordinary brown hair just hung to her shoulders instead of billowing out in a wave like Sally Whitlow's hair.

"You just can't stand it about her hair," he said.

"Well, I don't see how it can look like that. It looks like she just came out of a hairdresser's. But we've been on this boat for five days."

"Some people don't have to wash their hair more than once every two weeks."

"That's what's so annoying. I bet it always looks like that."

"But otherwise she's okay?"

"I guess so."

"You know, I like you just exactly the way you look."

"Somebody ought to lock you up," she said. "You ought to be in an institution." She opened her mouth and laughed and laughed.

He set down his suitcase and took her by the arm.

"Look," he said. "The line's starting."

It took them quite a while to work their way forward. When they were at last standing on the quayside, the other passengers were beginning to form up in front of the three guides. They walked past the French-speaking guide and came to the English-speaking guide, who had been nice to John about changing the tickets.

"You will know the island of Rhodes is supposed to be the island of roses," she was saying. "*Rhodos* means a rose. But it is more probably truly the flower you see here, the hibiscus." She gestured towards some beds of red hibiscus flowers.

"Let's find that hotel," he said. "Let me carry that. She said it wasn't very far away."

They set off towards the town. In front of them half a dozen cab drivers stood beside their Chevrolet taxis. The drivers began to call to them as they came nearer. Two rushed forward to carry the bags. Larsen lifted his head to the side and said no in Greek. He had to say it twice, and Amy said no thank you.

The hotel was small, new, and looked clean, but the room was small, too. There was just room enough to stand up between the bed and the window. The shutter was down because of the sun.

"Can you ask him if there's a shower?" Amy asked. The man who had shown them the room beckoned them out again and down the hall. There wasn't any shower, but there was a bath. They took the room and began to unpack. They didn't take out much, as they were only staying the two days.

"I'll go see about the car," John said.

"There must be a bus."

"But it would be nicer by car. And we'll need it tomorrow."

"It's your money," she said.

He went out of the hotel, rented a car for two days, and drove it back. Amy walked out the hotel door as he was putting the key in his pocket. She had been sitting downstairs near the door, watching out for him.

They got in, and John took out the map he had been given at the garage.

"I think I'm okay, but if you see any signs that say *Petaloudes,* sing out. That's us."

"Does *Petaloudes* mean butterflies?"

"I don't know. It might. It sounds like it ought to mean petals."

"That's because of the way they look when they fly. Like petals," she said, and made her hands do butterfly motions.

He looked at her face. She was looking happy, and was calm enough. He started the car.

Once they got clear of the town, the roads began to wind and to climb steeply. And the island was lusciously green, unlike the art book photographs of the rest of Greece, where temples which turned out later to be made of grey, orange, or honey-coloured stone appeared stark white under annihilating sunlight and set in landscapes of sand and rock and cracked, impoverished earth.

"It seems to be way up in the mountains," he said.

"I wish it were the right time of year."

"So do I, but we can see the place, anyway. It's nice to see a couple of places that are just pretty without all the history."

"And maybe they'll have postcards. Oh! Oh, John! Stop the car."

He slammed on the brakes.

"What is it?"

"I forgot to mail my postcards."

"Jesus H. Christ, Amy. You could have killed us."

"I've got to mail them," she said, reaching for the door handle.

He pulled her back.

"One hour isn't going to make any difference."

"No!" she said. She started to scream, "No, no, no! I've got to!"

He shook her by the shoulders and then held her head between his hands.

"Just calm down, now. Just relax. We can buy lots of postcards in a few minutes, and then we can send them all together."

"But——"

"We can send them all together, and everything will be all right. Okay?" He kissed her on the nose three times.

"Okay?"

"Okay."

He started the car again. Luckily they hadn't been on a corner when she had made him stop.

They drove around more corners and the road kept banking upwards, and then suddenly there were lots of trees very close to the road.

They did not speak. He kept his eyes on the road but was thinking, *So, we're not going to get out of it so easily.* And the right half of his body seemed to have taken on the sensitivity of a third eye; if his wife were to make another dash at the door handle, or perhaps towards him, trying to get at the wheel, he would know it even though he was looking ahead through the windshield.

The road levelled out, went down, and then up again. The air was cooler, the coolness seeming to come from the trees. Perhaps it really did, he thought—released oxygen or something, causing a freshness around the trees. But perhaps also part of the sensation was induced by a mental reaction to the green colour. The previous spring, the university store had had a large pile of notebooks on sale, the paper of which was a peculiar green colour, and inside the cover of each notebook you could read a statement to the effect that "research had shown" green to be extremely soothing to the eyes. He had bought one and found the colour irritating, but there might be something in the idea after all.

All these things were connected: the eye, the mind, the body. Hip bone connected to the thigh bone. Yet even when the whole business was going right and healthy, it was fundamentally mysterious. Research showed, but you could dig into your past till you were blue in the face and it still wouldn't help you to feel confident walking into a room full of strangers if that was the sort of thing that had always made you nervous. Research could probably stop you washing your hands fifty times a day, but then you'd start something else, like picking your nose. Or worrying about postcards.

They came over a ridge and began to descend into the valley.

"This is it," he said. He guided the car up a slope and around to the right where there were three other cars parked under the trees. They could see the weathered wood railing and the steps going far up the mountainside, and the two lower ponds and the little waterfalls between. Everywhere was the sound of water.

"It's pretty," she said.

He locked up the car and took her arm. He led her past the postcard stands and made sure that he didn't seem to be trying to distract her attention. And she didn't notice.

They began to climb the stairway. The wood didn't look very solid. Down below, where there were other railings around the watercourses, the wood looked yellow, like bamboo, and the water was a vivid green, even greener than the trees. Three people, slung with cameras, came down the path and passed them. It was very narrow, and John had to pull Amy back from the edge. There were more people farther up, and it looked like a long climb.

"Do butterflies need a lot of water?" she asked.

"I don't know, Amy."

"It's a nice place for them, though. Think of having a place where you go to every year like this. They fly for miles and it's the same place they've been coming to for generations."

"Yes," he said. "It's nice."

"I wonder why people don't do those things. I mean, why don't people have places they go to? Migrating and hibernating and all that. It's very strange when you think about it. But then it's very strange if you suddenly wonder why not."

They climbed to the level of the third pool and looked down at the emerald circular ponds in their nests of yellow railings, with the sun dappling over everything through the leaves of the overhanging trees.

"It looks like some place in Africa," he said. "I wonder what makes the water so green. Maybe it's very cold."

They stood there for a while and then she looked farther up the path. He could see that she was suddenly frightened of going up to the top. She looked back down at the water again.

"It makes you dizzy to look all the way down."

"Yes," he said. "It's a long climb to the top, too. How are your loafers holding out?"

"Oh, they're okay. John, did you ever think—you know, people who say there isn't any life after death think it's because it would be so peculiar. But it's even more peculiar to be alive in the first place, isn't it? So why not?"

"Well," he said, "I don't know. I think it's one of those things you believe in or you don't. I don't believe it has much to do with thought. I mean, you're predisposed to believe one way or the other. And I don't think it has much to do with how you feel about the sacredness of life, if that's what's bothering you. Do you want to try going to the top?"

"I'm sort of tired," she said.

"As a matter of fact, I've had enough of a climb, too."

They began the descent.

"It's being on board the boat for so long," he said.

"But we walked all over Delos and Crete."

"But your legs get to feel different."

At the bottom of the path she saw the postcard stand and made a beeline for it.

"Oh!" she said, picking up one card after another. "Oh look, they've got pictures of all the butterflies." She handed him a picture of a leafy tree with a brown trunk. He didn't see any butterflies. Then he looked more closely and realized that the entire trunk of the tree was composed of hundreds of butterflies lying next to each other.

"That's amazing," he said.

"Aren't they pretty? It looks like they're just sleeping there." She kept picking up more postcards. "Just sleeping," she cooed.

The woman behind the stand had caught the spirit of the thing and began to select better and better pictures to be looked at.

"Look at this one, John," Amy said, and handed him a picture of a flight of pink butterflies taken against a background of dark leaves. If you squinted your eyes they looked exactly like flamingoes flying in formation.

The postcard-seller was even shorter than Amy Larsen. The top of her head only came up to Amy's chin. She began to talk in French about the butterflies, and handed John a piece of paper which had the history of the place written on it.

"What's she saying?"

"Wait a sec. Her French is worse than mine." He interrupted her and asked why the butterflies chose that particular spot. It seemed a nonsensical thing to ask, but the woman answered him straight away: it was because of the trees, because of the resin in the leaves.

"Isn't that interesting," Amy said. Then she picked up one of the things on the tray full of keychains, paperknives, cheap unworkable ballpoint pens, and other souvenir objects.

It was a green-enamelled brass frog with red glass eyes. Its head was on a hinge and the mouth opened up into a spout.

When you lifted the head, the belly of the frog became an ashtray and the bottom jaw a cigarette-rest. She clicked the head up and down several times, and then bought the frog, though neither of them smoked.

They walked back to the car. A Greek soldier passed them on their way. Two other cars had pulled in to the left of theirs, and six soldiers were standing leaning against the fenders. Amy's hands were clenched on her postcards as they walked forward. John unlocked the car door, got in and leaned over to unlock the other door, and pulled the handle back.

She sat down on the seat and left the door open. She put all her postcards up on the dashboard and set the frog beside them. John got the map out of the door pocket. He left his door open, too. Now that they were away from the coolness of the water, the heat was noticeable.

"Why are they all looking at me like that?" she said.

"Soldiers always look at girls, honey."

"They're looking at me like I was some kind of a freak."

"You're just freakishly Nordic, that's all. Probably your hair."

"My hair is dark."

"Not in this country." He opened the map. "We've got time to go someplace else. We could go visit this temple. That's on the other side of town, but we'd have time."

"Okay," she said. She began to click the frog's head up and down.

"Do you like my frog?"

"Sort of."

She opened the head again and looked into the bowl of the frog's belly.

"It's built just like me. Slim as a lily down to my tiny waist and from there on in like a battleship. Like a kangaroo."

"The ideal female shape," he said, punching the map to make it fold up again. He looked to the left and saw that the soldier they had passed had returned, and three of the men were drinking out of bottles.

"Lucky I bought so many stamps," she said, and took a ballpoint pen out of her purse.

"You cleaned them out. Would you like something to drink?"

"No, thanks."

"I'm thirsty. I'm going to see if they're selling soft drinks back there."

"I'll write my postcards."

"Okay. If they've got any ice cream or something like that, would you like that instead?"

"No, thanks."

He got out and closed the car door after him, knowing that she would be crouching over her postcards, having dragged her hair over most of the left side of her face because the soldiers were looking at her. And then, of course, she really would look like a freak.

At the postcard stand the woman sold him a fizzy lemonade, opened the cap, and gave him a straw. It wasn't very cold. He walked back to the car and drank most of it there. Beside him Amy was writing away furiously. He drank through the straw and put his right hand on the back of her neck and then squeezed her shoulders.

"It isn't inherited, Amy," he said.

She went on writing. He finished the lemonade and looked at the postcards she had finished, lying beside the hideous frog. The date, still complete with year, was on each, and the left-hand side crammed with minute writing. He got out of the car and looked around for a basket or some sort of container to put the bottle in, but there wasn't one. The soldiers had stood their empties at the foot of one of the trees. He put his bottle down beside the others and went back to the car.

He waited till she had finished writing the postcard she was working on, and said, "All set?"

"I haven't finished yet."

He appropriated the remaining cards.

"How many have you done?"

"Wait. One, two, three—six."

"Well, that's quite a lot. We'll leave the rest till we get back to the hotel. You wouldn't want to get stuck there without any and have to go out and buy some new ones."

"But if I finish these, I can send them off and get some more later."

"Nope. Right now we're going to see that temple."

He put all the written postcards into the outside pocket of her purse, leaned over her, and closed her door. She kissed him on the cheek.

He started the car and gave her a hug with his right arm.

"Better put that away," he said. "I don't want it to fall off."

"It can't break. It's brass or something."

"Supposing I had to put on the brakes suddenly? It could hit one of us in the eye."

She put the frog in her purse and he backed the car out and down the slope and on to the road. He hadn't expected the kiss and it had made up for a lot of things.

They were halfway to the town when she said, "I've got to go to the bathroom again."

"Didn't you go at the hotel?"

"Yes, but I've got to go again."

"Can you wait till we get into town?"

"No."

He looked for a field with bushes and finally found one, pulled over to the side of the road, and stopped. She bolted out the door and ran across the field, the handbag, which contained wads of Kleenex as well as everything else, clutched to her chest.

He leaned forward over the wheel and closed his eyes. A car passed on the road. He sat up again, then leaned back on the wheel, and by mistake sounded the horn. When she returned through the field, she said, "What's the rush?"

"No rush. We've got plenty of time."

"You were honking the horn."

"Oh, I leaned up against the wheel. I didn't mean it to hurry you."

They drove on, back through the town, and he decided to be smart and get her to mail half the postcards so that she wouldn't pull another stunt like the one earlier in the morning.

"How nice you are to remember. It just slipped my mind," she said, ducking out of the car to put the postcards in the slot. He had made sure that she took the ones she had written on instead of the others; they were all stamped. She had bought one hundred air mail stamps in Heraklion. That wasn't counting the stamps she had been buying for two weeks. He hadn't even known she had brought the money with her, and then she had simply said, "Oh yes, just in case of emergencies."

They drove through the town and he kept along the shore road. It wasn't so far as he had thought.

"Look," she said. "There's a temple."

He overshot, and parked the car off the road where he had stopped, and they walked back along the tar road. On either side of them grew flat fields full of wildflowers. They could see the tops of the orange-yellow temple columns, only three and a half of them left, the three entire ones with the epistyle on top. And when they moved into the field and then downhill, they could see some big trees in the distance over to the right, and ahead beyond the building, the ocean dancing with light.

"Oh, I like it," she said. "It's like the bones of a lion. Is it Apollo's?"

"I think so, but I may be wrong. I should have brought the guidebook along."

"Let's just walk around," Amy said.

They walked hand in hand, looking at the temple, the fields, the sea. A fresh, light wind blew inshore.

"That's nice, to have a breeze," she said. "It was hot in that valley once we got away from the water."

"Let's sit down."

They walked forward into the columns and sat on a broken slab of stone. The remains of the temple looked smaller and much less grand from inside, but so did every temple he had ever seen except the Parthenon. They sat looking in the direction of the ocean. He wanted to talk to her, and realized that he couldn't.

The first days in Athens had been all right. And the trip through the Peloponnese had started out all right, too. They had arrived in Corinth near lunchtime and gone through the gates. Amy had been hopping up and down with anticipation, since they could already see it: a temple islanded in a sea of yellow flowers, just like the picture on the cover of his highschool second-year Latin book. They had gone in and sat down inside the temple, and after a while had had the place to themselves. It was very hot for the time of year, he had thought. The sun had come straight down. And when they had left and come to the gate, it had been padlocked and there was nobody around. "I'll climb over and hunt somebody out," he had said. And she had told him no, that she was climbing over, too. And up she had gone, over the wire fence. He had been worried that she would slip and fall, and had tried to stop her, but she had gotten angry, and had gone over like a bundle of laundry, and then had been so proud of her athletic ability and laughed with pleasure. Later in the day she had had a bad headache from the sun, and he hadn't felt so well himself, but he had thought for the first time in a long while that everything was going to be all right. They had stayed at a hotel on the beach, where they were the only couple in the whole place, and that was all right. And then in Olympia, the weather had been beautiful and there were pine trees everywhere with the wind making swooshing noises in the branches, and that had been nice. But then they had gone to Mycenae, and that was the place where he had become really worried about heatstroke. The sun kept pounding down like lead over them. She had been holding a branch of orange blossoms he had yanked off a tree from the car window. And they had walked around the ruins for about fifteen minutes, and sat down so that he could read the guidebook aloud. He had been reading for quite a while before he noticed the stupefied look on her face. "This is a terrible place," she had said. "It makes you feel that people have been murdered here. Not just one or two people. Hundreds. Thousands. It's monstrous and squat and barbaric and awful." Not seriously, in an exasperated way, he'd asked, "Well, would you like to go?" And the look had left her face and she had said, "Yes, please." Nauplia had not been a wild success, but not a disaster, either, and on the day they had gone to Epidaurus, he had felt everything take a turn for the better. They had gone to see the theatre, and she had insisted on climbing all the way up to the very last row of stone seats, where they had sat down. "Oh, what a wonderful place," she had said. "What a wonderful place. I only wish it was the right time. To see the plays here. It wouldn't even matter that we couldn't understand them." And while they were sitting there, with the enormous theatre going down, down like a huge bowl in front of them, about four busloads of Greek schoolchildren in dark blue uniforms had come running on to the stage, three teachers following along behind. They had been able to hear every separate footfall. The children had fanned out over the stage and then climbed up and seated themselves in the first five rows. And the head teacher, a man, had stood on the centre stone and given them a talk in a perfectly ordinary tone of voice, and from where they had been watching, way up in the topmost row, he and she had been able to hear every syllable as clear as a bell, although they could not understand the language.

They had reached for each other without saying anything, and with her hand in his he had thought that he would never forget this, he could never forget it as long as he lived, and it would always make him feel good just to think about it. Later in the day they had gone through the museum and seen the reconstructions of how the columns had been arranged in a snail-like interior passage of one of the shrines. They walked around and around, looking at the design which changed at every point. He did not mind reconstructions unless they pretended to be the real thing; he found it very difficult to visualize what the ruins would have looked like with the inner walls and a roof on top. But these passages in the museum had the original marble capitals set on top of the columns, and they were carved with lily patterns, which had the strength and delicacy of living plants. That was what all the business of classical things was about: if once they hit that balance, the result was an impression of reality so strong that it was unearthly, and as wonderful as if they had created a breathing human being. They had both been happy that day. But then there had been the drive back to Athens and difficulty about the hotel, where the staff had read the date the wrong way around, or rather, the European way. Then the boat, where their cabin was very cramped. But still he had had the feeling that it was going to be all right.

If only it hadn't been for the postcards.

"Enough?" he said, and looked at his watch. She nodded, and they started walking back to the car. As they came out on the road, they saw two little girls with bunches of flowers in their hands. When they crossed over to the car, the children smiled at them and gave them the flowers. Amy said thank you in Greek, and John said thank you, and then looked suspiciously at Amy, who was awkward with children, but not knowing more than six words of the language, seemed to feel for once that she wasn't expected to join in any coy questions and answers, to play the "aren't we cute" game habitual to so many children because the parents enjoy it. The only children she really felt comfortable with were somehow eccentric, like his nephew, who had given her a long stare through his thick-lensed glasses, held out his hand, and said, "Hello. This is my guinea-pig. His name is Winston. Would you like to see my train set?"

Still smiling, she took the flowers from him and put them together with hers. The children were friendly, but standing with their arms relaxed at their sides, so it didn't look like a bid for money, but he was upset about the whole incident. Amy got into the car, which he had forgotten to lock, and he brought out a handful of coins from his pocket and gave one of the smallest to each of the little girls. They seemed surprised and very pleased. They clutched each other and giggled, and as he turned the car and headed it back towards town, they waved. Amy waved back, but they drove to the hotel in silence.

In their room he read out parts of the guidebook to her. She had put the flowers in one of the basin glasses, and lay flat on the bed with her arm over her eyes.

"It's nearly time to join the group for lunch," he said.

"With group," she murmured. She rolled down and buttoned the sleeves of her blouse, which she had turned up on the way to the temple because only he could see her arms, and she had suddenly become self-conscious about the hair on them.

"Everybody has hair on their arms," he had told her.

"But not like mine. Mine are like a sailor's."

"Well, you could take it off if it bothers you. It doesn't bother me."

"No, that just makes it grow thicker."

She got up off the bed to go out to the bathroom again. He washed his face and hands. Before they left the room he put his arms around her.

"How do you feel?"

"All right. I just don't feel like it, that's all."

"Not at all?"

"No. I'm sorry. I don't know why you're so good to me."

"Don't keep saying that. As long as you don't get worried about anything, everything will be okay."

"I hope so," she said.

They walked to the other hotel. Three buses were parked down the street from the entrance. He looked at his watch again and they hurried through the lobby and were shown into a dining-room where only two couples were eating, and out on to a terrace with a green and white striped awning above all the tables of the group from the boat. The English-speaking guide nodded from a distance and the waiter sat them at a table where two old women were speaking French together and a German couple were eating in silence, cameras laid out at rest before them in leather cases, like a cowboy's six-shooters in their holsters. The meal consisted of a very good moussaka and some dark green vegetables that looked like tiny parachutes. John had wine and Amy drank one glass. Afterwards they ate a fruit salad with ice cream, and were served instant coffee because so many tourists wouldn't believe that the real Greek coffee was coffee at all. But since it was a very good hotel, the coffee was poured from a pot. The Frenchwomen took out cigarettes and blew the smoke in the direction of the Germans. The German took out a cigar.

"Want to walk around the hotel?"

"Sure," Amy said.

They strolled back through the dining-room and into the front lobby.

"La plage?" John asked.

The man behind the desk called a bellboy over and spoke to him. The boy gestured towards the Larsens and began to lead them ahead down a wide carpet with palm trees in tubs against the walls. Amy looked around at the impressive surroundings. When John caught her eye, she pulled a face at him. They went down some stairs and were gestured towards two doors, the changing-rooms, one for men and one for women.

"Pas pour baigner, seulement pour voir," John said in his half-forgotten French. He only really remembered enough to understand, not much to speak.

"*Oui, ça va,*" the boy said, indicating the door for women. They both walked in, and saw through the open doors ahead, the beach and the sea. There were no guests on the beach because it was mid-day, but maybe also because it was out of season. Yet everything had obviously been cared for, just the right number of deck chairs set up at the back of the promenade, the right number stacked, fresh paint on everything and the green and white striped beach umbrellas in place.

"What a wonderful hotel," Amy said.

"It sure is. We've got to stay here some day. We should move out and stay here now."

"No," she said, "we can't afford it."

They went back out of the changing-room and up the stairs. He thanked the boy and gave him a tip, and asked where the washrooms were.

"This time I've got to," he said.

"I will too, just in case. And before the mob gets off the terrace."

They separated and he told himself that she was still thinking about it, she would never be able to forget what he had said that time about not being able to afford it.

The three buses took them to the foot of the fortifications, and they all herded forward over a bridge below which lay a dried-up watercourse filled with red hibiscus and purple bougainvillea and palm trees, and some pink flowering bushes that he didn't know the name of. At the very bottom of the decline it looked as though crops were being grown.

"I have a feeling that guide was wrong this morning," he said. "I'm sure the flower of the island was the rose. I'm sure it was in ancient times anyway, and probably till very recently. Sounds like the kind of interesting misinformation that makes a hit just because it's wrong."

"I haven't seen a rose since we got here."

"No. It wouldn't have been a modern rose, anyway. Just the simple kind with five petals."

They passed under the great stone archway. Then they started up the narrow street and lost the English-speaking guide.

"I'm tired," Amy said.

They stood to one side to let the others stream past and John looked around, but there was no place to sit down. Up the street, guides were explaining the history of the different places where the crusaders had had their headquarters.

"I'm okay," Amy said. "I just want to get out of this place. There isn't any room, and such a crowd. I can't breathe."

"Let's cut through everybody and go on ahead."

"Okay."

He took her by the hand and pulled her forward. The other people were going off into the courtyards at the side and looking at the inscriptions and carvings. He dragged her by the hand till they came out ahead of the group. There was still no place to sit down. They kept walking, Amy with her head down. He saw she was in a bad mood and he was worried. They came to postcard stands and shops, but she didn't notice. The road broadened out into a modern road but became ever steeper and there seemed no end to it. He stopped walking. She stopped, too, looking straight ahead and bad-tempered. He sighed and put his hands in his pockets, and looked back down the road and then up the slope.

"There's a camel," he said.

"Where?"

"Hanging out in front of that store. A picture of a camel."

"Don't like camels much," she said.

"He looks a little tacky, I must admit."

A few other people from the group came up behind them and walked on ahead.

"They're selling lemonade over there," he said, and began to walk forward again slowly. She followed, her head down, her whole attitude mulish.

"I can't stand that fizzy stuff they have here."

They walked on, passing brass pans, andirons, jewellery, clothes.

"There's another frog just like yours, only bigger."

"As a matter of fact, I hate it. I don't know why I bought it. Maybe because it was so ugly."

"For God's sake, honey, cheer up," he said. "Don't like this, don't like that. You're a real bundle of fun today, aren't you?"

She kept her head down, lips tight together. They moved through the street and more people kept coming up behind them. Suddenly her arm shot out and went under his elbow. He took his hands out of his pockets and felt her arm wrap around his back and her hand settle at his waist, gripping him through his clothes like a small tree-living animal.

"I like you," she muttered. "I like you all right."

"That's more like it." He put his arm around her shoulder and with his free hand tried to lift her head.

"Glad to hear it," he said. "Tell me some more. Tell me about how you like me."

She looked up. There were tears on her face. She put her other arm around his neck. "I love you," she said, as though she were drowning. "I love you. I love you so much sometimes it makes me want to throw up."

They had stopped in the middle of the road and there was still nowhere to sit, only shops and their doorways. Her body had gone heavy in his arms as though she might sink down to the ground. He half lifted her over to the side and, still held in his arms, leaned her up against a shop window. There were clothes and beads hanging from hooks, and brass objects up on tables. He had pushed aside a hanging rack of peasant blouses to find a solid place. On each side of them was a table strewn with knick-knacks. Her hands around him started to knead at his back and she was breathing as though she would choke.

"Let's go back to the hotel," he said.

"I don't think I can walk that far. Oh, what's happening? It just came all over me—whoosh. I don't think I can walk at all."

He thought he knew what was happening, but it might be something else.

"Listen, Amy, are you in pain?"

"No, no. Not pain. Just feels so strange. Feels so weird. I'm burning up."

He got a good grip on her in case she fell, and smoothed her hair and kissed her on the neck and face. She turned her head from side to side.

"Whoosh, just like that?" he said.

"Oh God, John. I feel like one of those women who can't get to the hospital in time and have their babies in a cab."

She was laughing, now, with the tears still on her face, and her face red, and her breath still panting. A crowd of people pushed by them up the street, the Fischers among the group.

"Okay, kids, break it up," Mr. Fischer called over. "Just look at them, going into a clinch in the middle of the street. In the middle of the day, yet."

Mrs. Fischer made as if to come over to where they stood locked around each other, hunched against the window. She was wearing a pale blue jersey suit, carrying the jacket over her arm, and looked hot.

"Are you all right there?" she asked.

Amy turned her head. "I'm fine," she gasped. "I'm fine. It's just that I love him so much."

Mr. Fischer smiled, took his wife by the arm and tugged her away.

"Now why don't you say nice things like that to me?" he asked her.

"You get rid of that beerbelly, Superman, and you'd be surprised what I'd say to you."

"Is that right?" he said.

John watched them going away up the street with the others, and saw Mr. Fischer make a playful lunge at his wife, and heard her voice saying, "Not my new girdle, darn it!"

"I feel so hot," Amy said. "Don't let go."

"I won't let go."

"John, something's happening to me."

"You're telling me."

"Oh Jesus, do you think I'm going crazy?"

"Not a chance. You're doing fine."

"Don't let go of me or I'll fall over."

"I won't let go of you."

"I think I'm dying," she said. He held her as tightly as he dared, and felt her back and shoulders jump. Then she was like a sack of potatoes and he was holding all her weight. A voice said, "Are you having any trouble?"

He turned his head and found himself looking into a bespectacled woman's face inches from his own. There was a battery of rhinestones at the top of the lenses.

"Just a private domestic argument," he told her.

"Oh," the woman said, and moved away.

Amy took her hand from his neck and stood straight on her feet again.

"Better?" he said.

"Yes. What happened?"

"You're kidding."

"Is everybody looking at me?"

"Just me."

"Everything's all right, isn't it?"

"It's fine. Everything's fine. Do you think you can walk?"

"Oh yes, I'm fine now."

They started to walk with the other people from the boat. He kept his arm around her and looked at her face. She looked happy.

"Is that it up there by the trees, where all those people are sitting on the wall?"

"I think that's just where we assemble. I can see the French-speaking guide."

"I passed out, didn't I?"

"Sort of."

"But I feel fine now. Maybe it's just the heat."

"I don't think so," he said. "Let's skip the museum and go back to the hotel and do it together next time."

"Oh, it wasn't," she said. "I felt as though I was dying."

He started to laugh.

"Honestly!" she said.

They reached the wall, which went up the square like a ramp. The buses were parked below, and the entrance to the next building on the tour was across the square. She sat on the wall and he stood beside her. The people around them were speaking French.

"Everything's all right now, isn't it?" he said. "About that other business, I mean. It's like I told you, the doctor said it couldn't be inherited. Not possibly."

"Shut up about this inheriting stuff. I'll inherit you right on the nose if you don't quit talking about it."

"Okay, I just want you to know."

She looked past him and yawned. "This is a nice place," she said.

"Yes, it's nice."

"I like this place."

"Good."

"Only it's a little hot right in the sun."

"We can move over to the entrance there."

He helped her down off the wall and they started to cross the square.

"Oh, John, I've got to go to the bathroom again."

"I don't believe it."

"I mean it."

"We'll miss the group."

"That doesn't matter." She looked from one side to the other. "Down that other street. There's a café."

"All right," he said.

She marched off quickly down the street. The café was crowded with working men sitting out at the tables. Without hesitating, she stepped through the open doorway, through the hanging plastic strips for keeping flies out, and went inside. There were a few more tables, but most of the men were standing up at the counter. They all looked at her. He felt like a man in a cartoon, his head turned away while his dog strains on the leash to get at a lamp post. She went straight up to the counter, said hello in Greek, and then asked in clear American French, *"S'il vous plaît, lavatoire."* The man serving didn't understand. She repeated it. John stepped up beside her and reeled off *sotto voce* all the various cognates for toilet he knew. Finally, hoping that it wasn't an indecent gesture, he made motions of washing his hands, and that seemed to get across. The man called into the back room and a boy in an apron came out. He explained something to the boy in Greek, and Amy bustled forward and out into the back room. Then there was silence. John ordered a coffee and felt uncomfortable. Gradually people began to talk again, but not much. The coffee was very hot and sweet. He had finished it long before she came out again.

She was still looking happy, and did not seem to mind the fact that everyone was looking at her, although she was normally so self-conscious. She said thank you in Greek to the man behind the counter, which seemed to gain her the approval of everyone, and they left.

"I was beginning to wonder what had happened to you," he said. "I had visions of you waking up in Rio de Janeiro, doped to the eyeballs and forced to lead the rest of your life as a white slave."

"Ha!" she said. "It was just miles away and like a real old farm privy. I'm dying to wash my hands. They have a little garden out back there, full of flowers."

"Did it have a half moon on it?"

"No," she said, and laughed.

There was no one to be seen in the square. They went through the entranceway of the building across the square from the wall and couldn't see anyone there, either. Then they found a guard and asked where the museum was. He walked back with them and pointed up the street to what looked like another part of the fortifications.

"This must be it," John said.

"I can hear them inside."

The guard at the door tried to sell them tickets and John pointed ahead, saying, "Group" until he let them in.

It was a small museum, cool inside, with several lovely busts and funeral reliefs and a small kneeling Aphrodite, which was famous. There was also a bust of Alexander the Great as a youth, hair down to his shoulders and the nose knocked away. John looked closely at this, liking it very much, and decided that portraits of Alexander never looked ruined if they had been damaged, because somehow you had the feeling that it had happened in battle. He was still thinking about the idea and looking from a three-quarter view at the bust, when Amy from the other side of the room announced in a loud, isolated voice, "There aren't any postcards in here."

His head went around fast, and he saw her turning from side to side and glaring. People were beginning to bunch around her as he reached her side.

"Where are the postcards?" she demanded. In an even louder voice, imperious, she called again for the postcards.

He moved her away by the arm.

"They're outside, honey. This way," he said. He wanted to go through the floor.

"I don't see any at all," she said, still loudly, but not shouting.

"Right out here. I'll show you."

Behind them the Germans were making comments. They passed the man of the couple who had sat at their table for lunch. He had a pair of sunglasses folded in one hand and his cameras around his neck, and was standing up like a boiled slab of meat with his eyes turned coldly on Amy. *Oh God,* John thought, *oh God, oh God.* He got her out into the hallway with the desk and its racks of postcards, and the belligerence left her immediately.

"Oh good," she said, "they have lots. And pictures of the town, too."

She started to thumb through the cards, smiling.

"I don't want that one," she said, lifting out a picture of the Aphrodite.

"Why not?"

"Well, I couldn't send Mother a picture of a naked woman, could I?"

"Why not? It's a work of art."

"It's a naked woman. Look. They'd never let it go through the mail."

"Sure they would, Amy. It's a postcard."

"Well, it isn't right. And Mother wouldn't like it anyway. It isn't the kind of thing you'd want to send your mother. Specially if she's sick."

She put the card back, and chose seven others.

"That's enough, now," he said. She still looked peaceful and composed.

"Where can we sit down? I want to get them off right away."

He led her out of the room and over near the entrance to a place where the wall jutted out into a shelf. They sat down and she put the cards beside her and opened her purse. He picked up the postcards and took away two and put them in his pocket, not in the same pocket the others were in, since she might notice. She put stamps on the five he had left her and began to write.

"Do you think she can understand all the things you're writing?"

"Sure. The nurse can read them out."

That hadn't been what he had meant.

"And she can look at the pictures," Amy said. She wrote quickly, putting the cards down one by one as she finished. He picked one up and read it through. It was perfectly lucid. Then he looked at the date at the top. He picked up the other cards. On all of them it was the same day and December, 1963; the day they were married.

"Do you mind if I just add my regards?"

"Go ahead. That would be nice."

She was working on the fourth card and beneath her hair her face looked full of sweetness, and serene. He took his ball-point pen out of his pocket and changed the dates on the cards, inking out the date she had written. He did the same for the last two, and quickly read through her messages. She had described every chink in the walls, every corner of the hotel they were staying at and the hotel where they had had lunch, and what they had eaten, and what they had seen, not to mention the historical parts.

"Well," he said. "All we need now is a mailbox." He kept the cards in his hand and she packed up her handbag and they stood up. When they came out into the sunlight the change of temperature was a shock. They walked hand in hand.

"I see one," she said. "Isn't that lucky?"

They came up to the mailbox and he said, "Do you want to put them in, or can I this time?" He didn't want her to see the dates.

"Oh, you can."

He pushed them in.

"Aren't you being nice to me today?" she said, smiling up at him brilliantly. "Mailing my postcards and everything. Aren't you nice to me."

"My pleasure, Miss Amy," he said.

She hugged him, and he smiled at her and hugged her back. *It's going to be all right,* he was thinking. *It's got to be all right. This is Amy, her face and eyes and mouth and hair and the way she looks and all the things about herself that she thinks are ugly which I love so much, and she's the only person who's ever understood me and it's just got to be all right.*

They walked down the street with their arms around each other. They passed the café where she had had to go to the bathroom. She took his other hand in her free one and squeezed it and held on to it, and they kept walking slowly, a bit like drunks tied to each other. Her hand was much smaller than his and damp, and still clung the way a tree animal clings to a branch. He began to sweat.

"It's hotter in the sun," he said, and took a handkerchief from his pocket. He hugged her shoulder to him as he took away his hand.

"But it's nice," she said. "I like this place."

He wiped his forehead and his upper lip, and put the handkerchief back in his pocket.

"So do I," he said.

They turned a corner and passed four more tourists coming up the street. They passed by a man selling honey and almond cakes, and turned in to a narrow street where there was shade, and saw a donkey carrying a load of sacks, and walked under a hanging wall of bougainvillea flowers. He began to sweat again.

Theft

"Look out, Jake," I said, "there's a big stone in the middle of the road."

"Where?"

"Straight ahead, right in front of you. Hold on. Over to the left a little ways. Mind you don't bump into it."

"Can't bump into it. Can't even see it."

"Right up there." I pointed at it in the dark. "A big goddam boulder, right in the middle of the road. Who'd want to put a thing like that there?"

"Where?"

"Right there, right in front of you," I said, and fell over it.

"Where are you?" he started to call. "Hey, where did you go?"

"I'm down here. By this big boulder."

"What boulder?" he muttered. And he fell on top of me.

"Jake, I think maybe I'm drunk," I said.

"Who, me? I'm not drunk."

"Me. Do you think I'm drunk?"

"I don't know. Do you think so?"

"I believe maybe I just might be. Just a little."

"Let's have another," he said. "Where did it go?"

"I think you're sitting on it."

We had another, and then another. And one more. And he said for about the tenth time that night, "Well, how's it feel to be a father?"

"Fine. Feels good. Feels grand. God almighty, I'm glad it's over."

"Nothing to it. I told you it was going to be all right, didn't I?"

"Sure. It's all right now. But wait till it happens to you. Man, I been scared before. Not like that."

"Why scared? Happens every day. That's nature. Annie says she'll be aiming for eight. Eight, she says. At least."

"Eight. Holy God."

"What she says. And I want to be there when it happens."

"You're crazy."

"Why not? That's life. That's important. I'd want to be there."

"Let me tell you," I said, and I thought I was going to start crying, but it came out laughing, "let me tell you, it was almost death. They said she almost died. I'm so glad it's over, I'm just so damn glad it's over."

"Have another," Jake said.

I took some and held on to it.

"Listen. You want to be there when it happens? Look, I wasn't even there and I felt like you can't imagine what. All week I been all cramped up and sick with it, like I was the one having the child. You just don't know. Here, have another."

I passed it to him and he dropped it and we had to hunt around.

"Got it," Jake said after a while. "What you doing going dropping it right on the ground like that? I thought you was handing it over."

"You dropped it."

"Who, me? It's all right. Plenty left."

"Have another."

"Don't mind if I do."

I leaned my back against the rock. It was still so dark you couldn't see much.

"Well?" Jake said.

"Well what?"

"You said have another. Let's have it."

"You're holding on to it."

"Who, me?" he said. After a little he began to laugh. I didn't know what was so funny but I started to laugh too.

"You're right," he said. "I had a hold of it all the time. Do you think maybe I'm drunk?"

"Who, me?" I said.

"Here, have another. How's it feel to be a father?"

We both got laughing. When we stopped it was at the same time, so it sounded very still afterwards. I felt quiet and better.

"I'll tell you, Jake," I said. "It's quite something. It makes you feel strange. I expect you get used to it, but it makes you feel like—makes you feel real awestruck. When you think about it, it's a big thing."

"Sure. Sure is. I'll drink to that. What are you going to name him?"

"I think we'll have to name him after Uncle Ben."

"You ain't going to name him after me?"

"I wanted to, but Maddie said how it would mean so much to him and Annie says she thinks it's right, seeing how he practically brought us up."

"I was only fooling."

"No, I meant it. I did want to. We'll name the next one after you."

"Right. And we'll name one after you, too."

"One of the eight."

"I'll drink to that," he said. We both drank some more and sat quiet for a while. I got to thinking how good it was to have the worry over but how funny we should be sitting in the middle of the dark, in the middle of the road, up against a big boulder that shouldn't be there.

"Hey Jake, I don't know about this rock. Who'd want to go and do a thing like that?"

"Like what?"

"Go and put a big rock in the middle of the road like that,

where somebody can come along and get hurt. I think we should push it out of the way."

I gave it a shove but it was too heavy to move. I tried again and my hand slipped.

"Leave it be," he told me. "Wait till daylight and I'll help you move it."

"All right. All right, we'll leave it. Let's have another."

"Funny it should make such a difference—names. You remember when I used to tell you the names of the stars?"

"Sure," I said. "I remember."

"Funny it should make such a difference. Why people remember a name a long time after they'll remember anything else, after they forget what went with it. Did you ever think: names are very old things. Old as the stars. Pass them down from way back, and then people give them to children when they're born. Funny way to start out."

"I've forgotten most of them," I said.

"Which?"

"Names of the stars. A long while back. I was ashamed to say, because of all the trouble you took and then me going and forgetting."

"That's all right. Everybody does. Remember some things and forget some things. I'll teach you again sometime. Not tonight. No stars tonight. It's going to rain."

"We'll name the second one after you," I said.

"Right. And we'll name one after you. The first boy. Unless Annie's got some name she won't give up."

"You mean it?"

"Sure," he said. "Promise."

He fell asleep first. During the night it rained and when day-break came we saw that we weren't in the middle of the road; there wasn't any road at all. We were lying in somebody's field, miles from home and feeling like nothing on God's earth. I've only been drunk twice in my life and that was the first time. Almost eight years ago.

"You," the foreman calls, "you there, boy, you dreaming?"

"No, sir," I say.

I'm not dreaming, I'm just trying to stay on my feet. If I could dream it through I would, right on through the day. What I do is more like just thinking or remembering, anything to take my mind off being hungry. I didn't start on it till after the fire and now I have to do it every day.

It's best if you can do it to singing or to counting, out loud. The new man gets nervous if there's too much of the singing, he thinks every song he doesn't know might be a protest song. Up he walks in his Godalmighty way like he's saying to himself: here I come, boys, here I come. And tells us not so much of the singing, it slows down the work.

I can do it in my head now and I expect it's what happens to soldiers; they say soldiers can be sound asleep and still keep on marching once they've got the rhythm. That's the way it happens. Sometimes I begin by saying over words to myself. Or names, or following the line of a song without sounding it. Then I can imagine pictures of things, people, or places, and go on from there. Just remembering back a week will often take you into a string of things you haven't thought about for a long while, and they can keep you going.

I think about my mother's voice sometimes. She could sing. And I think about my father, though only a couple of memories and they're like the ones of her, blurred and hard to get at. I remember looking into his face but not what the face looked like. I remember being held in his arms and being small enough to be held like that. Clearest of all, I have a picture of being out walking with him. He lifted me up and carried me on his shoulders—that's all I remember of it, like a picture I can stand away from and look at: me riding on his shoulders and looking up ahead, seeing the sky. But it's very strong and always when I think of him it leads me into other thoughts, I think how I did the same thing with Ben when he was smaller.

They say he was a great man, at least that's what everyone said till after Aunt Mary died. Then Uncle Ben started saying, "Yes, he was a great man all right, such a fine character, such high principles. He was such a great man and had such strong principles your Mama died of work." A long time later I said to him, "I don't know what he was like, I was too young. Aunt Mary saw him one way, you saw him another way—leave it like that. I only saw him like a child, I only remember him lifting me up on his shoulders and looking at the sky."

"Yes, that's what he was like," says Uncle Ben in a bitter voice. "He'd lift you up and show you the sky. Some it cured and some was killed by it."

I don't know if he was such a high-principled character. Maybe he was just wild, like Jake. And a man people would always be talking about, with a kind of public reputation. Like Jake; I've seen him walk down the street and have people come up and follow him, follow him around like dogs, just to be near him. And I've seen it the other way around, name-calling when he walks by, and the kids rushing out to throw a stone after him as soon as he's out of range.

After the fire Jake asked me, "You haven't been joining any of those freedom organizations, have you?"

"No, I thought that was your field. You still fighting for our racial equality?"

He didn't answer one way or the other, just said again, "You sure about that?"

It might have been. They asked me to, all right, kept hanging around, trying to sound me out and talking: injustice, freedom, exploitation of labor, all those things. I didn't let on what my political views were, just told them the truth: that I didn't have the time to join anything no matter how good the cause. I know those boys—sit around talk, talk, talk and when they're through doubletalking each other, out they go and beat up some poor fool who's just trying to make an honest living and never did nobody harm. I don't spell freedom like that.

They went away and a couple of weeks later came back a second time. Then they tried to bribe me. Dragged in Maddie and the kids and said what a better life they'd lead and so on. So I told them: Look, I had all those milk and honey lies from the competition and I'm not buying, thanks all the same. And I told them to beat it.

I don't think it was that, but you can't tell about these things any more.

"Just asking," he says. "It don't seem like it could have been accidental."

And I said, "Look, Jake, strange as it may seem, working your guts out from the age of sixteen on don't leave a man much time for long discussions on what we're all going to do when we rule the world. What do you think, now?"

He said it looked to him like a pretty unprofessional job but he'd ask around. Maybe it was a freak thing, a mistake, or what Annie said: "Maybe just somebody wanting to put you out of action so they could get their hands on that famous job of yours." I can believe that. She laughed when I took her seriously, but I don't think it's at all unlikely. Anyway, it couldn't have come from very high up otherwise Jake would have found out, working with one foot on each side of the line like he does.

"What's that you're doing there, dreaming?" says the foreman.

"No, sir."

"We don't pay you to just stand around with your mouth open catching flies."

He's got a neck like a bull, a thick bulge at the back under his hair. Not muscle; that's fat. Fat from forty years of overeating.

"Hustle it on up there," he says.

"Yessir."

The second time I got drunk was with a stranger, an old man they called Little Josh. It was the year of the big riot when they first started calling the army in and I first heard what martial law meant, that if you show yourself you're a dead man and they say you were looting. I'd lost my job and went to work with the fruitpickers. I walked all night to get there so I wouldn't lose a day's work and worked on through as soon as I arrived. I've never seen people work like that, sometimes through half the night, because we were paid by the basketload, and falling asleep under the trees whenever it hit them. There were some women there and children too. A lot of knifings in the night, a lot of drinking, and one night a man hung himself from a tree and nobody noticed, they worked all around him till daylight. That was the first time I'd seen a hanged man: mouth open, tongue out, swollen, suffocated.

We were allowed to eat all the fruit we wanted and I couldn't believe it to begin with because we can't afford to buy it at home. It tasted so sweet, the way you imagine flowers would taste, but if you try to live off it you get sick. Some of the women there set up stands where they sold bread and fish fried in oil, and now whenever there's fish being fried it reminds me of that time, being bone-tired, sleeping on the ground, and the smell of the fruit and trees everywhere, even in your clothes.

The second week I was there an old man joined the group; he was short and had a squashed-in face and walked leaned-over a little, which made his arms look longer than they should be. He stood looking at the trees, ready to choose his workplace, and somebody made a remark. A few others joined in and soon there was about seven of them poking fun at him. "That's all right, Grandaddy," I said to him. "Don't pay them no mind. You work along with me." I pointed out my place, we walked over to it, and started in. Little Josh he was called, and I couldn't believe he only had two hands—he was picking nearly twice as much as anybody else.

The night we got drunk everyone was eating and drinking in an abandoned place up on a rise in the land. There were still some walls standing, a few stone steps up the hill, and a lot of roots growing through it all. I remember they had fires going, cooking, and I was being eaten alive by the bugs. When we left five men came and leaned over the edge of the wall to see if I'd fall down the steps. I turned around and said, "You think I'm going to fall down, don't you?" One of them said yes, the others said they just wanted to see we were all right. "Well, I'm not going to," I said, turned back around, and nearly fell down the steps. Little Josh had the same amount and he was still sober long after everybody else was blind. There was a full moon out. And stars. He told me next day that before I passed out I'd pointed out the stars to him, naming them in a very loud voice as if they were being given names for the first time.

I only started thinking this last week about being drunk. Because it's the same feeling; not the happy lifted-up feeling while you're drinking. Like what you feel when you wake up afterwards: shaky, tired, and your head hurts. That's what going hungry is like.

That morning I left before Maddie could ask me what I'd eat. I had the feeling if I didn't get up on my feet quick and start walking, I'd fall down. I got to work early, which they never notice, only if you come late. And it was so bad I couldn't even work the trick with thinking and remembering.

It was a Thursday. They got us both on the same day, two hours apart between the two arrests.

Naturally, if I'd known about Jake I'd never have tried it on my own. But there were all those weeks behind me, of Maddie asking "what did you eat at midday", and me telling her lies. The first few days it was easy to make up a pretend meal. Later I'd begin to repeat.

"You had that yesterday," she says.

"So?"

"Are you sure you're eating all right? You can't stint yourself with the work you're doing. You'll get sick. Then where will we be?"

"You quit fussing. I'm eating fine," I say, and it was a lie again. I hardly ever ate lunch since the fire, when we lost the livestock.

Then I'd ask her what she and the kids had had. She'd say they'd had the leftovers from the night before. One evening that week I say, "Isn't this what we had last night?"

"Yes. You don't like it?"

"I thought you said you finished it off at lunch."

"There was a lot left over," she said.

Sure. Believe it every time. The children aren't getting any fatter, either, and that means she goes without hers altogether. I saw them from the field one day, off in the distance a lot of kids scrabbling around the ditches over by the spring. But I recognized my two. And the foreman, seeing me look, said, "What some folks will allow, letting it get so the children got to go digging in the ditches, eating the weeds out of the creek. Their folks should be ashamed. Letting them run loose on private property like that."

"Yessir," I said, and knew for certain then that Maddie was lying too.

"That's theft. That's what those children will grow up to," he says. "It's the parents' fault. That's what's wrong with all the young people nowadays—their parents don't set them an example. I'd give those kids a good hiding, you can bet, if I was their father."

"Yessir," I said. And I can believe it. Because nobody ever burned you out and taxed you into the ground. I can see you beating your own kids for being hungry. Bet you're real thick with the tax men. Never had to say "Yes, sir" while you were hungry right down to your bones and saw your children starve.

I used to walk through the market at midday. It's amazing how the bare smell of food can keep you going. Even watching somebody else eat sometimes helps, though you wouldn't think it. And even more curious is the way a real meal in the evening, if you take it slow, can be invested with the taste of the best things you could wish for.

Sometimes at the end of the day I'd beg scraps off the tradespeople in the square. They were good about it, they knew how it was. But at noon you couldn't ask since they had to make their living too, and sell as much as they could before the end of the day. The soldiers had plenty of food of course, and kids used to hang around them, pick up whatever they threw away. That might have been a good idea for me to try. Yet I never did know a soldier who'd dish out so much as a crust to a grown man, though he'd give anything to a child. Part of it may be natural sentiment, but I believe they also consider it actually unlucky to refuse a child. Say no to a man and the only had luck is his own that you refused.

That afternoon in the market I couldn't stand it any longer. The weeks seemed like months, and while I thought that, began to seem like years. All the way through in my chest and legs and belly I could feel all of that time I'd gone without food.

It was bread set out to cool. And I smelled it from a long way off. From beyond the fruit and vegetable stands and the basketware it led me, pulled me, right through the crowd. Sweet and warm, giving off fragrance like a tree in bloom.

If Jake had been along he'd have known how to handle the situation. He says just never give your right name and you'll be all right. With the political atmosphere like it is they'll never bother to pick you up on the street again unless they recognize you. And that's unlikely, because they think we all look alike. Or if it's one of ours working for them, chances are he'll let it go unless it's for something so big that he'd get a recommendation out of it.

Jake was very relaxed when he toted things off. He knew all the right lies to tell, and the right names to say, and he'd state with great confidence that so-and-so had sent him to collect the article because he had an account there. "Oh, aren't you Mr. so-and-so and isn't this such-and-such a street?" he'd ask. And then he had a charming manner of apologizing while he handed the thing back, and a self-assured way of asking directions as to how to get to the mythical place he'd mentioned.

I'd never done it before myself.

I walked blind, straight to it. I saw it sitting there, fresh and new as a baby, and just put my hand on it like it belonged to me, and walked off with it.

I hadn't taken but ten steps before there was a hand on my shoulder and the law and the military were standing all around.

"Where'd you get that?" one of them said.

I started to eat the bread because I was goddamned if I was going to go to prison and be punished and all the rest for something I hadn't even enjoyed.

"What are you doing there?" said a second one.

I kept cramming the bread into my mouth, all new and sweet and soft, and thought: whatever comes now, whatever else happens, it's been worth it.

"Cut that out, you. That's stolen property you've got there," said the first one.

I kept on eating.

"Leave go, I said," the first one told me.

They began to push. I got my face into the bread and had my elbows working, but in the end it was more of a fight than I could manage without my fists and anyway they kicked the remainder out of my hands. About half the bread was left; during the scuffling they stepped all over it till it flattened out into the ground.

They punched me in the head just as routine procedure and kicked me a couple of times the way I've seen them do to other people, and took me off. Theft, resisting arrest, and striking an officer in the pursuit of his duty. They told me the charge on the way. The younger one seemed very impressed by the sound of it. He kept jerking my arm up behind me while they dragged me along, and saying, "Oh, you're in trouble. Are you in trouble. Are you ever."

They took me all the way into the center of town. First they made me wait while they talked over what they were going to do with me. I think that lasted about an hour but I'm not sure, because it was like I gave up time as soon as I knew it was all really happening and jail at the end of it. Then one of them said, "All right, that's it," and they took me outside again and to the prison.

It was one of the old-fashioned kind, going all the way down into the ground below floor-level. Some of the building consisted of the original solid rock. And they put me down, under ground, into a room where the cells were hewn right out of the stone. No windows, only a view through bars into the center of the place where the jailer and a friend sat at a table and threw dice.

The first person I noticed when they brought me in was Jake. He didn't say anything, so I gave no sign and was glad I'd told them a false name.

There were six cells in all. Two big high-ceilinged ones on either side of the entrance, then two on each of the side walls. It was really a triangle-shaped place; the side walls came together in a point of rock and the roof sloped down at the join. The ceiling was also stone and gave you the feeling that at one time the whole thing had been a big natural cave with hollows. Jake was in one of the small end cells and they stuck me in the other one, so we were next to each other but almost close enough to touch, and because of being at the triangle-point where the side walls met, we could see each other's faces.

It wasn't too bad. High enough so the top just cleared my head when I stood up straight, though it was smaller and lower near the far wall, with hardly room for your head if you were sitting down.

The jailer went back to the entrance where he stood around talking to the soldiers. His friend followed after, lingered for a time, and then went out. I had a feeling he was supposed to be on duty someplace else and was making a retreat while the jailer kept the others busy. They were all in uniform, the jailer and his friend, too.

"Did you give your right name?" Jake said.

"No."

"That's the style."

"What did they get you for?"

"Stole a horse."

"A whole horse? What for?"

"Not to eat, you fool. To plow. One of the horses they were using for crowd control. I had a buyer lined up and everything. Had it walking behind me quiet as you please when that fake beggar on the corner—you know, by the fruit-juice stand—"

"I know him. Paid informer."

"Oh, I know that. I been paying him too. But it looks like yesterday the military priced him out of my range, because he was the one pointed me out."

It sounded like small-time stuff, not the kind of thing Jake would let happen. But I know he still picks things up now and then just to keep his hand in, he says, and for fun.

"Bad luck," I said.

"He'll think so if I get out."

"What do you mean if?"

He tapped his foot against the wall.

"This place feels damn solid. Looks like some kind of security prison. Four armed men standing behind the jailer when he opens up to give you your provisions. Not so easy. Not so easy at all. I never been in one like this before."

"But they'll have to take us out to be tried."

"Tie us hand and foot, like as not."

"Do they usually do that? I thought you said these boys were pretty easy-going."

"Not any more." He kicked the wall again.

"Hell, all I did was steal a little bit of bread."

"Bread? Caught out for lifting a hunk of bread? Oh, Seth, goddamn. You fool, you."

"All right, all right. They got you too, didn't they?"

"Why didn't you wait till I was with you? A beginner's trick like that. I don't suppose you even thought of going up to it with your coat over your arm."

"No, I never thought of that," I said. "I'll remember."

"You do that. And you can remember never try it alone, too. Not till you got somebody to show you how. Lord, whatever possessed you?"

"I was just hungry as hell."

"Why didn't you ask me for a loan?"

"Cut it out."

"Why not? We've got plenty."

I didn't want to go into all that again. We've borrowed enough off him already. Sure, he's got plenty till they catch him for getting it. And the more he gives away, the more he's got to go against the law.

I said, "Listen, Jake, what with the last time I paid any taxes and what you gave us after the fire, that's more than any man should be asked to lend."

"I'm not any man. I'm kin. You should have asked me."

Sure. The way things stood I wouldn't be able to pay back what he'd already given us. Not for years. Maybe never.

"Let's stop talking about it. It makes me sick to think about it."

"And what about Maddie? And the kids? Maddie says—"

"What?"

His face changed and he shut his mouth. So she'd asked him. She never told me.

"Well," I said, "how much is it now?"

"She didn't want you to know. Don't tell her I said anything. I'm glad to give it, Seth. Honest. I worry about you."

"I'm all right."

"No you are not."

"You're right, I'm not."

"A long time ago somebody told you honesty's the best policy. And you been sticking to it a long time after you figured out honesty's the fastest way to starvation."

"And dishonesty lands you in jail."

"Only if you get caught."

"Well?" I said. "Well?"

I grabbed hold of the bars and gave them a shake. Built for keeps. They were solid as a mountain wall.

One of the soldiers out beyond the entrance laughed. I could just see them around the corner. They were drinking together and the jailer appeared to be telling them a tall tale of some sort, acting out the different voices as the story went on. One of the men wiped his mouth with the back of his hand and said something that made the rest of them laugh too. They weren't looking in our direction.

"Do they beat you up or anything?"

"Not yet. I don't think it's likely. The jailer's all right. He's a good man."

"He looks like some kind of a clown."

"He is," Jake said, "but he's all right."

I began to wonder what would happen to Maddie; whether she'd have enough to live on, whether she'd guess what had happened to me, or think I'd been killed, or maybe think I'd left her. She couldn't be thinking that.

"Listen, Jake. If I try to get word to Maddie, they'll find out my name, won't they?"

"That's all right. You just leave it. Sam, you know Sam, he saw me when the law came on the scene. He'll tell Annie. She'll come over here and she'll see you, then she'll tell Maddie."

"You think she'll be all right?"

"Sure, Annie will see she's all right. She'll look after them."

"I just wish I could see her, right now. They'll let her come see me?"

"Sure. It'll take a while for the word to go around."

I thought of her sitting at home in the evening, waiting for me to come back from work. I imagined the kids asking questions when it began to get later and later and still I didn't come. And what her face would look like when Annie told her, what she'd say: not this on top of everything else. And when she finally came to visit me, looking through the bars, any other woman would say: How could you, how could you be so foolish or so selfish or so cruel to us, as if we didn't have enough trouble already. But she would ask me if I was all right, if I was well.

"I don't know if I can face her," I said.

"Well, what do you want? First you're scared she won't be able to come, then you don't think you can face it."

He told me I never should have taken up crime in my old age, you had to start young while you still had a sense of humor. He was smiling, the way I'd seen him look at Annie when she sulked, but harder.

"I bet the job's gone," I said. "Bet somebody else is doing my work right now."

"Most likely."

"I never missed a day in nine years. Not even when I was sick."

"That was your trouble."

Outside the entrance it sounded as though the group of men was beginning to break up. Two of them went down the hall and the jailer leaned around the corner and gave Jake a friendly kind of look. Jake nodded to him and started to talk again, but he dropped his voice.

"Tell you the truth, Seth, most of these jailhouse shacks you can bust through the wall with your thumbnail, but this one is over my head. I tell you, I never seen one like this before, not even the military cells. And I don't like it. I think something's going on. You been listening to the news lately?"

"Politics, you mean?"

"We got them on the run, looks like. Arrests going on in batches, in bundles. All this week they've been clamping down. All along the line. And it's started up at the top somewheres. Scared stiff. I don't believe there's one empty jail in town."

"You think they put us in here just because they don't have room anyplace else?"

"Could be. I hope that's why. Hope it ain't because they think we're special. You haven't been joining any of those freedom organizations, have you?"

"You asked me that once before already."

"I wonder maybe did somebody burn you out because you joined something or other. I wondered at the time."

"Because I didn't join, maybe. They asked me."

"Oh, my Lord. And you refused. So that's it. What did you tell them?"

"Just told them to go to hell."

"I see. Did you ever hear from them again?"

"Nope. They had somebody follow me a while back, about five months ago, but he never spoke to me and at least nobody was hanging around the kids or Maddie, which really would've had me scared. He just used to dog me around the place, him and a friend. They didn't even stick very close except in crowds, so they wouldn't lose me. And then they quit all of a sudden, about five months back, like I say."

"Sounds all right. Makes sense."

"You don't think there's a connection, do you? That they were just waiting to arrest me?"

"No, not any more. Not if that's all there was to it. I was just thinking about the time element. No, you're in the clear there. They've got better things on their minds by now, I expect."

Worse things, I'd say. I've seen some of those men around town. In the crowds. All last week and the week before, when there's that feeling in the crowd, sort of agitated but just waiting, like kindling about to go up, I've spotted them.

He said, "Something's happening for sure. I mean something more than what I know already. A lot of people are keeping their mouths shut that never used to."

From the entrance I heard steps and the sound of something being moved, maybe a table. The jailer came in and walked over to us. He was a stumpy gingery man, going bald at the front; large in the shoulder and walked with a bit of a limp and a funny rolling, like he might have been a navy man. He rubbed his hands together and gave me a big smile through the bars.

"Hungry?" he shouted. "Food!"

I couldn't believe it. I thought it might be the beginning of one of those mental tortures you hear about.

"You no want? No hungry today?"

"Yes, sure. I'm hungry."

"Good-good-fine."

He said it all in one breath and he had a funny way of talking, like he was putting on an accent or something. He smiled again and thumped his chest.

"Homer, that's me. Foreigner. My mother she is Greek, but I been citizen a long time now—fully qualified reliable citizen, keep the law. But I know, you know—before. Before I'm so respectable, I been on the other side of the bars, your friend Adam can tell you."

"Adam?"

"Oh, so sorry, I think you friends already." He jerked his thumb at Jake. "Adam," he said, and then nodded his head at me and said, "Abe."

"How do," Jake muttered, and glared at me.

"I hear you talking and I think you know each other already."

"Just passing the time of day," Jake said.

"Yes, is good. So I put you next door. Is sad, it make you worry behind bars when you get nobody to talk to. Is true, yes? Me, I talk all the time."

"It's the poet in him," Jake said. "Tells me he's got poetic ancestors, ain't that right?"

"My name," said the jailer. "Is name of greatest poet of Greece. Homer. You know Homer?"

"Can't say as I do," I said, "but I never been out of the country. This Homer a big man over there in Greece?"

"Biggest. Biggest poet we got. But he is dead a long time. He lived hundreds of years before now, centuries before now. We got other poets, but Homer he is the best. You got poets too?"

"I expect. Fraid I don't know much about it."

"Sure," Jake said. "Everybody's got poets. But it's always the same story—the good ones died a long time ago and the ones we got now aren't any good. Five hundred years from now people will say somebody was the poet of his time today and it'll be some poor fool you never heard of. Must be a hard life living five hundred years faster than everybody else. I'd just as soon leave it alone."

"Ah but the glory!" says Homer.

"Sure. You figure it out. These poets and people don't begin to live till they're dead. So think about it: who's got all this glory? Dead men. Right? You can keep that. Besides, all the best poets are anonymous anyhow."

"Anonymous," says Homer, like he was trying out the sound of it.

"Seems to me if you're going to be a great man, be one in the world, where it counts. If you're looking for glory. Life after death ain't the kind of glory I'd be interested in."

"Your friend Adam, he is a philosopher, isn't it?"

"No," I said, "he's just got a good line and likes a fight."

"Is what I mean. Same thing. Got a good line, like a fight, it's what I call philosophy."

He turned and walked back to the entrance and yelled at someone outside. A voice answered back and he called again. This time it was probably an order, since nobody said anything but there was a lot of moving around.

"Adam?" I said. "What the hell?"

"Damn, you fool. See to it you don't mess up on it again."

"What kind of a joker is that anyway?"

"I told you, he's all right."

"I just hope he wasn't joking about the food."

"No, that's for real. They fed me once already."

"When did they pick you up?"

"An hour before noon, about then. They brought me straight here, even gave me a drink. It's all right. When did they get you?"

"About two hours after. But they dragged me around first, took me to about three different places inside this big building and made me wait."

"Did they ask you a lot of questions—I mean specific questions about people you know or business you might be involved in?"

"Just name, age, and where I lived. Most of the time I think they were arguing about who was responsible for me and whether I should be charged according to where I said I lived or where they made the arrest or what. Then I believe there was some complication about the charge being under the civil administration or the military authority—is that right? I wasn't paying much attention, I was all beat out. Does that have something to do with the trial, whether we'll be tried under some kind of martial law? I always thought martial law just meant they killed on sight."

"Did you find out which one they charged you under?" Jake said.

"I don't rightly know."

What I remembered most about the waiting was the young soldier who'd been set to keep an eye on me. He was the one who hadn't dared to beat me up too openly, but while we waited he went stiff as a plank with the strain, hoping I'd make a move so he could watch the others come kick my guts out. I kept wondering what sort of a man he'd be in five years' time, whether he had a girl or a mother, whether he wouldn't want her to see what his face looked like looking at me. Or if there was some person, anybody, for him who he wouldn't ever want to find out exactly how he was wishing the hurt on me, not out of hate but just to see it happen.

I smelled food.

It came around the entranceway and filled the place like a rain-bearing wind. The jailer came in, with four others and the food. Jake told me quickly not to try for a break.

"The one on the left is mean as hell. I think I've seen him around before, he's probably a retired professional fighter. And Homer's a lot stronger than he looks—got me in the neck when I made a move last time. Don't try it."

They opened the door, made me stand back so I had to crouch down against the wall, and they set it all down on the floor. Then they closed up again.

The smell was so good and so strong it made me dizzy. I sat down with my back to the bars and took the bowl on my knees, telling myself all the time to take it slow or it would make me sick. I don't think I'd seen so much food together in one meal for two years. It almost made me feel like crying. And when I took the first mouthful it felt all surprised, as though I'd just eaten it ten times over in my thoughts and the taste of it should be different. They'd given us something to drink, too, like Jake said they would. With every swallow I kept reminding myself to go slow, and hoping I wouldn't get so drunk I'd forget to call him Adam or that I was supposed to be Abe.

"How you doing, Abe?"

I turned my face around to him.

"Fine."

"If you could see what you look like. My, like you just been through some kind of mystical experience."

"If I'd known—if I'd known I was going to eat like this, I'd have *tried* to get in."

"It's just good luck," he said. "We're lucky to have Homer. All the jails I been in, nobody ever gave me food like this. See, the jailers get this allowance from the state for feeding prisoners. Most of them just pocket it. And some of them work it double, take the money and claim they get in more prisoners in a week than they've seen in a month. As busy making up names as we are. The officers are in on it too most times, or they know about it and let it go till they need a favor. I told you, Homer is all right. He don't even hold it against me for trying to break."

It took a long time and I was full before the bowl was empty, but I hung on to it and kept chewing real slow and washing it down between mouthfuls. Then I wondered about what to do afterwards. The only thing in the cell besides me and the walls was a straw mat at the back. And there was a funny, close smell about the place that I hadn't noticed so much while I'd been standing.

"Jake," I said, "you know, it isn't all that strong, but this place smells like they been keeping wild animals in it."

"That's us, society's wild animals."

"What do I—"

"Adam, Adam," he added. "Lord, will you remember it? You may be in the clear politically, but I'm not so sure they'd like it if they knew a few things I'd been up to lately. It's all right this time, he didn't hear. Just remember."

For a moment I thought the food would come up. I began to sweat and as soon as I felt it coming out I knew I'd been sweating in waves ever since they closed the cell door the first time.

"Sure," I said. "I'm sorry. I'm just not used to—"

"Take it easy. Don't get all panicked. What were you saying?"

"Oh, about what you do when you've got to relieve yourself in this place, just do it against the wall or where?"

"Ask Homer, he'll hand you a pot for it. I figure it's his own idea—I've got a mark on the wall over here and drawings by about five ex-prisoners. They never had it so good in this place till they hired Homer."

The whole bunch came back and we went through the unlocking again so they could take away the bowl and all, and I asked Homer.

"When he gives it to you," Jake says, "take it in the hand you aren't going to use to eat with, and then don't put that hand near your mouth again till you can wash it. Wipe it on your clothes if you have to. Be on the safe side."

"What do you mean?"

"What I say. And another thing, I haven't exactly seen anything moving yet, but I'd stay away from that straw job if you can help it. If you want to sleep, curl up on the floor near the bars."

"Not exactly the comforts of home."

"It's pretty good compared to the others. In that respect, at least."

He didn't say anything about the walls or even look at them, but he was thinking about them. I didn't mind for the moment. It went in patches, thinking about what was going to happen to us, and sweating, and then putting it out of my mind. Right then I was thinking about Maddie again.

*

Later on Homer came in. He gave me the pot and some water and came back again a spell later and stayed to talk. He told us all kinds of stories from all over the world and had us both laughing. It was going fine between us and I was feeling good, almost proud about saying Adam or just leaving out the name every time I wanted to say something to Jake. Once when Homer stepped away to speak to a man at the entrance Jake said his stomach turned over every time he thought I was about to come out with his name, but I was pretty sure I could handle it now. There was just one time where I suddenly felt bad, when Homer was in the middle of a story and I wondered if they were all his or whether he'd collected some of them from the men he'd been in charge of and if maybe some of those men had been put to death.

Jake started in then, and he was in good form. Nobody can tell a tall tale like Jake, specially the ones where you have to keep a straight face till the end, and he had Homer wheezing and coughing and practically dancing over the floor with laughing.

I once said to Maddie I wished I was made like that, always joking and laughing and not taking the world seriously. And she said it only looked that way with Jake because he was so energetic and he'd always had that joking way and the gift to make other people laugh when he wanted them to. But really it was all put on like an actor, and underneath Jake was very serious. "A lot more than you," she said. But I never could see it, unless she meant political things. "Aren't I serious?" I said, and she'd said, "No, you're just worried," which was true enough.

I asked Homer finally, "Are you a navy man?"

"Who, me? No, not for anything would I go near the navy. Never."

"I just thought, no offense, the way you walk."

"Oh," he said, "oh, I break my ankle, is nothing. No, I get the choice a long time ago. You see, me and some others, they catch us for taking things. Oh, we were very young but we do it for years, all together working like a team. And the law says well you can choose how to be now, in a hole for life or you go into the forces. So what do I do? My mother is in the country illegal and I know so many boys die in the navy living so close like they do, freeze in the winter and burn up in the summer, wet all the time and no sleep—nothing. Three man I know kill themselves there. No, I don't touch the navy, is slavery. I say, I go into the army and serve the country, become a respectable citizen, earn money, travel maybe. And is what I do. Is not bad life, the army. And people have respect. Is no matter where you come from, how poor, if you're a good soldier you can put that behind. And other people also forget. Is democratic."

"Sure," said Jake. "Don't you think that's a damning indictment of a country, that the only way a man can become a first-class citizen or anything approaching it is to join the military? Though of course your case ain't quite the same as ours."

"You can join," Homer said. "Why not?"

"Why not? Oh, I know the army. But do they call it by its right name? Exploit a place here, free a place there—everybody's still at peace but meanwhile everyplace is being occupied and there are a lot of corpses lying around wherever the army's been. And if you look at the ordinary soldier, why, under normal conditions he'd be in the place of these people he's supposed to be guarding or freeing or occupying or whatever they call it from day to day. People with no rights. He comes from someplace where he's got no rights and the army knows he'll join it to get hold of them. Then they make him take away the rights of other people just like him. I don't see how anybody can be such a—"

Suddenly he began to cover up. It sounded all right if you didn't know him and hadn't been looking for the pause before he started to unsay everything. I didn't think Homer would care in any case.

"Politics," Jake said. "I expect you've got politics in Greece, too."

"Don't speak of politics, she drive me crazy. All Greeks talk about politics, always. Always. Since beginning of time. We invent politics, I tell you."

He asked me if I held such strong views as my friend Adam.

"Not exactly," I said. "I sort of agree, but not for the same reasons. I got no grudge against the military, or the law either. Not really, when you think about it. I mean, somebody's got to keep order. But I don't know. I almost did join up with the forces, it sounded pretty good. Food and pay and travel maybe, all that. But I've seen too many folks go that way. They say it's such a wonderful life; follow the rules and work hard, and on your free time there's no responsibility and you're your own man. You get drunk and get into fights, have all the women you want, and nobody holds it against you. It's expected you're going to cut loose and go wild when the discipline lets up. Wherever you go there are always girls around and drink and everybody thinks you're so big because the army's big. Well, that's all right when you're eighteen or twenty or for a couple of years more. Gets the wildness out of you. But I've seen men, forty or fifty years old, and they're still leading that life and doing all those things, the things you do when you're eighteen or twenty, and still thinking that way: how good it is to be independent and tough and not be tied down. Those men, it's as if they never grew somehow. And they're the ones that feel very strong about the army, get tears in their eyes when they remember how good it's been to them. Just because they've made the army into what they should have had if they were grown men. Work, get married, have a family and work for them—that's what a man should do."

"Lots of men in the army has families," Homer said.

"Sure, I know. The army'd rather have them single, though. And I was talking about career soldiers, that's what I'd have to be. Otherwise you get in there and get married, say, and then you can't get out because you need the pay twice as much, and what else are you fit for except soldiering if you've been in there for four or five years? You'd have to start right at the beginning and you can't do that because you got a family to support. And you're only half a family man besides, because you see more of the men you work with than you do of them. And when you get your time off, most of these men will try and talk you into going with them to hit the town, and they'll keep picking at you if you say no, tell you you're going soft, and make you think you're not a real man any more if you just want to have a quiet evening alone with your family. They're wrong. They're the ones don't know what it is to be a man. But it's hard to stand up to that kind of thing, especially if they're your friends, challenging your manhood like that. In the end you're only half a soldier and half married and you can't give your best to either side."

"You don't have to give the best," says Homer. "You act sensible and do not worry about the pride, it works out all right. Lots of soldiers have their families to live with them."

"And a lot of them only think it's going to work out easy that way and then find out it's harder than they imagine. The way things are, it's easy for army families to break up."

"But lots of men has their family come along and no trouble," says Homer.

"Sure, I know. The family ain't too happy about it, though. It takes a real solid marriage for it to work. Even then, I know of cases where they split up. It's just that you can only have the one or the other all the way. Sometimes it works out. That's mostly when the boys go in there for the money and save it up, send it home, and don't get married till they're out. But that's dangerous, of course. I could have done that, I suppose. Go in to fight, right into the frontliners—that's where the money is. But we were too poor to take the chance. Even allowing for me being scared to die, I couldn't afford to—no honest, it ain't so funny. Say I lasted two years and get killed, well what happens to my family in five or ten years? That means they're one worker short for the rest of their lives. And now I got a family of my own. I could have joined the military yesterday. Sometimes I got so desperate I thought I'd maybe do that. But the way the political situation is now, you know they'd never send me out of the country. I'd have more value to them here. They'd stick me right here in the middle of the city, keep me on home ground, so the next time there's a big riot I'd be out there doing crowd control. And who'd be in the crowd? Some day I might come face to face with my best friend or my wife or even my kids. So you see I can't, the choice isn't really there. It doesn't make sense to say I could join. I couldn't, not the way it's set up."

"You married?"

"Yes, married young. Are you?"

"Oh yes," Homer said. "But I'm not so young when I marry. She's back home. Across the water. I save to bring her over."

"A Greek girl?" Jake said.

"Girl?" Homer laughed. "I tell her, she like that." He drew a picture in the air with his hands, showing us his wife's shape. "A woman!" he said loudly. "A big woman, built big."

"Big as that?" said Jake. "That's something you can hang on to in a storm, all right."

"You bet," said Homer, and winked. We all laughed.

"Plenty storms in marriage, I guess. She is not beautiful. But I miss. She has a pretty voice, soft. And she is funny—no, is fun. Fun to talk with, not stupid. She make you feel good. Is most important of all, isn't it?"

"Yes," I said.

Jake shrugged and said he'd never thought about what was the most important thing of all.

"I got the one I wanted, anyway, that's important. Only I like them a little smaller."

He put his hands through the bars and shaped a curve out and in and out, and looked at me.

"What do you say, Abe?" he said.

I wondered what would he do if I came out with it and told him: I say that's my sister you're talking about so freely. He was enjoying himself, putting me on the spot when he knew there was a doubt about how far he could push me, and whether I'd remember his name right. It's strange to have a friend like that, so close you know each other like your one hand knows the other, but you don't understand, like I still don't understand how Jake doesn't worry or how it is he's got to walk right on the edge, always, and thinks it's fun.

He said, "I always found those big girls give you a lot of working space, but in the long run most of them are kind of low on activity. Make you do the whole job yourself. I like something with more action."

Homer leaned his hand up against the wall just far enough away so Jake couldn't grab him if he wanted, and said, "Is lots of men play the trumpet, but not all of them can make her sing."

"There's one on you, Adam."

Jake was smiling, and said, "That's pretty good. I'll have to remember that one."

"You married too?" Homer asked him.

"That's right."

"Children?"

"No."

"You?" he asked me.

"Two. A boy and a girl. One of each."

"Is good. Me too. My boy Alexander, twelve year old, and the little girl is ten, Cora. We disagree about the name, so we just call her Cora which means girl. My wife has a beautiful name, is Phyllis, which means a green bough."

"The which?"

"A green bough. How you name your children?"

"Ben, he's seven, going on eight. And Mary. She's, oh almost six now. Every time somebody asks me I have to think. They grow so fast. And my wife's name is Maddie, Madeleine."

"Madeleine, is nice. But you are young to have a boy eight year old."

"Twenty-five," I said. "I told you, I married young."

"You ever regret?"

"Not about that, no."

"Is very young," he said.

That's what they said when we got married. And afterwards somebody always says don't you have second thoughts about it now. I don't see it, like asking a man does he regret being a man, does he have second thoughts about his own family. Everything else could go, and does, and that's the bitterness. But if that went, that's your life, the people you love. Jake says it's freedom and ideas that move the world, but the men who keep pushing freedom and ideas know that's a lie, and if instead of just burning us out they'd tried to do something to Maddie and the kids, they could have had me doing what they said, for a while anyway, till I figured out how to stop it. They know that. They just must have thought I wasn't worth their time.

"It's been hard sometimes. It would have been harder alone."

"Twenty-five," said Homer. "If I was twenty-five again, oh, that is young. Me, I am forty-seven. Forty-seven."

"Old enough to be my old man."

"No," he said. "I was not here then."

He turned to Jake, who was laughing at what he'd said.

"You are older a little?"

I thought how funny it was that out of the two of us Homer liked Jake better, but I was the one that trusted Homer. I forget just when it was I began to trust him, but now I'd have told him anything about me and I didn't believe he'd carry it to anybody else. But Jake didn't trust him. He never trusted anybody unless he'd known them nearly all his life and even then you could count the ones he really trusted on your fingers. And there were things he wouldn't let people know just because he said it wouldn't be good for them to know.

"Oh, I'm bowed down with age compared to him."

"How old?" asked Homer, and Jake decided to tell him.

"Twenty-nine."

"Old? That is young. Very."

"Young for some, old for others. I'm no spring chicken any more."

"What's that?"

"Just a phrase. Means not in the first flush of youth, not green, not younger than most. Old Abe there is what you call green."

"Green?"

"Lacking in experience."

Homer thought about that and I thought: that's why he likes Jake better, because of being experienced, which is true, though Maddie always said not to mind. That day after I lost my temper she said not to mind, she'd rather have a fool with a good heart any day than a worldly man who said bitter things. "He's what you call cynical," she said. "And you don't know what he's thinking. I know, when you get mad you just roar and break things and lash out, and when you think something you say it. But what it is he thinks, Jake never shows, not anything. It makes me nervous. I wonder it don't make Annie nervous. Maybe he shows it to her. I'd rather know where I stand." And I told her, "Annie knows where she stands, all right." That was early, when we were first married, and I was ashamed to lose my temper, I didn't believe it could happen where you were contented. Some little thing it was, and all my life I been careful not to get mad like that, because being stronger than most through the chest and arms and shoulders, you have to be careful or your own strength can turn against you and break you. Like I never like to get into fights or even be in crowds that might be about to demonstrate or something, I always try to avoid it, because I get that feeling once I was in I'd kill somebody. Or hurt somebody by mistake. And you can get so you like it, I've seen that happen too. Once when we were kids, I remember, hitting Jake harder than I'd thought, turning around and seeing the blood on his face, and it made me want to die. He didn't say a thing. It's as though you can't hurt him. And he still loves a fight, but not for anger. For fun. I know when he's angry: he gets very calm, his voice goes gentle, and it's worse than if he hit you or shouted or smashed something. Like that day he came in the door and he'd heard the rumor the neighbors started, saying the Lord had put a judgment on him for his way of life and that was why he and Annie didn't have any children and wouldn't ever. He put down something he was carrying and said very quiet, it only took one spiteful tongue to take away the good name of a thousand people and what did it matter to him, what the hell. Annie tried to run out of the room but he caught her by the elbow going around the doorway and just said, "Let's have my dinner, it's been a long day."

We talked a little more and Homer left us for a while. He said there was a friend he had to see. As he walked off through the entranceway he called out, "Don't run away."

"A lot of speechifying you been doing," Jake said. "You don't usually talk so much."

"It's the worry."

I thought how all the time, even when I was talking, I kept thinking about things that happened a long time ago. And thinking about Maddie and Jake and Annie and my life, like I was far away someplace or like maybe inside I knew I was never going to see any of it again.

"Quit that. Nobody knows, we may need all the energy we've got in a while. You just quit worrying and sit tight. Keep your eyes on me and if there's ever a chance for a break, I'll give you the sign."

"I just can't stop wondering."

"Well, try."

"I thought you said we couldn't break out of this one."

"Not yet. Later, when they take us out."

I thought: I should have tried to get away before they brought me here. At the time I never even thought of it, I couldn't think of anything except I'd been caught. Not till they closed the door.

Homer came back in with a friend, the same one I'd seen him with when they first brought me in. They sat down at the table in the center of the room and played dice again. They were talking in a language I didn't know the sound of, so I guessed it must be Greek. The friend spoke it slowly and let Homer correct him every now and then. In the middle of the game Homer turned around and said, "You gamble?" Jake told him yes but he didn't always play it straight.

"Nobody else I gamble with does either, so it works out the same."

"I used to play," Homer said, "here, with men in the cells, but just pretend, no real money. One day a man's widow come to me and she swears her husband dying words was I owe him twenty-five thousand and she is to collect. You see, we play very high because is pretend. So now I don't do that no more."

The friend didn't do much talking. Just once he looked us both over and said to me, "You fight?"

I didn't understand.

"Fight. You fight ever, for money?"

"No," I said. "I don't like it. With the money or without. I figure why hurt people you don't even know."

"You got the build."

"Not me," I said, and pointed to Jake. "He's the one fights. He's been a boxer."

"I mean wrestling, that's the game. Too short in the legs to box. You'd be all right as a wrestler."

Jake was giving me a long, dirty look. The man said to him, "Where you box?"

"Oh, just here and there."

"Professional?"

"No, just amateur stuff."

"With the army?"

"Against the army."

"You know Big Quint? Old One-Punch Joe and the Sicilian Lion and Cassius what's-his-name?"

"I did," Jake said. "But a long time ago."

"And Killerboy Dexter? What a slugger that one was—and a fine left he had too, that fooled a lot of fighters. I suppose that was before your time. Best of the young ones coming up is that boy Rufus, comes from somewhere up North, someplace outside Syracuse, around there. Rufus—I forget his other name. I hear they're keeping him hid on a farm down in the country somewheres, training him with some of the oldtimers. Rumor is they're grooming him for the Olympics, but nobody admits to seeing him fight yet. Everybody just says he's the best coming up. A lot of money's started changing hands on that boy. I'd bet myself if I could be sure. You hear anything on that score?"

"I wouldn't know anything about it," said Jake. "I haven't been around to the gym for a couple of years now."

"Wrestling's the game," the man said, and he went back to the dice.

It was hot. And it was getting darker. All the light came in from the entranceway and now that the sun was beginning to move, the place was almost in total darkness. Homer had brought a light in and put it on the table, and there were two more lamps up on the walls in front of the middle cells. But from where we were the light came dim and uneven and the place seemed cruder than before as the sun went. I began to long for air and the light that was still shining outside.

Another man came in suddenly and said something to Homer. The game broke up and all three went out.

"Listen," Jake whispered to me. "You're so nice and friendly today, but we all know already what a pal you are, so let's just have a little less of this exchanging birthday dates and how old people were when they got married and what's your great-grandmother's name and where you were when and what's your favorite color, right? And if you can't shut up about your own life-story, just at least leave mine out of it. What are you looking so pleased about?"

"I was just thinking about Homer and his wife. Shaped like a whale, with a name that means a green bough. That's nice."

"You goddamn fool," he said.

There was some shuffling around outside and a loud, firm voice I hadn't heard before. Homer's friend mumbled something and Homer began to talk, too. The big voice went on, lower and impossible to tell what it was saying. When he came back in Homer told us there'd been a big riot about two hours ago.

"Lots of arrest. Then there was two small riots in a different part of the town. Everybody say it look like she was plan like that, to take away attention and let the leaders escape. That's what they look for now because there are so many and you can't arrest allbody. Is bad, riots. Lots of people they don't even know there's riot going on, they just standing there doing nothing. Then the law bring them in to me, saying this is a dangerous criminal, and sometimes it's just girls and boys, so young and all beat up. Once I have a mother and child in the cells, very dangerous, they tell me. What they call—agitators, is it? Very dangerous agitators, this mother and child."

"How long do you keep them?" said Jake.

"Oh, that one, I mark it down and let them go, and lose the record later. That was on the other side of town, bigger jail and always full. Also I work with my friend, you see him? The one just leave. We have arrangements, you know."

"How'd we stand for an arrangement here?"

Homer looked over at the entranceway, rubbed his chin, and moved over to Jake's cell, right up near the bars.

"Here is different. I don't take the names, so I can't fix."

"But you got lots of friends in that department," Jake said. "Ain't that right?"

"Some, yes."

"I got friends too. What do you say to combining?"

"Not for theft," Homer says, and he pointed at Jake. "You, you do something. You know what the law is, but you do that anyway. I only fix it if people are here by mistake."

"It was a mistake. Mistaken identity. They mixed me up with somebody else. Some fool yelled stop that man, and I looked around, saw him going around the corner, and the law grabbed me instead. I tried to tell them at the time, but they were so all-fired happy to get their hands on anybody at all, they wouldn't listen."

"No?" said Homer. He didn't believe it.

"Truth," Jake said. "What do you say?"

He shook his head.

"No bad feeling, I do it if I believe is just. But is not so bad, you get out soon."

"Not soon enough. Look, Homer, you know how it is."

"Enough. Don't say no more, you make me angry. Sure, I know how it is. I always take what is coming to me. You do the same now.

Is not so hard. I know how it is, so I know also what stories people tell the jailer and how you try to make sympathy and so on. See, I used to do it too, she's the first trick after telling the story to the law. All the things you say, I say them a long time ago."

"No harm trying," said Jake.

"Understand, I have sympathy, yes. What do I care? so they catch you, they take away what you try to take, so you don't profit. I think people should be charge money as punishment for theft. Charge them more money than the value of what they try to steal and give it to people they steal the thing from. You can't pay the charge, you can work it off. Then for small things, why make a thief stay in jail? Is not sensible. Because nobody is really hurt by it, not like hurting somebody's health or murder or other things. But that is personal opinion of mine, I don't let that change my mind. Is a question of law, you know. I know what is law. You know what is, and you know before you come to my jail. And also, here it is more difficult than any other place I been. Very difficult. Other people are working here that I don't know. This place here, even if I think you are bad-treated when they bring you in, when they take you out, I cannot change it. Is my job, is my job to see you stay here till they have a trial. What else happen is not my job. Beside, I could help at the beginning if you get arrested by the regular authority, but it was soldiers bring you in, isn't it? I got no friends high up there, up at the top where you need. Only with the local force I got friends high up. All I can do with the army is fix food and transportation and transfer, not take the name off the record."

I remembered what Jake said about how rickety the other jails were and how the best time to try for a break was when they took you out into the street.

"Could you get us transferred to a different place?" I said.

"Not now. All the jails is full now. But later, if they keep you here a long time, maybe."

"Thanks."

"No, no thanks. I only say maybe and if. It depends maybe on how many arrest they make with the riots and how they do the trial. Sometimes after riots they try all together in a block, get the jails clear quick, but sometime they wait and wonder who they got, specially if they think this riot was plan careful, not just a lot of people standing around. I see later if there's another place. But is too difficult, then I don't push. You understand is difficult for me without giving reasons why I change you. It use to be easy. I could do something even here, four, five month ago. Not now."

Jake asked him how long he expected they would keep us here.

"Hard to say. Maybe they keep you a long time here to wait for the trial. I hope is what they do."

"Like our company, do you?"

"Sure, sure, you and me we get along, right? I understand, you joke. Is not that. I mean, if they decide fast, give you a quick trial, it is with military trial and you get a harder sentence."

"But I was under civil arrest. I only met up with the military when they handed me over."

One of Homer's friends looked in at the doorway and said something. Homer turned around to answer him from where he stood.

Jake said, "Listen, Homer, if you would, there's something we'd both appreciate."

"Unlock. Yes, I bet."

"No, just if you could find out exactly how they've charged us, civil or martial law, and when they plan to try the cases."

"Sure, I do that anyhow. I always do that for my prisoner to save the worry."

"But don't lean too hard on the questions if it looks like some official's going to let it slide. I mean, if there's a holdup maybe I could get someone to change things from the outside, if you see what I mean."

"Sure," Homer said. "Is fair enough. Good luck to it. I cannot say exactly till the end of the day, maybe till tomorrow when they have gone over the day record. But I ask around, I find out what happen to your record, who got it, what they think happens to you. Meantime, I think you have company tonight—I hear there is some arrest to be transferred here, and maybe more people from riots, we see. Hope it don't mean you must double up. I keep saying to them it looks big but is small, only big walls is all."

"You're right there," said Jake.

He sat down on the floor. I'd been sitting on mine for some time, even though Jake had told me not to stay on the floor too long and not to sit totally still there because you'd lose the strength in your legs, and we might need it for a break later on. He kept moving back and forth and doing a kneebend up and down every once in a while. But I didn't believe any more it was going to be a question of getting out. Now I believed in the trial and didn't think it was going to be as bad as I'd imagined. I was feeling generally better about the future, except for what was going to happen to Maddie and the kids, and how she'd take it. If I was away for a long time, Annie could look after them. Jake always had plenty of money put by for when he was up against the law. But it couldn't turn out to be such a long time, not for just a piece of bread, I didn't think. I wasn't sure about the horse.

"Do you think they'll try us about the same time?" I asked him. "I wish it could be together. What's it like at the trials?"

He started to say something, but Homer came in again and sat at his table. People kept walking by and talking outside and the place seemed more open and lighter because now it was near sunset and the light was coming in on the slant. You could see it lying like patches of sand or like dust on the floor at the entranceway. Men came in, asking Homer things and going out again, talking to each other in the passageway. Then there was a commotion outside, a lot of voices and then stillness and right afterwards laughing and whistles and voices that seemed to be humming like water. Homer got up to see and went out the doorway. Jake stood up in his cell and then I did too.

"Another prisoner?" I said.

"A woman, bet you anything. Probably Annie."

Homer came back in sight. Annie was standing behind him, next to an officer who held her by the arm and grinned down at her. She said something to him, looking back into his face in a measuring sort of way, and almost smiled. He laughed and let go of her.

"I leave you to talk," Homer called, and waved his hand towards us so she could see we were at the far end. Then he turned and motioned the other man to follow him out. Annie walked forward from between them, alone, across the center of the floor. She had her head up and walked easy, keeping her eyes on the side of the room where Jake was.

It was strange to watch how she was and know she didn't know I was there, or looking at her. Stranger than seeing somebody you know walk by in a crowd. She looked hard. Full of devilment, able to take care of herself, and ready to talk back. It made me almost shy, seeing her, the way she was when she wasn't at home and wasn't a sister—a woman coming to see her husband in jail, which was a thing she'd done lots of times before.

She sauntered up near the cell, flicked her eyes past me, lazy and sneery, and then looked. She stopped in the middle of walking so she nearly tripped, and her face changed.

"You? I thought it was Jake."

"Right behind you, honey," he said. She whipped around.

"You, oh you—this is the last straw. Lord, this is the limit. It's all right for you to go taking chances, but why you have to drag my kid brother into—"

"He didn't," I told her.

"This was one he done all by his own fool self," Jake said.

She turned around again and curled her fingers closed on the bars of my cell and leaned forward like she wanted to put her head through.

"Ain't you ashamed?" she said. "And what's Maddie going to do now you landed yourself in this place? Ain't you shamed?"

"No," I said, "I am not." I started to explain, but she didn't want to listen. All the time I was talking she was giving me her own talking-to. I couldn't listen to her and talk at the same time, and I suppose she couldn't have been listening to me either, for the same reason. But it didn't seem important. At the time it only mattered that I was getting the explanation out.

"I was hungry," I said, "and I stole some bread. That's all there was to it. I was hungry enough so's I didn't bother much about who was going to be looking at me. That's all there is to it. I'm not ashamed, I'm just worried, sick with the worrying. And you don't make it any better. Do you think I like being here?"

"You should have thought. Oh my Lord, why didn't you come to me and say? You should be—"

"Cut it out, Annie," Jake said.

I said, "Listen, you'll tell Maddie, won't you? And tell her not to worry."

"Not to worry?"

"And see there's somebody can look after the kids for a while, so she can come and see me. I got to talk with her."

"I bet she'll enjoy that, walking through that line of studs out there and at night-time, too."

"How many out there?" Jake asked.

"About ten."

"Come over here, Annie."

She dropped her hands. They came away from the bars all at once as though they'd been stuck there instead of holding on. She went over to Jake and he put an arm through the bars and around her shoulders.

"They been giving you a hard time?"

"Just the usual, saying things. Asked me how much I cost."

"How much did you say?"

"Told them to ask my husband."

He put his other hand through and started to touch her face and neck. I had the feeling I shouldn't look and turned to the side, to the wall.

"Something I want you to do for me," he said. He began to tell her names of people and where to go and what to say.

"Keep your eye on the entrance, will you, Seth?"

He started whispering something to her and she answered, and after a while sighed and said all right. Then he squeezed her to him against the bars and drew his arm back so it was just lying along her shoulder. She turned around and told me not to fret, that she'd see Maddie was all right and try to keep her from worrying. She looked tired.

"Somebody coming."

I could just see Homer's head moving into view and another man's hand, waving fingers in the air as he walked. Jake looked, too.

"What were you giving him the eye for?"

"Who?" she said.

"That tall number had you by the arm when you came in. Who is he?"

"How should I know? He was standing outside. Said he'd show me where you were."

"You have to play up to him like that?"

"I didn't play up to anybody. Anyway, who's talking? I bet you missed me last night, didn't you?"

"I missed you," he said. He was looking over her head at the other man and his face turned peaceful and set, getting angry.

"If I died," he said, "you'd get married again before the year was out, wouldn't you?"

She didn't move for a while. Then she lifted his hand, knocked his arm away, and walked back to the entrance without looking at either of us or saying goodbye. Jake leaned up against the side wall and ran his hand over the bars where she'd been.

"What are you looking at?" he said.

"Just looking."

He let go of the bars and turned his back.

I've seen it happen so many times before and every time it jars me up, because I don't understand how it can be. I've lost my temper with Maddie, hit her because I couldn't help it. But I never wanted to hurt her. And afterwards, knowing I'd hurt her, I felt as scared and miserable as if I'd killed her, so in the end she was the one who had to comfort me, though she was the one got hurt. With Jake and Annie it's different, they set out to hurt each other. That's what I can't understand about it, that they love as much as we do, and still they can plan out a hurt the way you would prepare a pleasure.

He's treated her so bad sometimes, not beating her around, but just saying something mean. She does the same. Both of them wild with the notion that the other one could be fooling around with somebody else. And all of it is uncalled for. I don't believe either one of them has stepped over the line since they got married. But they talk about it all the time, and threaten each other with it, and hint it might be so. At first I used to think it happened because they didn't have any kids, that they needed an extra thing to be in their marriage. But then I met up with other married people who were jealous that way, with two or three kids, and that just meant two or three more weapons in the battle as far as they were concerned.

Jake said to me once I was lucky I wasn't jealous. "I got no cause," I told him. "You don't either. So why be jealous," and he answered, "There don't have to be cause. You're born that way or born without it. Jealous means jealous from the start—possessive."

Maybe that's what it is, that people just have different ideas about what belongs where. So if you are jealous that way, you imagine it should be possible that a body is yours when you have possessed it, and everything inside the body. I know he thinks that way about other things, like a horse or something like that belongs to the man that can take it, and if you can't hold on to what you've got you don't deserve to have it. I don't hold with that—I don't approve. When I stole, I knew it belonged to somebody else. I knew it perfectly but I took it anyway. But for Jake, the horse was his as soon as he began to lead it away. Finders keepers is what he thinks about things, about objects.

But about people, how can you say that? I told him, the people you belong to, it's in your mind, in your soul. They could be a hundred miles away and living with somebody else but it would be the same inside you, wouldn't it? And you could belong to somebody who never belonged to you, who didn't give you a second thought, not even if you were married. "I'm not talking about love," he said, "just who she sees in the afternoons." I'd only be worried if Maddie didn't love me any more. As for anything else, I don't think it would happen, but if it did it wouldn't be the end. "You don't even have any cause, Jake," I told him. "And even if you did, you know where her heart is, so can't you stop treating each other like that?" He said, "A change of bed can cause a change of heart."

I couldn't get anywhere talking about it with him. Maddie used to talk to Annie too, after a quarrel, till we got dragged into it that time and I had to tell them. I told them both it was all right for them to get into these fights and come ask us to take sides, but in a week they'd be together again and meanwhile they'd have broke up our home so in the future they would have to settle it alone. Mostly it was just all the talk that went on, that's what I couldn't stand. Both of them, it's as if you could almost see them sewing or weaving with the words, as if they are ornamenting—a jab here, a stitch there, and it's obvious they enjoy it, but it makes my head ache. I figure if you think something, then say it and don't take all day over it, but if you aren't sure what you think, shut up till you've made up your mind.

Jake can talk. Like anything. I think he used to make up his mind while he was talking. It's not so much like that now, he's quieter now. But at the wedding when he came with Annie, Maddie's mother said, "Can he talk? That boy could steal the brains right out of your head with his talk." Now he keeps a lot to himself because of politics, and you don't know all he's thinking.

"Will you quit looking at me like that?" he said.

"Just looking."

"She'll get over it. It don't mean a thing. Just keep her so mad she won't have time to think about anybody else till I get out."

I said, "You know if anything happened to you she'd kill herself."

"Maybe."

"You know she would. Maddie's the one would get married again."

"You think so?"

I'd never thought about it before but now it seemed like I'd known all the time.

"Sure, and I'd want her to. If anything happened to her, I'd get married to somebody else again too. Not right away, but I would. I couldn't live alone like that. And neither could she. It would be worse for her—I'd want her to get married again. How'd she live with two kids and no man in the house? It's bad enough you'd have the grief, why should she be unhappy too?"

"You wouldn't be jealous?"

"What do you mean, jealous? I'd be dead. But I'd like to know she's all right. I'd like her to get married again to somebody would make her happy."

"You mean you'd want her to love some other man? Really, like she loves you now?"

"Yes, I would. After I'm dead." I wouldn't want to leave somebody and have the world turn black and be dead to them whenever they think of me not being there. Much better if they think of me kindly and know I want them to be happy. For the children, too. Isn't that love?

Jake said, "Well, you don't know what it is. My, I feel like I'd be jealous even after I was dead."

"That's why she wouldn't be able to go on afterwards," I told him. "You wouldn't either. Think about it. What would you do if anything happened to Annie?"

"I don't want to think about it. I don't know."

Homer came in with his keys and began to unlock one of the middle cells.

"She is pretty, very," he said. "Lots of what you call it? Temperament. We got girls like that at home."

"You got everything back there," Jake said.

"Sure. I have a cousin like that a long time ago. You say something and her eyes flash and she tell you to go to hell. Then she wait till everybody leave her alone and she cries, cry like she will die. Is pride, is wonderful in a woman."

"You know all about that too?" Jake said.

"Two years ago, three years ago—well. Now I am feeling old. Is the job, maybe." He went over to the other middle cell and unlocked that one too so the doors stood open.

Jake said, "Is there anything you don't have over there in Greece? By my count you invented poetry, politics, philosophy, women. What else is there you don't have?"

"Money," Homer said.

"How about religion, did you start that too?"

"You very religious?"

Jake laughed. I heard shouts out in the passage and stamping feet and a roar of people coming closer. And then an armed guard burst through the entranceway, about seven of them, and they were dragging eight or nine people with them.

"Five in here," Homer said, and stood back. "Rest over there."

The soldiers began to cram them into the cells. They were young kids, looking not more than nineteen or twenty and two of them girls. All of them were kicking and hitting at the military and calling them paid tools of the government and hired butchers of imperialist tyranny and things like that. Then they started shouting names and dirty words, the girls too. But they must have come from good families; they were rich, you could see that. Most of the boys, about five of them, were dressed like me, dressed to look like a poor man, a fieldworker. But if you looked you could see their poor man's clothes were made out of real quality stuff.

The doors shut and they quieted down just for a moment. That's the bad time, when the door closes and you know there's no choice any more. But then they decided to put up a good front, and they yelled even louder than before, calling Homer names and jeering at him. I could see five of them, four boys and a girl. And if I got down into the corner I could see the other four on my side of the wall. But I didn't like the feeling of having those five all able to look straight into my cell with nothing I could do about it except turn my back. I got into the other corner and stood sideways so I could turn around whenever I wanted to, and watched them.

Homer waited for them to get quieter and then he and the friend he'd been playing dice with, the one who liked wrestling matches, started to hand in water and pots and things. One of the boys got his arm through the bars and poked the wrestling man hard in the eye. He grabbed the arm and twisted it and I heard a snap. "You've broken my arm," the boy yelled, "my God, he's broken my arm!"

The girl in the cell started to scream: "You dirty bastard, you filthy motherfucking son of a bitch." The ones in the other cell were shouting, "Police brutality, imperialist pig," and then all of them smashed the pots against the bars and the walls and threw the water out over the floor and began to throw the broken pieces into the center at Homer and his friend. There was water and smashed pieces everywhere, and they begin to sing. One of the freedom songs, one of ours.

Homer stood by the table and put his hand to his friend's face, looking at the eye. Then he took him by the arm and they both walked out, leaving everything on the floor. The singing went on.

When they'd finished there was a silence. The reaction's coming, I thought. "Hey, how's your arm?" one of them said from the other side. I moved over and looked out to the side and could see him with his face against the bars. I thought he must be the leader; he'd started the song. He had a little beard and a sunburn. I imagined he must have worked hard for both of them. The others were all very white from sitting up late at night talking about politics. Jake says I should be aware of what's going on but he didn't appear to be too set on them either. I looked over and saw him yawn and do another kneebend.

Back in the cell I could see, one of the boys said, "What a filthy place. I've got to pee." "Go ahead," one of the others told him, "give them some work to do for all the money they're getting beating people up." The girl and some of the others began to giggle. "Me too," said another boy and then they both did it against the wall while the rest cheered. After that they were quiet for a while. I could smell it coming through the place, a hot vegetable smell, going sour. There seemed to be less air than before.

A couple of them sighed and mumbled to each other. One of the boys said, "Well, what are we going to do to fill in the time?" and put his arm around the girl. I supposed she was his girl because she let him and they began to kiss up against the bars.

One of the boys looked embarrassed and turned away, but the others looked on while they kissed. Then they began to do more, he started to undo her clothes, and I thought: Lord, they're going to, right where everybody can see. But the girl appeared to be bored and pushed him away. "I'm not in the mood," she said. He nuzzled up to her again and said, "Come on, you're always in the mood, aren't you?" She took his arms away and said, "Cut it out," and moved away from him, one elbow out with her hand on her waist and holding on to the bars with the other hand. She tossed her hair back from over her eyes and stayed like that. I saw her face; she was still trying to look bored. And I thought: that one's just lost her forever, and it's a good thing. That's what they come to jail for, to get right down to real life, to the truth, and if you're looking for it there, that's where you'll find it.

Someone was crying outside in the passage. Everybody looked. "Beating up some poor kid," one of them said, and the crying went on. Homer and his friend came around the corner of the passage and out through the entrance, supporting a man between them. He was one of us, and he was still crying and had trouble standing. But he wasn't hurt, I didn't think. It must have been grief. Because he was crying the way people do when it's all over, and everything around you disappears so you can't even see what you're looking at and you don't care any more. They put him in one of the big cells, the one to the right of the entrance, and closed the door. Homer said something to him but the man couldn't answer. He sat down on the floor and kept on crying, running his hands over his head and face and not even bothering to turn away.

One of the kids called out, "What did you do to him? Are you proud of that? What did you do to that man?" Homer didn't look around. He went back outside with his friend and came in again alone and began to clean up the floor. The kids said things to him, trying to get his temper, but he kept on cleaning, not looking at them and his face resigned, not grim like I would be. When he finished, he stood up, holding all the broken pieces.

He said to them, "There is three men outside, your fathers or your uncles or something. They pay to get you out. They also pay for destruction of government property, for this. Men come in here and I try to make it clean as possible because it is bad enough to be in jail without the discomfort. You think I got lots of these? You think with all things going on so fast the state has time to give me supplies? No, I buy things myself and I keep the place clean myself and if I don't, there come diseases. Now you go piss on the wall and what happens if twenty more people come here and no time to clean it up? You do not think of other people who come after you, they have to live with all the things you break and make dirty."

"That's tough," one of them said. "You're making me cry." And another one said, "That's what you're paid for, isn't it?"

"I am pay by your fathers and uncles and the rest. They are rich and they treat me all right. When you have money, twenty years from now, you will pay me. But you will treat me like dirt. That is the difference," he said, and went out. The man in the front cell kept sobbing and I began to feel bad and tired from all the noise. I sat down on the floor.

"Hey," one of them called. He was in the cell on my side. I thought it was the voice of the tanned one with the beard. He was calling to Jake. "What are you in for, brother?"

"Brother, hell," Jake said. "I never seen you before in my life."

"We're on your side," the voice explained. Jake didn't answer, and the voice said again, "What are you in for?"

"Child rape," Jake said. A few of them laughed, and then it sounded like the laugh was dying out and they weren't sure, because his face hadn't changed.

"You're kidding," the voice said.

"No," Jake told him, and turned away.

"How about you?" another boy said from the cell that looked into mine. "What are you in for?" He smiled and I had that feeling that we were tied together, like when somebody you don't like smiles and it's as if you're standing at the other end of the line, his smile jerks up one on you, and you don't want it to happen, it makes you mad that it might respond all by itself, because you don't like the person. I thought against it so my face didn't move and I didn't answer him, and turned my head to the wall like Jake.

The man at the far end kept on sobbing. Some more of the kids tried to speak to us but I wasn't playing. Neither would Jake, which surprised me. He knows all their ideas and the language they use. I don't understand it and I'm damned if anybody is going to do that charity thing to me: we are sorry for you, we sympathize, we're fighting for your betterment, stand here like a monkey and look pleased and think how good we are. Or they give you food and clothes which you're not in a position to refuse, and when they leave they've robbed you of your honesty, your smile tied to the one they have that says: aren't you grateful, don't you like us, isn't it a lucky thing for you that we think about you once a year. They get very uncomfortable and vexed and sometimes scared if they think you're laughing at them behind their backs, and then they don't come back the next year and your kids have to do without, like you.

I heard Homer's voice and a lot of steps coming in. The military was back. "They buy you out," Homer says, and began to unlock the cells. One of the kids said they hadn't asked anybody to buy them out and they were going to stay there as a protest against police brutality. The soldiers began hauling them out. The one with the hurt arm came out quiet enough, wanting to get to a doctor. Some of the others put up a fuss. The girl from the other side suddenly kicked one of the guards for no reason at all, it looked like. He swore and let go and she kicked him again.

His friend who was standing next to them pulled back his fist and hit her in the breast. She screamed all the way out and was crying and saying, "You coward, you dirty coward."

Then they were out in the passage, the sound of them going, and it was quiet except for the man who was weeping.

"Did you see that?" Jake said. "Got him on the shinbone twice before they ever thought of laying a hand on her, and she'll go home and show her bruise and tell how she was roughed around by the hired imperialist thugs who've got nothing better to do all day than beat up women and kids."

"I thought you liked those kind of people, protest and rights and all."

"Not from them, it's too late for it now. It was a nice gesture, very helpful in the beginning, but we don't need them any more, they're just in the way. Besides, it's a kind of mental slumming for most of them. We want them out in the streets when they're landowners and senators and running import-export businesses like their folks, when they've got the pull to change the laws, change everything. But I bet, I bet you anything, in twenty years when they've got the family holdings and the house and everything, they'll be taking their kids on vacations to a little villa outside Rome or someplace and voting themselves tax reductions so they can keep what they got. And once in a while they'll boast to the kids about how they went through that stage too, they were idealists and right in the middle of the violence, where the action was."

"Singing our songs," he went on. "They've got songs of their own—why don't they work on that? They take it from us and they'll drop it in a few years. Retain the sympathy, of course, a lot of good that does."

"You're always saying people should fight for their rights."

"Sure, sure. If you know what they are and know what you're doing. I'm just sick of all this idealism running around the place. It's like an epidemic, everybody's got it. Trouble with idealism is it kills people. I'm not interested in motives, I just want something that works out without too much strain on everybody. Man, you talk with some of the people I know. Fanatics. Got a lot of schemes but what's in their minds is that they want to take over the show. Just the system all over again, we'll get on top and then we'll stomp on you for a change. And the people who've really got something to cry about, can you move them? Hell no. If there's a takeover they'll still be at the bottom. And all the ones that complain and won't lift a finger, think if everything was distributed equal nobody'd ever have to work again—I'm sick of all of it."

"Well, they wouldn't. Have to work again."

"You're crazy."

"Not what I call work, not what I been doing for the last nine years every day."

"That ain't work, that's slaving."

Homer came in again and started to clean out the floor of the cell and scrub the walls.

"What about them?" he said. "Did you hear the things that girl was saying? If that's my daughter I throw her out of the house and never come back, you bet."

The weeping man calmed down a little and started to moan. Every once in a while he'd break into sobbing again, but it was quieter. He had his head down on his knees and his arms around them.

"What's his trouble?" Jake asked.

Homer came over and said in a low voice that the man had stabbed his wife.

"Dead?"

"Instant, just like that. The neighbors say they quarrel all the time, shout. He never beat her, maybe he should. This time they shout at each other across the table and there's a knife there on top. He says he don't mean to hurt, all he mean was to shut up the shouting so she would listen. He is heartbreaking, he loves her very much. The neighbors say is true what he says, no other man, no other woman, just being angry. Very sad. They will try it as accidental I hope. He says he wants the trial right now, wants to die."

"Poor bastard, poor fool," Jake said.

Homer went back to scrubbing down the cells. I had to use the pot and then I thought I'd sleep. All day I usually move around, I never knew how tired you get if you stay shut in. And I was feeling the bruises and beginning to stiffen up from when they pushed me around making the arrest. They can tell who's rich and who isn't and who's got friends. They never roughed Jake around unless he got in first. He looks too smart and too important.

I stretched. Homer began to whistle and to hum. I lay down on the floor and put my head on the stone, cold and hard. Then I changed around and put my arm under my head and closed my eyes.

I must have gone right under. When I woke up a man I'd never seen before was talking in whispers to Jake, saying goodbye. I sat up and watched him leave and saw Annie at the entrance, going out with him into the dark hallway.

"How long was I out?" I said.

"Not very long. She says Maddie's coming later. Uncle Ben will walk her here, and Annie's going to look after the kids."

"She still mad at you?"

"No," he said, "no, we made it up," and smiled.

"Good."

The man who'd killed his wife was still sobbing quietly.

"Has he been at it all this time?"

"No, he let up for a time. He only started again a little while back. Homer says they're moving him on later."

"I hope we don't get any more rioters."

"So does Homer. It cuts down on the food."

"That's funny, you know, I thought it would make me feel sick. I did feel sort of unsettled, but not sick. And I'm hungry again. Already."

"It's the idea. Watch out for that. You know in your mind you'd like to keep on eating all day long. But your stomach can't take it. So take it slow."

"Is there any news?"

"Not much. Not good. I got Joe to hunt out my army friends."

"Virgil?"

"Him and others. They don't know anything, don't know where to begin. I never knew such a total breakdown of grapevines. We'll just have to sit it out till something comes through."

Homer came in and unlocked the other cell by the entrance, the big one on the left.

"Another noisy one," he said. "I put him far away as possible." While he was speaking four guards came in with the prisoner, squirming and writhing in his clothes like an animal in a sack, and muttering to himself. He was the strangest looking thing: all gawky, skinny as a reed and dressed in rags that were covered in dirt. His hair fell all over his eyes and below his shoulders and even from a distance I thought I could see things hopping off him. He stuck out one long bony leg while they tried to move him along, and you could see the toenails on his bare feet, longer than I imagined nails could grow, like the nails on his hands, black with dirt. And there were sores on his legs, which were the color he was all over, a kind of livery yellow.

"Blasphemers," he blared out in a voice like a trumpet call, but it made you want to laugh. Then it broke, and he trilled what he was saying in a high quavering voice that sounded as if it was coming from a completely different person.

"Repent, the day is at hand. Oh ye ungodly, ye of little faith." He screwed his head around and I stepped back farther into the cell. His face gave me the kind of sinking feeling you get when you see blood, but that kind of fascination, too. I'd never seen anybody like that, so that you felt revolted but you couldn't take your eyes off him. They say snakes do it to birds.

"Goddamn, we've got the whole works now," Jake said. "A week in this jail and you could write a history of the world."

"Unrighteous and ungodly," said the stranger. "Pharisees, Pharisees!"

He had great blazing eyes and inside his beard a loose mouth full of rotten teeth. When he called out "Pharisees" the eyes rolled up and his face went all meek and mock-pious, so for a moment I was sure he was putting on an act for some reason.

They shut him in the cell and Homer turned the key and stood back, brushing off his clothes. The stranger rattled the bars and sang out, "Eaters of offal, ye that persist in the ways of the ungodly, Pharisees!" He went on like that, his eyes roaming over the rest of the cells for a while, but none of us gave him a reaction, so he turned around and sat down with his back leaning against the bars, and scratched his head and muttered to himself.

"What kind of a thing is that?"

"Some religious nut," Jake said. "Some kind of faith-healer probably."

"Why's he in here? He looks sick."

"Maybe he was preaching to the multitudes or something when the riots broke out. Start screaming and kicking enough and they pull you in. Some of them do it for the food and a place to sleep for the night."

Homer came up to Jake, who said to him, "I got a complaint to register about the way the tone of this place is going down. It's turning into a regular sideshow. What's the world coming to when a man can't find any peace and quiet even in jail?"

"You tell me?" Homer said. "You tell me. Food is soon."

"And drink?"

"Sure, drink too. Coming soon," he said, and went out.

"I could do with a drink," Jake said.

Lots of things I could do with, I thought. The air was still heavy and thick and the place had the sense of something wild having passed through and gone, time coming back and sitting there slow. I was thinking I hoped they'd put me out to do hard labor because I couldn't take a lot of this, being shut in. Maybe you got used to it, though. I planned the first thing I'd do when I found out how long the sentence was going to be. It would be to do what all the others do, so they tell you: find someplace where I could mark off the days one by one.

"Goes by slow when you got to wait it out," I said. "I wish we knew one way or the other right now without a trial, what the sentence is."

"I know right now. I know they aren't going to keep me in for long. Not if I can help it. I been sentenced three times and never yet served one. Don't let yourself slide back that way. Do you want to be cut off from the world for the next ten years?"

"Ten years for a piece of bread?"

"Lord, Seth. Don't you know anything?"

That's what he always said when we were kids. Nobody would believe he was older because he was so small, it took a long while before he got his growth. Maybe that's why he likes to fight, because he's never forgotten how he used to have to. "Don't you know anything?" he'd say, and pretty soon they weren't laughing any more, everybody was taking orders from him.

"Don't you know anything? You don't imagine they're going to go easy on you because you give them some hard-luck story, do you?"

"For taking a piece of bread? What do you think they're going to do, cut my hand off or something? They couldn't give me more than six months, could they? I never stole anything before."

"So you say. But wait till you hear what they say. Wait till some man stands up and says, yes that's the one that burned down my business last year, and some woman says she's positive you're the one raped her grand-daughter just a week ago, she remembers your shifty eyes, and swearing up and down on oath and a dozen witnesses to prove it. Asking you where you were on such-and-such a night three years ago and looking triumphant when you say you can't remember. Don't you know that? If every man was just charged with the crime he's done, everybody there is would be in jail for something. Hell no, you get arrested and you're a representative for all the ones who never got caught out."

I thought it couldn't be like he said, he was trying to scare me about it. Maybe he figured if I got too relaxed I'd drop some hint about his political doings. I wasn't all that relaxed; my hands were sweating again.

Homer and the four-man guard came in with the food. First they went to the cell on the right, where the man was moaning to himself about his dead wife. He didn't raise his head from his knees or move in any other way. Homer gave his keys to one of the others, went into the cell himself, and laid the provisions down on the floor while the ex-fighter stood behind him. He locked up again and the man still didn't move. Then they went over to the left-hand cell and started to open up. The religious nut jumped to his feet and began chuckling to himself. "Stand back, there," one of the guards said and he moved a little way back, but he kept pacing back and forth, making noises to himself like he was agreeing with something someone was saying to him, and holding his arms out with the fingers bent like claws.

Homer went into the cell and was about to set the food down when the religious nut made a dash at him, knocking everything out of his hands and sending it way up into the air. The food and drink and water splashed all over the inside of the cell and on the walls and over Homer and the guard by the door. The nut shrieked out, "Get thee behind me, get thee behind me, spawn of the devil," and began to dance around the cell. The ex-professional stepped forward and cracked him across the mouth. And he let out a yelp, not sounding like pain, sounding like some kind of a love-sound a woman might make. They closed the doors on him and Homer went out into the entranceway with the fighter, leaving the other three men behind. The religious nut capered around his cell and began to harangue them, saying, "Man shall not live by bread alone but by every word that proceedeth out of the mouth of God." His voice kept changing, sometimes loud and strong as a whip cracking and then going all quavery and high and his face would turn back to that mealy-mouthed humble look. When he said "mouth of God" he lifted his right hand and pointed his finger up at the ceiling, throwing his eyes up dramatically.

He went on parading in front of them, stalking back and forth and shouting out a long string of stuff at them. He said, "I am the living bread, the living bread which came down from heaven, and if any man eat of this bread he shall live, he shall live, live forever. And the bread that I will give, the bread, the bread that I will give is my flesh. My flesh which I give, my flesh which I give, give for the life of the world."

"I know what's wrong with him, all right," one of them said. "Is that your trouble, sweetheart?" He laughed.

A second one said, "God, it makes you sick, look at him."

The religious nut was panting with excitement and his mouth was wet.

"I knew a nut like that once," the second one said, "went around hammering nails into his hands. It's a sex thing, gives them some kind of a kick. They run around shouting at people till somebody beats them up—that's what they want. Did you hear him squeal just then? Loves it."

The third guard, a good-looking boy and younger than the others, said, "You shouldn't laugh at crazy people."

"What's eating you?" the first one said. "You got religion all of a sudden?"

"I just don't think it's funny, that's all. They can't help it. Some of the things they say aren't so crazy—they're just like everybody else, only it comes out scrambled. He's not hurting anybody, is he? Everybody's a little crazy, every religion's a little crazy."

"Not everybody," the second one said. "And not every religion. Is that what you meant to say, *every* religion is crazy?"

The younger one shrugged, and said he just didn't think it was funny and besides it was unlucky to laugh at crazy people.

"Crazy? Why, he's a goddamn raving pervert," the first one said.

The religious nut kept muttering all the time they were talking about him. As soon as they stopped he got their attention again and said, "The hour is coming, the hour is coming when the dead shall hear the voice of the son of God. I am the son and he that honoreth not the son honoreth not the father that sent him. The hour is coming. I am the son of God, I am the son of God. As soon as they hear of me they shall obey me, the strangers shall submit themselves unto me."

"What did I tell you?" said the first guard.

"It is God that avengeth me and subdueth the people under me. He beat them small as the dust before the wind, he cast them out like the dirt in the streets."

"Who are you calling dirt, you bastard?" the second guard said to him, and started to put his arm through the bars.

Homer came back in with the other one and said sharply, "What you doing making him shout like that? Come on, this is time for working. What you think, you can stand there all day? The food is getting cold." He shooed them into the passageway and came over to us, not looking at the religious nut who was still mumbling and shouting and hopping up and down. He shouted, "I receive not honor from men. Blessed are they that hear the word of God, but I know you, that ye have not the love of God in you. I am come in my father's name and ye receive me not."

"I'd like to receive him," I said. "Right in the teeth, I'd like to."

Homer said, "This day is the longest day in my life, I bet. First one thing, then another. Why they get him started like that? And I got to clean that up too. And now the other one start to cry again, no wonder. Oh, I am feeling old as one hundred today. And there is more people coming tonight. When I sleep I don't know."

"Who is he anyway?" Jake said. "What's he in for? Exposing himself to little girls, or what?"

"Is a mistake, all a mistake. I don't know why they send him here. He is sick and crazy. This is a jail, not a place for sick peoples. I ask his name to put it on the record and he just keep saying: I am the son of God. Like that, in a big echo voice and turn his eyes up. What he is arrest for I don't know because nobody send the charge record and he is transferred from someplace else. What a mess in my jail all day."

"Try a little of that Greek philosophy," Jake said.

"My philosophy for today is this," Homer says, and made a gesture with his hand.

Jake laughed. "Is that Greek, too?"

"Is international, yes?"

The food came in with the four guards, first to Jake's cell, next to mine, and then they all went out. I had some of the drink first and felt better. That man was crying again but the other one had stopped, and I began to eat.

Suddenly he started up again in that high, quivery cooing voice.

"I know you, that ye have not the love of God in you," he said. "I am come in my father's name and ye receive me not. My God, my God, why hast thou forsaken me, why art thou so far from helping me and from the words of my roaring? Oh my God, I cry in the daytime but thou hearest not, and in the night season, and am not silent. But thou art holy, oh thou that inhabitest the praises of Israel. Our fathers trusted in thee, they trusted, and thou didst deliver them. They cried unto thee and were delivered, they trusted in thee and were not confounded."

I began to feel let down and sad again. The noise kept going on, sometimes soft and sweet and sometimes bleating out strong and showing off. The soft voice was the worst, it made you feel crawly inside.

"But I am a worm and no man," he went on. "A reproach of men and despised of the people. All they that see me laugh me to scorn, they shoot out the lip, they shake the head, saying: he trusted on the Lord that he would deliver him—let him deliver him, seeing he delighted in him. But thou art he that took me out of the womb, thou didst make me hope when I was upon my mother's breasts. I was cast upon thee from the womb, thou art my God from my mother's belly. Be not far from me, for trouble is near, for there is none to help."

I turned around in the cell and put my back to the bars, feeling terrible all of a sudden and wanting to cry. I thought: if that man who killed his wife starts up again I won't be able to hold it back.

The voice went on: "Many bulls have compassed me, strong bulls of Bashan have beset me round, they gaped upon me with their mouths as a ravening and roaring lion. I am poured out like water and all my bones are out of joint. My heart is like wax, it is melted in the midst of my bowels, my strength is dried up like a potsherd. And my tongue cleaveth to my jaws, and thou hast brought me into the dust of death. For dogs have compassed me, the assembly of the wicked have inclosed me, they pierced my hands and my feet. I may tell all my bones, they look and stare upon me. They part my garments among them and cast lots upon my vesture. But be not thou far from me, oh Lord, oh my strength. Haste thee to help me."

"Seth?" Jake said, and I turned around. "Not hungry?"

"It's that goddamn nut. That awful mealy-mouth voice and the words so beautiful. What is all that stuff he's been spouting?"

"That? That one's a paslm. He's praying. The rest of it he's grabbed from all over the place, quoting from lots of different parts of the scriptures and getting them all mixed up."

"It's that voice, that awful voice. Can't they shut him up?"

"He'll stop it if you leave him alone. He wants an audience, that is all."

"I can't stand him," I said. "I hate him."

"Shouldn't hate."

"Why not? I'm beginning to think there's lots of things I hate. Never had time to think about them before."

"It's bad for the digestion," he said. "Besides, you hate somebody, that means they got a hold over you. They got you right in their hand."

"I don't see it. What is that, religious morality? All they tell you about in religion, it's full of hate. Hating all the ones that don't agree with you."

He began to tell me a story about a boy that lived next door before his family moved near us and we got to know each other. This boy took a dislike to Jake, a real hatred. One day the boy was making fun of him and Jake turned around and told him he wished he'd die. Next week the boy hung himself. I didn't believe it.

"It's true," he said.

"I mean I don't believe he would do it just because you said that."

"Lots of things people do. Specially when they build up hate like that and don't know how to get rid of it. If you're going to hate you should know why and what it is and how to keep it in control. Otherwise it can turn around and fall back on you. Why do you think you hate him?"

The voice had stopped now and I felt easier.

"I just can't abide his sicky-sweet psalmsinging voice. I don't mind so much that he's a nut."

"What's wrong with the voice?"

"Gives me the cold shakes," I said. I began to eat, to feel filled with the taste of it, and it was much better and I thought about seeing Maddie soon.

Jake sighed. He said, "A brother-in-law that's got the cold shakes, a weepy homicide case, a religious maniac who thinks he's the Messiah and a jailer who's a Greek philosopher—Lord, do I pick them."

"Do you remember when you were religious?" I said.

"A long time ago, that was."

I remembered. I remembered he even thought he had a calling and would go into it for life. Some of them are like that. They say a reformed sinner makes the best man of God because he can know and understand other people's weaknesses and help them to peace the way he found it. And it works the other way, too—the ones who brood about religion suddenly throwing it over and going wild, like Jake, and they never go back to it. When they change like that it's lifelong. Not like me. All my life I could never make up my mind about those things and in the end I realized I never would. I remember Jake would say, "There's got to be something more, there must be. Sometimes I feel like it's all a reflection or like a shadow of the real thing," and to listen to him talk about the mystery of things, you'd get all calm and serene and inside you were burning with the knowledge that everything was completely mysterious and large and full of un-thought-of marvels. But I never felt that way by myself. It took Jake talking about religion to make it happen.

Then he changed. Once he said maybe God was just the way things happened, that everything that took place, all put together, made God. He said how he'd always wanted to experience what the scriptures spoke about: that God would talk to you. But that would mean God was a person and acted like a person, and if he was perfect and all-powerful he wouldn't be a person, because people are so small. Not just that they die, they're all-over small. All the believers who tell you you're doing something wrong or a thing or an action of yours is immoral because God wants this and God wants that; Jake said this God that's talking to them, that's themselves. That's their idea of what their good selves are like and what they'd wish to have happening in the world.

Then he got stuck on ideas. And he said religion was ideas but he wanted ideas that could handle people in this world, not deal with some world after death, which he'd never really taken to heart anyway. He began to get interested in politics. And he told me, like telling me I was lucky not to be jealous, "You're lucky you've got that instinctive certainty of what's right and what's wrong. I never had it." And by that he meant that I wasn't as smart, since I'd never gone into the question deep enough to find out that there's no such thing as right or wrong. Just how you happen to look at it, which was another thing he told me. I knew he was smarter, but some things he didn't see, for instance that I'd know when he said I was lucky to be this or that, that it was a way of telling me I had a place and it was just a notch below his. Some of the mistakes he makes with people—that's why, because he could misjudge those instinctive certainties. Not so much with strangers, there he was always all right.

And he made friends in the army and got them to give him information about where certain troops were stationed and what maneuvers they were carrying out, how long they'd be staying, how the communication lines were set up, and so on. Passing it on to freedom fighters and the protesters, I suppose, and I'm sure, I know, there's a name for that and a very special law that covers it, overthrowing the state and all. They've got his name in one place and his description in another, and nobody's put the two together so far, but Maddie says she wouldn't be in Annie's place for anything in this world.

One day he says to me, "Maybe you're right about it all being in the mind, who you belong to. That's the thing, to possess minds, to be able to influence people, make them change their minds and change their lives. That's the real power, to get other men's minds under your control." So that's what he does now, and I still don't understand and maybe never will. What on earth would you want with somebody else's mind? Bad enough you're stuck with your own.

"Thou didst make me hope when I was upon my mother's breasts," Jake said, "that just tears my insides out. I think that's what I liked most about it, just the words."

"You called me Seth," I said.

"Nobody to hear. Don't you start doing it or you'll trip up."

They came back and opened up to take the things away. I was feeling a little drunk, though it was hard to tell, sitting down. They'd given us more this time. When they went to the religious nut's cell and cleaned it up he began jabbering again and after they'd locked up he made a grab at one of them through the bars. Homer wasn't with them this time, he'd given the keys to his wrestling friend and you could see his eye was already swelled out a lot from where the protester had hit him. At the cell on the other side they took out the food but left everything else. And then they went out again.

Homer came back with a new set of guards, the night shift, I guessed. They had about six people in tow and put them into the side cells where the kids had been. They were all working men, most of them looking pretty much like me, and very beat up, looking tired and dazed and not talking or trying to push back. The religious nut quoted a lot to them but they took no notice. Two of them lay down on the floor. Homer and the guards handed in water and something to drink and pots, and came back later with food but not as much as they'd given us.

While they were eating the religious nut's speech dribbled off into muttering, then he quit entirely and sat down with his back to the bars. Homer came across the center of the floor, around the table, and said to me, "Is Maddie, yes?"

"Yes," I said and stood up. My heart started going all the way up through me and I hung on to the bars. He walked her across the room from the entranceway towards my cell and then went out, leaving us to talk. She looked shy and scared coming across the floor with all the men in the place.

When she got to the cell she put her arms through and up around my shoulders. All the hard work she does, and her hands so small. I put my arms through and held her close up to the bars and wanted to get my head through.

"Are you all right?" she said. "Are they feeding you all right?"

"I'm fine. Don't worry about me. I'm sorry, I'm sorry about all of it, Maddie. But you get Annie to stay with you and don't worry about me. It's you I'm worrying over, everything else is all right."

"Ben and Mary asked about you," she said. "Annie told them you'd gone to visit her cousin Liza, so I had to back her up. I didn't know you had a cousin Liza."

I had to laugh because cousin Liza was a family joke and a name to use for excuses when you wanted to get out of something. I was never sure we really had any cousin by that name; Annie knew more about those far-off cousins than I ever did. I remembered she once told me cousin Liza had been a notorious old woman who disgraced the family at some point and died about forty years ago.

I told Maddie and she relaxed a little and didn't look so strange. She gets that pinched-up look sometimes like she's a very old woman, and when she looks that way she also appears to be about four years old, all the ages come into her face.

Jake said hello, and she said hello to him and turned back to me. I wished there weren't any other people around, so I could really talk. It felt shaming to be overlooked by so many people and not able to speak really. I thought: this must be the worst part of being in jail for a long time—standing near the people you love but not quite able to touch them and not quite able to talk to them and sweating with the constraint; counting, all the time they are there, how much more time there is until they've got to go. So much to say, and unable to.

"Well," Maddie said. "Well, I'll look in tomorrow."

Just then the religious nut threw himself against the bars of his cell and pointed his finger at us, and bellowed out, "Daughter of Sodom, Jezebel, beware the sins of the flesh, beware!"

Maddie looked behind her and I looked, over her head, seeing him writhing himself up against the bars, moving in a jerky rhythm and roaring, "Beware the unclean lusts of the flesh, beware the guile of painted women that leadeth unto temptation! My judgment is just because I seek not mine own will but the will of the father which hath sent me."

I tasted the food coming back up my throat and felt Maddie in trembles between my hands, like from cold, and I couldn't take it any longer.

"Shut up," I yelled, "shut that goddamn bastard up, shut him up, Homer, make him quit!" And then it happened again like I always try to avoid, like a curtain of blazing light coming down over my forehead, getting mad and not knowing or caring any more, not hearing what anybody else was saying, just yelling that I was going to kill him when I got my hands on him.

Then I heard Jake, quiet, saying, "Easy, take it easy. You're making it worse."

I looked up and saw his face and felt the hotness begin to go and the shaking come on.

"That's just what he wants," he said. "Take a look. It's you he's interested in, not Maddie."

I looked and saw the nut with one foot through the bars now, weaving his body back and forth, and looking straight at me. His eyes were nasty and pleased, his mouth wide open and blood down the side of his face from where he'd been hit. Seeing me look, he started up again, started whipping himself into a frenzy, running his hands all over his body. But Jake got in first.

"Just don't listen," he said. "Now he knows he can get a rise out of you, he'll try it again."

I turned my head away and began to cry. Maddie smoothed her hand over my neck and said, "Oh Seth, oh Seth."

Homer came in then and said what was the trouble, what had happened.

'That crazy son of a bitch, insulting my wife."

Homer went over to his cell and the nut pulled his foot in and gave him a short lecture in his trumpet voice. Homer stood there without saying anything, and the nut slouched off into one of the far corners and sat down.

Maddie said, "Oh Seth, putting you in with horrible people like that."

I told her again not to worry, and touched her face and took her hand in through the bars and kissed that. She did the same with mine and Homer made a sign from the entranceway that it was time for her to go. She looked back as she went, and I thought: if that other one makes a remark or does anything at all, even coughs when she gets up close—But he didn't look at her and she went out with Homer.

Later in the night the guards came and took the homicide out of his cell. He'd stopped crying but he went with them blank-faced. I wondered if they were taking him to trial. Homer had quit work for the night. Before he went he'd promised us to remember about looking up the day records. The man who took over was one I hadn't seen before, very thin and grey-haired and sullen. All night long they were changing men in the middle cells, taking out the ones who were there and replacing them with others. I didn't think they could be rioters, only a few of them looked like they'd been in a fight. The rest were all ordinary looking men, some young and some older. They tried to sleep when they came in, but hardly had time because the guards were moving them so fast. I guessed finally that they were all being held for questioning about something. Jake said he was going to sleep. Over by the entrance the religious nut was rolled up in a ball in a corner of his cell. I was tired, but it had been so dark in the place for so long that I didn't think I could sleep. I lay down and kept watching the people going in and out.

Finally I thought I would sleep after all and make myself a dream. Maddie said once she didn't dream, she said she supposed that meant she didn't have any imagination, and looked embarrassed. I told her all it means is that she forgets them when she wakes up. I'm always talking about them since it means a lot to me. Some people don't care about it or don't like the thought of dreaming, or are scared by it, by the thought that they go someplace away from the body. Jake says you don't, it only seems that way, like being able to remember a face, you can close your eyes and call it up by thinking, and you don't truly leave. Maybe Maddie has dreams she doesn't want to remember; I'd want to remember even the bad ones.

When we were kids we used to compare. Annie dreams in black and white and repeats dreams and remembers what people say in them. Jake's are in color, like mine, and people in them talk but you don't remember what they've said, only maybe a word once in a while. Same with mine. But he dreams about people he knows and I don't usually unless they are far away. My little girl Mary is the strangest one—she's dreamed some things that have happened afterwards. She dreamed about the fire before it happened, and about Maddie's grandfather dying. Last week she said she had a dream about me, she dreamed I was in a big parade or some kind of celebration and we were all going somewhere to do something important. She said it scared her but afterwards she thought it must be all right because though she didn't see the end, the dream finished halfway, when I was in it I was looking happy.

I closed my eyes and tried for a good dream. I like planning them out just before you go under. Then they take over and change, of course, and the real dreaming begins.

When I woke up I didn't know where I was and then remembered and knew the dream had been a bad one. I'd had a feeling in the dream that I was all bent down and weak and couldn't move very well, and people I'd met a long time ago kept asking me what had happened to me. And the trouble was I was old, about a hundred years old with a long white beard. But I'd felt it in my body, withered up and broken and too feeble even to say what was wrong with me.

Jake looked like he was still asleep. The cell where the weeping man had been now had about six men in it, all asleep on the floor. The grey-haired man was also asleep, at the table, and the middle cells as far as I could see were empty with the doors closed. I thought I remembered Homer unlocking the empty cells earlier in the day and I wondered if that was a safety precaution, to add time in case somebody got hold of the keys and tried to lock the jailer in. Or maybe I'd misremembered and he hadn't really used the keys. I had that feeling you sometimes get after a bad dream, that you don't want to go to sleep again right away.

I lay there and waited and tried not to think about anything particular. Things from the past started to go through my head, like before at the beginning of the afternoon, making me go back to when we were all kids, as though I had to say goodbye to it.

I saw Homer come through the entranceway. He didn't make enough noise to wake the other man or the other prisoners, but Jake was suddenly up on his feet. I stayed where I was and half-closed my eyes.

"It's like I am afraid," he said. "They try you together."

"When?" Jake said.

"Now."

"In our absence?"

"Yes. It is going on now, is what I hear. Rumors everywhere, but that is mainly what I hear, and I think is reliable. Also I hear out of all arrest made yesterday only one or two come on any list at all. There was no time. Nobody is going to bother, it's either let them go or try them quick and the charge the same for all, sedition, incitement to violence, treason. You know."

"Both of us together?"

Homer flashed his hand out and said, "All of you, all in here right now. Seven, eight, nine, ten, they do it by the block."

"But we must all be in for different things."

"That's all I know, what I hear."

"Listen," Jake said. "You know we didn't exactly give our right names. I think they've got us mixed up with somebody else."

"Oh, I suspect that, is not that, is not because of any names."

"But the charge is straight theft, isn't it?"

"They don't say. I will tell you soon as I hear more."

He left and Jake sat down. He stayed like that, waiting, and I kept the way I was.

I slept again. Some dreams I have places I go to with fields and mountains, sometimes the sea. And in some dreams I have cities that I've never been to before. But the dream I had this time was just countryside, nothing particular, and I was walking in it and don't remember anything happening.

Jake was sitting the way he'd been before.

"Any idea what time it is?" I said.

"Sun-up, I imagine. It's hard to tell in here."

The other jailer was gone, and the other prisoners still asleep. I felt ghostly and cramped. Jake stretched and did kneebends and told me to do the same, but I couldn't face it. We waited. It began to get lighter and some of the men in the big cell by the entrance stood up and stretched. sat up or lay down again. The light grew, and time dragged.

Then there was some noise outside and people moving around, it sounded like a lot of them, talking and walking through the passageways outside. Once I caught sight of some lumber being carried by some of the military and jailhouse guards, down the corridor and past the entranceway.

"Barricades for another riot, I suppose," I said.

Jake held on to the bars and looked at me. Sometimes I've seen him go like that, looking steady as if he's looking straight through the world and out the other side, and it seems to be a face I've never met before but would never forget.

"What?" I said.

"Start doing those bends, Seth. And remember to make the break when I give you the sign."

"I don't see the use—"

"Just do what I say."

Homer came back while I was holding on to the bars and swinging my feet around. Seeing him from the side and then the back when he turned, he looked old and tired, like a different person, not like a man who would enjoy clowning around and laughing. He went over to Jake's cell.

"They decide," he said. Jake nodded.

I stood still to listen and it was so silent I could hear my eyelids creak when I blinked.

"Death," said Homer.

Over his shoulder I saw Jake's face, looking as though he'd known.

"The whole bunch of us?"

"Yes. It is martial law, for all of you."

"How's it going to be?" Jake asked. And Homer told us.

"I send for your families already," he said, and went out again. He hadn't looked at me.

I shut my eyes and swallowed, and heard it loud in my throat and in my ears.

"What martial law?" I said. "They couldn't have proclaimed it or anything till the riots started, that was hours after they caught us. I can't believe—"

"Hush. It's like he says. You remember what I told you, we'll make the break when they get us in the streets."

Out in the passage somebody started hammering. Soldiers came in and stood around the doorway. Homer came back in once more and talked to the others, the seven men on the right, and the religious nut. The men got up on their feet but the nut didn't seem to have taken anything in. He stood leaning against the bars, looking mopey. The other men began to talk, low and scared. One of them shouted out something just once and afterwards they went back to the same uneasy mutterings.

Guards came in and some of the soldiers were called away. The hammering went on and a sound of chopping, and then a group of people, women, came in and rushed for the right-hand cell. All hell broke loose then: screaming and crying. But I still couldn't believe it.

Two more guards came in, and Maddie and Annie with them. Maddie was running.

She reached me, saying, "They can't do it, Seth, they can't do it," and beat her head against the bars. That was when I believed it; when I held her face up, I saw it there in her eyes and believed it for the first time.

The place was loud as a storm now, it was hard to hear anyone. I said, "Listen, Maddie, we're going to try for a break in the street.

But I don't want you there, you hear? You stay away. I specially don't want you there if it won't work. Promise me. It's important. Promise me you'll stay away." I've seen it, mouth open, body twisted out of shape, swollen, suffocated.

"If it happens," I said, "come for the body after."

"Oh no, oh no, no, no," she said, "they can't do it to you, you didn't do anything."

"Promise, Maddie. Nothing's certain, it can go either way whether we get away or not. You stay away, please, I ask it."

"I promise," she said, and cried. A guard came to take her away but she wouldn't go. He lifted her away like a child and she looked back at me all the way. They were taking the other women out, too. One of the guards came for Annie, she was the last, and she hadn't made a sound yet, but when they touched her on the shoulder she crumpled to the floor, sobbing, and put her hands through the bars, holding on to Jake's legs. They carried her out. She was crying like the man who'd killed his wife, and didn't see me when her face was turned in my direction and looking at me.

"How's it going?" Jake said.

"I don't know. My throat's all tight. I got the jitters. I don't know if I'll be much use when it comes time."

"That's all right. Wait for me. Take it easy all the way till I give the sign. Then give it everything you've got for as long as you can. If it don't work out make sure they have to beat the life out of you to stop you getting away. It's better than letting them get us there."

Homer came back and asked Jake if there was anything he wanted done for Annie.

"I say it just in case, because I am married and father and so on. You try to break, yes? There's ten of you, is a chance."

"Don't miss much, do you?"

"Just in case, I keep an eye on her if you want."

"Don't he have any kin?" Jake said, looking over at the religious nut. "Nobody say goodbye to him?"

"I ask him but he keep saying he is the son of God and nobody else."

"Lord, not even a friend. What happened to the man that killed his wife?"

"They take him out in the night."

"Is he being tried quick, like he wanted?" I said.

"No, he is transferred."

"He was arrested after us, wasn't he?"

Homer said yes. "They don't need a trial for that one, he has another knife on him."

"You let him keep a knife on him?" Jake said.

"I see he does not get too close, to me or to the others. He wants the knife, he can keep it."

Jake looked over his head and saw the last of the guards go out the door. The hammering outside had stopped and it was quiet.

"Homer," he said, suddenly, softly, "unlock it. Now."

He looked into Jake's face for a long while. I felt the sweat coming down in floods and thought it must be possible to hear my breathing clear across the floor to the street outside. Homer walked to the table and got his keys and started back to Jake's cell.

He had the key out in his hand when four soldiers and two of the guards walked in through the entranceway. The guards sat down at the table and one of the soldiers called Homer by name.

"Coming," he said. More came in and stood up against the bars of the empty cells.

"Is too late," he said, and whispered to Jake. Then he said, "I get you fresh water," and went to say something to the soldier, going out afterwards.

"What's happening?" I asked.

Jake said, "Shut up."

We waited. The numbers kept changing in the room. It began to get hot. Finally more were leaving than were coming in, and when Homer came back there were only three left, leaning up against the entranceway, and all the rest were out in the passage, talking.

He came over to us and handed Jake some water through the bars. Then he did the same for me, and I saw he was handing me something else, too: a knife. Then he reached inside his clothes and pulled out a fistful of what looked like leaves.

"No chains, no tying up, I don't think," he said. "But maybe you can't get your hands free. Take these, is for the pain, in case."

"What is that?" Jake said.

"I know a friend get it for me," Homer said, and left, to stop one of the guards who was about to walk over to us and say a word to him. Homer edged him back to the entrance and they talked there.

"What is that?"

"Looks like just leaves." I began to chew them up. All the time I'd thought: don't ever take that stuff, that's the poor man's grave, pretty soon you just live on dope and aren't even hungry any more. Besides, they say it does things to your head, even when you stop and get over the craving for it, you're never right in the head again. I always thought it wasn't worth the chance you took.

"What are you doing? Holy God, Seth, it's them African weeds. Don't take it. How much did he give you? It'll knock you right out."

"For the pain," I said, and kept chewing, and wiped the juice off my mouth.

"Are you crazy? Are you out of your mind? Don't take it, it'll kill you, all that amount." He turned around in his cell and slapped his hand against the wall.

When I'd chewed up all the leaves I expected something to happen right away.

"It's all right," I said, "I just feel sort of full and sleepy."

"You fool, you fool, you damn fool," he said. "I'll try my best. Homer says he'll help as much as he can. Hide the knife. If you get your hands free, use it. And if it looks like they've got us for keeps, use it on yourself. Remember."

"Sure," I said, "I'll remember. I feel fine, everything in working order."

He sort of laughed at me and put his hand up to his eyes. "Oh Seth, goddamn," he said, and turned away.

"What's the matter? I'm just fine."

He turned back again and I saw the shine of where tears had been in his eyesockets. I'd never seen him cry before in my life.

"What's wrong, Jake? I know what you're thinking. You're thinking you're going to have to leave me behind."

He didn't answer.

"Want to say goodbye now?"

"Not yet. Do you think you can fight?"

"I don't rightly know. I suppose, when time comes. But I feel fine. I'm not scared any more."

Homer came in and three of the military with him, with an officer in charge. "Those first," the officer said, and Homer unlocked the big cell on the right, opened the door, and stood back beside it. The two soldiers moved the men out of the cell and more guards came in to hustle them along. One of the men didn't want to leave and sat down on the floor, holding on to the bars. After they'd taken them all out Homer shut the door.

"Not yet," the officer said.

Two more soldiers and two guards came in. Homer told one of the guards to be ready to take over, that he was going as an escort. Then we waited. The guard Homer had spoken to went out and another one came in to take his place.

"I don't think those leaves are all they're made out to be," I said. "Hey, Jake, I said I don't think—"

"I heard you. Take it easy."

We waited some more and then Homer unlocked the cell where the religious nut was. The two guards led him out and he walked quietly enough to the entrance and out. Then he came running in again, with both men holding on to him and his feet sticking out in all directions, it looked like, as they pulled him back and out. He was shouting, "Pharisees, blasphemers!"

There was a lot of noise coming from the passageway, it sounded like there must be about thirty or forty people standing out there, and they laughed as the religious nut was taken through. Then it was our turn. Two soldiers and the officer walked in front and on the sides and Homer and another guard took up the rear. I'd forgotten what the passage looked like, I hadn't noticed much when they'd brought me in. It was lined with soldiers from end to end. As we passed through, Homer handed his keys to the guard he'd spoken to.

We came to the door and stepped out, and I stood stock still, blinded by the sun. I thought we must have been wrong about the time; it felt more like midday than morning. But I couldn't be sure, couldn't be sure about what time it was or what day. It felt like a day that wasn't spaced like others, a day that was running like a river and would always be the same wherever you were set down in it, and might go on forever. The other guard jabbed me in the back. "All right," I said, and moved forward, but I was feeling strange, very good but strange, like I was another height of myself above where my feet were going.

We walked down the street and there didn't seem to be too many people around. Some stopped when they saw us and others just looked and kept on walking. Then we came to a knot of people who were shouting things; there were soldiers standing around, and in the middle was the religious nut, bending down, and I thought: they're beating him up and he doesn't know what's happening, I feel sorry for him. But then I caught a look at his face as we passed by. He had on that secret, smug, mealy-mouth look and I realized he was enjoying whatever it was, being in the middle of a fuss.

I noticed that all the sound had blocked out of my ears. It was very strange. My feet kept walking and I could feel Jake very tense beside me. I said, "Jake, you know, the sound's just gone," and I couldn't hear myself say it but I thought it must be coming out slowly and not all formed. He touched my arm, and that was strange, too. It felt like I didn't have skin any more but something else that felt all different. I said, carefully, "I think those leaves are beginning to do something."

Up ahead the seven men and their guard branched off down a street and started to head in the opposite direction from us. We went around a corner. There were more people now, filling up the side of the street and blocking the corners, looking as though they'd been expecting us. I looked behind and saw the guards and soldiers with the religious nut, following along behind. Then I saw somebody throw something but still I couldn't hear. More people began to file into the street till it was like walking between walls of them and I could see their mouths opening and their faces having expressions and their hands moving, shaking fists and cupping around their mouths. Then something else started, like I was going away and coming back again, seeing everything far and small and taking place from below.

And then it happened, suddenly. Like a wall breaking through, it happened far and then it happened near, as if it was all going on inside of me, and the sound came back, loud, people screaming and shouting and calling names and everything near, near. Whatever that stuff was, it hit me all at once, like nothing in this world, making me ten times bigger, lifting me right off the ground so I knew I could do anything, anything at all, I could jump over houses, I could fly. And I shouted.

"Now, Seth, now!" Jake yelled. Homer fell down, taking a soldier and the other guard with him, and I began to fight like it says in the stories when they slew ten thousand, hitting everything. People were yelling, "Get him," and a woman spit in my face and I saw Jake lifted like a swimmer coming up for air and lashing around him, and Annie hitting the officer with a stick and a piece of his tooth fly out, separate, into the air. I was down and being kicked and had dirt in my mouth. Jake called out, "Run, Seth, run, run," and I was up again, running into the crowd. And all at once Maddie was there. I called to her, "Maddie, Maddie," and had my arms out and she pulled me into the crowd, her breast coming into the crook of my arm, lovely and frightening to feel, like when we danced at the wedding. "Seth!" she shouted and they dragged at me from behind and tore me away. I saw the knife fall and took it up quick and hit everything, everybody, it was happening so near and so strong inside, burning and huge, and lifted me away with it, slashing, seeing the red come out. I fell again and I saw Annie, and two of them hitting her, and Jake on the ground with the others pulling him back and beating him on the face, and saw blood from his mouth and nose, and the religious nut screamed and screamed somewhere but I couldn't see him. All of them came down on me all of a heap and dragged me along, about five of them hanging on. Jake was saying, "The hell I will, the hell, lift it yourself you bastard, you son of a bitch." And then I thought how funny it was, how they were going to kill us and Jake had said don't take it, it'll kill you. I started to laugh. They punched me around the head and I still couldn't stop. My knees went under and I sat down in the dust and laughed and laughed. They got me on my feet and I went down again, and then up, laughing, and they had to carry me with my arms all limp, and laughing. Because it was coming from the center and blooming out, enormous all the way through the world, making my arms and legs all laughing too, like my face.

After that I didn't mind, about anything. I thought I had blood on my face but I didn't feel the hurt, and we went forward, the crowd shifting place and changing size, and I'd stopped laughing but I was happy, happier than I knew it was possible, and liking the noise and thinking what a fool I was never to take that stuff before, because I didn't know there were such things in the world and how it makes you feel, so fiercely happy. The procession went on, seeming happy and joyous, as if we were going to some wonderful thing, and all of it more beautiful and exciting than anything else that had ever happened or anything to come after it in the whole history of time. The people and the noise bright and singing and lovely, and strangely wonderful. I could see the sound, real, and I could hear the shape of the people and what the colors did, the inside of me out and free and the outside beautiful and changed, like being a god, and felt good and thought I never knew what it meant before.

Then I was standing and I saw Jake's face altered and large, far away and then near, and the sun and the sky, and a soldier near me.

"There," he said. A lot of people came up close and the military pulled me down to the ground and then everything stood still and at peace. I looked up and saw a soldier's face, I saw the sun on his cheekbone and his eye, spoked with light, perfect and close. I saw him take his arm against the sky and then there was a scream, and I knew it must have come from me though I didn't feel the hurt. But I looked at my hand and there was blood. I heard praying, and I thought it wouldn't be so bad after all.

The holes were there and the stones and they got the ropes on. I started to go up.

"Clear the area," the officer called. "Clear the area."

I went up and I went up and then I fell, all at once I fell.

And it began.

You always think it can't go on, it's got to have an end. And

I thought maybe I shouldn't have taken those leaves because they say that's what's wrong with it: it lifts you up but it drops you down afterwards lower than you were before. I wondered if that could be why and that was why it was hurting so much. I thought: could it go on like this to the end, never getting less but always more and more? Jake was there and the religious nut, and Jake called, "Goodbye, Seth," and I shouted, "Goodbye, Jake." Then he called to the religious nut, saying, "Goodbye, put in a good word for us when you get there," but he didn't answer.

They say it usually takes three hours. To me it seemed to be more like three days. I passed out and I came back again and I imagined I saw the light go and the stars come out white, very bright and pure. And I could hear my breathing, loud, reaching, as if I was trying to swallow all the cool darkness and its many stars which make you feel so strange and yearning to see, all of them so small and so many and not touching but looking as if there's a life there and a special thought in the way they are spread, specially right and like it could be no other way. It seemed to me I saw the dawn and that I was stiff as though I'd been sleeping in the dew, and that I was wet from making water in the night but hadn't known when it happened and couldn't believe I'd slept, because of the pain.

That was growing more. You hear, they always say, nobody can hurt you that much because when the pain is too sharp your body protects you and makes you numb against it so that the bad part only lasts a short while and after that you know you are over it and it can never be so bad again.

But this was more. I lost the feeling in my arms. Not numb. They had a different feeling now. A no-feeling. And the no-feeling hurt like they say of people who lose an arm or a leg: they will complain of terrible pain in the limb that is no longer there. I thought now, yes, it's happening, and this no-person is coming over me, starting at the edges, and I can feel him coming more and more, closer to the center of me where I still know who I am.

I remember the sun and what it did. Sometimes there were tears on my face, I think, and sweat all the time, and I was half blinded, trying not to look but wanting to now and then to make sure I could still see. Drying up, my eyes were drying up and no place to turn my head. Once there was a vulture moving slow in the air above me and I thought: not my eyes, not my eyes. And I shut them though it would have been no use. There is always something to lose, something that can be taken from you. Even at the end you don't think this is going on forever; nothing else does, so this has to stop too, you think, and at the end I'll be well again. Even when you know.

Three days and two nights I thought it lasted. Pulling and pulling. And a wind roaring in my ears. Not the sound of the crowd—that's my blood going by, like you can hear it jumping in your ear when you lay down your head to sleep.

I tried to moan then, but my voice was taken in my breathing, stretching for the sky with my mouth open and all dry down to my throat and beyond, drying up and burning out like grass on the hillsides in high summer when the sun stands hard above and kills the green out of them. First they go brown and then like ashes, grey. And lastly they are bone white, skeletons that were once gardens, and the dust blows from them.

I tried to look, to see Jake, but it was like looking into a wall of brass. My eyes opening, heavy and swelled, the glare striking deep into them, and closing up again slowly and not able to shut tight. I thought: it's too late now, I can't call, and it's too hard to look, eyes turning to leather and the no-person weighing down on me, blood falling through my ears.

I thought I heard the other one, the religious maniac, screeching high and thin into the air. And then I heard him clearly.

He was starting to pray again, quoting that psalm, saying, "My God, my God, why hast thou forsaken me, why art thou so far from helping me and from the words of my roaring?" And I heard Jake, from where he was, cough. And then I tried, my eyes wincing back from the light, to look, and I saw Jake heave himself and yell, all strangely misshaped like he was singing, "God almighty, why can't you pull yourself together and take it like a man?" And I blacked out again, not knowing whether he'd meant it for himself or for the other one.

When I came to, I thought it must be either dawn or sunset, the air still and calm, and I could open my eyes on it and see.

There was a terrible sound coming from somewhere. And then I placed it: the sound I was making in trying to breathe.

The things I knew now, it would almost have been worth it to find them out: how important it is to breathe. You gulp in the air, you fight for it and try to hold on to it and there is no holding.

Strong in the chest, that made me need food. But I knew now, all the things you need in life have to be stolen from somewhere, from the earth or from other people—food, water, warmth, you need them to live. But they can be taken from you. And you can live for a while and can come back to health after you have had fire and food and water taken from you. But the air—take away all the air just for a few moments and life is over. It is death to take that away, because it is free and freely there, the only thing in the world that is truly free. And you live on it as much as you live on food, but do not realize.

I thought I would look down for the last time. But something had happened to my neck and my head; I thought somebody must be holding me and pressing something against me there. I tried to move, and my face was like stone, and all the parts that could make it turn, like iron. I tried and I forced. And I tried it until it worked, stone coming into motion, iron bending, my head sideways, and I could look down.

I saw the hills and the trees and the city beyond, and below me some of the crowd still huddled behind the guards and some looking up, I thought. A shine came off something, a weapon or a helmet, and as I looked to see what it was, a breeze lifted the corner of a soldier's cloak and threw it back over his shoulder, showing the scarlet suddenly like a bird turning wing. I thought: quickly, turn your head back, quickly, or it will stay like this and you won't be able to look up again.

This time it was harder and took much longer. When I had my head up again my eyes were on the religious nut. He was dead by the look of him, and he looked at peace and beyond the moving of any pain. He looked somehow better that way, stretched out, better than he'd looked when he was alive. Being all skin and bones, he seemed to look right there, as though he'd meant to be there all the time and his body had fulfilled itself in the shape it took when he died.

Then I looked at Jake, and a smarting came into my eyes, needing tears. He was dead, you could tell, but not like the other one. You saw the agony of it on him, all of him, the strong body and the open-mouthed face, swollen, wrenched, disfigured with pain. And looking desecrated, shameful to look at, like butchers' meat if they did that to men. I wanted to cry aloud to him, and saw him like it was my own soul I was looking at but more than my soul. And wanted to call to him though he could not hear, hanging as he was bloody-armed from the cross and dead as the other one against the other cross that stood between us on the hill.

I was the last. And this is the last thing, I thought, the last I'll ever see.

I was looking at the sky. I saw it and I knew it as no man ever saw it before, looking into the heart of it, as no other man will ever know it.

I'd never noticed before just how it is, how it is a face that looks back and looks with love, and is arms that open for you. How sweet and calm it is. How blue. How it is lovely beyond belief and goes flying away into farther than can be known. And it goes on like that, on and on. Forever and ever. Without end.

Inheritance

When Carla's marriage broke up, everyone from her father's branch of the family felt obliged to load her with so much pity and advice that she didn't think she'd be able to last out the summer with them. Sometimes their kindness made her feel even worse: her Aunt Grace, for instance, had laid a hand on her arm and told her not to mind: time would heal the wound, and besides, think of how much worse it could have been – she might have had children.

When her grandmother died, that put the lid on it. She'd loved her grandmother. They'd always been able to talk together, rattling along like schoolfriends. In the last months of her life, her grandmother had done several things that other people considered eccentric, or even crazy. Carla knew better, because the old woman had explained to her beforehand: she'd said, 'It may not come now, but if it does, I want to be prepared. I don't like leaving things in a mess. And legal formalities can be intimidating to simple people – to the kind of people who live around here.' She was referring to old acquaintances; they included the cook, maid and handyman who had worked in and around the house over the past fifty years. She'd left most of them something in her will, but in addition she wanted them to have mementoes that wouldn't be taxable to the estate or come to them through the lawyers. She spent a lot of time on the phone, arranging for certain items of furniture to be collected and driven to the houses of friends. She sent cash through the mail – something everyone, even people not related to her, knew was crazy – and had it arrive safely.

Finally, one day, she asked Carla to get all the jewellers' boxes and silk pouches out of the safe. And she'd proceeded to put on every necklace, bracelet, pin and ring that she owned.

'Which ones do you like best?' she'd asked.

'The lizard pin,' Carla had said, 'and the gold link bracelet, and the ring with the tiny rubies – that's always been my favourite.'

'It's not valuable. Very ordinary stones.'

'I love it.'

Her grandmother had put the brooch and bracelet into her hand and slid the ring on to her finger – the same finger on which Carla had worn her wedding ring.

'And it fits,' Carla had said.

'Stop Minnie from being so scandalized. If you don't want to wear your wedding ring any longer, there's no reason why you should.'

'I wouldn't want to. But even if I did, I couldn't. It broke. It broke in pieces on the day he walked out. I just put my hand up on the edge of the sink when I was reaching down to get my heavy frying pan out of the cupboard, just as usual, and the ring fell into separate pieces. There must have been a fault in the metal. It upset me so much – more than almost anything else. The exact same day: can you imagine? It's enough to make you believe – I don't know.'

'Yes, there's no doubt these things happen. Nobody can explain them. I remember when Father was in the hospital; we were sitting together, waiting for news, and all at once there was a loud crash from the library: his portrait had fallen off the wall. Maybe you've guessed – we had the news shortly afterwards that he'd died, and it must have been at that very moment.' She picked out several other small pieces of jewellery to present to Carla. 'Promise me', she said, 'you'll wear them or you'll give them away to somebody else who'll wear them. What I don't want you to do is to put everything in a drawer somewhere and save it. It's the same with life, the same with love. You've got to use it, enjoy it – be happy with it. And if you lose it, so be it: never mind.'

'Oh, I'll wear them,' Carla promised.

'It took me a long time to learn that,' her grandmother added. 'It was a conclusion I came to really rather late.'

They got into the old Plymouth – the only car her grandmother still trusted – and Carla drove from one house to another. She'd stop the car, help the old woman out and then stand aside as the friend, ex-servant or acquaintance was asked, 'Which one do you like best?' As soon as the object had been handed over, her grandmother said that she had several calls to make and had to be going. Carla noticed that a nice etiquette was observed: towards the end of the day, the recipients were not asked to choose. Her grandmother would simply pluck some jewel from its place and say, 'I wanted you to have this.'

A few weeks later, she died. No pictures fell from the wall, nor were there other portents. Carla was desolate. The aunts and uncles started to divide up the furniture. She received instructions from her cousins about how to hang on to their share, too. Her father flew in for the funeral, but his wife didn't bother to attend. He looked and obviously felt uncomfortable, trying to give correct formal expression to feelings he hadn't possessed.

Carla felt sorry for him. They went for a walk through the woods on the trail starting from where the old stables had been. He asked her about her plans for the future.

'Go back to my job, I guess. I don't want to. I don't want to be in the same town with him. I'd like to make a complete break with everything, just go away somewhere. I really would.'

'You could come stay with us,' he told her. She was touched.

'In a year, maybe,' she said. 'I'd love to. I'll have to get things organized, think about money.'

'Oh, I'm sure we could get you the ticket. And Marsha would love it.'

Marsha wouldn't love it; she'd hate every minute, but she'd have to lump it. For a moment Carla thought she might take up the offer. She liked the idea, she said, but she wanted to wait a while.

Her grandmother had left her some money and a few stocks and shares, which she could either save or use immediately. If she dropped everything and just went wandering around the world, she could probably last for three years. And in the meantime, the business she'd built up over the past five years would fall apart.

She was a designer. She'd started out with the idea that she'd go into textiles and end up with her own range of fabrics and clothes. But she hadn't been able to fight her way into the profession. She'd done a few magazine ads and cartoons for the newspapers, and got her first good assignment through a friend: illustrating birthday cards. That had led to the Kassels, who ran a toyshop that stocked the cards. From her first week with them she was designing the toys and overseeing their manufacture, and getting the coffee and sandwiches ready in the back room while first Mrs Kassel and then Mr Kassel came to her for advice: crying, telling her that the family was breaking up and their lives were over and why hadn't they had a daughter like her. The business was booming, thanks to Carla – or, rather, thanks to her work and the Kassels' ability to push it towards customers with all the enthusiasm they felt for it; she could never have done that by herself. The business continued to prosper while the family did in fact split and Carla had to take sides. And her husband began to feel that she wasn't paying enough attention to him. It was still doing all right when she set up on her own and it was her turn to cry all over both the Kassels about her husband.

And now her own business was a success, expanding all the time. She could send in work while someone else held the fort for her. But not for three years. Three months, maybe. She thought hard about where she could go for three months only.

And suddenly she remembered the other side of the family: her mother's side. There was a little gang of great-aunts still living up in what had been her mother's home town. They'd all be pretty old now. She thought she ought to see them.

She told her father the next morning, the day of his flight out, that she'd decided to use the next couple of months looking up her mother's relatives. 'I've forgotten the name of the town they live in, though.'

He told her the name and wrote it down. He even remembered the right street. 'They're rather strange people,' he warned her. 'I thought so when I met them. Half of them can't even speak English.'

'That's all right. And maybe we won't like each other, but I just feel that we should try; that I ought to get to know them before it's too late.' She didn't say that – beginning with the break-up of her parents' marriage – she had started to fear the weakening of any family ties. Her fear might even have contributed to the ending of her own marriage. Families should stick together, she believed.

When she left her grandmother's house, the others were already busy with their own affairs and hardly noticed her departure. Two of her aunts had stopped speaking to each other because of what her father referred to as a 'misunderstanding'. But there had been no failure to understand. The two women both wanted the same thing, that was all: they were fighting over who was to get the Chinese jade buffalo. Carla was glad that her grandmother had given her the special pieces of jewellery outright, with her own hands, on that day of presentations. Twice during the plane flight up north she stopped reading her book, held her hand up and turned it to the side so that the light from the small airplane window shone over the bracelet and ring. She could remember them both from all the way back to the beginning of her childhood.

*

The part of town where her great-aunts lived was a place of broad avenues, green lawns and big trees. The houses too were very large and decorated with bannistered porches, balconies and verandahs. The district definitely didn't look like one where you'd find people who, as her father had told her, could barely speak English. Nor had the letter she'd received read like the work of an illiterate. On the contrary, the language had been precise – in fact, almost stilted, although grammatically faultless.

She lost her way among the peculiar numbering systems of the neighbourhood. As she was beginning to feel tired enough to risk the embarrassment of ringing a doorbell and asking for directions, she saw a mailman turn the corner and come towards her. He was a grey-haired man who looked as if he'd had the job for many years and knew all about the city. When she asked him, indicating her useless map, he said, 'Oh, the Countess. Sure.'

'Countess?'

'That's what she calls herself.'

There was no way of telling if the man thought her great-aunt was pretentious, silly, or actually out of her mind. He told Carla that she'd missed one of the turns and was in exactly the right spot on a parallel street.

'Just one block away,' he said, pointing. Then it was easy. She was held up only a few more minutes, and that was because she couldn't believe that the house with the number was the one she was looking for; it was about the size of a nice old country hotel.

She walked down the path, up the stairs to the porch, and rang the bell. The front door stood open, only the screen door was shut. Through it she could see a hallway, a table with flowers, the foot of a magnificent stairway; and an old woman tottering towards her, a uniformed maid at her elbow. The maid reached the screen door first and opened it. Carla stepped forward.

The old woman held out her arms. 'At last,' she crooned. 'My dear little Carla. Oh, what a joy – oh, if only your mother were alive at this moment.'

Carla allowed herself to be embraced, and she kissed the great-aunt on both cheeks. She also realized that she'd been led astray by what could genuinely have been described as a misunderstanding: there was nothing wrong with her aunt's education or upbringing – it was just that she spoke a different language. She was speaking German.

'Well,' the aunt said. 'Yes, lovely. Did your mother bring you up to understand German?'

Carla said, 'No, she wasn't – I was with my grandparents most of the time.'

'Of course,' the old woman said, switching to English. 'We tried to make them allow you to stay up here with us. But they wouldn't.'

'I learned French and German in high school.'

'Yes?'

'And I kept it up in college when I was bumming around Europe in the summer—'

The old woman lapsed into German again, asking questions.

'But I've forgotten a lot,' Carla went on. 'And I'm pretty slow. I was always stumbling around, even at my best. My accent was OK, but I never got the genders right. And that stuff about matching up the adjectives in the dative – well, I sort of skipped that side of it.'

'We'll have to do something about that. But not today – no, there's no need to be nervous. Now, where is your suitcase?'

'At the motel.'

'We'll have it brought. You'll stay here, naturally. I'm your Aunt Gisela, by the way.'

'You wrote the letter.'

'I wrote it. The others didn't want to answer. Ridiculous. Come in here and we'll have some coffee and I'll tell you about it.' She led Carla through a wide hallway, across oriental rugs, past furniture polished until it shimmered. In a far corner of the room where they sat down a grand piano gleamed as if made of patent leather.

The maid reappeared without having been summoned.

'Bring us some coffee, Agnes,' Aunt Gisela said. 'And the usual . . . sandwiches and cakes.'

'Crackers?'

'Cupcakes. *Kuchen.*' When Agnes had gone, she said, 'That's the one I still mix up. And she gets so angry if I want to send them back to the kitchen.'

'This is a wonderful house,' Carla said.

'Quite nice, yes. We had better in Germany. We had palaces.'

'Really?'

'Didn't your mother tell you anything?'

'I was only ten when she died. I can't remember that she ever talked about her family at all, not once.'

Aunt Gisela sat forward in her chair. She told Carla that she had come from an ancient, important and persecuted aristocratic family and that quite aside from the significance of being heir to a rich cultural heritage, there was the question of the actual property. Some of the buildings and estates were unavailable at the moment: they lay in Poland, East Germany and Lithuania. But there were others.

'One doesn't want things to go out of the family,' she said. 'Of course, it's important to have museums, but it's better that all those objects should be in daily use.'

Carla shifted her attention as Agnes brought the coffee. Her aunt said, 'Would you mind pouring? My hand is still steady, but sometimes I pour a perfect cup just half an inch beyond where it should be. All over the table, over the floor.'

Carla poured out the coffee and busied herself with the plates. She said, 'My other great-aunts—'

'Gerda and Ursula. You'll have to discount everything they say. They're old-fashioned and absurd. There are so few young ones in the great families nowadays. We have to forgive and forget.'

'That's what I think,' Carla said. 'Especially now. I wrote you: my grandmother just died. I think we should get together and be friends while we can. When people die, it's too late. But I wouldn't want to stay here in the house if they don't want me.'

'You are my guest,' Gisela said. In four bites she made a neat meal of one of the small iced cupcakes. She lifted her hand to the plate again. Her movements were exceptionally light and quick for a woman of her age. And she was extraordinarily thin for someone who was in the habit of gobbling cakes. Carla herself stopped at one and refused a second sandwich. She gave her attention to the family history: where they had all lived, how many houses and castles they'd owned, how many wars they'd been through.

'There aren't many of us left,' Aunt Gisela said. She raised her coffee cup and added, 'As you say: we can't afford to keep up family quarrels.'

Carla smiled, but she suddenly felt less welcome. She was glad that for the first night at least she'd be in the motel.

After their coffee, she was shown around the gardens at the other side of the house. They were bordered by four noble trees and were full of flowerbeds. The beds were laid out in an orderly way that made the whole of the back yard appear clean and regimented.

'This must take a lot of work,' Carla commented.

Her aunt nodded and said complacently, yes.

A little later, as the afternoon light was beginning to soften, she met the other two aunts: Gerda and Ursula. Ursula was tall, thin, dignified and not very talkative. Gerda was bunchily plump, had scanty brown hair, and stared at Carla, leaning close; in both of her eyes the iris was ringed in white. Carla wasn't sure what that meant, other than that it was something you often noticed in old people's eyes. It might just be a sign of age, not of disease or partial blindness.

'I see you're wearing the lizard pin,' Gerda said. Her eyesight was good enough for that, at least.

'My grandmother's.'

'I know. I remember. I have a photographic memory for jewels. If we'd been the right age, or from the kind of family that went into trade, I should have been connected with a jewellery business. Yes, definitely – I have a feeling for it, despite the unfortunate family failing. You too? You find yourself drawn to shiny objects and colour?'

'Not specially. I just have this strong sentimental attachment for the things I saw my grandmother wearing when I was a little girl.'

They sat down on the side of the room near the piano. Ursula began to play. She took every piece very slowly. Carla was invited to replace her at the keyboard; she had to explain that she'd never learned more than a few short works, had been bored by her music teacher, still couldn't read the bottom clef, and had begged to give up after a year.

'How you must regret it now,' Gisela said.

'Not at all. It was completely wasted time. I never had any talent for playing. I like listening.'

'One wouldn't expect you to be a Paderewski, dear. It's simply a necessary accomplishment.'

'I don't', Carla said, 'find it necessary.'

'Ah,' Gisela murmured.

Disapproval seemed to radiate towards her from all three women. She wanted to get up and go back to her motel and rest for a couple of hours. She'd almost reached the end of her time-limit for chat with strangers. Having to do part of it in German was an added strain. 'What's the family failing?' she asked.

'We're pearlkillers,' Gerda said.

'What's that?'

'Did you know that there were such people?'

'No.' She still had no idea what the phrase meant, either in English or in German.

'That's right,' Gisela said. 'It's true. Something to do with the chemicals in the skin.'

'Oh?'

'But I don't think little Carla is interested in hearing about that kind of thing.'

'Well, she should be,' Gerda said. 'It's a family characteristic. Did your grandmother ever wear pearls, Carla?'

'Yes, she had a long rope with knots between the pearls in case the string broke. She wore them all the time. One of my aunts has them now.'

'She wore them all the time because you have to. Pearls need to be kept in touch with the oils of the skin in order to retain their lustre. They can dry out if you keep them in a box.'

'There are some people', Gisela said, 'who have a theory that you should also wear them when you swim in the ocean – to return them to their home – but I can't believe the salt would be good for them.'

'Most of the ladies we used to know', Gerda continued, 'had pearls. And when they weren't wearing them, they made the maids wear them, to keep the pearls healthy. The younger the skin, the better it was supposed to be. But there are some people whose skin produces a chemical harmful to pearls – if they wear a ring for a while, suddenly they'll notice that the pearls have shrunk and almost withered back into the setting.'

'Pearlkillers,' Gisela said. 'Our whole family. You may be one, too. We had an aunt who didn't develop the symptoms till late in life; then she let one of the maids wear her pearls while she tried to find a buyer for them, and – guess what? The maid turned out to be a pearlkiller, too. We thought that was extremely funny.'

'And very suspicious,' Gerda added. 'Sometimes servants acquire the family traits out of affectation or a desire to emulate. But to be a pearlkiller presupposes an inherited tendency. Doesn't it?'

'I don't know,' Carla said. 'She might have had a family with the same kind of thing.'

'Servants don't have families. They're parasitic in that respect. They want the family they're working for. They love them and they hate and envy them. It's like biographers and the famous. What I could tell you about servants.'

'Has Agnes been with you long?'

'Agnes. That slut. A real camel.'

Gisela said quietly, 'We've had a certain amount of trouble with Agnes.'

'Oh?'

'She's been going out with some much younger man,' Gerda said. 'A fortune-hunter. He thinks we'd leave her our money. As if we would.'

'He must be half her age,' Gisela said. 'There can't be anything in it.'

'Don't deceive yourself. Agnes does it with anyone. She drinks like a fish, and then she doesn't care who it is. Yes, it's true. She goes to bars and picks up men and they go somewhere together. Some hotel that specializes in that kind of thing, I suppose.'

'We have no way of knowing that,' Gisela told her.

'Some of these old families, you know,' Gerda muttered; 'the servants even look a lot like the masters.'

'That could be psychological,' Carla said. 'Or psychosomatic.'

'Yes. There's also a word for family relationships that become substitutional.'

'What?' Gisela said.

'Subst—'

'Yes, I heard it. I just don't know what it means.'

'Ah. Let's say: the brother in a family commits a crime. He'd be punished, but then so would the other members – his parents and sister, and so on. They wouldn't be precisely what you could call guilty, but they'd be associated by virtue of their kinship. There would be a group liability. In German that would be called *Sippenhaft*. You understand?'

Carla said, 'Sure – it's so they won't be able to take revenge for the brother being punished.'

'I assume that's what's behind it.'

'Primitive.'

'And effective,' Gerda said. 'The cruel methods primitive peoples have of dealing with disease – they prevent it from spreading. There are other plagues, too, and epidemics. There are evil ideas, for instance.'

Carla sighed. The muscles in her neck and shoulders ached from having to sit at attention. She thought of saying that the methods of primitive peoples hadn't saved them from being wiped out by measles and the common cold; but that would simply lead Aunt Gerda to some new topic. Did they always talk like that – jumping all over the place and never letting up? Or was it just because she was a new face? She said, 'You know, I think I'd like to go back to the motel to rest for a little. I'm kind of tired out from the trip.'

'Oh, you can't go till after supper,' Gisela pleaded.

'Let her go,' Gerda said.

At the piano Ursula stopped playing. She lifted both hands from the keyboard in a concert-hall flourish. She looked at Carla. 'Your mother', she told her, 'betrayed her family.'

'She married an outsider, that's all.'

'We always marry Germans.'

'Or if you don't, you don't get married?'

'That's right. It's better than ending the way she did.'

Carla stood up. Gisela, slowly, tried to follow; she scolded Ursula for her tactlessness.

Carla moved quickly from the room. Behind her she heard the piano starting again. Ahead of her Agnes – large-nosed, thin-lipped, with her hair scraped into a bun and a smirk on her face – reached for the screen door.

'Carla dear, please wait,' Gisela begged.

As the old woman came wheezing up to her, Carla turned and held out her hands. 'Aunt Gisela, it's been really nice meeting you,' she said, 'but not the others.'

'They don't understand. They don't see anybody all year long. They forget how to behave. I'm the one who deals with everything. They haven't been out of the house and garden for over twenty years. I think your mother's engagement party was the last time they went out. And that was only to make a big scene and say they wouldn't come to the wedding. You have to understand. They're old.'

'Were they wonderful and kind when they were younger?'

'Well, I suppose they've always been difficult.'

'I'll see you tomorrow,' Carla said.

'Yes, please. Please, Carla. I want to ask a great favour of you. There's something I want you to get for us. My cousin, Theo, took it. It didn't belong to him – it belongs to us. You will promise, won't you?'

'I'll come see you tomorrow,' she said. 'I've got to go now.' Agnes swung the door ahead of her.

She ran down the steps and away.

She lay on the bed in her motel room and wondered if she'd have the nerve to pack up and just get out in the morning, leaving one of those messages that said, 'Called away suddenly'. But that was what other people had done to her all her life; she couldn't be the one to do it to someone else. She especially shouldn't do it to Aunt Gisela, who didn't deserve to be treated like that. Aunt Gerda would be a different matter. And the other one, Ursula: sane but nasty.

She also wished that she had a very large drink. She should have bought a bottle someplace. She wasn't the kind of woman who went into bars on her own. She didn't really want to go swimming alone in the motel pool, either, but if she just stayed sitting in her room, she might start thinking about her ex-husband again. She might even imagine how her divorced mother had felt after she'd left her child with its grandparents. Her mother had checked into a motel room – maybe a room very similar to that one: and had ended up cutting her wrists.

The view from the windows showed a parking lot and beyond it the old jetties. Across the river stood abandoned brick warehouses and behind them, pine trees. The sky was a firm, northern blue, only just beginning to darken. Even in her aunts' neighbourhood, among the large houses and plush green lawns, the sky had that look. It reminded you that nearby were the lakes as big as seas, and the unbroken miles of evergreen forest that used to be the country of the Indians.

Her telephone rang. When she picked it up a man's voice told her that he'd had a call from her great-aunt Gisela and he'd like to talk to her for a few minutes, in person, if she didn't mind. His name was Carl Raymond.

'That sounds like two people,' she said.

'What?'

'When did you want to meet?'

'I kind of thought right now. I could take you out for supper and we could talk. My uncle George is your aunts' accountant.'

'Oh,' she said. The information meant nothing, if true, but it persuaded her.

She took a shower and changed into a dress that was still slightly wrinkled over the skirt.

He was waiting at the reception desk. He'd been gossiping and joking with the clerk, who said to her, 'I didn't know you were a friend of Carl here, Miss.'

'We've never met,' she said. She put the key down on the counter and held out her hand; Carl shook it. He said he was glad to meet her: they had a lot to talk about. 'First of all, some food.'

'What's wrong with here?' the clerk asked.

'Go on,' Carl said. He took her by the elbow and led her out to a car. He told her, 'It's a long story, and I've just come off work. I'm going to need a drink before I can get it straightened out.'

'That's fine by me,' she said. She began to perk up. Always, she thought, just when she was ready to throw in the towel, something nice turned up. And she still hadn't learned that it always would: the pleasant and unpleasant ran in tandem. But whenever she began to feel dejected, she forgot: the bad times seemed to be going on for ever. Maybe it was possible that she'd inherited the predilection from her mother.

He parked the car and took her in to the kind of bar and grill that made the customers put on ties. The lighting was subdued enough to hide her badly-ironed skirt.

They each had two drinks. She got a good look at him while he was ordering the meal: he was tall and well-built, about her own age and had a squarish head, pale blue eyes, a strong-featured face, small regular teeth. His hair was straight and light, clipped short – almost like a crew cut, which made his ears appear to stick out a little. Most people would have considered him a good-looking man. She thought he was all right: nice but rather uninteresting. She'd grown too used to her husband's dark, frizzy-haired, ugly-romantic looks.

'Carl and Carla,' he said. 'That's sort of a coincidence, isn't it?'

'That's right. We sound like a comedy team.'

'Well, some kind of a team, anyway. I'll drink to that.'

'So you're an accountant?' she said.

'No, I'm in real estate. It's my uncle George who's their accountant. At least, he's still your aunt – your great-aunt – Gisela's, but there've been arguments with the other two. Maybe you didn't know it, but your aunts have a big reputation in this neck of the woods for—'

'Eccentricity?'

'And general cussedness. And when they don't have much to occupy their time with, they get on the phone and try to strike points against each other through a third person.'

'Uncle George.'

'And Uncle Bertram at the bank and my father, before he picked up and moved. He was in the same firm as one of their lawyers, Sandy Howe. Mr Howe used to say it was a lean week when one of them didn't want to change her will. Anyway, I guess they're an institution by now. Life wouldn't be so colourful without them. And they went through quite a lot during the war; during both wars, there was a lot of anti-German feeling.'

'But they've lived here for a hundred years.'

'They didn't mix. They wouldn't talk English. They wouldn't marry anybody who wasn't from a German background. My family was mostly German, too. A lot of this town was. But nobody else thinks of it that way. We're all American. Your aunts aren't. They never wanted to be. And they told everybody about their titles.'

'That wouldn't have made them disliked. That's something everybody laughs at. Even the mailmen.'

'It isn't democratic.'

'If it's true.'

'Oh, it's certainly true.'

'Really?'

'Without a doubt.' He began to tell her about the family's holdings in Eastern Europe.

Their food came and he continued to talk. She could see he was a man who could be driven to frenzy by the idea of large stretches of saleable land. She wondered if perhaps the three old women had decided to bamboozle him just for fun.

Over coffee he went on to tell her about the houses and estates they still had in countries that recognized their ownership. 'They're millionaires,' he said. 'Multi-millionaires.'

'Nice.'

'I just wanted you to know that if there's any difficulty about the estate, you could fight it.'

'What do you mean?'

'You're the heir, aren't you?'

'No.'

'Surely.'

'Not at all. They cut my mother right out of their lives when she married.'

'Your mother, but not you.'

'Me too, I'm sure. It's what they call *Sippenhaft.*'

'I think you're the heir. And if you weren't, you could claim it. You could certainly claim it against the parlourmaid.'

'Agnes? What's she got to do with it?'

'She's one of the ones who's put into the wills and taken out again every week. It's how they keep her there. They make a promise and then they fight and they break it, and so on.'

'What a life. How can she stand it?'

'Not much choice, I guess.'

'But how can she believe it? Obviously it's a game they play.'

'Nope. If they sign all the right stuff, it's real. It's binding. You could try to prove afterwards that the way they kept changing their minds was a sign of mental decay, and that they were being taken advantage of; but you'd have to fight it through the courts. You couldn't just throw it out.'

'Well, it's no stranger than anything else. I don't think it has anything to do with me. But thanks for the information.'

'Right,' he said. 'Just thought you ought to know.'

He took her back to the motel, walked her to her room, waited till she'd unlocked the door, and then pulled her back and kissed her on the mouth before saying goodnight. She went inside, shut the door and stayed looking at it. It was too short an acquaintance for him to be kissing her. And it was a long time since anything like it had happened to her.

As she was getting ready to go in to breakfast, her phone rang. Aunt Gisela was on the line. She sounded a lot more quavery than Carla remembered.

'Please, dear, I know it must have been upsetting yesterday, but I'm not feeling very well – I don't have the time to smooth things over the way I used to. Would you come over, please?'

'All right,' Carla said. 'After I've had my breakfast. But just you. Not the others.'

'They're very sorry.'

'I doubt it.'

'What's that?'

'I said I don't believe it. Ursula did the dirty work and Gerda thought it was a scream. They got a lot of pleasure out of hurting me. And I'm not letting myself in for a second dose.'

'Oh, no. I'm sure—'

'I mean it. If I see them, I'm walking out again. Agreed?'

'Yes, dear,' Aunt Gisela said.

Carla felt that she had taken action and made everything clear. Before the divorce she'd never spoken harshly or even decisively to anyone. She ate a large breakfast. Over her last cup of coffee she remembered that the evening before, she'd been ready to get out altogether. Now she really didn't know what she was going to do except that when Carl had kissed her at the door she'd been given the impression of having a lover again. She could even have asked him in. It all started so easily, she thought. Again. She'd been sure she never wanted anything else to happen ever again.

Aunt Gisela arrived panting in the front hall. She hadn't been quick enough for Agnes, who whipped the screen door open and afterwards deliberately slammed it so that it twanged like a harp.

'The humidity today,' the old woman said, her breath whiffling; 'or perhaps the pollen.' She drew Carla down a side corridor and into a pleasant study overlooking part of the garden.

'This used to be Albert's room,' she said. She waved her hand at a leather armchair large enough to have been the favourite reading-chair of a fairly big man. Carla sat down in it.

Gisela seated herself bolt upright in a straight-backed wooden chair. 'I must tell you some more about the family,' she said.

Carla leaned forward. Her aunt's narrative came out without pause, partly in English, partly in German, both broken by laboured breathing and a whistling from the lungs. Carla didn't dare interrupt. It seemed like the kind of speech people gave when about to be executed – it appeared to cover everything Gisela had ever thought or remembered about the family, and included statements to the effect that: they were all under a blight; they had done many great wrongs to several other large and important families hundreds of years ago; they had lost kingdoms, or places as good as kingdoms; they were of royal blood; some of the family, led by cousin Theo, had managed to swindle the others out of a very great deal of money and property and were living it up on their ranches in South America; Theo had absconded with something called 'Count Walter's Treasure', but it belonged to her – Gisela; he had ruined her when she was a girl and then laughed at her, and if there had been any consequences, she'd have had to – well, Carla knew what she'd have had to do. 'And now getting old,' she sighed. 'But if you get the Treasure back, Count Walter's, I'll be well again. And it's yours after me, you know. A part of your German inheritance.'

'I'll try,' Carla said. The old woman was in such distress that she'd have promised almost anything to calm her down.

'I'll pay all expenses, naturally. Carl is seeing about the tickets now. And he's agreed to chaperone you. It wouldn't be right for you to go alone.'

'Where?'

'He'll be in Germany at this season. Or possibly in one of his Italian villas.'

'But—'

'Then it's all arranged. I'm so glad.'

'Aunt Gisela, I don't understand.'

'Priceless. I'll be well again when you've got it.'

'I don't even have my passport with me.'

'You remember the number?'

'Yes.'

'Good. We'll be able to do something.'

'How? That kind of thing takes time. And doesn't Carl have a job someplace?'

'He's saved up a lot of vacation-time. You don't understand about Theo. Soon it's going to be too late. I'm too old now. We've got to have it.'

'Why?'

'If we die without the Treasure . . .'

'Yes?'

'I don't want to tell you.'

'When you say it's going to make you well: how's it going to do that?'

'By touch.'

'Is it a kind of relic or something?'

'Exactly. That's the word. Isn't it stupid – when I forget a word nowadays, I lose it from both languages. Occasionally I can get it again through the French or Italian. The mind is so weak, Carla. When you start wearing out.'

'And Carl would go, too?'

'He handles a lot of our business affairs now.'

'What happened to his father?'

'I believe they call it "mid-life crisis". He started to want young girls instead of his family.'

'Is Carl the only one?'

'There's another boy and a girl.'

'And their mother?'

'She's still here, complaining. You can see why he went. But she wasn't like that before he left. She's become a different person.'

Something made of metal clanked on to the floor just outside the door. It sounded like a bunch of keys. Aunt Gisela rose with an easy smoothness surprising in her condition. She opened the door.

Agnes stood outside, not looking in any way bothered; she said, 'Are you going to want lunch or what?'

'A light luncheon for two, Agnes. In here. And then you may leave us.'

'OK,' Agnes said. She slouched away.

Carla was on her feet, protesting that she had to go, she had to make phone calls about her business, she certainly couldn't spend more than a week on vacation.

Gisela over-ruled her. She said quietly, 'Yes, dear, yes,' patted her hand, smiled charmingly and added, 'but you know that I'm the one who really doesn't have time. I can see it running out as clearly as if it were sand in an hour-glass. Just this one thing for your old aunt, little Carla.'

The phone woke her up early. She'd swum back and forth in the motel pool for twenty minutes the evening before, had had a large drink with her salad-bar meal and slept like a log. They weren't supposed to give her a morning call; she had an alarm clock with her. It was still almost dark.

'Yes?' she said into the receiver.

'It's Carl. I've got some bad news.'

She thought something must have happened to Gisela – a stroke or collapse of some kind. Or, maybe after all the excitement of the day and the amount of talking she'd done, actually her death.

'Didn't you hear the sirens?' he asked.

'What?'

At some time around midnight, her aunts' large house had burst into flames. Carl had been wakened, since his family lived so near. Half the town had been there, and the whole of the fire department. The house had burned for hours. In fact, it was still on fire. And as far as anyone knew, there were no survivors. That meant her three aunts, a cook, two parlourmaids and Agnes, who – the police were assuming – had been the one who had started the blaze.

'Oh,' Carla said in the dark. 'Oh. I can't take it in.'

'Go back to sleep. I only called up because I didn't want you to hear through somebody else. My uncles are going to be handling most of the paperwork, I guess.'

'Shouldn't I go out there?'

'No. There's nothing you could do. There's just a big crowd of people watching the place burn to the ground. It's OK about the passport, by the way. Or maybe you won't want to go, now that they've passed on.'

'I don't know,' she said. 'I'll have to think about it.' She said goodbye and lay back in the bed. She wondered about Agnes and whether the act of arson had been revenge for being cut out of a new will. She thought about the three old women surrounded by fire, then she pushed that thought away and went to sleep again.

*

In the first week they covered north and middle Germany and were headed towards the south. Uncle Theodore was always at some new address; he'd also sold a lot of his former property. Gisela evidently hadn't kept up with his movements as well as she'd imagined. All the telephone numbers Carl had unearthed were out of date. Even the exchanges were different. Sometimes the new occupants they met would become interested and dispense friendly information and advice, none of which was of any help in tracking down the missing relatives; or, at least, not during those first few days. But Carl usually managed to get another address out of the people they interviewed – his German was better than hers – and so they moved south.

'It's like the treasure-hunts my grandfather used to invent for us,' Carla said. 'At Easter, when we were children: you began with a poem that was a riddle. It led you to a certain place, where you'd find the next clue. And at the end there was a present.'

'Lots of candy? A chocolate egg?'

'No, we had that anyway. The present was usually a book.'

'Bavaria next,' Carl said. 'We've even got castles on the agenda.'

'Aunt Gisela told me the really big estates were in the east. Some of them were in Poland and Czechoslovakia.'

'So they're all collective farms by now?'

'One of them's a sanatorium and another one's a kind of health farm, where people can do their exercises in beautiful surroundings. It had a famous park.'

'Doesn't it make you feel strange to know that your family owns those places – that they're actually part of your inheritance?'

'No,' Carla said, 'definitely not. One ordinary apartment is going to be plenty for me. What makes me feel funny is knowing I've got all these relatives like Uncle Theodore and Aunt Regina, and I've never met them. And now I can't even find them.'

'We'll get you there,' he assured her. 'Plenty of time. I've got six weeks.'

'Five, now.'

'And we've got two good clues: Munich and Naples. Maybe we

should split up for a couple of days. That might cut down on the time. How's your Italian?'

'It isn't. Only phrases from operas: *Ah, patria mia. Perfido amore.* And so on. That's about it.'

'And I can ask what time the train goes and how much things cost. What do you think? I could go there and phone you in Munich. OK?'

She thought it over while they ate lunch outdoors on a terrace crammed with iron tables, each of which had a striped parasol sprouting from a central bar that went up through the middle of the tabletop like the trunk of a tree. They were surrounded by Scandinavian and American tourists. Carla figured that she could find her way around another German city all right, but she wouldn't have any idea how to go about making a phone call from one country to another, between two languages, neither one of which was her own.

'All right,' she agreed.

'I'll miss you,' he said.

She smiled. He meant that he'd miss sleeping with her. All the time they were still in America, nothing had happened. And on the first night they'd spent in Germany, he'd come into her hotel room and that was that.

They'd visited one or two places not on the list: she'd always wanted to see Heidelberg, so they'd gone there and had their picture taken together with what seemed like hundreds of other tourists; there were Americans all over the town, even though the summer was almost over.

And they'd made a detour to a little church they'd been told about, which was supposed to be architecturally interesting. As they'd approached the place in their rented Volkswagen, Carla had suddenly seen the building; it stood on the top of a hill, among other gently rounded slopes planted with wheat that had already been harvested. The stooks were lined up in the fields, the sky embellished with puffy clouds, and the whole day was like an illustration from a volume of nursery rhymes. The church itself was of a dark, honey-coloured stone; the front looked like a Carlsbad clock one of her father's aunts had owned.

Most of the other tourists there had been German. They were taking photographs of the outside, and talking in lowered voices inside. As she and Carl entered, the change from bright light to the murky interior was abrupt. Carla had stood still. With one hand she'd held on to Carl. With the other she'd twiddled nervously at the small ruby ring her grandmother had given her in the spring.

'This way,' Carl had whispered. She'd followed him until they stood side by side, looking into a glass box let into the church wall. Inside the box was what Carla at first took to be a ceremonial robe laid out in splendour. And then all at once she realized that within the robe was a corpse. There had been fourteen of the things, each in its private showcase, all around the inner walls. They were supposed to be saints.

'I'll miss you, too,' she told him.

She got so lost in Munich, and so often lost, that she ended up taking taxis everywhere. It was pointless in any case; the two houses she was looking for, and of which she had several fine photographs, didn't exist. In one instance, the street itself was no longer apparent. Everything had been bombed and built over.

She walked around the museums and in the evening went out to a performance of a ballet. When she got back to her hotel, there was a message that Carl had telephoned. He called again at midnight.

'Any news?' she asked.

'Lots. And I've talked to Uncle Theodore.'

'Well, finally.'

'Not completely. I talked to him on the phone. He's in South America.'

'I don't believe it.'

'And he wants us to come see him.'

'Just hop across—'

'And he's arranging the flight and paying for everything. And,' he added, 'he says he's just dying to see you.'

They walked out of the airport into a thrashing crowd as noisy as a political demonstration. A lot of the people looked as if they were in fancy-dress. Everything suddenly seemed utterly strange to Carla – almost as though she'd been put into a different century. She didn't even have the sense that she might have known the place from pictures in newspapers or on television.

Carl held her by the arm. He had a way of nipping her upper arm with his hand so that his thumb made a large, painful bruise. She didn't complain. She thought that if he let go, they might become separated. And if that happened, she wouldn't stand a chance. The noise and crowd and heat would overwhelm her. She felt nearly ready to pass out as it was.

He found a porter and then a cab. They drove away from the airport, through part of the city and to a highway. She sat silent, his arm around her shoulders. The taxi turned off the main road and started to climb. They were going up into the mountains.

'Look,' he said.

She made an attempt to take in the landscape and the views, but she was too tired to appreciate anything. She tried to sleep. She wished they hadn't left Europe.

It was evening when she woke. The taxi had stopped and their luggage was being moved to a horse-drawn carriage. Carl shook her as she began to close her eyes again. When she saw the horses waiting and got a second look at the carriage, she said, 'My God, it's like one of those fairytale things.'

They both wanted to sit outside, up with the coachman, who kept signalling back towards the doors with his whip and repeating some instructions.

'What's he saying?'

Carl told her, 'He wants us to get in.'

'Why?'

The man put the whip down and made flapping movements with his hands.

'Owl?' Carl asked.

'Bats,' she said. 'I'll bet that's what it is. Let's go.' She climbed into the coach and sat down on the seat. As soon as Carl joined her, the wheels rolled forward. She said, 'This is unbelievable.'

'I guess the roads aren't very good.'

'If they're no good for a car, they'd be a lot worse for one of these things.'

'Pretty comfortable, actually. If Clark Gable could do it in a phone booth—'

'We could fall out on the doorstep before we realized we'd arrived. I could have bruises in a lot of new places.'

The night came down around them, the road grew bumpy. At one stage, while they were negotiating a sharp turn, something slapped hard against one of the windows from the outside. Carla was suddenly wide awake.

'A bat,' Carl said in a sinister voice. 'Coming to get you.'

'Couldn't have been. It was huge. Maybe it was a condor. Or a big rock.'

'A rock would break the window.'

'It's so dark,' she said. 'There isn't a light anywhere.'

They drove for half an hour more before they saw lights, which seemed from the outline to be coming from a castle of some kind.

'They don't have castles here,' he told her.

'Well, a big house. An enormous house. See?'

Carl put his face to the window. He didn't speak.

She said, 'I've got a feeling it's like something I've seen before. It looks a little like one of those photographs. Maybe they built it that way on purpose, as a copy of what they'd left behind. Carl?'

'It's big, all right,' he said.

'You slept well?' her great-uncle Theodore asked. In daylight he didn't look so peculiar. When she'd arrived – cold, sleepy, stumbling into the light – he'd struck her as odd, and incredibly old, and irretrievably foreign. She and Carl had been introduced to the entire indoor household, who were lined up in the front hall to meet them. The other great-uncle, Erwin, had appeared senile and dwarfish rather than – as now – diminutive and charming. And her great-aunt Regina, in a floor-length green and black dressing gown, had given an impression of dramatic malevolence; she now seemed merely grumpy and theatrical: a heavy-faced old woman who dyed her hair black, as she must have been doing for nearly forty years. She also wore, even at breakfast, a great deal of strong-coloured make-up. Another woman – a frail figure in white, who had gestured tentatively from a landing the night before – still hadn't come downstairs.

'I slept like the dead,' Carla said. 'Isn't Carl up yet?'

'Roderigo is showing him the estate. He woke early, with the others.'

She sipped her coffee. The first thing they'd done as she'd sat down was to warn her about the strength of their coffee.

She wondered why Carl hadn't come to her room. She didn't even know where he was sleeping. As soon as the servant had shown her to the room she was to have, he'd hurried Carl down the corridor, and that was the last she'd seen of him. She thought it was strange. He was only a recently acquired boyfriend, but the others didn't know that; they had been told that she and Carl were engaged. That was supposed to make the whole question of bedrooms easier and perhaps less offensive, if anyone thought that way about it.

'Was Roderigo the man with the moustache?'

'The manager, yes. They'll be back for lunch. And in the meantime, perhaps Kristel –'

'Kristel is in her study,' Regina said.

'Or Regina?'

'I have to do my exercises.'

'And I, unfortunately, am occupied with business matters, but—'

'I should be delighted', Erwin said, 'to show little Carla the house and gardens.'

Erwin was waiting for her in the hall when she came down from brushing her teeth. She was beginning to get a better idea of the structure of the house. It was built in storeys, on several levels of the mountainside. The gardens too climbed up and down screes of rock into which stone steps had been cut. There was a wooden handrail that would have been useless if anybody had really needed to lean on it. Uncle Erwin skipped along nimbly at her side. For a man of his age he appeared astonishingly agile and supple in his movements. All the great-uncles and aunts of the family must have been hitting eighty at least, possibly ninety and upwards.

'Did the family build the house?' Carla asked.

'No, it was here before. It was a convent, or a monastery, or something like that. And a fortress. So often these places are like that: they have some treasure, and so they have to be in a position to defend it. There are a great many sacred buildings in the area from the same period. Most of them are partly ruined. They were lucky to have water here. That's why they survived so long. We added a lot, of course. Look.' He raised his arm towards the windows and towers above them. He started to explain which walls had been added when. Carla lost interest.

He went on, 'There are three main gardens. Everything else is extra. The vegetables are over on the other side. Now, be careful and watch where you put your feet. The mist comes up and makes the rock slippery. And there's a kind of moss – that can be just like ice when it's raining.'

He led her down a stone staircase between two walls dappled green and grey with lichen, and into an arcade of white-blossomed bushes. Everything in the first garden was white.

The second garden was almost all full of red flowers, though there were pink and orange shades too, and some yellow. The last garden was purple, blue and grey. 'We wanted black,' Erwin said, 'but so few flowers are truly black and the only ones we could think of won't grow here.'

'A black garden? Why?'

'Because of the flag, of course. Red, white and black.'

'I thought the flag here was—'

'The German flag, Carla dear.'

'Oh? Well, I guess now you've got the American flag instead. And England and France.'

'Yes. Unfortunate, but it will have to do.'

He walked her down to the front of the house, where they climbed into a carriage. The sides of the vehicle were open but there was a canvas top. Erwin gave orders to the driver in a language Carla didn't understand. As they started to move, she told him about the night before and about the bird, or whatever it was, that had bumped into them.

'Probably an owl,' Erwin said.

'We thought it might have been a bat.'

'Bats never make a mistake like that. They have their own system of radar. But an owl, or another kind of bird, might have been caught by the shine of the windows.'

'Do you get a lot of bats around here?'

'Thousands. And they're the real thing, you know – the vampire bats. They come into the fields at night and attack the cattle. And also the horses. We have to be careful. Of course the local people here say that we're vampires, too – our family.'

'Why on earth?'

'It's a figure of speech. Because we're rich. We suck the blood from the poor. At least, according to them. The truth is that we're civilized and educated and they're just ignorant peasants. And we pay them to do work for us.'

'You own the land they live on?'

'That's right. And so do you. You're a member of the family.'

She was shown a model village, a rug-weaving factory and a fish farm. The workers were Indians of all ages. A lot of them were very light-skinned. Most of the adults, both men and women, had a scar on their foreheads. Carla didn't hear a single laugh, or even any talking, among them. They worked slowly, with concentration.

Erwin made a detour so that she could see what was happening in a pool at the other end of the hatcheries. He led her up close. A large, jittery crowd pressed forward behind her. When two men emptied a pail of scraps into the water, the pool appeared to boil with activity. The crowd moaned, at once sickened and gratified. 'It's the fish,' Erwin said. 'They're like piranhas.'

'You breed them?'

'Not really. We like to keep the pool full. Everybody knows what can happen to whatever falls in. The idea of being deliberately pushed in, or even thrown, is one that fascinates our employees. They seem to regard it as a form of insurance we hold over them – a warranty of their good behaviour. I understand that mothers even threaten their babies with it.'

'But, that's terrible.'

'No, no. It's like a legend now. It's, ah, a focus of attention to which other things are referred. You understand?'

'I don't think so,' Carla said.

'Well, it doesn't matter. Let's just say – everyone would miss the pool if we decided to get rid of it. And the people who'd miss it most of all are the ones who are the most afraid of getting thrown into it.'

They spent the rest of the morning looking at meadows and pastures and views that spread away from them like an ocean of cultivated land. The family holdings appeared to be of about the same acreage as the state of Connecticut, or possibly even more extensive than that.

'And the forests,' Erwin added. 'We sometimes speak of them as the jungle. And all the places where you can find butterflies. Kristel is our great lover of butterflies. She can show you.'

'Was that the woman in the shawl?'

'That was the housekeeper, Maria. Kristel didn't come downstairs last night. She hasn't been well.'

'Oh? I hope it's not serious.'

'It's never serious,' he said. 'She likes the pose. Her mother was an invalid – romantic and glamorous: had hundreds of lovers. One always assumed that her fatigues were brought on by an excess of amours. Or perhaps a heightened artistic sensibility. I remember her very well – a marvellous woman. Poor Kristel isn't quite up to that standard. And she doesn't have the acting talent.'

'Oh,' Carla said again. Erwin gave directions to the driver to turn the horses and they went through a gully that was bursting forth in yellow bushes even high up, where it didn't look as if the roots would have anything to hold on to.

They reached the house again and were let off near another walled garden, so that Carla could be shown the vegetables. She stepped over a low-growing branch of pink flowers and clutched at the corner of a stone outcrop. They had followed the paths around to the other side, where the vegetables joined up with the flower gardens. The blue air beyond rose above them like another mountain. The combination of flowers and talk and the steep climb between dangerous turnings was beginning to confuse her.

She said, 'You know, I think I've still got a little jet-lag left over. I feel sort of dizzy.'

Erwin put out a hand to steady her. 'How selfish of me,' he said. 'I should have thought. It's probably the altitude, too – most people feel that straight away.'

She didn't see Carl until just before lunch. He was coming down the main staircase as she was going up. She asked, 'What happened last night?'

'There you are,' he said. 'This place is driving me crazy. I couldn't find my way back to your room, and then I almost got lost again when somebody turned out the lights. Jesus, did you hear the crying?'

'No.'

'Roderigo says everybody thinks it's a ghost.'

He started to tell her about the tour he'd been given. She thought how healthy he looked, and how happy. He even seemed a little too cheerful – like a commercial for a cereal. He told her, 'This place is fantastic. The whole thing. It's like a private empire. Really.'

'And by rights Aunt Gisela should have had her share of it. Maybe it was all hers.'

'First I've heard.'

'She told me that. She said: "Theodore stole the Treasure from me." '

'She was kind of gaga towards the end of her life.'

'"Count Walter's Treasure" – that's what she called it. At first I thought it was her way of alluding to something else, like her emotions or her honour. You know. But she would have been almost a generation older – well, not quite that much, but I think she was too old to have had any kind of an affair with him when she was young. She was way up in her nineties – at least ten years older, so it couldn't have been in her youth: he'd have been too young for her back then.'

He said, 'I know these older women that keep on moaning about being ruined by younger men.'

'Is that right?'

'Wishes.'

'Carl, has Uncle Theodore said anything to you about how long we're invited for?'

'It's indefinite.'

'My work isn't indefinite,' she said.

Over luncheon Uncle Theodore talked about the history of the estate and the founding of the family fortunes in that part of the world. Regina listened to him without comment. She shovelled her food purposefully into her mouth and chewed. Aunt Kristel had risen from her sickbed in order to attend the meal. She had shied away from both young people, saying, 'Please – if you'll forgive me: my hands hurt today.' And she had placed the hurting hands in her lap. 'Some days', she murmured, 'are worse than others.' Carla was just as glad to avoid the physical contact. Kristel's whitely desiccated face and hands were alarming: they had a leprous look.

She shot a glance at Carl but he was turned to Theodore in an attitude of interest and expectation. She looked down at her plate. The meeting with her aunts and uncles was one she'd felt she had to have, but it was hard for her to believe that she was related to these people. They seemed grotesque. She couldn't understand how Carl was able to play up to them, unless he was simply impressed by their wealth. *To the end of the week,* she thought: and then she'd be saying goodbye.

'Goodbye?' Uncle Erwin said. 'But – we shouldn't dream of letting you go so soon.'

'I have to get back to my work.'

'Yes, the child is right,' Theodore agreed. 'We're retired. And the young have their own lives.' He sighed. 'But stay to the end of the week at any rate. We'll have a few parties. Show you around the neighbourhood and boast a little.'

'Yes, parties,' Kristel squealed. The onrush of gaiety made her look momentarily imbecilic as well as ill. She raised her afflicted hands in the air and made a few dancing movements with them.

'I'll send someone down to the village,' Theodore said. 'Have you any preference for a day? I'm afraid the best we can do is Tuesday or Thursday. Let's make it this Thursday. Then we'll be able to keep you a bit longer.'

'All right,' she said. Everyone around the table smiled. She wondered why she'd ever had the feeling that they might not be willing to let her go.

That afternoon she and Carl had tea with Theodore, who talked about the duties of running such a large estate and the difficulties of growing old without heirs. 'You have to leave everything to foundations,' he said, 'and do it in such a way that the next generation won't be forever quarrelling about what you really meant.'

Carla said that she agreed with her grandmother: you should just give your possessions away and let the other people do what they liked with them. She twisted and turned her grandmother's ring as she said so. It wasn't easy to speak up against Theodore.

'One or two trinkets', he told her, 'are hardly to be compared with a huge amount of land.'

'But the principle's the same. The future may be completely different. The way people live, the circumstances of their—'

'The future,' Theodore stated, 'can be controlled from the past. Good planning ensures that the future will be as one wants it. We have to look ahead, that's all.'

'No one's ever been able to do that.'

'I agree with your uncle,' Carl said.

'Oh?'

'Certainly. It's only a question of organization. It's political.'

'Really,' she said.

'That's right. And', he looked at Theodore as if for confirmation, 'the systematization of heredity.'

'What does that mean?'

'It means: the great thing about graduating from the Neanderthal and Cro-Magnon stages is that once you've got a good brain, you can get the people with less brains to work for you. And if you're only reproducing with your own kind, your people become more and more intelligent, while theirs become progressively stupid and degenerate, and finally unable to run their lives without being governed by someone else.'

'But does inheritance operate like that? I thought it was supposed to skip around; you know – the similarities show up on the tangent and between generations that are three or four steps apart.'

'No,' Carl said flatly. 'All you have to do is look at greyhounds and horses. It's a matter of breeding.'

Uncle Theodore nodded. He looked approvingly at Carl. It was easy to see where the theory had originated. Carla said, 'Even if that were true – which I don't believe – would it be right to deny people equality just because they're stupid or underbred?'

Theodore took over. 'It's definitely right', he answered, 'to prevent them from taking up a position of power for which they're completely unqualified.'

'If you change people's circumstances and upbringing and education, you change their qualifications.'

'No. There's nothing you can do with poor stock.'

She was irritated enough to push the argument further, even though it would break up the tea-drinking. She opened her mouth to begin and then saw that the others all sided with Theodore. It was better to drop the subject. She said, 'Well, I don't agree.'

Kristel giggled and said she'd always felt that debates on these big political subjects were best left to the men. Regina threw her a look of contempt.

'The future is our job,' Theodore said. 'As well as the present.'

Carla raised her cup to her lips. Maybe the mania for control – like the whole line of reasoning – was connected with the fact that these people had no generations to come after them. The future meant children. Now, at last, she was glad she didn't have any. She remembered one of the quarrels she'd had with her husband; suddenly she could even recall, as if echoed intact, the tones of their voices as they'd yelled at each other. 'When are you going to get pregnant?' he'd shouted. And she'd screamed back, 'When you stop sleeping around.' 'I'm not going to stop,' he'd told her. 'I like it. It's a hell of a lot more fun than you are right now.' And so forth. It had gone on and on. And all that time she'd wanted children, yet she'd known that no matter what he said, he'd walk out on her as soon as she had any. She hated him more than anything in the world and wished that she could kill him again and again – once wouldn't be enough.

She was gripping her teacup tightly and staring down at the rug. She still loved him, which made it worse. The marriage couldn't have ended any other way, but she kept catching herself at wishing: if only things had been different. The future might be determined by the past, but the present seemed to her always uncontrollable and chaotic.

Kristel finished her last cup of tea as she pressed flowers into the pages of a book for Erwin's collection. Regina occupied herself with some kind of crocheted scarf. And while Theodore took Carl upstairs to look at some old papers that concerned the estate, Carla walked up the opposite staircase, to her room. On her way she passed the three paintings that gave her the creeps: a landscape of blasted trees and ruined temples lit by a livid glare that made the stone columns look like old, naked legs; a still-life vase full of rotting flowers, with a cup and saucer sitting on the table in front of it; and a mythological scene that showed a convocation of centaurs: these bearded, hairy creatures were grouped in a circle, though most of them had their muscled backs towards the viewer, and within the tight huddle they formed, appeared to be doing something singular, perhaps unpleasant, possibly unspeakably gross.

Regina had told her the names of the painters, who were apparently well-known. Regina was extremely proud of all three. They were, she said, prime examples of German culture.

Carl came to her room before they went down to dinner. He said, 'I won't see you tonight. Your uncle is initiating me into some kind of ceremony. It's for men only.'

'What kind of ceremony?'

'I don't know. Some club the ranchers have, maybe.'

'I hope it isn't anything political. From the way they've been talking, you might end up covered in swastikas.'

'Don't be silly.' He sounded as pompous and didactic as Theodore, but unlike Theodore, he wasn't the kind of man you could be afraid of. There was a hint of shiftiness about him. He'd probably done something crooked with her great-aunts' money, she thought. He'd probably been friendly with Agnes.

'What are you looking like that for?' he asked.

'I was remembering what you told me about older women,' she said. 'How they fell in love with younger men.'

'It isn't just the older ones here. It's all of them. Haven't you noticed? There are a lot of blond children on the estate. And grown-ups, too. Theodore told me: it's in our interest to have as many workers as possible. And it isn't as if they mind.'

'Who mind?'

'The women. They come to us naturally, of their own free will. They reject their own men.'

Us? she thought. She said, 'Why do they do that?'

'Because', he said, perfectly seriously, 'we're superior.'

It wasn't worth getting angry about, but the effort of putting up with him was beginning to wear her down. He was still good-looking and she still felt tolerance and a certain affection for his body, but not so much now for his face or voice. And all at once she wondered about the fire at her aunts' house: how it had really started, and if someone had deliberately set it, or had even been told to.

'I guess it's like the lobotomies,' he said. 'They think of it as medicine.'

'What's medicine? Are you talking about sex? What does lobotomy have to do with it?'

'When you took the tour with Erwin, didn't you see how many of the Indians have a scar right here on their foreheads?'

'Yes. It's the way they get rid of the poison from some kind of insect. It's trepanning, not lobotomy.'

'Whatever you want to call it. They go to Erwin, crowds of them, and ask him to do it. Theodore, too; Erwin taught him how. No insect bites, no infection – they just want the operation. And afterwards they feel better. A lot of them want it done over and over.'

'There isn't any reason for it? They aren't sick?'

'They're all completely well. I told you: they just want the operation. Apparently it goes way back. The Incas used to do it, too.'

'The Incas used to cut the hearts out and eat them.'

'That was the Aztecs.'

'I can't believe it.'

'It's all in the history books.'

'Jesus,' she said.

'I don't know. They really do feel better afterwards. And a lot of civilized people believe the same: they want somebody to run their lives, fix them up, change their luck.'

'That's horrible.'

'If it makes them happy?'

'It can't,' she said. 'To have an unnecessary operation can't make them happy.'

'But it does,' he told her.

Carla sat between Regina and Kristel on the back seat of a horse-drawn carriage. They were shielded by screen curtains and covered with a green canvas top, in spite of which she'd already been stung by a gnat.

They had a driver named Eusabio. He'd stopped the horses so that the ladies could admire the view. In the distance, outcrops of rock massed together into a chain of spiky hilltops. At the top of one of the high peaks was another monastery; they'd seen three already.

'Now, this is really interesting,' Regina said.

Kristel murmured, 'I don't feel well.'

'I've got a bit of a headache myself,' Carla admitted.

'Nonsense,' Regina said. 'You'll both feel better once we've had some exercise.'

'I'm not walking all the way up there,' Kristel wailed. 'That's how Frieda got sick. You kept pushing her.'

Erwin turned around from the front seat and smiled at Carla. 'You mustn't think we're like this all the time,' he said.

'Oh, shut up,' Regina told him.

'Usually', he added, 'we're much worse.'

Regina rose from her seat. She climbed down to the ground. Erwin followed, saying that they'd be back soon. Eusabio drove the carriage forward slowly and stopped under the shade of some trees. They waited. Carla fanned herself with a piece of paper she'd found in her purse; she always kept a supply of paper by her in case she wanted to jot down an idea for a design.

'I hate these places,' Kristel said. 'They aren't my idea of Christianity at all. I remember the way churches used to be – the way they still are, on the other side of the world. God knows what the people here really believe. They're all like animals.'

'I got the impression they were very devout.'

'They like ceremonies. They love all these ceremonies about death and entombment. The ideas, the ideals, mean nothing to them.'

The glare coming off the rocks was beginning to make Carla sleepy and slightly dizzy. She looked down at the fan she was holding, and noticed that on part of the paper she'd begun a picture of one of her cat-boxes; the paper must have been in her bag for months: the drawing divided the sitting cat at a point lower than the one she'd finally chosen. And the completed boxes had been put into production before the previous Christmas. She considered telling Kristel about the German church of the fourteen saints. But it wasn't worth trying to shock these people.

'I feel sick,' Kristel said.

'Was Frieda the one who couldn't walk? Was she always—'

'Healthy as a horse till her eighty-sixth birthday, when she made a pig of herself on Elvas plums and brandy.'

'Didn't she have a disease like—'

'Oh, everybody knows what was wrong with her. Disappointed in love, that's all. And Regina – well. She was the scandal.'

And you? Carla thought.

'Regina would still be a scandal if anybody'd take her. It's a disgrace. And now she's so righteous.'

'And you?'

'Me?'

'Do you like living here?'

'Oh. Of course. I'd rather be back home, naturally, but this was where Theo wanted to take us.'

'Where's home?'

'Berlin, Dresden, Leipzig.'

'And the last time you were there?'

'I went back once on a visit with Erwin in 1931. We had a lovely time.'

'I see,' Carla said.

'I love parties. Are you looking forward to yours?'

'My what?'

'Your initiation ceremony.'

'Oh? Initiation into what?'

'Into the family.'

'Is that the same kind of thing Carl was doing last night?'

Kristel looked suddenly as if she'd said more than she should have, and knew that it was too late to do anything about it. She flapped her hands, laughed, and said she had an idea that the business with Carl was some sort of contest that had to do with the Indians.

'Like what?' Carla asked.

Kristel shrugged. She didn't know, she said. And maybe, Carla thought, she didn't.

'But I've seen your dress, and it's beautiful. It's just wonderful. It's silk and satin and all covered with little glittering jewels and shining white, like a wedding dress.'

'Oh?'

'Yes. Right down to the floor. And there's a veil that goes with it.'

Carla turned her head. Kristel was looking straight out into the landscape; her face glowed with eagerness. It was impossible to tell if she was lying, or remembering some other event, or imagining a thing that had never been.

'And you'll be wearing the family jewels. Including the Treasure – they had such a time getting it away from Gisela before we left home.'

She caught Carl as he was turning out of the hallway leading from her landing. 'What's going on?' she said.

He was in evening clothes. Something about them didn't look right. They fitted perfectly, but seemed antiquated, especially the jacket. 'Aren't you ready yet?' he said. 'I thought you were trying on your dress. We aren't supposed to see each other.'

'Carl, what is all this?'

'It's just to make them happy. Some kind of pageant-thing they do. The Indians believe it makes the grass grow, or something.'

'You're kidding.'

'Anyway, hurry up, will you? We don't have much time. And I want a drink first.' He ran on down the stairs, moving easily, his head up, not having to look down at his feet, which she always had to do on staircases.

She went to her room and began to pack. She started with the dresser drawers and the medicine chest in the bathroom. After that, it was only her two dresses and the trousers and extra skirt.

She opened the wardrobe door and stepped back. A mound of shiny white material bounced out at her – part of the lower half of a very long dress. It was like uncovering a light. And there seemed so much more of it than should belong to a single dress. She tried to push it in again, so that she could get to her clothes. The voluminous heaps of it sprang back at her. The whole garment reminded her of a filled parachute and a newsreel she'd once seen, that had shown a landed airman who'd had to fight with his still-billowing chute. It was all over her. But as she reached up to squash some of the material into place, she caught sight of the bodice, still on the hanger, and stopped. She'd never seen anything like it: delicate lace, interwoven with tiny pale jewels in leaf and flower patterns, criss-crossed by knotted and curled ribbons in all shades of creamy white: tinted in pastel colours like the dawn.

As she stood there examining the workmanship of the dress, there was a knock at the door and Regina stepped into the room. 'I'll help you with it,' she announced. 'You'll need someone to snap up the inside straps, otherwise the folds won't lie right. The others are no use – they always get so hysterical about parties.'

'This must have taken years to make,' Carla murmured. 'Hundreds of people must have worked on it.'

'Only about ten, I think.'

'Where does it come from?'

'From here. It's been in the family for generations.'

'When was it—'

'Hurry up,' Regina ordered. 'Take off your clothes.'

The door opened again. Kristel and the housekeeper, Maria, burst in. Kristel looked even more sickly than usual – her skin was almost like a cheese going bad; but Maria was grinning with excitement. She made a grab at the buttons of Carla's blouse. Carla pulled away.

'Calm down, Maria,' Regina said. 'Here, hold the train free.'

Carla began to undress. She kept her underclothes on, and her sandals. Regina and Maria stood on chairs and lifted the dress down over her head.

'The shoes,' Kristel pointed out.

'Nobody's going to see the shoes,' Regina said. 'The dress is too long on her, anyway.'

'And the Treasure. My God, how could we have forgotten it?'

'I didn't forget,' Regina said. 'Hold her hair up, will you?'

They dragged her hair up and back, and began to stick hair-pins into it. They jammed the veil comb on top and batted the netting out of the way; it floated backward like a ghostly shadow of herself. Kristel turned around and took a bottle and glass from a bag she'd left near the door. She poured out a liquid that looked like sherry, and handed the glass to Carla. 'Drink this,' she said. 'It's traditional.'

Carla was reluctant, but the drink smelled good.

'Go ahead,' Regina told her. 'Be careful not to spill.'

Carla drank.

She drank three glasses while the other women fussed over

her – shoving rings on to her fingers, skewering diamonds into her sleeves, pinning and clipping sapphires across the headband of her veil. When they were ready at last, she felt drunk. They guided her out of the room, holding her skirts to protect them as she squeezed sideways through the doorway. They led her along a corridor, down a staircase and to a landing bordered by a balustrade. Down below she could see a congregation of people and heard the hum of their voices. Far off in the background she picked out Carl, who was talking to her great-uncle Theodore. She felt like yawning. Over in the right-hand corner a group of men with musical instruments sat in chairs. Such a large gathering, she thought: what was it about? And what was she doing there at all, surrounded by these weird old women? She should be at home, designing toys. Any minute now she'd begin laughing the silly laugh that came over her when she hit the best stage of inebriation – the first, where she felt terrific.

'You wait here with her,' Regina said. 'I'll be right back.'

'Where are you going?' Carla asked.

'To get the Treasure.'

'Better hurry up, before I fall asleep.'

'You shouldn't have given her the third glass,' Regina said to Kristel. 'Idiot.' She stomped away, turning abruptly and entering a room just beyond the corner. The band started to tune up. Kristel snivelled miserably; she muttered that her hands were hurting.

Carl looked up. Although he was so far away, Carla could tell that he was staring at her with an especially expectant, approving look. Some of the other people below had also caught sight of her, or rather, of the dress. The band gave out a few screeching chords, pulled itself together and swung into a jaunty tune. Regina came swishing back around the edge of the bannisters. She was holding a box covered in black velvet. She handed it to Carla, saying, 'Here. Put it on.'

Carla lifted the lid. It snapped open so that the contents were hidden from the others, but she could tell that in any case their attention was all on her face. She stared downward. 'What is it?' she asked.

'The largest pearl ever discovered,' Regina said importantly. 'Absolutely perfect, unique, and – of course – priceless.'

Carla smiled drunkenly down into the box, at the black velvet stand, the heavy, glittering linked chain, the elaborate gold and enamel setting, and inside it the large sunken blob of shrivelled brown matter that resembled a piece of burned meat.

'Well?' Regina said.

'Wonderful,' she answered. 'Priceless.'

I See a Long Journey

Flora had met James when she was going out with his younger brother, Edward. She'd been crazy about Edward, who even then had had a reputation for wildness where girls were concerned. She'd been eighteen, Edward nineteen. James was thirty-one.

She'd liked him straight away. He was easy in talking to her: relaxed and completely open, as if they'd known each other a long time. In fact, in a way she did know him already – not just through Edward, but from her older sister, Elizabeth, who had gone out with him for about two months a few years before. He had had many girlfriends and mistresses, naturally. He was agreeable and amusing, well-known everywhere and well-liked. He was also the most important of the heirs.

When he proposed to her, she thought her decision over carefully. She wasn't in love with him but she couldn't think of any reason why she should turn him down. He'd become such a good friend that she felt they were already related.

After the marriage, Edward changed along with everything else. The barriers came up all around her. Where once, on the outside, she had felt shut out of their exclusive family, now – on the inside – she was debarred from the rest of the world.

There had been a time at the beginning when she had fought. If it hadn't been for the money, she might have succeeded. Their quarrels, misunderstandings and jealousies were like those of other families. And she was like other girls who marry into a group of powerful personalities. She was tugged in different directions by all of them. They expected things of her. They criticized her. They tried to train and educate her. When she was pregnant for the first time, and when she had the child, they told her what she was doing wrong.

But that was the stage at which she found her own strength: she clung to the child and wouldn't let them near it. They had to make concessions. It was the first grandchild and a boy. She was sitting pretty. She could take her mother-in-law up on a point in conversation and make her back down.

Shortly after the birth a lot of pressure was taken off her anyway; Edward formed a liaison with a girl who sang in a nightclub. He was thinking of marrying her, he said. He wanted to introduce her to his parents – her name was Lula. His mother hit the roof about it. She described the girl as 'an unfortunate creature: some sort of half-breed, I believe'. Quarrels exploded over the breakfast table, down in the library, out in the garden. In the kitchen, of course, they were laughing.

She met Lula. Edward took them both out to lunch. Flora wasn't nervous about it: she even tried to put the other woman at her ease by saying that she too had once been an outsider to the family. But Lula wasn't going to accept anyone's sympathy. She put on a performance, talked loudly, looking around at the other people in the restaurant, pinched Edward under the table and went out of her way to throw as many dirty words as possible into every sentence. Then she stood up abruptly, declared that it had been so very, very nice but she had to run along now, tugged Edward by the hair and left.

'She isn't like that,' he said.

'You don't have to tell me. I could see. She'll be all right when we get together next time.'

'She really isn't like that.'

'I know. I told you – I recognize the camouflage. I liked her fine.'

'I think you made her feel unsure.'

'And I'm the easy one. Wait till she meets the others. She'll have her work cut out for her.'

'They gave you a rough time, I guess.'

'It's all right. That's over now.'

'It's mainly Mother.'

'It's the whole deal.'

'But things are OK between you and James?'

'Oh, yes,' she said. 'But we're in the thick of everything. If you and I had married, we could have escaped together.'

'But we didn't love each other,' he said matter-of-factly. It upset her to hear him say it. Someone should love her. Even her children – they needed her, but she was the one who did the loving.

'Besides,' he told her, 'I'm not sure that I want to escape. Even if it were possible. And I don't think it is.'

'It's always possible if you don't have children.'

He said, 'It's the price of having quarterly cheques and dividends, never having to work for it. Think of the way most people live. Working in a factory – could you stand it?'

'Maybe it wouldn't be so bad. If you were with somebody you loved.'

'Love doesn't survive much poverty. Unless you're really right down at the bottom and don't have anything else.'

Was it true? If she and her husband were lost and wandering in the desert, maybe he'd trade her for a horse or a camel, because he could always get another wife and have more children by the new one. It couldn't be true.

'I'm sure it would,' she said.

'From the pinnacle, looking down,' he told her, 'you get that romantic blur. Wouldn't it be nice in a little country cottage with only the birds and the running streams? It's the Marie Antoinette complex.'

And at another time he'd said, 'Love is a luxury for us. If I were on a desert island with the soulmate of all time, I'd still have the feeling that I'd ducked out. I guess it's what they used to call "duty".'

'There are plenty of others to take over the duties,' she told him.

'And they'd all think: *he wasn't up to it.* And they'd be right.'

It took two years for the family to wean Edward away from Lula. Then they set him up with a suitable bride, an Irish heiress named Anna-Louise, whose family was half-German on the mother's side. One of Anna-Louise's greatest assets was that she was a superb horsewoman. Flora liked her. The boys' father, the old man, thought she was wonderful. His wife realized too late that Anna-Louise was a strong character, not to be bullied. Flora was let off the hook. She didn't allow her mother-in-law to take out on her or her children any of the failures and frustrations she had with Anna-Louise. She put her foot down. And eventually her mother-in-law came to her to seek an ally, to complain and to ask for advice. Flora listened and held her peace. She was learning.

James was the one who helped her. He guided her through her mistakes; he was the first person in her life to be able to teach her that mistakes are actually the best method of learning and that it's impossible to learn without at least some of them. He warned her about things she would have to know, strangers she was going to meet. She was grateful. But she also saw that he was part of the network and that all his actions, though well-meant, were aimed at making her just like the rest of them, whether she wanted to be or not.

It always came down to the question of money. The money made the difference. They were one of the richest families on the Eastern seaboard. Flora's own parents were from nice, substantial backgrounds; they'd had their houses and companies and clubs, and belonged to the right places when it had still been worth keeping up with that sort of thing.

She'd known people who knew the cousins, who gave parties at which she would be acceptable – that was how she had met Edward. Everyone knew about them. Everyone recognized their pictures in the papers. To marry into their ranks was like marrying into royalty, and a royalty that never had to worry about its revenues.

Her marriage had also changed her own relatives irrevocably. It was as though they had lost their thoughts and wishes; they had become hangers-on. They name-dropped with everyone, they could no longer talk about anything except the last time they'd seen James or Edward or – best of all – the old man.

They were all corrupted. One early summer afternoon Flora sat playing cards with James and Edward and her sister, Elizabeth, who had married a cousin of the family and thus, paradoxically, become less close.

Flora thought about the four of them, what they were doing with the time they had. All except for James were still in their twenties and they were like robots attached to a master-computer – they had no ideas, no lives. They were simply parts of a machine.

She wondered whether James and Elizabeth had slept together long ago, before she had become engaged to him, and thought they probably had. An exhaustion came over her: the artificial weariness enforced upon someone who has many capabilities and is consistently prevented from using any of them.

The doctors called it depression. She worked on her tennis, went swimming three times a week, and helped to organize charity fund-raising events. She made progress. Now she was an elegant young matron in magazine pictures, not the messy-haired girl who had run shrieking down the hallway from her mother-in-law's room as she held her squealing baby on one arm and then slammed and locked the door after her. She would never again stay behind a locked door, threatening to cut her throat, to go to the newspapers, to get a divorce. James had stood on the other side of the door and talked to her for five hours until she'd given in.

And now they had their own happy family together and she moved through the round of public and domestic duties as calmly and gracefully as a swan on the water. But the serenity of her face was like the visible after-effect of an illness she had survived; or like a symptom of the death that was to follow.

*

James thought they should take their holiday in a spot more remote than the ones they usually chose in the winter. He was fed up with being hounded by reporters and photographers. And she was nervous about the children all the time. The house had always received a large quantity of anonymous mail and more than the average number of unpleasant telephone cranks. Now they were being persecuted not just because of their wealth, but because it was the fashion. Every day you could read in the papers about 'copy cat' crimes – acts of violence committed in imitation of something the perpetrators had seen on television or in the headlines of the very publication you had in your hand. If there had been a hoax call about a bomb at some large public building, it was fairly certain that the family secretaries would be kept busy with their share of telephone threats in the next few days. Everyone in the house was on speaking terms with at least ten policemen. There had been many crises over the years. They counted on the police, although James's mother, and his sister Margaret's ex-husband too, said they sometimes thought that most of the information these nuts and maniacs found out about them came straight from the police themselves.

Anna-Louise's entry into the family had brought further complications, adding an interest for the Irish connections on all sides. Anna-Louise herself wasn't afraid. She wasn't in any case the sort of woman who worried, but on top of that, her children hadn't been put in danger yet, whereas Margaret's had: her daughter, Amy, was once almost spirited away by a gang of kidnappers. 'Fortunately,' Margaret told friends later, 'they got the cook's niece instead. She was standing out at the side of the back drive, and it just shows how dumb these people are: It was Sunday and she was wearing a little hat, white gloves, a pink organdie dress and Mary Janes. If they'd known anything about Amy, they'd have realized she wouldn't be caught dead in a get-up like that. As a matter of fact, at that time of day on a Sunday, she'd be in her jeans, helping MacDonald in the greenhouses.'

They had paid handsomely to get the niece back; good cooks weren't easy to find. But they'd cooperated with the police, which they wouldn't have dared to do if Amy herself had been the victim: it would have been too big a risk, even though in that particular case it had worked and they had caught the three men and rescued the girl. Flora later began to think it would have been better for the niece not to have lived through the capture; she started to crack up afterwards and developed a bitter enmity towards Amy, who, she told everybody, ought to have been the one to be seized.

The incident had taken place when Flora was in the beginning months of her second pregnancy. It brought home to her how difficult it was to escape the family destiny: even the children were dragged into it. And though it was only one of the many frightening, uncomfortable or calamitous events from the background of her first few years of marriage, it was the one that turned her into a woman who fretted about the future and who, especially, feared for the safety of her children. James tried to soothe her. On the other hand, his friend and chauffeur, Michael, who kept telling her everything would be all right, seemed at the same time to approve of the fact that she worried. She thought he felt it was a proof that she was a good mother.

'If we go too far away,' she said to James, 'the children –'

'We have telephones and telegraphs, and an airport nearby. It isn't any worse than if we were going to California for the weekend.'

'But it's so far away.'

He asked, 'What could we do, even here, if anything happened?' The question was meant to mollify, but it scared her even more.

'The doctor says you need a rest,' he insisted. She agreed with that. It seemed odd that a woman should live in a house as large as a castle, with nothing to do all day but easy, pleasant tasks, and still need a rest. But it was true.

'Michael will be with us,' he added.

That, finally, convinced her. If Michael came along, nothing bad could happen, either at home or abroad. She was distrustful of even the smallest disruption to her life, but she wanted to go. And she would be relieved to get away from the menace of all the unknown thousands who hated her without even having met her.

You couldn't be free, ever. And if you were rich, you were actually less often free than other people. You were recognized. The spotlight was on you. Strangers sent you accusations, threats and obscene letters. And what had you done to them? Nothing. Even the nice people were falsified by the ideas they had of your life; those who didn't threaten, begged. Everyone wanted money and most of them felt no shame at demanding it outright. They were sure they deserved it, so they had to have it. It didn't matter who gave it to them.

She too had been altered, of course. She had made her compromises and settled down. Of all the people connected with the family only Michael, she felt, had kept his innocence. His loyalty was like the trust of a child. When he drove her into town to shop, when they said hello or goodbye, she thought how wonderful it would be to put her arms around him, to have him put his arms around her. She was touched and delighted by all his qualities, even at the times when she'd seen him thwarted or frustrated and noticed how he went white and red very quickly.

'All right,' she said. 'If Michael comes too.'

'Of course,' James told her. 'I wouldn't be without him. There's a good hotel we can stay at. I don't think you'll need a maid.'

'I don't want a maid. I just want to be able to phone home twice a day to check if everything's all right.'

'Everything's going to be fine. You know, sometimes kids can get sick of their parents. It won't do them any harm to miss us for a week or two.'

'Two?'

'Well, if we don't make it at least two, half the trip's going to be spent in the plane, or recovering from jet-lag.'

*

They had parties to say goodbye: the friends' party, the relatives', and one birthday party for Margaret's youngest child, which coincided with a garden club meeting. Flora's mother-in-law directed the gloved and hatted ladies around flowerbeds that were to be mentioned in the yearly catalogue. Her father-in-law put in a brief appearance at the far end of the Italian gardens, shook hands with a few of the women and came back to the house, where he stayed for quite a while looking with delectation at the children digging into their ice cream and cake. Flora smiled at him across the table. She got along well with him, as did all his daughters-in-law, though Anna-Louise was his favourite. His own daughters had less of his benevolence, especially Margaret, whose whole life had been, and was still, lived in the always unsuccessful effort to gain from him the admiration he gave so freely to others. That was one of the family tragedies that Flora could see clearly. No one ever said anything about it and she'd assumed from the beginning that, having grown up with it, they'd never noticed. It was simply one more truth that had become acceptable by being ritualized.

The birthday room was filled with shouts and shrieks. Food was smeared, thrown and used to make decorations. One boy had built a palace of cakes and candies on his plate. There were children of industrialists, oil millionaires, ambassadors, bankers and heads of state; but they looked just like any other children, grabbing each other's paper hats while one of them was sick on the rug.

Michael too was looking on. He was enjoying himself, but he was there to work. He watched with a professional, noting glance. If anything went wrong, he was there to stop it. His presence made Flora feel safe and happy. She began to look forward to the trip.

The next evening, it was the grown-ups' turn to be sick on the rug. Five of their guests had to stay over for the weekend. On Monday morning Flora and James left for the airport.

At first she'd wanted to take hundreds of photographs with her. She'd started looking through the albums and every few pages taking one or two out; then it was every other page. Finally she had a fistful of pictures, a pile as thick as a doorstop. James chose twelve, shoved the others into a drawer and told her they had to hurry now.

The children waved and smiled, their nurse cried. 'I wish she wouldn't do that,' Flora said in the car. 'Bursting into tears all the time.'

'Just a nervous habit,' he told her. 'It doesn't seem to affect the kids. They're a pretty hard-bitten bunch.' He clasped his hand over hers, over the new ring he had given her the night before. She tried to put everything out of her mind, not to feel apprehensive about the plane flight.

They were at the airport with plenty of time to spare, so he took her arm and led her to the duty-free perfume, which didn't interest her.

'There's a bookstore,' she said.

'All right.'

They browsed through thrillers, war stories, romantic novels and books that claimed to tell people how society was being run and what the statistics about it proved.

They became separated. The first James knew of it was when he heard her laugh coming from the other side of the shop and saw her turn, looking for him. She was holding a large magazine.

'Come look,' she called. The magazine appeared to be some kind of colouring book for children. There was a whole shelf full of the things. After the paper people in the drawings were coloured and cut free, you snipped out the pictures of their clothes and pushed the tabs down over the shoulders of the dolls.

'Aren't they wonderful?' she said. 'Look. This one's called "Great Women Paper Dolls". It's got all kinds of . . . Jane Austen, Lady Murasaki, Pavlova. Look at the one of Beatrix Potter: she's got a puppy in her arms when she's in her fancy dress, but underneath it's a rabbit. And –'

'These are pretty good,' he said. He'd discovered the ones for boys: history, warfare, exploration. 'As a matter of fact, the text to these things is of a very high standard. Too high for a colouring book.'

'Paper doll books.'

'You've got to colour them before you cut them out. But anybody who could understand the information would be too old to want one. You wonder who they're aimed at.'

'At precocious children like ours, of course. They'll think they're hysterical. We can send them these. Paper dolls of Napoleon and Socrates. Look, it says here: if I don't see my favourite great woman, I may find her in the book called "Infamous Women Paper Dolls". Oh James, help me look for that one.'

'Flora,' he said, 'the children are here. We're the ones who are supposed to be going away.'

'Yes, but we can send them right now, from the airport. Aren't they funny? Look. Infamous Women – how gorgeous. Catherine di Medici, Semiramis. And in the other one – here: an extra dress for Madame de Pompadour; the only woman to get two dresses. Isn't that nice? She'd have appreciated that.'

She was winding herself up to the point where at any moment her eyes would fill with tears. He said, 'Who's that one? Looks like she got handed the castor oil instead of the free champagne.'

'Eadburga.'

'Never heard of her.'

'It says she was at her worst around 802. Please, James. We can leave some money with the cashier.'

'Anything to get you out of this place,' he told her.

After they'd installed themselves in their seats and were up in the air, he said, 'What was the difference between the great and the infamous?'

'The great were artists and heroic workers for mankind,' she said. 'The infamous were the ones in a position of power.'

The speed of her reply took him by surprise. He couldn't remember if it might have been true. Florence Nightingale, he recalled, had figured among the greats; Amelia Earhart, too. But there must also have been a ruler of some sort: Elizabeth I, maybe? Surely Queen Victoria had been in the book of good ones. And Eleanor of Aquitaine had been on a page fairly near that. He was still thinking about the question after Flora had already fallen asleep.

*

They arrived in an air-conditioned airport much like any other, were driven away in limousines with smoked-glass windows and were deposited at their hotel, where they took showers and slept. The first thing they did when they woke up was to telephone home. They didn't really look at anything until the next day.

They walked out of the marble-pillared hotel entrance arm in arm and blinked into the sun. They were still turned around in time. Already Flora was thinking about an afternoon nap. They looked to the left and to the right, and then at each other. James smiled and Flora pressed his arm. The trip had been a good idea.

They strolled slowly forward past the large, glittering shops that sold luxury goods. You could have a set of matching jade carvings packed and sent, jewellery designed for you, clothes tailored and completed in hours. James said, 'We can do all that later.' Flora stopped in front of a window display of jade fruit. She said, 'It's probably better to get it over with.'

They stood talking about it: whether they'd leave the presents till later and go enjoy themselves, or whether they ought to get rid of the duties first, so as not to have them hanging over their heads for two weeks. Michael waited a few feet to the side, watching, as usual, without seeming to.

They decided to do the difficult presents first – the ones that demanded no thought but were simply a matter of knowing what to ask for and choosing the best. They handed over credit cards and traveller's cheques for tea sets, bolts of silk material, dressing gowns, inlaid boxes, vases, bowls and bronze statuettes. By lunch-time they were worn out.

They went back to the hotel to eat. Light came into the high-ceilinged dining-room through blinds, shutters, curtains and screens. It was as if they were being shielded from an outside fire – having all the heat blocked out, while some of the light was admitted. About twenty other tables were occupied. Michael sat on his own, though if they had had their meal anywhere in town, he'd have eaten with them.

James looked around and smiled again. 'This is very pleasant,' he said. He beamed at her and added, 'I think the holiday is already doing its job. You're looking extremely well after all your shopping. Filled with a sense of achievement.'

'Yes, I'm OK now. Earlier this morning I was feeling a lot like Eadburga.'

'How's that?'

'At her worst around 8.15, or whenever it was.'

He laughed. It had taken her years to say things that made him laugh and she still didn't know what sort of remark was going to appeal to him. Sometimes he'd laugh for what seemed to be no reason at all, simply because he was in the mood.

They went up to their rooms for a rest. She closed her eyes and couldn't sleep. He got up, shuffled through the magazines and newspapers he'd already read, and said he couldn't sleep, either. They spent the afternoon making love, instead.

'Dress for dinner tonight?' she asked as she arranged her clothes in the wardrobe.

'Let's go someplace simple. I've had enough of the well-tempered cuisine. Why don't we just slouch around and walk in somewhere?'

'You wouldn't rather get the ptomaine at the end of the trip rather than straight away?'

'Well, we've got lists of doctors and hospitals a mile long. We could get a shot for it.'

'Will Michael be coming with us?'

'Of course,' he said.

'Then I guess it's safe enough.'

'In a pinch, I could probably protect you, too.'

'But you might get your suit creased.' She made a funny face at him.

'I love vacations,' he told her. 'You're definitely at your best.'

'I told you: I'm fine now.'

'They say most of the jet-lag hangover is caused by dehydration, but the big difference I've noticed this time is the change in light.'

'Well, it's nice to be away for a while. There'll be at least three new quarrels going by the time we get back, and they'll be missing us a lot.'

'We might take more time off sometime. A long trip. A year or so.'

'Oh, Jamie, all the sweat. I couldn't do it so soon again, setting up a whole new household and uprooting the children from all their friends.'

'I didn't mean I'd be working. I meant just you and me away from everybody in a lovely spot, somewhere like Tahiti. New Caledonia, maybe.'

She said again, 'Would Michael come too?'

'I don't know. I hadn't thought.'

She pulled a dress out of the hanger and decided that it wasn't too wrinkled to wear without having the hotel maid iron it.

'I guess he'd have to,' James said.

'He wouldn't mind?'

'Kelvin? He never minds anything. He'd love to.'

She'd have to think. If it had been Michael asking her to go away with him to the South Seas, she'd have gone like a shot. But the more dissatisfied she'd become with her life, the more reluctant she was to make any changes.

She said, 'Well, it's something to think over. When would you want to make a decision about it?'

'Three weeks, about then.'

'All right. We'll have to talk about the children. That's the main thing.'

She was still worrying about the children as they started towards the steps that led to the elevators. There was an entire puzzle-set of interlocking staircases carpeted in pale green and accompanied by carved white banisters that made the whole arrangement look like flights of ornamental balconies. If you wanted to, you could continue on down by the stairs. James always preferred to ride in elevators rather than walk. Exercise, in his opinion, was what sport was for; it wasn't meant to move you from one place to another. Locomotion should be carried out with the aid of machines and servants.

'Let me just call home again quick,' she suggested.

'You'll wake them all up. It's the wrong time there.'

'Are you sure? I'm so mixed up myself, I can't tell.'

'We'll phone when we get back from supper,' he said.

They had been on other trips together long ago, when the telephoning had become a genuine obsession. Now they had a routine for it: she mentioned it, he told her when, she believed him and agreed to abide by the times he designated. The whole game was a leftover from the unhappy years when she'd had no self-confidence and felt that she kept doing everything wrong.

Michael stepped into the elevator after them. He moved behind them as they walked through the lobby.

'Look,' Flora said.

The central fountain, which earlier in the day had been confined to three low jets, now sprayed chandelier-like cascades of brilliance into the three pools beneath. Tables and chairs had been set out around the display and five couples from the hotel were being served tea. As Flora and James watched, a group of children rushed for a table, climbed into the chairs and began to investigate the spoons and napkins. A uniformed nurse followed them.

James said, 'Like some tea?'

'Unless Michael doesn't –'

'Sure,' Michael said. 'I'll sit right over there.' He headed towards the sofas and armchairs near the reception desk. Wherever they were, he always knew where to find the best spots for surveillance, and probably had a good idea where everybody else might choose to be, too. He'd been trained for all that. You couldn't see from his walk or from the way his clothes fitted that he carried guns and a knife, but he did. Sometimes it seemed incredible to Flora that he had been through scenes of violence; he'd been in the marines for two years while James was finishing up college. His placid, law-abiding face gave no sign of the fact. But she thought how upsetting the experience must have been to him at first. Even killing didn't come naturally – especially killing: somebody had to teach it to you. And boys weren't really cruel or bloodthirsty unless they had a background of brutality.

Michael's background, she knew, was quite ordinary. He was a child of an undergardener and one of the parlourmaids at the house. Once she'd asked him how he'd managed to get through his military training and he'd told her that he'd been lucky: he'd been with a group of boys who'd become really good friends. And, as for violence, he'd added, 'You got to be objective, say to yourself this is completely a professional thing. Like render unto Caesar. You know?' She had nodded and said yes, but had had no idea what he'd been talking about.

They sat close to the fountain to enjoy it but not so near as to be swept by the fine spray that clouded its outpourings. James had also taken care to station himself, and her, at a reasonable distance from the children, who looked like more than a match for their wardress.

Their nearest companions were a man and woman who might have been on a business trip or celebrating an early retirement. They gave the impression of being a couple who had been married for a long time. The woman looked older than the man. She had taken two extra chairs to hold her shopping bags and as soon as the tea was poured out she began to rummage through her papers and packages. She looked up and caught Flora's eye. Flora smiled. The woman said, 'I couldn't resist. It's all so pretty and the prices are just peanuts. Aren't they, Desmond?'

The man's eyes flicked to the side. 'We're going to need an extra plane to take it all back,' he said. His head turned to the stairway and the main door, warily, as if looking for eavesdroppers.

'Not here,' his wife told him.

'Only damn part of this hotel they let you smoke a pipe is in your own room. Place must be run by the anti-tobacco league.'

'Do you good,' his wife said. She began to talk about silks and jade and porcelain. Flora guessed before the woman started to quote numbers that they were going to be several price-brackets under anything she and James would have bought. On the other hand, like most rich people, she loved hunting down bargains.

The couple, whose name was Dixon, went on to tell their opinions of the city and of the country in general. They regretted, they said, not having made provision for trips outside town to – for example – the big flower festival that had been held the week before, or just the ordinary market mornings. They were leaving the next day. Flora saw James relax as he heard them say it: there wasn't going to be any danger of involvement. He began to take an interest in the list of places and shops they recommended. Flora was halfway through her second cup of tea and could tell that James would want to leave soon, when Mrs Dixon said, 'What I regret most of all, of course, is that we never got to see the goddess.'

'Oh,' Flora said. 'At the festival?'

'At her temple.'

'A statue?'

'No, no. That girl. You know – the one they train from childhood, like the Lama in Tibet.'

'Not like that,' her husband said.

'Well, I just couldn't face standing in line for all that time in the heat. But now I really wish I'd given myself more of a push.'

'I haven't heard about the goddess,' Flora admitted. James said that he'd read about it somewhere, he thought, but only remembered vaguely. And he hadn't realized that the custom had to do with this part of the world.

'Oh, yes,' Mr Dixon told him, and launched into the history of the goddess, who was selected every few years from among thousands of candidates. The child was usually four or five years old when chosen, had to be beautiful, to possess several distinct aesthetic features such as the shape of the eyes and ears and the overall proportion of the limbs, and could have no blemish. 'Which is quite an unusual thing to be able to find,' he said. 'Then –'

'Then,' Mrs Dixon interrupted, 'they train her in all the religious stuff and they also teach her how to move – sort of like those temple dancers, you know: there's a special way of sitting down and getting up, and holding out your fingers, and so on. And it all means something. Something religious. There are very strict rules she's got to obey about everything – what she can eat and drink, all that. Oh, and she should never bleed. If she cuts herself – I forget whether she has to quit or not.'

'She just has to lie low for a few days, I think,' Mr Dixon said.

'And she can never cry – did I say that?'

'And never show fear.'

'Then at puberty –'

'She's out on her can and that's the whole ball game. They go and choose another one.'

'So people just drive out to her temple to look at her,' Flora asked, 'as if she's another tourist attraction?'

'Oh no, dear,' Mrs Dixon said. 'They consult her. They take their troubles to her and she gives them the solution. It's like an oracle. And I think you donate some small amount for the upkeep of the temple. They don't mind tourists, but it isn't a show – it's a real religious event.'

Mr Dixon said, 'She's very cultivated, so it seems. Speaks different languages and everything.'

James asked, 'What happens to her afterwards?'

'Oh, that's the joke. She used to spend the rest of her life in seclusion as the ex-goddess. But this last time, the girl took up with a young fellow, and now she's married to him and –'

' – and there's the most terrific scandal,' Mrs Dixon said happily. 'It's really turned things upside-down. I guess it's like a priest getting married to a movie star. They can't get over it.'

'Matter of fact, I wouldn't want to be in that girl's shoes.'

'Why?' Flora asked.

Mr Dixon shrugged. 'A lot of people are mad as hell. They've been led to expect one thing and now this other thing is sprung on them. They're used to thinking of their goddess as completely pure, and also truly sacred. I guess it can't look right for her to revert to being human all of a sudden, just like the rest of us. See what I mean?'

Flora nodded.

'She's broken the conventions,' James said, which didn't seem to Flora nearly such a good explanation as Mr Dixon's, but she smiled and nodded again.

*

They took a long time deciding where they wanted to eat their evening meal. In the beginning it was too much fun looking around to want to go inside; they had discovered the night life of the streets, full of people going about ordinary business that might have taken place indoors during the daytime: there were open-air barber shops, dress stalls where customers could choose their materials and be measured for clothes; shops that stocked real flowers and also stands that sold bouquets made out of feathers and silk.

'No wonder Mrs Dixon had all those piles of packages,' Flora said. 'Everything looks so nice.'

'Under this light,' James warned. 'I bet it's pretty tacky in daylight.'

Michael grunted his assent.

'Don't you think it's fun?' she asked.

'Very colourful,' he said. She wasn't disappointed in his answer. It gave her pleasure just to be walking beside him.

She would have liked to eat in one of the restaurants that were no more than just a few tables and chairs stuck out on the sidewalk. James vetoed the suggestion. They moved back to the beginning of richer neighbourhoods and he suddenly said, 'That one.'

In front of them was a building that looked like a joke: dragons and pagodas sprouting everywhere from its roof-tops. The lower floor was plate glass, which reassured the three of them – that looked modern and therefore unromantic and probably, they expected, hygienic. 'We can rough it for once,' James said. Through the downstairs windows they could see rows of crowded booths, people sitting and eating. Most of the patrons appeared to be tourists – another good sign.

They entered and were seated all on the same side of a table. Flora had hoped to be put between the two men, but the waiter had positioned Michael at James's far side. Opposite her an old man was eating noodles from a bowl. He stared determinedly downward.

They looked at the menu. As James ordered for them, a young couple came up and were shown to the remaining places; he had a short beard and wore a necklace consisting of a single wooden bead strung on a leather thong; she had a long pigtail down her back. They were both dressed in T-shirts and bluejeans and carried gigantic orange back-packs. They made a big production of taking off the packs and resting them against the outside of the booth. When the old man on the inside had finished eating and wanted to get out, they had to go through the whole routine again. Once they were settled, they stared across the table contemptuously at the fine clothes the others were wearing. They seemed to be especially incredulous over James's outfit, one which he himself would have considered a fairly ordinary linen casual suit for the tropics.

James switched from English to French and began to tell Flora about New Caledonia. It meant that Michael was excluded from the conversation, but he knew that this was one of James's favourite methods of detaching himself from company he didn't want to be associated with. It only worked in French because Flora's limited mastery of other languages wouldn't permit anything else. James had always been good at learning new languages. As a child he had even made up a language that he and Michael could use to baffle grown-up listeners. Occasionally they spoke it even now. Flora had figured out that it must be some variation of arpy-darpy talk, but it always went so fast that she could never catch anything.

The back-packers spoke English. He was American, she Australian. Their names were Joe and Irma. They spent their whole time at the table discussing the relative merits of two similar articles they had seen in different shops. Some part of the objects had been made out of snakeskin and, according to Irma, one of them was 'pretty ratty-looking'; on the other one, so Joe claimed, the so-called snake had been an obvious fake, definitely plastic.

'It's like those beads you got,' he said. 'Supposed to be ivory, and you can see the join where they poured it into the mould in two halves and then stuck them together. Why can't you tell? How can you miss seeing it? If you keep on spending money like this –'

Irma muttered, 'Well, it's my money.'

'We should be keeping some by for emergencies,' he said. She sulked for the rest of the meal. She chewed her food slowly and methodically. Flora wished the girl had picked everything up, thrown it all over her companion and told him to go to hell. He was staring around with disapproving interest at the other diners. He wasn't going to feel guilty about hurting his girlfriend; he hadn't even noticed her play for sympathy.

Flora said in French, 'Could you really go for a year without work?'

'Sure. I'd work on something else,' James said. 'We'd get a nice boat, sail around.' He added, 'The food isn't too bad here.'

'Wait till tomorrow to say it,' she told him.

*

The weather next morning looked like being the start of another wonderful day. All the days were wonderful in that climate at the right time of year. They both felt fine. Michael too said he was OK. Flora called home.

She got Margaret on the line, who said, 'We've missed you. Anna-Louise is on the warpath again.'

'What about?'

Anna-Louise's voice came in on an extension, saying, 'That isn't Margaret getting her story in first, is it? Flora?'

'Hi,' Flora said. 'How are you all?'

'The natives are restless, as usual.'

Margaret tried to chip in but was told by Anna-Louise to get off the line. There was a click.

'Children all right?' Flora asked.

'Couldn't be better.'

'Are they there?' She waved James over. They spent nearly fifteen minutes talking to the children, who said again how much they loved the paper doll books and how all their friends thought they were great and wanted some too. James began to look bored and to make motions that the conversation should stop. He leaned over Flora. 'We've got to hang up now,' he said into the mouthpiece.

They were the second couple into the breakfast room. 'Are we that early?' she asked.

He checked his watch. 'Only a little. It's surprising how many people use their holidays for sleeping.'

'I guess a lot of them have jet-lag, too. That's the trouble with beautiful places – they're all so far away.'

He spread out the maps as Michael was seated alone at a table for two several yards beyond them. Flora had them both in view, Michael and James. She felt her face beginning to smile. At that moment she couldn't imagine herself returning from the trip. The children and relatives could stay at the other end of the telephone.

James twitched the map into place. He liked planning things out and was good at it. She, on the other hand, couldn't even fold a map back up the right way. She was better at the shopping. Now that they were used to their routines, they had a better time sightseeing. In the early days James had spent even more time phoning his broker than Flora had in worrying about the babies.

She remembered the young couple at dinner the night before, and how much they had seemed to dislike each other. Of course, it was hard to tell anything about people who were quarrelling; still, they didn't seem to have acquired any of the manners and formulae and pleasing deceptions that helped to keep lovers friendly over long periods. She herself had come to believe that – if it weren't for this other glimpse of a love that would be for ever unfulfilled – she'd have been content with just those diplomatic gestures, plus a shared affection for what had become familiar. If she had been free to choose at this age, her life would have been different. Everybody was free now; and they all lived together before they got married.

James put a pencil mark on the map and started to draw a line across two streets.

Maybe, she thought, she'd been free even then. The freedom, or lack of it, was simply ceremonial. Rules and customs kept you from disorder and insecurity, but they also regulated your life to an extent that was sometimes intolerable. They protected and trapped at the same time. If it weren't for habit and codes of behaviour, she and Michael could have married and had a happy life together.

It had taken her years to find out that most of her troubles had been caused by trying to switch from one set of conventions to another. The people around her – even the ones who had at first seemed to be against her – had actually been all right.

She said, 'You know what I'd really like to do? I'd like to see that girl.'

'Hm?'

'The one the Dixons were talking about at tea. The goddess.'

'Oh.' James looked up. 'Well, maybe. But don't you think the idea is going to be a lot better than the reality? Following it up is just going to mean what they said: standing in line for hours. Do you want to spend your vacation doing that?'

'And if you don't, regretting that you never did. I would like to. Really. You don't have to come, if you don't want to.'

'Of course I'd come, if you went.'

'Could you find out about it? It's the thing I want to do most.'

'Why?'

'Why? Are there goddesses at home?'

He laughed, and said, 'Only in the museums. And in the bedroom, if you believe the nightgown ads.'

'Please.'

'OK,' he promised. 'I'll find out about it. But it seems to me, the one worth looking at is going to be the one that went AWOL and got married.'

'She didn't go AWOL. She was retired.'

'A retired goddess? No such thing. Once a god, always a god.'

'If you become impure as soon as you bleed, then you can lose the divinity. Women –'

'All right, I'll find out about it today. Right now. This very minute.'

'I'm only trying to explain it.'

'Wasted on me,' he told her.

'Don't you think it's interesting?'

'Mm.'

'What does that mean?'

'I'll see about it this afternoon.'

Over the next few days they went to the botanical gardens; to the theatre, where they saw a long, beautiful and rather dull puppet play; and to a nightclub, at which Flora developed a headache from the smoke and James said he was pretty sure the star *chanteuse* was a man. They got dressed up in their evening clothes to visit the best restaurant in town, attended a dinner given by a friend of the family who used to be with the City Bank in the old days, and made an excursion to the boat market. Half the shops there were hardly more than floating bamboo frameworks with carpets stretched across them. Bright pink orchid-like flowers decorated all the archways and thresholds, on land and on the water. The flowers looked voluptuous but unreal, and were scentless; they added to the theatrical effect – the whole market was like a view backstage. James and Flora loved it. Michael said it was too crowded and the entire place was a fire-trap.

'Well, there's a lot of water near at hand,' James said.

'You'd never make it. One push and the whole mob's going to be everybody on top of theirselves. They'd all drown together.'

'I do love it when you get on to the subject of safety, Kelvin. It always makes me feel so privileged to be alive.'

A privilege granted to many, Flora thought, as she gazed into the throng of shoving, babbling strangers. She suddenly felt that she had to sit down.

She turned to James. 'I feel –' she began.

He saw straight away what was wrong. He put his arm around her and started to push through the crowd. Michael took the other side. She knew that if she really collapsed, Michael could pick her up and sling her over his shoulder like a sack of flour, he was so strong. He'd had to do it once when she'd fainted at a ladies' fund-raising luncheon. That had been a hot day too, lunch with wine under a blue canvas awning outdoors; but she'd been pregnant then. There was no reason now for her to faint, except the crowd and the lack of oxygen.

There wasn't any place to sit down. She tried to slump against Michael. They moved her forward.

'Here,' James said.

She sat on something that turned out to be a tea chest. They were in another part of the main arcade, in a section that sold all kinds of boxes and trunks. A man came up to James, wanting to know if he was going to buy the chest.

Back at the hotel, they laughed about it. James had had to shell out for a sandalwood casket in order to give her time to recover. When they were alone, he asked if she was really all right, or could it be that they'd been overdoing it in the afternoons? She told him not to be silly: she was fine.

'I think maybe we should cancel the trip to the goddess, though, don't you?'

'No, James. I'm completely OK.'

'Waiting out in the sun –'

'We'll see about that when we get there,' she said flatly. It was a tone she very seldom used.

'OK, it's your vacation. I guess we could always carry you in on a stretcher and say you were a pilgrim.'

He arranged everything for the trip to the temple. The day he chose was near the end of their stay, but not so close to the flight that they couldn't make another date if something went wrong. One of them might come down with a twenty-four-hour bug or there might be a freak rainstorm that would flood the roads. 'Or,' James said, 'if she scratches herself with a pin, we've had it till she heals up. They might even have to choose a new girl.'

In the meantime they went to look at something called 'the jade pavilion' – a room in an abandoned palace, where the silk walls had been screened by a lattice-work fence of carved jade flowers. The stone had been sheared and sliced and ground to such a fineness that in some places it appeared as thin as paper. The colours were vibrant and glowing – not with the freshness of real flowers nor the sparkle of faceted jewels, but with the lustre of fruits; the shine that came off the surfaces was almost wet-looking.

As they walked under the central trellis a woman behind them said, 'Think of having to dust this place.' A man's voice answered her, saying, 'Plenty of slave labour here. Nobody worries about dust.'

'Glorious,' James said afterwards. And Michael declared that, 'You had to hand it to them.' He'd been impressed by the amount of planning that must have gone into the work: the measuring and matching, the exactitude.

Flora had liked the silk walls behind, which were covered with pictures of flying birds. She said, 'I guess you're supposed to think to yourself that you're in a garden, looking out. But it's a little too ornate for me. It's like those rooms we saw in Palermo, where the whole place was gold and enamel – like being inside a jewel box. This one would have been even nicer made out of wood and then painted. Don't you think?'

'That would fade,' James said. 'You'd have to re-do it all the time. And in this climate you'd probably need to replace sections of it every few years.'

They kept calling home every day. The weather there was horrible, everyone said. Anna-Louise had a long story about friends of hers whose house had been burgled. And one of the children had a sore throat; he coughed dramatically into the receiver to show how bad it was.

'They need us,' Flora said. 'That was a cry of despair.'

'That was the standard performance,' James told her. 'There's one who hasn't inherited any bashfulness. He'd cough his heart out in front of fifty reporters every day and do retakes if he thought it hadn't been a really thorough job. No hired substitute for him. It's going to be a question of how hard we'll have to sit on him to keep him down. Worse than Teddy was at that age.'

'He sounded pretty bad.'

'You're the one we're going to worry about at the moment. One at a time. Feeling faint? Claustrophobic?'

Flora shook her head. She felt fine. They strolled around town together and sat in a public park for a while. They'd chosen a bench within the shade of a widely branched, symmetrical tree. Michael rested against the stonework of a gate some distance away. While he kept them in sight, he watched the people who passed by. James pointed out a pair of tourists coming through the entrance.

'Where?' Flora asked.

'Right by the gate. It's those two from the restaurant we went to our first night out.'

'Irma and Joe,' she said. 'So it is. And they're still arguing. Look.'

The couple had come to a stop inside the gates. Joe leaned forward and made sweeping gestures with his arms. Irma held herself in a crouching posture of defence: knees bent, shoulders hunched, chin forward. Her fists were balled up against her collar-bone. The two faced each other still encumbered by their back-packs and bearing a comical resemblance to armoured warriors or wrestlers costumed in heavy padding.

James said, 'She's just spent all her money and he's bawling her out.'

'You give it to him, Irma,' Flora said. James squeezed her hand.

They stayed on their bench and watched a large group of uniformed schoolchildren who – under the supervision of their teachers – went through what seemed to be the usual class exercises and then began to play some game neither Flora nor James could understand. Two of the children passed a book through the group while the others counted, telling off certain players to skip in a circle around the rest. They they all sang a rhyming verse and formed up in a new order.

At last he said, 'OK?' and stood up. She got to her feet. In the distance Michael too stepped forward.

They were three streets from where the hired car was parked, when Flora caught sight of a yellow bowl in a store window. She slowed down and, briefly, paused to look. James and Michael moved on a few paces. She turned back, to ask James what he thought about the bowl, and a hand closed gently over her arm just above the wrist. She looked up into a face she'd never seen before. For a moment she didn't realize anything. Then the hand tightened. At the same time, someone else grabbed her from behind. She dropped her handbag. Gasping and mewing sounds came from her throat, but she couldn't make any louder noise. She tried to kick, but that was all she could do.

Michael and James were with her almost immediately, hitting and kicking. Michael actually threw one of the gang into the air. Flora felt herself released. She fell to her knees, with her head against the glass of the window.

'Here,' James said, 'hold on to that.' He thrust her handbag into her arms and pulled her back up. She still couldn't speak.

They hurried her to the car and drove back to the hotel. Michael came up to the room with them and sat on the edge of the bed. James said he was calling in a doctor.

'I'm all right,' she jabbered, 'all right, perfectly – I'm fine. I'm just so mad. I'm so mad I could chew bricks. The nerve of those people!' She was shaking.

Michael stood up and got her a glass of water. She drank all of it and put her head down on the bed.

'That's a good idea,' James said. He and Michael left her and went into the sitting room. She could hear them talking. Michael said, 'The cops?' and James said, 'Tied up with police on vacation. Besides, what good?'

'No hope,' Michael answered. 'Anyway, weren't after money.'

'Bag.'

'No, arm. And left it. Her, not the. Alley right next. A few more seconds.'

'Jesus Christ,' James said. 'That means.'

Michael's voice said, 'Maybe not,' and Flora began to relax. She slept for a few minutes. She was on a beach in New Caledonia and Michael was sitting beside her on the sand. There was a barrel-vaulted roof of palm leaves overhead, like the canopy of a four-poster bed. She could hear the sound of the sea. And then suddenly someone stepped up in back of her and her arms were grabbed from behind.

She woke up. She almost felt the touch still, although it had been in her dream. She stared ahead at the chairs by the bed, the green-and-yellow pattern of the material they were upholstered in, the white net curtains over the windows where the light was beginning to dim away. She thought about the real event, earlier in the afternoon, and remembered again – as if it had left a mark on her body – the moment when the hand had closed over her arm. Once more she was filled with outrage and fury. *The nerve,* she thought; *the nerve.* And the terrible feeling of having been made powerless, of being held, pinioned, captured by people who had no right to touch her. That laying of the hand on her had been like the striking of a predator, and just as impersonal. When she thought about it, it seemed to her that she was picturing all the men as much bigger and stronger than they probably were, and perhaps older, too. They might have been only teenagers.

She wanted to forget about it. It was over. And James was right: it would ruin what was left of their trip to spend it making out reports in a police station. What could the police do? These gangs of muggers hit you, disappeared around a corner and that was the end of the trail. Once in Tokyo she and James had seen a man on the opposite sidewalk robbed by two boys. His hands had suddenly gone up in the air; and there was the pistol right in broad daylight, pointing into his chest. It could happen so fast. It was the kind of street crime she had come on the holiday in order to forget.

But you had to be prepared. These things were international. And timeless. All the cruelties came back: torture, piracy, massacres. The good things didn't return so often because it took too long to develop them. And it took a whole system of convention and ritual to keep them working; wheels within wheels. She was part of it. To keep the ordered world safe, you had to budget for natural deterioration and the cost of replacement. Nothing had a very high survival rate – not even jade, hard as it was.

She thought about the pavilion of jade flowers and wondered whether it was really so beautiful. Maybe in any case it was only as good as the people who liked it believed it to be. James had loved it. Michael hadn't seemed to like it except for the evidence of the work that had been put into it. He might have disapproved of the extravagance rather than been judging the place on aesthetic grounds. She felt herself falling asleep again.

When she woke it was growing dark. She got up, took a shower and changed. The three of them ate together in the hotel dining-room, drank a great deal, had coffee and then even more to drink afterwards. They talked about law and order and decent values and Flora was tight enough to say, 'We can afford to.' They agreed not to mention the incident to anyone at home until the trip was over.

James had a hangover the next day but read through all his newspapers as usual.

'Any mention of our little drama?' she asked.

'Of course not. We didn't report it. A few other muggings here, it says.'

'Maybe they're the same ones.'

'Nope. They'd have gone for the bag and left you. These are all cases of grab-and-run.'

'You mean, they wanted to kidnap me; get you to pay ransom. So, they must know all about us, who we are, what you can raise at short notice.'

'Maybe they check up on everybody staying at big hotels. Maybe they saw your rings. Or it might just be that they know a good-looking woman when they see one: probably thought they could sell you to somebody.'

'What?'

'Sure. Hey, look what else. It says here, the ex-goddess was stoned outside her house yesterday morning.'

'Yesterday morning we were pretty stoned, too. Or was that this morning?'

'A mob threw stones at her. They were some kind of religious group.'

'That's disgusting. That's even worse than trying to kidnap people.'

'She's all right, but she's in the hospital. That ought to mean she's OK. It only takes one stone to kill somebody.'

'Disgusting,' Flora muttered.

'And interesting,' James said. 'In a lot of countries it's still the traditional punishment for adultery.'

*

Their hired car drove them down the coastline. They took a picnic lunch, went for a swim and visited two shrines that, according to their guidebooks, were famous. On the next day they spent the morning trying to find material for curtains to go in a house belonging to Elizabeth's mother-in-law. Michael kept close to Flora all the time; their clothes often brushed as they walked or stood side by side.

On the day of their visit to the goddess it looked for the first time during the trip as if it might rain. James went back up to their rooms and got the umbrellas. On the ride out into the country they heard a few rumblings of thunder, but after that the skies began to clear and the day turned hot and muggy. The umbrellas sat in the car while they entered the temple precincts.

They were checked at the main gate, which looked more like the entrance to a fortress than to a religious building. Flora saw James stiffen as he caught sight of the long row of invalids sitting or lying on their sides, their relatives squatting near them on the ground. She remembered his joke about pilgrims. It wasn't so funny to see the real thing. He never liked being in places where there might be diseases. Most of their travelling had been carefully packaged and sanitized to avoid coming into contact with contagion or even the grosser aspects of simple poverty. You could have all the shots you liked, and it wouldn't help against the wrong virus. She knew that he'd be telling himself again about the number and quality of the hospitals in town.

The officials looked at their papers, spoke to the driver and interpreter, and let them in. The pilgrims stayed outside on the ground. Flora wondered how long they'd have to wait, and how important it was to pay over money before you were granted an interview; or maybe the goddess did a kind of group blessing from a distance. If she wasn't even allowed to bleed, she might not be any more eager than James to get close to the diseased masses. Even when inside the courtyard you could hear a couple of them from over the wall, coughing their lungs out. The smell of decay that hung around the place might have been coming from the same source.

They were escorted across a vast, open space, through an archway, into another courtyard, across that, and to a third. The long-robed official then led them up on to the porch of one of the side buildings, around the verandah and into an assembly hall. It felt dark and cool after the walk in the open. About seventy people waited inside, some sitting on the floor and others – mainly Western tourists – either on the built-in wood bench that ran around three of the walls, or on fold-up seats they'd brought with them. There were also low stools you could borrow or rent from the temple.

The official swept forward towards a door at the far end of the hall. Two more robed figures stood on guard by it. Flora's glance flickered lightly over the other people as she passed. There weren't many children there, except for very small babies that had had to be taken along so the mother could feed them. Most of the believers or curiosity-seekers were grown up and a good proportion of them quite old. A lot of them were also talking, the deaf ones talking loudly. Perhaps the fact that one figure was on its own, not turned to anyone else, was what made Flora notice: there, sitting almost in the middle of the dark wooden floor, was Irma, resting her spine against her back-pack. Joe wasn't with her. And she looked defeated, bedraggled, lost. Maybe she'd come not because this was a tourist attraction, but because she needed advice. She still looked to Flora like the complete guru-chaser – one of those girls who went wandering around looking for somebody to tell them the meaning of life. Yet she also looked desperate in another way, which Flora thought might not have anything to do with religion or philosophy or breaking up with a boyfriend, and might simply be financial. She was so struck by the girl's attitude that she almost forgot about the goddess.

They were rushed onward. The sentries opened the double doors for them and they went through like an awaited procession, entering and leaving three more hallways, all empty and each quieter than the last, until they reached a room like a schoolroom full of benches, and were asked to sit down. Their officials stepped forward to speak with two middle-aged priestesses who had come out of the chamber beyond – perhaps the place where the goddess was actually sitting. The idea suddenly gave Flora the creeps. It was like visiting a tomb.

She whispered to James, 'Did you see Irma out there?'

'Yes.'

'I'm glad she's split up with him, but she looks terrible. I think she must be broke.'

'Probably.'

'I'd like to give her something.'

'No.'

'Not much, just –'

It would mean so little to them, Flora thought, and so much to the girl. It would be even better to be able to tell her she'd done the right thing in leaving that boy and could choose a different man now if she wanted to, and this time find one who'd really love her.

James said, 'You've got to let people lead their own lives.'

Of course, it was assuming a lot. Irma might not have broken up with Joe at all. They might be meeting again in the evening after seeing the sights separately. Even so, it was certainly true that she had run out of money. There had to be some way of helping her out, but Flora couldn't think of one. Could she just hand over some cash and say, 'Did you drop this?' Maybe she could say, 'We were in the restaurant that night and you must have left this behind, it was lying in the corner of the seat and we've been looking for you ever since.'

'She'll fall on her feet,' James told her.

'For heaven's sake. It looks like she's fallen on her head. Can't we do something?'

'I don't think so. And I don't think we should. But if you still feel the same after we get through with this, we'll see. You'll have to figure out how to work it. And don't invite her back in the car.'

Flora stared upward, thinking. She saw for the first time that the ceiling beams were carved at regular intervals with formal designs and they were painted in colours so bright that they looked like enamelwork. She'd been right; that kind of thing was much more interesting than the jade pavilion. She thought: *I'll just put some bills into an envelope and use the story about finding it in the restaurant.* It was a shame when people ignored their good intentions because it was too difficult or too embarrassing to carry them out. She usually kept a few envelopes in her pocketbook.

The interpreter came back to their bench. 'Who is the seeker of truth?' he asked.

Flora looked blank. James said, 'What?'

'Is it you both two or three ask the goddess, or how many?'

'Just one,' James said. 'My wife.'

The man withdrew again. He spoke to the priestesses. One of them clapped her hands, the other went into the next room. The robed official spoke.

'Arise, if you please,' the interpreter told them. Michael moved from his bench to stand behind James. The three of them stepped forward until the official put up his hand against them.

The priestess came out again, leading a procession of eight women like herself. They walked two by two. In the middle of the line, after the first four and in front of the next four they'd kept a free space, in which trotted a midget-like, pink-clad figure: the goddess herself.

She was like a ceremonial doll only taken out on special occasions. Her robes reached to the floor. On her head she wore an elaborate triple-tiered crown of pearls and rubies and some sparkling greyish glass studs that were probably old diamonds. Long, wide earrings dangled from her ears and continued the framing lines of the ornamentation above, so that the still eyes seemed to float among the shimmering lights of crown, earrings, side panels and many-stranded necklaces.

All dressed up, just like a little lady, Flora thought; *what a dreadful thing to do to that child.* And yet the face that gazed out of all its glittering trappings was not exactly that of a child: enormous, dark eyes; serenely smiling mouth; the lovely bone-structure and the refinement of the features were like those of a miniature woman, not a child. Above all, the look of utter calmness and wisdom were strange to see. The girl could have been somewhere between seven and eight years old, although she was about the size of an American child of five.

The procession stopped. The official beckoned to Flora. She came up to where he pointed. The child, who hadn't looked at anything particular in the room, turned to her with pleased recognition, like a mother greeting a daughter.

Flora bowed and smiled back, slightly flustered but tingling with gratification. *This is weird,* she thought. *This is ridiculous.* But as the procession wheeled around, heading back into the room it had come from and gathering her along with it, she knew she would follow wherever they went and for however long they wanted her to keep going. She was actually close to tears.

The room was not a room, only another corridor. They had to walk down several turnings until they emerged at a courtyard of fruit trees. They entered the audience chamber from the far side.

The goddess seated herself on a wooden throne raised on steps. Like the rafters in this room too, the throne was carved and painted. She sat on a cushion of some ordinary material like burlap, which made her robes appear even more luxurious by contrast. Her tiny feet in their embroidered magenta slippers rested on one of the steps.

A robed woman, who had been waiting for them in the room, came and stood behind and a little to the side of the throne like a governess or a chaperone. Flora wondered if in fact the woman was to be the one to hand out the answers.

The little girl smiled prettily and said, 'Please sit.' She indicated the hassock in front of the steps to the throne. Flora knelt. She was uncomfortable. Her skirt felt too tight and her heart was thumping heavily. She raised her glance to the child and met, from out of all the silks and jewels, a look of happy repose.

'Speak freely,' the child told her in a musical voice. 'And say what is in your heart.'

Flora swallowed. She could hear the loud sound it made in her throat. All at once tears were in her eyes. She saw the figure before her in a blur, as if it might have been a holy statue and not a human being.

She began, 'I don't know what to do. Year after year. My life is useless. I have everything, nothing to want. Kind husband, wonderful children. I feel ashamed to be ungrateful, but it never was what . . . it never seemed like mine. It's as if I'd never had my own self. But there's one thing: a man. He's the only one who isn't corrupted, the only one I can rely on. I think about him all the time. I can't stop. I can't stand the idea that we'll never be together. He's only a servant. And I don't know what to do. I love him so much.' She ended on a sob and was silent.

She waited. Nothing happened. She sniffed, wiped the back of her hand across her cheek and looked up for her answer.

'Love?' the goddess asked.

Flora nodded. 'Yes,' she mumbled. 'Yes, yes.'

'True love', the sweet voice told her, 'is poor.'

Poor? Flora was bewildered. *Pure,* she thought. *Of course.*

'It is from the sky.'

The chaperone leaned forward towards the jewelled head. 'Godly,' she hissed.

'Godly,' the child repeated, smiling into Flora's anxious face. The densely embellished right sleeve raised itself as the girl lifted her arm. The small hand made a lyrical gesture up towards the heavens and back in an arc to the ground: a movement that described beauty and love falling upon human lovers below, uniting as it touched them – bringing together, inevitably, her life and Michael's without greed or insistence.

'Yes, yes,' she stammered again. She felt stunned. She knew that she had had her answer, whatever it was. It would take her some time to figure out exactly what it meant.

The child hadn't finished. 'You must rise above,' she said thoughtfully. 'You must ascend.'

'Transcend,' the chaperone corrected.

'Ascend,' the child repeated.

Flora nodded. She sighed and said, 'Thank you.' She started to get up. The chaperone came forward and, without touching, showed her the direction in which she should go. For a moment the woman blocked any further sight of the child. She indicated that Flora should move away, not try to catch another glimpse of the goddess, not to say thank you again; the interview was over.

She walked clumsily from the chamber and staggered a few times as she followed two priestesses back to the waiting-room. She bowed farewell to everyone. She let James take her by the arm. As they were ushered out, she leaned against him.

As soon as they passed outside the main gates, he began to hurry her along.

'Why are we going so fast?' she complained.

'Because you look terrible. I want to get you back into the car. You look like you're ready to faint again.'

'You're going too fast. I can't keep up.'

'Try, Flora,' he said. 'We can carry you if we have to.'

'No.'

'Christ knows why I let you talk me into this. What did she do – say she saw the ace of spades in your palm, or something? Jesus.' He and Michael bundled her into the car and they started on the drive to town.

She fell back in the seat. She still couldn't think clearly. *I must ascend,* she thought. It might be painful, but it would be necessary. *Did she mean that I have to rise above earthly love?* Maybe what the goddess had meant was that in the end everyone died and went to heaven, so it wasn't worth getting upset over unimportant things.

And perhaps the girl had also meant exactly what she'd said about love – that it was from heaven, freely given and necessary, but that rich people never had to feel necessity; if a friendship broke down, or a marriage, or a blood relationship, they somehow always managed to buy another one. Life could be made very agreeable that way. But love was what the goddess had said it was – not pure: poor.

'Well?' James asked.

'Better,' she said.

'Thank God for that. What did the creature do to you?'

'She told me I had to rise above.'

'Rise above what?'

'Oh, everything, I guess.'

'And that's what knocked you out – the Eastern version of moral uplift?'

'I just suddenly felt sort of . . . I don't know.'

He bent towards her, kissed her near her ear and whispered, 'Pregnant.'

'No.'

'Sure? You've been close to fainting twice.'

'Yes,' she said. 'Yes, I'm sure. No. What did you think of it all, Michael?'

'Very interesting indeed,' Michael answered. 'It's another way of life.'

'What did you think of her? The goddess.'

'Cute-looking little kid, but skinny as a rail underneath all those party clothes. You wonder if they feed them enough.'

'Those hundreds of people on litters believe she can cure them.'

'Yeah, well, they're sick. Sick people believe in anything.'

'Maybe they're right. Sometimes if you have faith, it makes things true.'

James groaned slightly with impatience.

Michael said, 'It's deception. Self-deception always makes people feel good. But it wouldn't fix a broken leg, if that's what was wrong with you. It might help you get better quicker, once a doctor's done the real work – see what I mean?'

'Yes, I see,' she said. He didn't understand. But there was no reason why he should. James said that she was tired and upset. 'We'll be back soon,' he assured her. 'And let's have an early lunch. I'm hungry as hell from getting up so early.'

'Is it still morning? You didn't think much of her, either, did you?'

'I thought she looked great, really fabulous – the dress, like a walking cyclamen plant, and the whole effect very pretty but a bit bizarre: like a gnome out of a fairy-tale. What I don't like is how she's knocked the wind out of you. They aren't supposed to do that. They're supposed to give comfort and strength. That's the nature of the job.'

'She did. She gave me something to think about, anyway. All the rest was me trying to get out what I wanted to say.'

He held her hand. He didn't ask what her request had been. He probably thought he knew; he'd think she'd have wanted to know something like, 'Why can't I be happy?' Everybody wanted happiness.

The car speeded up along the stretches by the coastline. They opened the windows and got a whiff of the sea before returning to the air-conditioning. Flora breathed deeply. All beaches were the same: salt and iodine, like the summers of her childhood. New Caledonia would be like this, too.

They reached town before noon. James ordered the car to wait down a side street. The three of them got out and walked to one of the nice restaurants they had tried several times before. Flora was all right now, except that she felt bemused. She could walk without any trouble but she couldn't stop thinking about the temple and the goddess. She especially couldn't stop remembering the expression of joyful serenity on the child's face. It seemed to her that if she kept up the attempt to recapture the way it looked, she wouldn't have to let go of it.

The whole business had gone very quickly, as matters usually did when well-organized, and paid for, in advance. And now they were having a good meal in a comfortable restaurant; and only at that moment did Flora recall that she'd meant to go up to Irma on her way out and hand her some money in an envelope.

'Eat,' James said.

She shook her head.

'Just a little,' he insisted.

She picked up the china spoon and looked at it. She put it into the soup bowl. James watched patiently. When the children had been small, he was always the one who could make them eat when they didn't want to, and later, make them brush their teeth: he let you know, without saying anything, that he was prepared to wait for ever, unchanging and with arms folded, until you did the right thing. Authority. And he never bothered with modern ideas about explaining things rationally. If the children asked, 'Why do I have to?' he'd answer, 'Because I say so.'

She began slowly, then ate hungrily. Before the coffee, she went off to the ladies' room for a long time and while she was there made sure that her face and hair looked perfect. She even thought of brushing her teeth with the travelling toothbrush she carried in her purse, but she'd be back at the hotel soon – she could do it there. James smiled approvingly as she emerged.

They sauntered out into the hot, dusty street again.

'Museum?' he suggested, 'or siesta?'

'A little nap might be nice. Is that all right with you, Michael?'

'Sure, fine,' Michael said.

James stopped on the corner. 'Where was that museum, anyhow?' he asked. 'Down around that street there somewhere, isn't it?'

Michael looked up. He began to point things out in the distance. Flora kept walking around the bend as the street curved to the right. She drew back against the buildings to avoid three boys who were standing together and talking in whispers. But as soon as she was clear, two others came out of the doorway. She started to move away, but they came straight towards her. And suddenly the first three, their friends, were behind her, snatching at her arms. It was the same as the day before, but this time she screamed loudly for Michael before the hands started to grip over her eyes and mouth. She also kicked and thrashed while they dragged her along the sidewalk. Right at the beginning, except for her own outburst, all the violent pulling and shoving took place to the accompaniment of low mutters and hisses. Only when James and Michael came charging around the corner did the real noise begin.

The gang had guns. The man now left alone to hold Flora from behind was jabbing something into her backbone. She knew it was a gun because she saw two of the others pull out pistols. They went for James. The voice behind her yelled, 'Stop, or we kill the woman.' Flora kept still, in case her struggling caused the weapon to go off by mistake. But Michael had his own gun in his hand and was crouched down in the road. He shot the two who were heading towards James, the third, who was waving a pistol in the air, and there was a fourth explosion landing someplace where Flora couldn't see. The arm around her gripped so tightly that she was suffocating. The voice, sounding deranged, screamed into her ear, 'You drop the gun, or I kill her!' She knew he meant it. He'd do anything. He might even kill her without knowing what he was doing.

Michael didn't hesitate. She saw him turn towards them and the look on his face was nothing: it was like being confronted by a machine. He fired right at her. She should have known.

She didn't fall straight away. The man who had held her lay dead on the ground while she swayed above him. She knew she'd been shot, but not where. It felt as if she'd been hit by a truck. And suddenly she saw that there was blood everywhere – maybe hers, maybe other people's.

She should have known that a man formed by the conventions of the world into which she had married would already have his loyalties arranged in order of importance, and that the men and male heirs to the line would always take precedence over the outsiders who had fitted themselves into their lives. James was central; she was only decoration. As long as one man in the street was left with a gun, that was a danger to James. In Michael's eyes she had passed during less than three minutes from object to obstacle. He'd shot her to pieces, and, using her as a target, killed the gunman behind her.

James had his arms around her. He was calling out for an ambulance. There were plenty of other people on the street now. And she thought: *My God, how embarrassing: I've wet my pants.* But what she said was, 'I'm bleeding,' and passed out.

*

She woke up looking at a wall, at window-blinds, at the ceiling. Everything hurt.

It was still daylight, so perhaps she hadn't been there very long. Or maybe it was the next day. It felt like a long time. She was trussed like a swaddled baby and she was hooked up to a lot of tubes – she could see that, too. And she was terrified that parts of her body had been shattered beyond repair: that they would be crippled so badly that they'd never move again, that perhaps the doctors had amputated limbs. The fear was even worse than the pain.

Someone got up from behind all the machinery on her other side and left the room.

James came from around the back of her bed and sat in a chair next to her. He looked tired. And sad, too. That was unusual; she'd hardly ever seen him looking sad. He reached over and put his hand on her bare right arm, which lay outside the covers. She realized that she must be naked underneath; only bandages, no nightgown.

'You're going to be all right,' he told her.

She believed him. She said, 'Hurts a lot.' He smiled grimly. She asked, 'How long have I been here?'

'Twenty-four hours.'

'You haven't shaved.'

He kept squeezing her arm lightly and looking into her face. She thought she was about to go back to sleep again, but he caught her attention by saying her name.

'Would you do something for me?'

She said, 'Of course. You're always so good to me.'

He put his head down on the bed for a while and sighed. He really did love her, she thought, but she'd never believed it before.

'If you could talk to Michael,' he said. 'Just a couple of seconds. He feels so broken up about how it happened. If you could just let him know you understand.'

'I understand,' she said.

'I mean, tell him you forgive him. He hasn't said much, but he hasn't been able to eat or sleep, either. Or shave. Can I tell him to come in?'

She suddenly sensed that everything was draining away from her, never to return. She tried to hold on, but it was no use.

'Flora?'

The horror passed. She felt better. The fear had left, along with all the rest. She knew that she was going to die.

'Yes,' she said. 'Tell him to come in.'

James went away. She heard his footsteps. And Michael's; heard James saying, 'Just a couple of seconds. She's very tired,' and saw him moving away out of the room as Michael sat down in the chair. She turned her head to look at him.

He was smiling. Even with her head to the side, she could see his expression exactly: a nasty little smile. His drunken uncle had been chauffeur and pander to the old man and his cousins; and, of course, Michael would have taken over the same office for the sons. She should have known. It was that kind of family: even the employees were inheritable.

Everything was obvious now, and especially the fact that Michael's unshakable politeness and deference had been an indication of his distaste for her. He'd give up pretending, now that he knew she was dying. It was more than distaste. It must be a real hatred, because he couldn't help it any longer. He wanted to show her, even with James just outside the door.

'I want you to understand,' he said quietly.

'No need,' she answered.

'You got to understand, it's for him. Far as I'm concerned, I don't give a shit. You've just got to tell him you forgive me. Then it'll be OK.'

Everything would be all right. It was simple, if you had that much money. When they reported the attack, James would see to it that everyone thought she'd been shot by the kidnappers, not by Michael. Who would question it? Two respectable witnesses; and dead men who were known criminals. The hospital would get a new wing, the police force a large donation. It would be easy. It would have been easy even if they'd deliberately set out to murder her and hired the men to do it.

'If it was me,' Michael said, leaning forward, 'I'd be counting the minutes till you go down the tubes. "Oh James dear, look at that, oh isn't that perfectly sweet? Can I have the car window open, if it's all right with Michael: can I have it closed, if Michael doesn't mind?" Pain in the ass is what you are. I mean, I seen plenty: one to a hundred I used to mark them, and you rate down around ten, sweetheart. A real lemon. "Am I doing this right, am I doing that?" I told him, "Jimbo, this one's a dud." And he just said, "No, Kelvin, this time I'm choosing for myself." He wouldn't listen.'

James could do it right next time, she thought. He'd marry again, perhaps quite soon, and be just as content. He'd probably go to New Caledonia after all, maybe with another woman, or just with Michael. Someone else would bring up her children, no doubt doing it very well. They'd have the photographs of her, so everyone could remember how pretty she'd been; she had always taken a good picture. The family would be able to choose the new wife, as they'd chosen for Edward. She'd been crazy about Edward; that was how everything had started. It was enough to make you laugh. But she had to stop thinking about it. She had to ascend. All the events in the house and all the holiday travelling would still go on, only she wouldn't be able to have any part in them. She had to rise above.

'I forgive,' she said. It was becoming difficult for her to speak.

'I'll get him,' Michael told her. He stood up.

'Wait.' She started to breathe quickly.

He leaned across the bed to look at her face. He said, 'I'll get somebody.'

'Michael,' she said clearly, 'I loved you.'

He stepped back. The smile vanished. He looked revolted, infuriated.

'I loved you,' she repeated. 'With all my heart.' Her lips curved together, her eyes closed, her head moved to the side. She was gone.

Michael began to scream.

The sound brought James running into the room, and two nurses after him.

Michael caught Flora up in his arms. He shouted into her closed face. He tried to slam her against the wall. James pulled him back. 'It's all right,' he said. 'Stop.'

'Bitch,' Michael yelled at Flora. 'Take it back. Take it back, you lousy bitch.'

'Calm down,' James said. 'She forgives you.' He got his arm around both of them and tugged. Michael let go, dropping Flora's body. She fell face downward. The nurses stooped to pick her up from the floor.

James and Michael stood grappled together, their faces wet with tears and sweat. Michael stared at the wall in front of him.

'It's all right,' James told him. 'She understands. Don't worry. After people die, they understand everything.'

No Love Lost

They walked in silence, seeing a corner of the house in the distance, then a larger part and finally enough to hope. Neither of them said anything until they were inside.

It was dark, dirty and squalid. Every corner stank.

'Well, at least it's still here,' his wife said. 'And they left the roof on.'

Some regions weren't so lucky: everything had been burned to the ground. He'd already heard that his parents' house – on the other side of town – was gone; it was like knowing that a friend had died. And now every time he remembered, the loss grieved him. He never wanted to go back: to look at the hole in the ground where the house had stood or, worse still, to see some other building put up to replace it. The old schoolhouse was burned out, too.

The churches remained, although the windows were broken and fires had been lit in the interiors. But it isn't easy to burn stone. The houses and temples of God are usually built to withstand anything but a direct hit; the house of stone and the heart of stone.

His wife looked everywhere: the walls, floor, ceilings, the staircase and the rooms upstairs. Her eyes moved over the slashed, gouged and cracked surfaces, the smashed steps, the ragged and waterlogged pieces of carpet. All the time that she was going up or down – moving restlessly past shattered window frames and over filthy floorboards – she kept hold of the baby. At last she returned to the front room downstairs, wrapped the baby in her shawl and put him in a torn cardboard box on the ground. She told one of the older children to stay and keep watch, in case there were rats. Then she walked through the doorway and out.

He didn't notice at first. He was still circling through the rooms, remembering that this dilapidated, sorry hovel had once been home and telling himself that – like so much else over the past four years – it had died. What particularly distressed him was the little room next to their bedroom. It had been the safe nest where they'd put the first child when she was old enough to sleep alone but within earshot. Obscene words had been carved deep into the walls and the place had the reek of a sewer.

In a daze he turned back to the bedroom and looked out into the paved yard. Once upon a time they had had fruit trees, vegetables and flowers.

He saw his wife, hands free, striding away from the house. He thought that she was finally walking out on them for good.

He reached the front door faster than he could think what he was doing. Later on he'd thank his good instincts that he hadn't hurt himself going down the uneven, pitted stairs.

'Where are you going?' he yelled at her. She disregarded the question. Ever since he'd been discharged from the army with a missing hand, she'd ignored his threats. When he'd shout at her, she wouldn't respond and she sometimes didn't even seem to hear: she'd simply stop listening whenever she felt like it.

'Go next door on the other side,' she told him. 'If anybody's there, say you're looking for food and go to the next house. If nobody's at home, take anything you can find: floorboards, anything metal we can use. Look for where they hid the ax. If there's only one person left, use your judgment.'

He had no idea what she meant, although it came to him not long afterwards that she was giving him a command to kill whoever might be living or hiding in a neighboring house; as long as it looked as if he could get away with it. His own children would be all right: she would have entrusted a knife to the oldest boy.

At least there wouldn't be any mines, she said that evening. You could never tell, of course, how stupid men could be. Usually they planted mines only if they were sure they wouldn't be retracing their steps or coming back another time from a different direction. Mining the landscape was a thing you did to destroy an oncoming enemy in country where you hadn't grown up and where your friends and relatives wouldn't be spending the next quarter of a century having their limbs blown off as they tried to work the fields.

There wouldn't be mines planted near their house because, having taken it once, the enemy had intended to come back and take it again, even though this time they'd lost.

But, as his wife also said, anything was possible.

She talked quite a lot like one of his commanding officers – a good soldier and a decent man but someone who at a certain depth was unfeeling. It was as if ordinary rules of behavior – and emotions normally considered natural – were kept at the shallower levels of his consciousness: beyond that point you couldn't find them and he'd operate on purely practical principles, without squeamishness. He was a man who would do what had to be done, no matter what that was. If it could help your survival to kill someone, you did; it would be stupid not to. If you had children to think about, it would be criminal not to.

His wife was now his commanding officer. He didn't mind. She was good at it.

He'd been a soldier for nearly three years. At first he'd liked the life. And since for a long while he and his friends were seeing everything from a distance and had no casualties in their unit, he wasn't afraid. They joked. They drank. They had all sorts of luxuries not available to the civilian population. And they despised civilians. They thought of them as sheep who would run this way and that once the gates were open or one of them fell through a gap in the hedge: instantly a whole field of sheep would be pushing and shoving, trying to get through the same opening, do the same thing – to copy, to follow. Soldiers were the ones who told them where to move, how to protect themselves, what to do. Civilians had no personalities; they were simply part of a vast herd: women, children, old people. They were dull and slow beyond belief and helplessness had become a way of life to them. That was why, as long as he was in the army, he felt no pity for anyone who complained of being stolen from, raped or tortured. What did they expect? Nothing that happened to any of them could be so bad as what might happen to him and his friends. Capture could sometimes be worse than injury. They all knew stories about soldiers who killed themselves with their own weapons rather than risk being imprisoned, beaten, tortured, mutilated: there was nothing people wouldn't do to each other, given the opportunity. Even without the expediency of war, cruelty could become a habit.

For a while everything had been fine, even in bad weather. It was a schoolboy's dream of what life could be when you were grown up: you and your friends would go around in a gang all day long, picking up girls when you felt like it and moving on to new places, and new girls.

No civilian had had any meat for months but in his company they had food, alcohol: anything they wanted. And if they didn't have it, they'd find out where it was and then go and take it. One of the few good things about being in the army was that although you were under orders, in your own outfit there was freedom. You could do what you liked and if anything went wrong, your friends were there to back you up. And there were times when life was fun. He'd laughed a lot.

He'd even sung. To keep themselves from being bored, he and his friends made up a silly song they'd sing to each other whenever they were in a good mood or drunk, or when one of them had managed to invent another addition. The song was about a poor boy – the youngest of three brothers – who was offered a chance to attend the royal celebrations at a king's palace, where he'd be given as much food and drink as he wanted and would also take part in a competition: he'd be allowed to kiss the princess and she'd select her husband from among the competitors. She'd choose the one who gave her the kiss of true love. There were many passages in the song of alliteration and polysyllabic words, with whole verses composed of things listed alphabetically; and by tradition certain phrases were always shouted in unison.

One of their company came up with a completely new version one night during an epic spree. It went on for what seemed like hours – stanza after stanza, all rhyming and in a strange combination of the hilarious, the beautiful and the scatological. Everyone wanted a copy afterwards, especially since they'd been too drunk to remember more than a couple of consecutive lines. The poet hadn't had any copies, not even a written one for himself. It was all in his head, he told them. And he was killed the next afternoon. That was their first death.

Their good luck lasted a long while but as soon as it broke, everything went at once. They were in the thick of things day after day, all the time. And he was terrified. He lived with the knowledge that in a split-second he could lose both legs and an arm and his eyesight. He stayed mildly drunk whenever he could: never enough to make him incapable of saving himself but the right amount to blunt his sense of danger and to keep him ready to fight, turning all his fear into rage.

As his friends were picked off around him, he retained the ability to laugh. What else could you do? One morning a man in their outfit woke up speaking sounds without any meaning. They tried to talk to him but he didn't seem to understand a word – he'd just give an idiotic smile at whatever was said to him. They thought that he must be suffering from some kind of brain damage brought on by the constant firing; or even the result of a stroke. But they didn't know and they never found out. They had to leave him behind with a rescue team that was blown off the road a week later.

Once, for three days, he thought that he'd gone deaf but his hearing returned; it came back when they pulled out of the action. And then he felt the pain: to hear again suddenly, with such acuteness, was maddening.

His wife and children were out of the fighting at that stage, evacuated to a different sector. When he was given leave, he'd go back to a place that looked normal. The silence was unnerving after the constant, overwhelming noise. He couldn't sleep.

His wife didn't want to sleep. She wanted to make love all the time or, rather, she needed to be pregnant.

She was pregnant again and he was back in the unit with his friends when he was in the explosion. He never found out what had caused it: grenade, gunfire, a hit from the air, even a sniper's lucky shot at the fuel tank. The noise, the light and burning and pain all seemed to come at the same time. If he and the others hadn't been relaxed and inattentive after their leave, they might have noticed some warning sign. Then again, they might have missed it if things had been the other way around: if their senses had been dulled and confused by fatigue or boredom – too many months without a break.

He was lying on the ground and twitching uncontrollably. All around there was screaming and a terrible smell. Then they were carrying him. He saw the fire. As they put him into the jeep one of his friends came running up behind the others, reached forward and dropped something into his lap. 'Here,' he said. 'They can do anything nowadays. You never know.'

It was a hand, perfect almost to the wrist and then like something on a butcher's slab. He looked down at his left arm and the bloody pulp pulled into a bandage at the end of it. He passed out.

He came to in a field hospital where the doctor bent over each man in turn, making a quick decision about the order of operation.

He held out the detached, dead hand.

'What's this?' the doctor asked.

'They thought you might be able to sew it back.'

'Me and the lace-makers' guild,' the doctor snorted. He took the hand. He said, 'It isn't yours. Look. It's a right hand. That's the one you've still got.' He started to move away. Over his shoulder he asked, 'Are you right-handed?'

'Yes.'

'You've been lucky,' the doctor told him, and turned to the next man.

Everything had become a matter of luck over the past few years. And luck was crazy. Being caught behind the fighting could sometimes be as dangerous as being sent into action. When the lines moved, everything else changed, too.

First came the bombardment. Everyone ran away. People died or got lost on the run. They couldn't find anywhere to stay because the ones in front of them were running, too. Finally they reached the city, where some were taken in and others were put into camps. The fear was that as soon as the enemy was near enough, all the people in the camps would force their way into the city, would have to be accommodated and then, in the ensuing siege, would ensure that everyone starved.

But while he was still recovering, the tide reversed. A third force joined the soldiers behind the fleeing civilians. Together they turned around and routed the enemy, taking back the land that had been lost.

He was discharged to go and live with his family. At that time his wife was housed in a place where she shared with three other families. Humanitarian aid societies doled out a bread portion to all of them. She was about to give birth. One of the children was sick and running a high fever. The authorities wanted to take the child – a baby girl – to an isolation ward. His wife wouldn't hear of it. She nursed the girl herself until all at once it became clear that there was no hope. Then she put the child in a corner and told everybody to stay away from that part of the room. She sent him to find a doctor. Everyone he asked said the same thing: he was on a futile search. No one with any medical knowledge could be found outside the hospitals, where the staff stayed and worked as if condemned. The hospitals had become the end and the beginning: childbirth, medicines, narcotics, the black market, the dying.

His wife gave birth in their quarter of a single, crowded room, where she was seen by a male aid worker the next day; he took her temperature and pronounced her fit. From its corner in the room the body of the sick child, now dead, was removed. They were given a receipt. Within a few days they received notice to collect the remains. His wife tore up the paper as soon as it arrived.

'How are we going to find her now?' he asked. 'All the reference numbers were on that.'

'Leave it,' she ordered. 'They make you pay to reclaim anything.'

'We can't just leave her. Our own daughter?'

'It isn't going to do her any good, is it?' she snapped. 'We need everything we can save. For food and medicine. Suppose the baby gets sick – what would you do?'

Since he was still recuperating, he put up with everything from her. He was so conscious of his own wound that it didn't occur to him that she too might be suffering the effects of war.

The children were nervous of him. They behaved as if he were a stranger. At some moments they'd look fixedly at the place where his left hand ought to have been, at others they'd turn their heads quickly in order to escape being caught in the act of staring at a disability.

He gave them the creeps. The realization pained him as much as would the loss of their love. And perhaps it came to the same thing: they didn't quite shrink away but whenever he approached too near, he could feel their dread. He told his wife, whispering into her ear at night. She answered softly, 'Give them time. They'll get used to you eventually. You're their father but they don't know you yet. It's all going to take time.'

It made him feel better to talk to her. What made her feel better was to make love, even so soon after the last birth. Once or twice he asked if she thought they really should: what if she got pregnant again?

She finally said to him, 'I can't do without it and if I don't get it from you, I'll get it any way I can.'

As soon as she was pregnant again, she calmed down and he understood: that unless she was carrying a child or nursing a newborn baby, she couldn't feel that there was any point in going on. There had to be something in her life that hadn't yet been ruined.

He also understood that she had allowed their daughter to die because the child was a girl, not a boy, and not the favorite daughter and because – if the aid workers had taken the child away in time to save its life – the family would have had to accept a cut in the bread rationing. His wife had made all those decisions while he was unaware of what she was doing.

When he saw the extent to which their lives had been determined and directed by her, he was amazed. The slight edge he felt of queasiness, even horror, actually increased her desirability. But he knew that with such a wife he couldn't afford to lose his strength.

He did exercises to keep the muscles limber in his shoulder and arm. He walked. Whenever he lifted a weight, he remembered to balance it and not to favor one side. He learned to use the left arm again. The doctors had promised him an array of implements that would fit onto a socket at the end of his healed stump: various builder's tools, a plastic hand without moving parts and the traditional pirate's hook. He hadn't really believed in the hook, but just as he healed well enough to be ready for the ingenious tool kit with its many ultra-modern gadgets, he was offered an artificial hand and a hook. Nothing else, he was told, was available; the other choices had now been discontinued. He refused the hand. It was unshaped: no indication on it of joints or knuckles, and it had a dead color like a plastic toilet seat. He chose the hook, with all its historical connotations of violence and romance. And after more exercises, he found that it was useful.

During those initial days of homecoming, their scavenging wasn't very organized. They wasted time by not conferring and by forgetting to take essential equipment with them. But as soon as they felt established, they began to fear the arrival of others. They'd have to hurry if they wanted to furnish the house, gather food and other supplies and remove from the neighborhood anything that could be used as building material.

The first things they took were beds and mattresses. After that, anything: in no particular order of importance. Most of the nearby houses were in the same condition as theirs but they did find a child's wheelbarrow that had been hidden, or possibly lost, under the foundations of a collapsed terrace by the old market gardens. Every single pane of glass had been shivered out of the greenhouses but there were still seeds, roots and bulbs.

They stripped enough wood from the walls and floors of neighboring houses to rebuild their own place and also to amass a good stock of firewood. Nothing would last through the winter, of course. To feel at all hopeful they needed the gas and electricity back, the running water, the telephones. But they had enough fuel to cook with.

They unbricked the well down behind the abandoned orchard and he volunteered to drink the first cupful. They had heard so many stories about booby traps and poisoned wells that he expected to die, but the water was still pure. Some of the old trees, gnarled and decrepit as they were, had been scarred and split, and some had been chopped down. The stumps were left but there was no sign of the wood. Others had just been hacked up – splintered and torn and probably shot at for target practice or for fun. But most of the trees had been left. A few bore small, bitter apples. One or two rows contained trees on which all the fruit, though minute, was edible and even sweet. To pick one of the tiny apples and hold it close to his face, breathing in the smell – and then to bite into the fruit and taste the sour sweetness – was a delight and, while it lasted, an astonishment.

Later in the next year, catching a whiff of fragrance blowing from the blossoming old trees, he'd think he was back in his boyhood again, loving and in love, with a soul unbroken: before he'd lost his hand, before he'd killed or done the other things he'd done, or seen everything that he'd seen.

He tried not to remember the trees that used to stand directly behind the house; they had brought the loveliness of spring up to the windows and its honey breath into all the rooms. In the autumn they had supplied large, luscious fruit that could be stored through the winter or made into bottled preserves. They had had apples and plums. Those were the trees that the enemy troops had used for firewood, simply out of laziness, because they were the ones nearest to the back door.

They had flour, some dried meat, salt and three precious bags of potatoes. Before they set out on their first well-planned plundering expedition, he went to the place where he'd buried an ax before joining up. It was still there. That was a triumph: the moment when he felt that, no matter how bad things were, he'd come home.

His wife inspected all the gardens in the area. She came back carrying a sack full of roots and leaves. One of the children proudly steered the wheelbarrow at her side; it was heaped with dusty bulbs: that was what they'd be eating and they'd be very pleased with it. Anything that fell under their eyes was like a forest creature caught in the cross-sights. They were like wild animals themselves: always hungry, always looking at everything with greedy eyes; criminals and murderers, he thought. How could you teach your children anything when they'd been through this?

And what did he tell them, anyway? *Don't get caught. Don't lose what you're carrying. Don't let them find the stuff on you. If anybody stops you, fight like hell and if they try to tell their side of the story, lie your head off.*

He still knew how to handle the kids but sometimes he didn't understand them. You couldn't teach them not to touch each other, not to touch themselves, not to touch insects or animals if they could find any in the destroyed landscape. They chased whatever hopped or crawled. They wanted to eat everything growing and anything they could pick up off the floor. You couldn't even prevent them, after all that had happened, from doing things that were dangerous: trying to grab a pan of scalding water off the edge of a table, swallowing a bottle of something without thinking that it might be harmful. You had to keep an eye on them all the time. That was bad enough. The children who were in real trouble were the ones who stopped whining. They'd sit in a corner all day, silent. They wouldn't eat. They'd say, 'I feel sick,' and not long after that they'd come down with the same infection everyone else had, but they'd be the ones to die.

One day he put down the load he was carrying, and straightened up to rest for a moment. He listened. The silence was enormous: a gigantic emptiness. You could have heard a cough or a hammer blow for miles. There couldn't have been a bird left alive in the country. And the pets they'd had: cats, dogs – where were they? Somebody had pushed them into a cooking pot and made gloves out of the skins, undoubtedly. Vermin, on the other hand, were plentiful, both big and small.

After years of living with shelling so unremitting that he had come to believe his full hearing would never return, his ears now strained for sound. He loved the slight pattering of leaves moving in a breeze. And he missed the song of all the many different kinds of birds he remembered. Now that the troops were gone, the birds would come back; but until they did, their absence remained another sign in the landscape of recent and comprehensive disaster.

The silence at night was entire, completing the darkness.

As they were settling back in, others were being moved and uprooted again. Some had official approval to go back to what had once been home, where – like him – they'd find the house gutted, the furniture gone, the inner walls defaced and in places knocked down or with holes punched through them. But they'd be lucky.

In many areas families found their houses occupied by people who would wave a set of papers at them, saying that they'd been granted the property by a provisional committee for something-or-other.

In their own district, enemy occupation was recent; the civilians had been moved out in a hurry to the nearest safe place, which meant that nobody else had been allocated their land. Not all the houses were left, of course. A number of families returned to an empty space; they were taken to the center of town and put up in deserted shops, old warehouses, churches and any other large construction that still had a roof.

The government officials in charge of housing installed families and went away, taking their papers with them and saying that food and clothing would follow. But what was on paper had ceased to mean much. Most people made themselves as comfortable as they could: begging for what they could get and taking more when your back was turned.

For weeks he was the only man in the area over twelve and under sixty-eight. When the others arrived they were on stretchers or on crutches.

Soon the time might come when the most nearly able- bodied men would band together to form a guard or sentry unit for protecting the weaker households from theft and damage. But at the moment nobody could be spared. Just as there was no extra food, there was no free time.

The quiet held – the limitless, eerie silence after years of fighting and months of being walled up under bombardment. It was as still as the moment after snow stops falling.

You could imagine that the world had gone backward a few centuries to a time when everything depended on harvests and you walked to the next village to buy and sell on market days.

They weren't really in a village, just out in the country on the outskirts of a small town. The town had been hit by air power, but not badly, since there had never been much there. A few kilometers away a larger town had had the paper mill and the gasworks bombed, neither of which had been of military importance, although from the air they might have seemed good targets. The troops who had been dropped there had stayed for a few days and moved on.

Everyone was afraid of the armies coming back, even of their own soldiers returning. Now that he was a civilian, he had thoughts and feelings like the people he'd once held in contempt. When he remembered some of the things he'd done, he didn't mind. Everybody else had done the same: just as bad and – most of them – worse. None of that was important. It was important to be alive. And to stay alive. He'd been doubly and especially fortunate: to be alive and to be out of the whole dirty business; because, as far as any of them knew, there was still fighting going on in other parts of what had once been their country. The official reports didn't say it was fighting. They called it negotiating.

About a month after other people started to reclaim houses in the nearby town, an old woman stopped him at the end of the lane and asked if she could have some apples from the orchard. He said, 'You'll have to ask my wife about that.'

'Your wife is a hard woman.'

'My wife is a fair woman. That's why we're still alive. Her first duty is to her own family.'

'What can I do?' the woman complained. 'We're starving.'

'I don't know and I don't care,' he told her. 'I've done my stint for other people and I've learned that as soon as they've got what they want, they forget what you gave up to help them. You're the same. You want something and you don't mind where you get it from. Look around you. Where am I going to find a single thing extra? And if I do find it, it's going to be for us. We're all in trouble. And we've been in trouble for a long time.'

She stood there, too dejected to speak. What he said was true and she still didn't have anywhere else to go. He wasn't sure that she was even from around there. He didn't recognize her, which didn't mean much: hardship could obliterate faces and personalities. His arm shot out, pointing to the distance. He said, 'You can take some apples from the far end of the orchard, but make it fast and don't do it again. And next time, ask somebody else.' He turned his back. He heard her running away to fill her shawl and her skirt. She hadn't thanked him: she'd asked God to reward him.

God was asked to do so many things, especially at times when He didn't seem to be there. One of the Army's men of God used to say to them, 'Now, boys, just because our Lord is on vacation at the moment, that doesn't mean that He's forgotten about us.' He'd been a well-meaning man. They'd all thought he was a fool. He'd continued to pray over one dying soldier until the man began to scream, 'Oh shut up, just shut up and let me die in peace.' And when he'd tried to skip to the end, to get the important words said at least, the man's brother had stood up and belted him.

After he'd seen death once, he began to expect it. It was all around, just waiting for its time. Even in years of peace, when it was usually hidden away, it was natural: a part of life. Other losses began to strike him as equally shocking but not natural: the loss of mental and spiritual power in everyone, including himself, and in the country at large – a draining away of honesty and fair dealing: an overall abandonment of principles, a general debasement.

Few of the changes were immediate. There were stages and developments, as in the growth of plants or the progress of a disease. The moral decay he saw had been going on for years but because he had been part of it, he hadn't been particularly aware of it. The fact that it dismayed him meant that apparently he still had some virtue left: just enough to cause him pain without doing good to anyone else.

He remembered a time during his recuperation: they were all in a shelter, waiting for the bombardment. There were so many people that his main worry was of the air giving out, although as soon as he thought about that he began to sense the claustrophobia and impending panic in everyone around him. That reminded him that an outbreak of hysteria could be worse than mild suffocation. The hands and hair, the bodies and clothing of strangers were pressed tightly to him – sometimes even in his face. A child suddenly complained, 'Something bit me,' and a few people laughed, which broke the tension. But shortly after that a woman screamed, 'My necklace – it's gone!' She started to call out, 'Thief, thief,' but a crowd of other voices told her to quit. Before the fighting, a lot of people would have murmured, 'Poor woman.' And even a year after it had begun, they would have thought: *Stupid bitch, why didn't she hide it better? Necklaces aren't to wear, they're to sell.* But finally most of them, like him, envied the thief and asked themselves why they hadn't been lucky enough to spot the necklace so that they could have stolen it themselves.

His wife was good at sneaking away with things: food, clothing, small objects – anything that caught her eye. He never commented. He'd notice what she'd managed to steal, or get the kids to steal, and he'd be glad of his share.

Their neighbors were back; first one family, then two more, and at last all of them who were still alive or not caught between borders and behind lines. He and his wife lied about how long they'd been at home. They made it seem that they'd arrived a few hours ahead of the others, and had spent all their time cleaning and scrubbing and unbricking the well. 'No fuel?' they said; 'no, we're in the same state. We're all in the same boat.' 'Yes,' the children agreed, lying expertly. Telling lies was a peacetime skill as well as a wartime necessity.

He had beds and mattresses. Other people were lucky if they owned one blanket to share among the whole family. Everything was obvious, of course. The neighbors knew. And he knew what they thought of him. But everyone realized that nobody else – and certainly none of them – would have acted differently. The laws of the lawless were in operation: *First come, first served; finders keepers, losers weepers.*

After the neighbors came the refugees: twenty thousand of them in a procession that looked like a picture of the damned let out of Hell. This time the aid workers were at the head of the column instead of the tail end. They'd learned that if they didn't introduce and explain the distribution system, householders would simply beat up anyone who came to the door. As for a slowly moving line of unarmed people, most of them related to the enemy – that presented an opportunity for reprisal without injury. Even the smallest children turned up with sticks and stones.

Two immense refugee groups were herded across their territory. After that, the numbers were fewer, although his wife said that the neighboring district had had fifty thousand marched through.

When the count dropped, the so-called friendly refugees joined the human flood and the housing system began. In the first settlement they had eight orphaned children billeted on them. He'd managed to rebuild the big bed so that all the refugees could sleep in it, jammed up against each other like sardines in a can. His wife was allocated food rations for the orphans and – as long as her family was taking care of refugees – for herself and her husband and children, too. They were given bread. There was nothing else. For six weeks they had bread. And they were grateful.

One late evening he headed for home with a pile of lumber on his back. The light down by the horizon was a strange, bruised purple. All he could hear was his breathing and his feet moving. As he thought about how his children were growing up in a world without school and books and religion, he heard the howling of a dog. He stopped, and heard it again. It had seemed immeasurably far away at first but while he was listening to the repetition, he placed it: the sound must be coming from the quarry, which meant that it had to be human.

He told his wife about it and she said, 'Forget you heard it. Don't interfere. Nobody falls in by mistake nowadays.'

Since there was no longer any local or national economy as people had once known it, he set up a business of exchange and reciprocal favors, which he ran together with a man he happened on while out walking or, as he called it, foraging. He was always looking for anything that could be used in some way.

The man was middle-aged and husky, yet despite his look of strength there was a sadness about him. He didn't talk much. When he did, there was a melancholy in his voice, too. Before the war he'd been a cellist in a symphony orchestra, so he said. Below the knee his left leg ended in a wooden peg that he'd made himself while he was in the hospital, waiting to be released. He introduced himself as 'Peg-leg'. He said that everybody was going to remember him by his disability in any case, so he might as well get used to it. And nothing was going to be the same again after all this mess, so it wasn't such a bad idea to begin with a new name to go with the new life; otherwise it could break your heart to keep thinking about how things used to be. 'Is there any work around here,' he asked, 'for an ex-soldier?'

'That depends. What can you do?'

'Anything.'

'You can work with me,' he suggested. 'I'm a carpenter: beds, tables, chairs, doors, window frames. Even roofing.'

'I could learn all that.'

'Where are you living?'

'I'm not anywhere,' Peg-leg told him. 'I was passing through, but now I'll find someplace. I can stay and work with you till spring. Then I'll move on.'

They'd meet in the morning and start off to town together to look for jobs to do. There was plenty of work for carpenters. He liked Peg-leg because he was serious, a good worker and, like himself, injured. In the hospital, and whenever he'd met people around that time, he couldn't understand the tactlessness that made them all say the same thing: *Lucky it wasn't the right hand.* But now he knew that that was the truth. Without his right hand, everything would have been difficult, every movement unnatural and perhaps never possible to relearn.

At home his wife struggled with the children and with the orphans, whom she resented. He was glad to get out of the house every morning, even in the worst weather. And when it was a fine day, his spirits would rise as he breathed the clear air and looked at the trees and, off in the distance, saw Peg-leg waiting at the gate where they met. One day he felt that he'd woken from darkness into light; he was well again. He might be missing one hand, but he was alive and healthy and still young and still a man who could find work and feed his family. And he was out of the fighting. And he had a friend.

*

They got through the worst of the winter and his mind was filled with the thought of a new pair of boots. His wife dreamt of the moment when life would become so normal that a dentist would move to a nearby town and she'd be able to find the time and the money to make an appointment.

There wasn't a day when somebody in the house didn't have a bad cold. Sometimes they were all down with colds and fevers, except his wife: she couldn't afford to be sick, she said.

The birds started to come back and there was a hint of spring in the softer winds: it wasn't quite there but it was anticipated. He began to notice – in the mud and melting snow – the tracks and droppings of small animals. One day after a long thaw he saw two cats and a dog. He warned everyone in the family: a tame animal, reverting to the wild, could be as dangerous as any genuinely wild creature never on friendly terms with man. Occasionally it could be worse, because it would be fearful and full of mistrust. It could attack, unprovoked. It would almost certainly carry diseases; a bite or scratch might be fatal. It wouldn't be a bad idea, he said, to carry a stick.

Just as what was left of the flower bed began to produce

green shoots under the retreating snows, the orphan children were moved on. He saw them waiting outside the front door for the truck that would take them away. They were skinny and hollow-eyed, their clothing in tatters. His own children were beginning to look well tended and fatter in comparison. And, following the example of their elders, they had been using every opportunity to persecute their weaker companions. He'd never said anything, because the house – together with the food and the children – was his wife's business. But now he was touched by pity at their malnourished, hopeless look. He went to where she hid the food. The child on guard asked, 'What are you doing?'

'You shut up,' he answered. He took the refugee children a few scraps – enough so that they'd have something to get them through a long journey. They ate the food straight away. 'I hope they find you some place better than this,' he told them.

There was no better place. The whole country was exactly like his own neighborhood except that in the cities it was easier for your neighbors to steal from you and there was a greater danger of sudden bombardment and siege.

'I'm sorry we didn't have more to give you,' he added. The children listened with a dead look on their faces. *You did have more,* they were thinking, *and you gave it to your own children.*

When the aid workers arrived, one of the orphans – an undersized little boy, who had been in the habit of following him around – ran back, snatched up his right hand and pressed his face to it.

He felt the small hands and a warm wetness, as if the child had licked his knuckles. Then the boy turned and ran off.

His wife was standing in the doorway, holding the baby, who was screaming. 'Did he bite you?' she asked.

He'd have felt better if he'd been bitten. The gesture had probably been meant as a kiss.

'I thought the little bastard was going to bite you,' she said. 'That's all we need. Make sure he didn't break the skin.'

He didn't bother to look. Who could afford medicine? And black-market medicine was likely to be adulterated with so many substances that it could kill you all on its own.

'Imagine if they were ours,' he said.

Their children would be all right. They were adept at every dirty trick of the petty criminal. If they had to, they'd kill and eat any family chosen to take them in.

She looked at him in a way that told him his weakness was disgusting. 'We've lost the bread ration too,' she said.

'There'll be more.'

'No. They're moving all the kids out.'

'They'll bring us some others.'

'How do you know? Maybe they will, maybe not. You don't know. I've seen people starve to death. Nobody starves in the army. You only find out about that when you're captured.'

Or sent back, wounded. 'We'll see,' he said.

The refugee children were counted and loaded into the trucks and then counted again. One of the aid workers said that the orphans' place would soon be taken by others – in fact, someone should call about the transaction in the afternoon. His wife looked up at that. 'How many?' she asked. 'No idea,' the man answered, in the way many people with a little power had acquired over the past years: you could tell from the tone of voice how good it made them feel to be able to give you – truthfully or untruthfully – information you didn't want or no information at all when you really had to know.

As soon as the trucks were out of sight, one of the children mentioned food: could they have something to eat? As a present, like the orphans.

It wasn't exactly tattling, so he couldn't feel angry. He told them again that the orphans didn't have anything. Another one of the children piped up, 'Those aid people have to give them so much food every day, or else they're arrested for keeping the money.'

'But they may have a long trip before they get to where they're going. I told you.'

'You gave them our food?' his wife screamed. She came at him from the doorway and hit him across the face. The blow made a loud noise. His cheek, ear and eye burned with the impact. She called him a stupid son of a bitch. Ordinarily he would have let things go until she calmed down, especially in front of the kids and while she was holding the baby against her hip, but this time he knew that it was important for him to keep his authority. When she came at him again for a second try, he punched her in the breast and then slapped her hard on the side of the face. She landed several feet away, gasping and on her knees, with the baby setting up a piercing cry. The children crouched against the wall.

'It's all right,' he told them. 'Your mother needs some time to rest. Let's go for a walk.' He held out his good hand. 'Come on,' he coaxed. For a terrible moment he was afraid that they might run away. But the smallest girl finally moved towards him in short, tottering steps, holding out her arms for him to lift her up. And after her, the others followed.

He led them out of the house, and began to tell them a story as they walked. Their need for stories was almost as great as their hunger for food. They were always begging to be told a story, usually one that they'd already heard.

He knew that he had won. When they returned to the house, his wife would regret what she'd done; she'd think that she had deserved to be punished. And he'd appear to be apologetic too, although he'd taken care not to strike her too hard. If he hadn't been injured, he'd be able to handle her with a softer touch: he didn't like hurting her. But if she was going to hit him in front of his own kids, she'd better be prepared to be laid out flat. He was the man of the house, after all. The children had to respect him. If he'd still had both hands, he'd have slung her over his back, carried her to the old millpond and dumped her in from the wooden bridge – that was what they'd done centuries ago to the witches and the gossips and the whores.

The children began to ask questions about the story he was telling. He answered and went on. He threw in a few extra jokes. They all began to enjoy the walk, the fresh air, and being together. He turned the story into the nonsense tale he and his army friends used to recite when they'd been drinking: about the poor boy and the contest to win the hand of the princess and give her the kiss of true love.

The version he used for them was always heavily censored. Some sections were his own invention. For instance, as he told it, the boy started to have good luck when he paid attention at school and his studious efforts brought results at the end of a year – a year and a day: the teachers at the school awarded him one of the entrance tickets to the palace dinner. Many tickets had been distributed throughout the length and breadth of the land but they weren't given to just anybody, because you had to earn prizes and treasures in this life. If you didn't earn them, you didn't deserve them.

He could have chosen other stories but since this was the one all the children liked best, he knew he could slip in some moralizing and get away with it. He was surprised to find that many of his interpolations, and even the offshoots into the sententious, produced requests for more, just as if they'd been part of the original fabric.

The food list was especially good; the main portion represented the combined efforts of his combat unit over a period of years. But the best sections had been made up one winter's night by a friend of his to whom rhyme came easily – a lighthearted young man who'd been blown to pieces in the same explosion that had taken away his own left hand.

The children would listen, entranced, sometimes joining in. And then they'd insist on having everything repeated. One of the best-loved sections described the clothes everyone at the palace wore to the ball before the kissing contest began. They loved the clothes and the food, the names of the characters, the music of the words, the fact that it was all unreal and sounded silly and that there was also a beautiful princess in the story. And, of course, that the hero won and everything ended happily.

Only the children who were seriously ill failed to respond to the poor boy and the princess.

In the army the favored verses were the ones that dealt with the 'kissing', which involved the princess trying out all the men, and vice versa, until the hero – the poor boy – won.

'For true love is sweetest,' he told his children, 'and true love is best, and whoever finds true love is happy and blest.'

When they returned from their walk, his wife was standing in the doorway, breathing out a narrow cloud like a banner. The air was cold enough to see your breath, but he'd smelled the nicotine from a distance. He stopped in front of her and held out his hand. From behind her back she produced the cigarette. He took a drag and handed it to her again. He half-closed his eyes as he exhaled. That was when it was best: on the way out, where you could look at it in the air, while you were still tasting it.

They stood like that, sharing the cigarette until it was finished. He let her have the end. She stuck a toothpick through the last of it. When there was almost nothing left, she squeezed off the fire, stepped on it and saved the few unburned strands to be collected with others and made into a fresh cigarette.

That was their conversation, their apology and explanation.

Neither of them mentioned the beating. They showed each other no sign that they wanted to hold on to the memory of violence nor to the knowledge that everything had taken place in front of their children. The kids would find out about marriage soon enough, just as they were discovering everything else; not that every marriage was the same. In this one, he knew, the day when he allowed his wife to get away with striking him in the face, whether she did it in public or in private, was the day when she'd make up her mind to replace him with a different husband. She had vigorous ideas about what a man should do and be. Some things she wouldn't stand for at all. At other times she'd pretty much ask to be kept in her place. Sometimes what she wanted from him was to know what he expected from her. He still thought that they'd be all right as long as he trusted his instincts and they didn't talk about any of it.

Where on earth had she managed to find a cigarette? From one of the aid workers, of course. But what did she have to offer in exchange? Nothing, while he was there. A promise – that was all she'd have to bargain with: a look in the eye, which she could deny afterwards. Unless she didn't want to.

He admired her quickness of wit, her suspiciousness and cynicism. Before the fighting started she was so different that he could hardly remember what she'd been like. He could only recall a vague picture of the way she'd looked: fresh, eager, delicately slender. But he'd been different, too. He had no idea what he'd been like – a nice, decent young man, probably. Now he was like everyone else – like a ragged, mean-looking cur that snuffles around the garbage piles at the back of a village.

They waited for the aid workers to bring supplies and another consignment of orphans – perhaps a batch of them hardly old enough to feed themselves: children who had to be closely supervised. Maybe there would be even more than in the first distribution.

The term 'aid worker' was relatively new. They used to be called charity workers. People no longer knew what the word charity meant. They didn't know the meaning of love or pity or how similar or different they were; they saw no strict divisions between compassion, condescension and contempt. The weak went under. If you didn't want it to happen to you, it was to your advantage to make it happen to somebody else. That would give you a better chance.

Sometimes at night he thought he could hear the howling of dogs. If real, and not simply a thing he imagined while he was waiting for sleep, the sound would be like the first howling he'd heard, and probably coming from the quarry. Abandoned mines and quarries were good places to keep prisoners or to bury them. You could fit a lot of people into a mine: put them in, station armed guards on the heights and blow up the entrance. And even more could be thrown into a disused quarry, although usually the intention there would be to free them at some stage because they'd remain visible.

Nobody talked about the quarry and everybody knew. It had a long history. Since his return, the only time he'd heard it mentioned openly by anyone except his wife was when a stranger had laughed about it, saying in a whisper, 'The divorce court where you don't need to bother with lawyers.'

When he was a child, life was orderly. Parents were strict; indoors they told their children: *Don't keep rushing everywhere. Don't jump around like that. Why are you laughing in that silly way? Be quiet.* Outside the house they said: *You're making a spectacle of yourself. Everybody's looking at you. Stop showing off.*

The teachers at school were also fairly uncompromising. They specialized in verbal castigation. Some of his friends preferred that. They knew how to defend themselves against it. He would rather have been strapped on the hands or whipped. That happened too, but none of it was too bad.

He had two close friends who followed or led him into escapades that ranged from the hilarious to the terrifying. Because they were such a small group, and because they never did anything really bad, they had no worries about betrayal from within. His brothers and sisters didn't know what he was up to and anyway they had secrets of their own that could be used against them if they told on him. So at the age when he was ready for adventure and adulthood, he and his two friends were climbing out of their houses at night and heading for the one place in the neighborhood where there were no rules: the abandoned quarry beyond the far side of town.

Once, when still a boy, he'd been persuaded to spend a night there on his own. It was almost like the more usual dare to stay overnight in a haunted house, except that there was a big difference between fear of unknown other worlds and fear of unknown genuine trouble. At the time so many stories were in circulation about the place and what went on in it that the quarry exerted an attraction nicely balanced between dread and longing. They all knew, even as children, that it was where people went to meet each other unobserved, to plan robberies, to hand over stolen goods, to see men and women who were disapproved of and 'to do it'. It was the latter activity that had become irresistibly fascinating to their imaginations. They wanted information. A prize had been selected: a ticket to something they also wanted desperately. He remembered that part only vaguely.

He and his two friends turned up at their usual meeting place and began the long walk to the quarry. In those days there were several sets of stairs leading down to the bottom, where by daylight the ground looked like a riverbed in time of drought: gravelly, full of dried bushes, sand and patches of mud and water. The place was huge, with divisions of landscape like the ones you might see in a large park gone back to the wild: the narrow offshoot like a tree-lined canyon, the uneven ravine bulged with sloping rock faces that were tilted and stepped like the overlapping waves of a sideways-moving sea; the clearings surrounded by scrubby undergrowth, the big open plains.

By luck they had chosen a cloudy night when the moon was full enough to allow some vision but not bright enough to make hiding impossible – just the sort of time and weather everyone wanted. And the ground was dry. His friends left him at a set of stairs covered by shadow. He'd agreed to meet them at dawn in the abandoned farm shack they used as a clubhouse.

He started down the steps, remembering as he moved not to trust the rotting handrails nor to look for complete safety in the stone below and by his side. Where the walls and stairs were worn, they could be slippery, glassily polished; and the stone had a method – peculiar to itself and treacherous – of retaining or breathing out moisture.

While he was undergoing his ordeal, his friends indulged in a midnight feast at their clubhouse. He expected that they'd be asleep when he got out but, because he'd promised, he did what they'd arranged: at three in the morning he climbed up the quarry stairs again and took the long walk back.

The others hadn't slept; they'd finished up the food and after that, all night long, they'd been telling stories. They wanted to hear everything. Without proof, naturally, they wouldn't hand over the prize.

He tried to tell them. As he talked, he grew less shocked, although there were some descriptions he didn't even attempt, nor could he convey the absolute terror he'd felt – not just at the idea of being caught, but at the sight of what was happening in front of him. He'd witnessed all sorts of activity, much of which he didn't even identify as sexual. He had looked on at gambling, knife fights, nakedness: men, women and children. There had been hundreds of people down there. Some groups had been peacefully eating and drinking around a fire – large parties, some of whose members would go off together into the straggly bushes and then drift back to the crowd. There had also been smaller gatherings where whatever went on was being forced on one or more people by others. No one interfered in any of the quarrels, which were loud. Yelling and screaming was ignored by the rest. Most people were drinking. As he talked about his adventure, it came to him that some of the bodies he'd stepped over and fallen against in an effort to remain hidden hadn't been dead but simply drunk, or asleep, or both.

His friends didn't believe half of what he told them. But since there was no question that he'd been down in the quarry and had seen quite a lot of what they imagined must be going on there anyway, they let him have the prize, whatever it was.

The days were warmer, but the real spring wouldn't come for over a month at the soonest and probably later than that. You could smell it in the air and feel it in the ground; that meant nothing. They could still have storms and weeks of freezing rain afterwards. Nevertheless, Peg-leg decided that the moment had come for him to move on. He announced his departure early one morning and said goodbye the same afternoon.

All at once it seemed as if a period of disappointment had begun. He refused to imagine that they might be heading for a stretch of bad luck: after what they'd gone through already, that would be ridiculous, although the thought of it was always near.

Until the aid workers brought new refugees and food-ration credits, they'd be living right at the edge. Without the extra bread, everyone felt nervous. Despite what they'd hoarded, most of their provisions were near exhaustion. Once the weather changed, transportation and travel in general would be easier. It was possible that that was what the authorities were waiting for.

Good weather was also needed for planting and putting the house in order. All he'd really been able to do before the cold months was to make the place watertight and as warm as possible:

to block the holes and board up the windows. A coat of fresh paint, whitewash and new windows would make the house look more normal again, less like a half-derelict construction behind which a family was barricaded.

If you'd approached the district at night, it would have been like coming to a place that had the reputation of being haunted. All the houses still standing were like his, and some much worse.

That was the prize, he remembered: for spending a night in the quarry – the reward was a ticket to a traveling fair. And he'd gone to the show they all called the Haunted House, which was actually named the House of Horrors. It was a collection of optical illusions and things that jumped out at you while you rode in the open car of a miniature train. The train carried a full load: children, parents, lovers, all laughing and shrieking. When you heard them calling out around the bend, you knew that there was something you should be prepared for. He'd whooped and cheered with the rest. He'd loved it. At no time was he so frightened as when he'd had to sit still and watch and be silent down in the quarry.

His first experience of women had also taken place in the quarry. He was interested in two girls at school and another who worked in a bakery. He used to have day-dreams about going out with them and about how much they'd let him do. His two friends were similarly plagued by futile dreaming. They were still trading lies and secrets when an older girl asked him if he'd like to come out on a picnic. He'd almost said no, not understanding that she'd used a code phrase. She'd been nice and hadn't laughed at him. 'At night,' she'd explained. 'You know. In the quarry. Have a couple of beers and cook some sausages over a fire.' Then she'd smiled, seeing that he'd understood. He'd said yes. And that was the beginning: going back to the place of terror to become an initiate, learning to feel at ease and to belong to the crowd of people who went there.

It didn't change the way he thought about the two other girls at school and the one at the bakery. But after a while it began to influence the way they thought about him. Only after he'd acquired the reputation of taking a girl to the quarry did he become someone to whom younger girls felt they could entrust themselves, while their parents were sure that they could not.

He was still in his teens when the quarry was declared out of bounds. First of all, several women were found murdered. Two were pregnant girls. Suspicion naturally fell on the man or men who might have fathered the unborn children. While investigations were still going on – and one man was already under arrest – more deaths occurred. The combination of methods used – strangling and knifing – suggested that more than one man was behind the crimes. The arrested suspect argued that despite his acquaintance with the dead girl he was supposed to have murdered, he hadn't seen her in some time and wasn't it likely that she'd been out at the quarry to meet another man who was the real father – or many men, who would pay cash for sexual intercourse, as a lot of people there did?

More bodies were discovered, including those of two young boys. The arrested man was released. No one ever found out who was responsible for any of the deaths.

After the killing of women and boys came the big fights between men. Family, religion, race and former nationality all helped to give the participants an incentive, as did the occasional winning or losing of some regional sports team at an important competition. Or the cause might simply have been the need to get into a fight.

As soon as the first men were killed and others badly injured, the friends and families came out in force. More men died; some of the women formed a protest group and went out to try to stop the fighting. They were beaten up by both sides. Three of them were hauled off to the far end of the quarry and raped. After that, the police stepped in. They entered with guns against a mob that knew the lie of the land better than they did and, greatly outnumbering them, took their weapons and beat them to a pulp.

The next stage was closure. The army took charge. Soldiers went down into the quarry, scoured every corner of it for human remains, broke and blasted the steps, railings and footholds from the rock face and removed the ladders. They used so much dynamite that no entrances remained, only a sheer drop from every point. The bad feeling they left behind quickly transferred itself back to the original sources of conflict. People thought, and said, that – as far as they were concerned – enemies didn't live in foreign countries: they lived right down the road and on the other side of town.

When the war began, there was plenty of hatred to call on. And once things were rolling, the few who had been neutral were sucked into the action. They became part of it. And then they hated, too.

*

They had three weeks of colds in the house. His theory was that the aid workers had brought sickness when they'd come to take the orphans away. One night the children got into a fight about something. There was screaming, shouting and crying – a general outpouring of misery and complaint that overwhelmed them all, including him and his wife. Afterwards he was tired to death. He woke up in the middle of the night and got out of bed. His wife turned over, murmuring, 'What's wrong?'

He said, 'I need some air.' He moved to the window and pulled the cloth aside. A wild, ghostly pallor flooded down from a full moon high in the sky. His hook was on the sill, where he left it every night before going to bed. The light touched it, making it gleam. She hated the hook. It wasn't that she was afraid of having him hurt her without meaning to if he rolled over in bed or flung out an arm in sleep. She just hated it anyway.

He felt his way downstairs and stepped out into the night. Everything was caught up in the moon's estranging glamor. He walked into the old orchard and roamed through the twisted alleyways. Long ago there had been a stone fountain near the center of the place, at least he thought he remembered something of the kind from his childhood, when the trees had belonged to a neighboring farm.

He couldn't find the fountain, nor any trace of stone or pipe-line. He stopped walking. It seemed to him that everything was gone. The wonderful light threw a momentary allure over the dreary muddle of ruined landscape and buildings. But there was nothing worth looking at in daylight. Beauty had gone from the world and from their lives.

The long delay of spring, the vanishing of the hope they had been given earlier in the year, made their poverty worse than before. What was left to offer a child like the one who had kissed his hand? When he thought of that sweet, inept gesture, he wanted to weep. But no tears came from him. That was gone, too.

If only they could get through the war – that was what he used to think: if only they could get through it, everything would be all right. But it was beginning to seem to him that nothing would ever be right again.

He kept going to work every morning, as usual. The days were empty, companionless.

Every crumb was counted as they waited for the next hand-out.

The aid workers didn't come back for another two weeks. When they did, they brought bedding, socks, mittens and food. A soldier who was traveling with them handed over a secret package of coffee, which he and his wife saved as if it were the gold of the fairy tales. Genuine gold was worth hardly anything any more and money was just paper. But coffee could get you out of trouble or buy you a favor. Sometimes coffee could even buy medicine. Cigarettes were also valuable, but not nearly so precious. All the soldiers still had cigarettes and matches. Coffee – even dried out, even ancient – was exquisite luxury.

The next morning their refugee arrived – only one: an old woman whose name and age they were never told because no one knew anything about her. She was simply being preserved as an example of the aid workers' goodness and proof that they were acting according to humanitarian principles. They'd given her a number.

She was carried into the house and placed in the center of the only decent downstairs bed they still had.

'Not there,' his wife objected. 'I know these old people. Their bladders work day and night. Put her over there. We'll rearrange things as soon as we can.'

The woman was shifted to a comer of the room where three of the children had been hanging around, full of curiosity about the aid people. As the workers lowered their burden to the floor, a stream of urine gushed from her; a steamy, stale odor filled the room. The children became hysterical, holding their noses and making sounds that imitated farts. One of the men who had helped to carry her muttered, 'Christ, not again.'

'See?' his wife said. 'I told you.' She signed the paper held out to her. As she handed it back, she asked, 'What can you tell me about her?'

'Nothing. She doesn't move but she isn't paralysed. She's old. Maybe she's sick, maybe not.'

'Does she talk?'

'She makes noises. That's all.'

'We should get extra rations for this. Somebody's got to keep cleaning her up all the time.'

'You get what's written down there.'

'Well, we'll do our best, but just look at her. I mean, she isn't going to last long, no matter what we do for her. It looks like she's had a stroke, anyway. Did a doctor see her before you loaded her into that cattle truck?'

'Doctor?' both the aid workers repeated. They laughed. One of them said, 'When was the last time you saw a doctor, Professor?'

The other one said, 'I expect that would be Dr Houdini you're referring to – we haven't seen him around for quite a while.'

The first one said, 'I guess he's done a disappearing act.'

After the two of them had left the house, they could still be heard, faintly: laughing as they got back into their open-sided van, banged the doors and started the engine.

That evening he helped to move the beds. They had to keep the old woman downstairs, where the smell immediately began to infiltrate everything around her. His wife said, 'We'll never be able to get rid of her.'

He answered in a low voice, 'They're sure to move her along soon. We aren't qualified to deal with her.'

'How qualified do you need to be to clean up piss and shit?'

'In a real hospital they might be able to get her speech back.'

'Oh my God, what for? Who's got the time for that sentimental garbage? Look around you. It's the children who need what this old biddy's using up. She's had her chance. And she had more than most – she must be a hundred if she's a day. She'd better stop making that noise.'

'She probably doesn't know she's doing it.'

'It makes me feel like hitting her over the head.'

'Don't forget: we're lucky to have a refugee with us.'

'You don't have to do the washing. Listen. There she goes again. Well, she can just lie in it. I'm not doing anything more till the kids are in bed.'

*

As he had feared, they went into a cold snap. It lasted nearly a week. All doors and windows had to be shut tight against the bitter daytime winds and the freezing nights. The old woman whined and groaned and the house reeked of her uncontrollable bodily emissions. Her mind might have been blocked by some unknown inner disaster, but the rest was without restraint. Whatever went in, came out. The stink reached every part of the house. After a while they began to taste it in the food they ate and even in the water they drank.

'She's as strong as a horse,' his wife said. 'She'll last for ever.'

'Hush,' he whispered.

'What for?'

He'd been told that people who were immobile and unable to talk – even people who were in a coma – could sometimes still hear. If the woman knew what they'd been saying from her arrival onward, she'd be in a state of anguish.

Outside the house the air was clear. He stayed away from home, going in to town or moving farther out into the country and working as long as he could, despite the cold.

Spring came at last, the real spring. Children who had hidden indoors for the past months came out to play. They formed gangs. Sometimes they took part in the ancient circle games and dances he'd grown up with. When he heard their voices from far away, he was reminded of his own childhood, his parents and the world that had been safe and happy before everything was smashed to pieces. But more often the games became like rehearsals for military activity. The gangs had leaders and bullies; the girls were excluded or beaten into submission. He could see the time coming when the older girls would be turned into whores until they became pregnant, after which their parents would throw them out of the house. And by that time the boys would have armed themselves with weapons to use against rival gangs; they'd already found tunes for the words they shouted as they strode back and forth, acting important. He didn't like to see them marching: it made him think that everything was going to happen all over again. But, of course, it would.

He concentrated on the vegetable garden, using the children as guards. They understood that their presence next to the newly dug and planted rows was essential. They never left the house except in a group, knowing that if anything were found to be missing at home, he or his wife would punish them for it after their return.

Everyone stole. His main worry, especially during the night, was the food. No matter how they tried to disguise it, anyone could tell that they had plenty now: enough to eat and to save, as well as seeds, bulbs and roots in the ground. Three of their neighbors had similar gardens but you could never have too much and – as his wife pointed out – those were just the people who would be the first to try out a midnight raid on somebody else because they could always say that the stolen produce had come from their own place.

The trees came into bud. People forgot their desire to have just one object that wasn't chipped, cracked, worn, torn, broken, mended or secondhand. They'd been given a fresh beginning and their world felt transformed.

The young ones longed for love and adventure while at the same time dealing in corruption and copying all the brutalities of their elders. They were busy trying things out. He took care to remain alert to what his own kids were getting up to, but it was impossible to keep all of them under control.

He couldn't even hold them down when they were at home. He used to step into the house to hear whispers and smothered, explosive giggles coming from the direction of the old woman's bed. She'd be whimpering and moaning as usual. And he'd find them pushing things into her mouth, pinching her, driving pins into her arms, pretending to stab her in the eyes with a stick. 'What are you doing?' he'd roar at them, and they'd scatter. But they were always drawn back. In their minds she wasn't human or even animal; she was an object – an object of amusement. Their favorite trick was to make her mew and cry in patterns, as if she were singing a song.

He'd tried to explain things to them until he realized the true horror: they understood perfectly well that the old woman could still feel pain and that their actions were hurting and frightening her. That was what they liked. That was the essence of the enjoyment.

If they behaved that way when they were young, what was their generation going to be like later? How would they treat ailing parents and grandparents or – when they had them – their own children? They had no respect for the weak and helpless: the old, the newly born, the sick, injured, crazed or blind. They accepted no responsibility for any of that. The young had been shown that even the strongest could die. They could see no point in prolonging the lives of the second-rate.

The spring was as lovely as in any year of peace. On some days it seemed like a season from an ancient age when all the world was beautiful, peopled by gods and goddesses.

They thought for a while that things might be getting better. It was even possible, they imagined, that the fighting might come to a stop.

They carried the old woman outdoors so that she could enjoy the fresh air. But her piteous whines and fearful gasps, her grunts and sighs, ruined the fine weather for them, just as when they were indoors she made the house unbearable. Feeble and miserable as she was, she seemed indomitable, whereas they were being worn down.

'She'll live for ever,' his wife said. 'She'll probably outlive us.'

One day he returned to the house for a bag of nails and a couple of hinges that were stored in the shed. On his way past the front door, he heard the old woman moaning. He stepped inside, where he found the children persecuting her again. He chased them out of the house and then went to the back, to collect what he'd come for. He crashed around in the cramped space, so angry for a moment that he had to stop and cover his eyes with his hands, thinking: *Be careful. This is how people have accidents. Calm down.*

They were just young, he told himself; they would learn. They'd change, like everything else. As soon as there was a genuine political settlement, the economy would stabilize and there would be enough for everyone. There would be celebrations, feasts, the ritual marking of days and years. Children would enjoy being innocent again and cruelty would recede from their minds. That was his hope, although he now saw little evidence for continuing to believe it.

In the distance he heard three of his children singing the alphabet song:

The Queen of Dalmatia, whose name was Aspatia, arrived in a grand coach and four. She had footmen and flunkies and uniformed monkeys and pink pearls right down to the floor.

They all sat down early and ate until late: pomegranates, pickles and pears; pasta, pies, parsnips and plump purple plums; peaches, pineapples and peas. Peacocks and partridges, pancakes and plaice; peppers and pretzels and palm trees. Prime poached, puce piglets and purest champagne that poured from the bottles like rain.

The Prince of Pomander ate a live salamander. He grimaced and gargled and gagged. He'd done it by accident but it set a court precedent much admired in Shiraz and Baghdad.

Oh, what delectable dishes they ate, from the lowliest up to the mighty and great. What speeches rang out through the old dining hall, what flirting and drinking and laughter went on. Oh, what a fine time they had, eating and talking and dancing away. All through the evening and into the dawn, everyone happy and glad. And the party went on the next day.

The sound of their voices drew away his fury. But he thought that it wouldn't be long now before they changed the nonsense rhymes to jingles that came close to the original obscenities of the old army version.

A military workforce came through with builders and engineers, leaving a restricted and unreliable telephone system and a low-level electricity supply that cut out just when you didn't expect it to. They were becoming a part of the modern world again. They had bottled gas, kerosene and intermittent running water that wasn't always safe to drink. They could get eggs, but not chickens, except on the black market. You could get anything there, so people said.

Occasionally you could catch sight of the big dealers going by, usually in the evening. There were always two cars: the bodyguards up in the front of the first one, with the boss in the back seat, sometimes accompanied by a henchman, and – in the second car – the women, in fur coats and diamonds and face paint you could see from a distance. They and their friends continued to do business without bothering most people; their fights were all with others of their own kind. Among the ordinary populace the general feeling was that they were providing a service no government was yet able to offer. Of course it was also true that if you went against them, they shot you; but everyone knew that. They were predictable and therefore less of a threat than, say, a roving band of deserters – that was the sort of thing that made everyone nervous, even the crooks.

By the time the leaves were out on the trees, his wife was saying that she'd rather live in a work camp than keep the old woman with them.

'What are we going to do without the extra rations?' he asked.

'I don't know. And I don't care. If you want her here, you can take care of her.'

'I'm working already.'

'Who isn't?'

'I don't understand why she doesn't die. She's in such a bad state.'

'She's alive because she's being treated like royalty in this house.'

'I guess if she died, we'd be issued with another refugee. One that would be easier to look after.'

'Don't you believe it. People like us have taken over the work of the hospitals. But this is beyond anything. If I ever set eyes on another one like this, I'll just let her lie there. We don't even have hygienic surroundings. They couldn't have expected her to last more than a couple of days. She should have died a long time ago.'

They stopped talking and stared at the woman, who no longer had even the look of someone who should be pitied. She was repulsive. She was the only one in the house who had a bed to herself although, God knew, nobody would want to use it after her. When she finally died, they'd have to bum it. Except that they wouldn't. They'd put the next refugee into it.

'You do it,' his wife said. 'It's your job.'

Over the next few days he found himself thinking at odd moments that it would benefit everyone, including the old woman, if he got rid of her; such a killing would be what was called 'humane', 'an act of compassion', or 'putting her out of her misery'.

It was even possible that the blubbering, whining noises she made were an attempt to ask someone to dispatch her rather than let her continue in bondage to her irreparably damaged body.

And maybe not. Perhaps she was just saying: *Feed me, love me, pity me, make me well again: help me.* But he'd seen plenty of hospitals where there were patients who just kept repeating, 'Oh God, let me die.' And they'd meant it. Lots of people felt like that. He could imagine feeling that way himself.

He didn't want to hurt her. That wouldn't be right. None of their troubles, including her own condition, could be considered her fault and certainly not the war, nor the system of refugee housing.

He didn't want to get caught, either. How could he dispose of her safely and painlessly? He thought about that during the next week and over the following months as the summer came and then reached its height and even with all the boards taken off the windows and the doors standing open, the oily tang of urine and the fulsome, barnyard stench of excrement reached every corner and expanded, ballooned, pulsated in the air. You could choke on it from the next room.

One day he realized that all day long he'd been thinking: *I hope I don't die like that.* Pretending to himself that his feelings were nobler than they were, he asked himself how she could want to go on living. It would be doing her a kindness to put an end to her.

He remembered his friends, so young and full of exuberance, who were now dead while a rotting piece of senility like this lived on. The mere fact of it enraged him. And the next moment, it filled him with sorrow. This thing had had a mother once. Once upon a time, a young woman had cradled a baby in her arms and looked lovingly down into its face; and it was to become this pitiable wreck.

Somebody should just hit her on the head with a shovel. He didn't want to do it himself. But if his wife did it, he'd accept it.

His wife wouldn't do it. She'd told him straight to his face that it was his responsibility. It was something he was just going to have to carry out without thinking: like breaking the neck of an injured animal.

*

The summer went by and the warm days of September. The crops were better than they had hoped for. They were able to save up towards the coming months. They were eating well for the first time that year; but their good fortune was spoiled by the old woman's presence.

It was bad enough in the warm weather when they could open the windows. What was it going to be like if she had to spend a whole winter with them?

Of course someone in her condition couldn't last much longer. He didn't think so, anyway. But his wife said, 'That old bag is just the kind who'll go on for another ten years, sucking it in at one end and pumping it out at the other.' He didn't like to hear her talk like that but he knew that her derision was a sign that she was looking for a fight. It was better to let her talk and not to make any comment.

'We've got to get rid of her,' she told him. 'We could get her out of the house and keep on drawing the rations.'

'Suppose they want to see her?'

'We could produce somebody. I heard of a case where five families lived off one old crone like this. They just moved her from house to house when the aid workers came around. It would be even easier here. You just give one of the officials a percentage.'

'And wind up in jail.'

'Not if you know the right ones. I could fix it. Just get her out of here.'

The rains began, followed by the first frost and then, near the end of October, a week of mild weather that was spring-like, almost summery. And suddenly, with the warmth, there was an outbreak of killing. As usual, there were some strangled girls, either pregnant or raped, but a lot more of the victims were children. He and his wife reminded the kids to be wary of strangers and over-friendly people. From the snake-eyed silence with which the advice was received, he began to suspect that many of the perpetrators were also children. That was certainly possible: war had awakened in the general population a readiness to kill. In any place where troops had gone through, there were always more corpses than seemed normal. Wherever there might have been hand-to-hand combat you could get away with it. People settled their quarrels as soon as they saw the first uniform go by.

His wife would do it if she had to. Even if she didn't have to. If she thought she could escape detection, she'd do it for a cup of sugar. It meant nothing to her.

How much did he mean to her himself? She still needed him, but he was damaged. As soon as other, able-bodied and younger men arrived back – on leave after a temporary cease-fire or with the occupying and peacekeeping forces or, should it ever be possible, at the end of the fighting – she might start looking around for something better. He had no idea now what she was like except that he feared she might be turning into someone who was stronger than he was and who eventually wouldn't have any use for him.

'I'm not going through a winter with that lump of disease in the house,' she told him.

'She isn't sick. She's old.'

'She's sick. I don't want the children to catch it.'

It was the children who brought everything in: colds, influenza, fevers, lice, bugs, fleas, skin diseases.

'We've got to get rid of her.'

'All right,' he said. 'I agree. But we can't make it look like an accident if she can't move, can we? And if it doesn't look natural, they'll get us for it.'

'She just has to stop breathing, that's all.'

'It'll show.'

'Then it's got to be the quarry.'

'What does that mean?'

'That's what everybody else has been doing. Not just our neighborhood. Everyone in the district.'

'Oh? Where did you hear that?'

'I keep my ears open.'

So do I, he thought. He still hadn't heard anything definite about the quarry other than the occasional hushed joke. And he'd assumed that the black-market traders would have been using it for payoffs and assignations if there had been any way to get in and out. There were rumors, but all of them seemed to refer to what had gone on before the fighting.

'They've been taking their refugees to the quarry, throwing them in and saying that they ran away. Nobody can get out down there. It's sealed.'

'And if somebody finds them? If the aid workers get to know about it?'

'Listen. This is the way it works: you take your refugees out there and throw them in. If you hit them on the head first, they don't last long and they can't tell anybody their names. You go back home and say they moved off, looking for more food or trying to trace their cousins, or something like that. Then you get new ones. All the aid agencies have is their names – they don't have time to make a record of anything else. Nobody official is going to remember what any of them look like. We aren't supposed to have them more than a couple of months, anyway.'

'But we aren't supposed to kill them.'

'You don't have to kill anybody. Once they're in the quarry, the rest of the bunch in there take care of things. They'd probably eat anybody healthy who just fell in. That's what I think happened to that missing boy – I think some of his friends pushed him in for fun and the quarry people ate him.'

'That's ridiculous.'

'Well, there isn't any food down there.'

'But they aren't animals.'

'They're starving, injured and sick. They see a nice, clean, well-fed young child alone and unprotected among hundreds of them – are you serious? They'd roast him on a spit.'

'Hundreds?'

'That's what I hear. Well, to start out with. Dozens, maybe. The rest will be corpses now. And bones. So. You get her out there and I tell everybody: her health improved so much that she just walked out on us.'

'The kids would be spilling the beans to everybody and his grandmother. They'd think it was funny.'

'I'll handle the kids,' she said. 'That's my department.'

He set off to walk to the quarry. He hadn't been there since before the war, when he'd lived in his parents' house on the other side of town. From his own place it wasn't far. It wouldn't take long.

As he walked, he thought about his wife. Where had she really heard those things? Women sometimes kept a piece of news away from the men of a community just as the men did from the women, but the problem of refugees was one that affected everyone. And surely the children would be talking about the quarry, if the story were true.

He could understand that something of the kind might happen. The time for pity and humanity was during and right after the shooting and bombardment: after the savagery of fighting. As soon as a year or so had gone by, the injured became a burden. But despite the lack of policing, and the makeshift nature of organizations in the district, people wouldn't feel safe committing such atrocities unless they thought they couldn't get caught. And the only reason they might feel that was if the aid agencies were in on some sort of swindle with them: handing the regular food ration to the families and dumping the refugees into the quarry to rot.

That made sense. And in that case, it would mean that she'd heard it from the man who kept giving her the cigarettes. So, had she been seeing him on the side? She was pregnant again, too. Was she pregnant by the other man? Was she in love?

*

The wind was behind him as it usually was if you were heading out of town from that point. That was why the quarry, the slaughterhouse and the tannery were all in the same general area. And it was another reason why his parents' house, now gone, had been in a better location than his and why his first long trek to the quarry had seemed such an adventure.

Despite the direction of the wind, as soon as he was close enough to see the outcrops of rock that marked the quarry boundary, he became aware of the smell: it was sporadically evident, moving in single, fugitive wafts and then the occasional full gust.

He circled the place, looking down. All the people he could see at the far end were entirely without clothes or shoes. They lay separately and most of them appeared to be dead but during his inspection one figure gave signs of consciousness. As he continued to walk, he caught sight of another: a man, wrapped in a few strips of cloth, who raised his head, crawled forward a few feet and lay down again. A crowd of noisy birds circled overhead. They landed near the bodies and flew back up, to come down at a different spot. A few desultory groans reached him: it was impossible to tell where they came from.

All at once he heard children's voices. Ahead of him, among the brushwood and scrub running up to the lip of the quarry, stood a girl and a boy: the girl no older than six and the boy possibly about four. They were throwing something down to one of the people below. He caught the girl's words: 'bread' and later – triumphantly – 'blanket'. A dark shape rose into the air and disappeared from view.

He wrapped his handkerchief around his hook and crept closer.

The children were so preoccupied that they didn't notice. He was right on top of them before they saw him. The boy screamed. The girl whirled around and stared, ready to run.

In an easy, conversational tone he said, 'Do you know somebody down there?'

'Anna,' the boy answered.

'Is she your mother?'

'She's our friend. She takes care of us.'

The girl pointed off into the bushes, and said, 'We found a ladder, but it's too heavy.'

'He could lift it,' the boy told her.

He said, 'I know those ladders. They're old. They've rotted. You'd hurt yourself on them. Haven't your parents told you to stay away from here?'

Both children looked down. The girl mumbled, 'We hear them crying.'

'Well,' he said vaguely, 'I'll see what I can do. But you'd better go home now. Nobody's safe here. And remember to keep away from the ladders. You could fall in there yourselves, you know. Go on.' He moved his good hand in an outward sweep. They stood still for a few moments, looked at each other and then ran.

He stepped forward to the quarry itself and peered over the drop. A middle-aged woman was standing directly below him, looking up. She was wrapped in the blanket the children had thrown down. 'Please,' she called up. 'For God's sake.'

Behind her stood a young woman, the only person he'd yet seen in the place who had on any clothes other than rags. She was not simply fully dressed: she was magnificently attired for the evening in sumptuous garments, the like of which hadn't been seen since before the war – a long, silky gown and a little velvet jacket with elbow-length sleeves. Her shoes, one of which was just visible beneath the hem of her dress, were of satiny black with an arrow-shaped stripe of some glittering substance at the front: metal or beads. Like the older woman, she was eating food from a piece of paper. There was no indication that anything had been taken by force; the two were evidently friends or had become allies through circumstance.

The older woman limped a step nearer. As she tightened her hand on the blanket he could see that she wore some kind of dark shift, possibly underclothing borrowed from her friend. 'Please,' she called out again, more desperately. Behind her the young woman crumpled up and threw away the piece of paper that had held the food. She made a graceful, swinging move forward, like the first step of a dance. 'Please,' she repeated. Her voice was stronger and fuller but also smoother and sweeter than the other woman's. As she spoke, she put her hands to the front of the dress underneath her jacket and pulled the material apart, showing him her breasts. 'Please,' she insisted, so softly that he could hardly catch the sound. It was as if he stood right next to her, close enough to touch, transfixed by her large, dark eyes, the kissing shape of her mouth after speech had left it, the beautiful breasts that she covered again.

'What's your name?' he asked.

'Maria.'

'And you're Anna?' he said to the older woman. She nodded. 'What's wrong with your leg?'

'It happened when they threw me in.'

'Could you climb a ladder?'

'Yes. But soon, please. Every hour we're weaker. We don't dare to fall asleep at the same time.'

He looked at Maria again. Her eyes held his, but she didn't add any words to what her gesture had already promised in return for rescue. He said, 'I'll try,' and turned away.

He followed the direction the little girl had indicated. After beating the undergrowth and shrubbery for a while, he found the ladder. It was old but long enough to reach to the bottom of the pit from one of the lower sides. Several rungs were missing, although the long sections looked all right; in some places they had been reinforced with metal. He kicked the wood. He tried its weight. He thought that he'd be able to get Maria out if he came back and put three more rungs in. He'd bring a rope too, in case they had to tie Anna to the lower rungs and haul her up that way. It would be easy if they had a car or a tractor or a horse – or any of several other things nobody had any more.

He didn't go back to look at them. Anything could happen between then and the next day. The ladder, for instance, might belong to a gang that was still using the place for smuggling or secret meetings, in spite of the gruesome recent addition of the living graveyard. He might return and find the ladder gone. The children's parents could be there, lying in wait for him, ready to deal with anyone who knew what they had done to the pleasant, gray-haired refugee who had been working as a nursemaid to their children.

He'd do what he had promised: he'd try. And they'd wait where they were, knowing that he'd expect them to be in the same spot when he came back.

A few drops of rain spattered down as he made his way home. At first he thought that he'd misjudged the hour and that the darkening sky meant an early evening, but the rain convinced him that he still had time to do everything: collect his toolbox, pick up some clothes and find the ropes he kept coiled in the corner cupboard to the right of the sink. The longest rope would certainly be enough. And there were two shorter ones.

As he walked, he scanned the houses in the distance. One of them would be the place where the two children lived. He wondered how the women in the quarry would be able to stand the cold and wet in a downpour. Thinking about the older woman reminded him of the old woman at home. What was he going to do with her now? If he hadn't met the children and Anna and

Maria, he'd have taken a quick look, come back at night and just shoved her over. But he'd have needed to borrow a car from somewhere, so maybe he'd have postponed any action till then.

The rain passed by. He came to the lane that led to his house. He'd have to think up something to tell his wife. He'd say that he'd decided to do what she'd been asking, and get rid of the old woman. So, he'd gone to the quarry. But there was a woman and . . . her daughter . . . who had been tricked, robbed and thrown in there with the others. And he was going to get them out. They could work in the house. They could take care of the children. And if she didn't like it, she could get out, because she sure as hell didn't do much herself nowadays. All she did was smoke black-market cigarettes one after the other.

He stepped over the threshold. The whimpers of the old woman started up as if renewing themselves in increasing frequency. And the smell was there. But his wife wasn't at home. And the children were out; they ought to have been back in the house at that hour. Maybe they were at a neighborhood party or walking home from a soccer game or doing work somewhere in order to earn extra money. But now it really was beginning to get dark and he didn't like the girls to stay out late unless they were with friends. Had his wife taken them all somewhere without telling him beforehand – had she left him? She wouldn't be able to manage on her own. And what man would take on a woman who had all those kids?

He heard another noise above the sounds of the old woman: the cries of someone in pain. They came from one of the back rooms where some of the children slept. He hurried towards the noise. Long before he reached the door, he must have recognized the grunts and moans for what they were. And as soon as he knew, he should have stopped, gone away to think, and laid a trap. But he didn't miss a step. He didn't seem to think at all, although something must have been taking place in his mind because he speeded up, going faster towards the door and not bothering to walk quietly. So, even though he had surprise on his side, they would have heard his approach before he came through the door.

He pulled the aid worker off his wife, swiped him across the side of the head with his hook and when the man produced the knife he'd reached for, jumped on the bed and started to kick him in the belly. His wife scrabbled around for the fallen knife. He slammed her in the face. Blood gushed from her nose and she fainted. He turned back to the man, but not fast enough.

He saw the fist coming at him, right in front of his face.

He woke with a headache worse than any hangover he'd ever had. The night sky was above him, irradiated by a half moon. Someone was bending over him: a woman – a beautiful woman. Maria.

He was in the quarry.

As soon as he understood where he was, he could smell the pungent reek: coming from all around him, especially from a large, lumpy shape lying on the ground ahead of him.

'Are you badly hurt?' Maria asked. 'Can you understand what I'm saying?'

He felt his jaw and tested the action of his limbs. He was still in his clothes and boots, but his hook was gone. He wondered if it had been lost during the fall. Of course not; it had to be unscrewed. He was lucky that they hadn't beaten the other half out of the bone; that could help to identify him, if anyone ever wanted to take the trouble.

He was sore, but that was all. No bones were broken, not even his jaw, and he still had his teeth. All the pain – except for his head – came from bruising, nothing more.

'They were in a hurry,' she told him. 'They threw the old woman over first. You fell right on top of her, with your arm under your head. Otherwise, you'd probably be dead.'

'This is the sandy side,' he said. 'Everybody knows that. They must have been scared. Or lazy. They must have known the fall might not kill me.'

A shadow moved behind Maria: Anna, still wrapped in her blanket. She sat down on the ground next to him, and sighed, saying, 'What difference does it make? We can't get out. You might be better off if you'd broken your neck.'

'They had a car,' Maria said. 'We heard it. I came over here to look. Anna stayed where we'd seen you in the afternoon.'

'How long ago did this happen?'

'Ten minutes, no longer.'

He sat up, thinking: *Thank God I haven't been here for a week and lost my strength.* The clothes and boots were a help, but not necessary. The missing hook was more important; without it he felt somehow unsure of his balance.

He told them about the stone steps that used to lead from the top. The stairs that went down to gravel and the ones that ended on solid stone had been left with projections and rough edges. The ones that led from stone still contained a long middle section of steps. Going up from gravel the stairs were more destroyed and higher, but less dangerous if you fell. It was a question of weighing advantage against disadvantage. He chose the stone. The women disagreed with him. He said, 'We'll see what it's like first.'

They walked across the quarry in the moonlight, Maria stepping daintily in her party shoes, Anna limping behind. Halfway over to the other side, someone began to follow them. He stopped to chase the intruder away. Anna said, 'Most of them are quiet till near the end, when they start to go crazy. That gives them a burst of energy every once in a while.' When the same form scuttled back, he turned around and kicked out at it. No one bothered them after that.

He put his hand on the rock face; it was cold but not wet. He wiped his hand on his trousers. He considered taking his boots off and decided against it. He longed for his hook.

'Stand back while I'm climbing,' he told the women. 'If I get out, I'll come back to where they threw me over the side. And I'll try to find the car. If I don't come back, I'll be dead.'

The first part of the climb was easy. At the still almost complete mid-section, he went up the steps without hesitation. Only after that did the ordeal begin, as he moved across jutting spars and ledges that broke under his weight, or leaned close to the rock wall to catch his breath and slow his heartbeat, only to find that the stone now seemed moist and slippery. He was running with sweat and gasping for air. His head felt ready to burst and he began to tremble. In the half-light his sense of distance was distorted so that he mistook shadow for solid ground. Pieces of rock crumbled away beneath him as he tried to find a safe place to stand and rest. But the longer he struggled, the clearer it became that there wasn't going to be any rest. He couldn't go back: he would never be able to repeat any stretch of the climb, much less do it again from the beginning; the trail was collapsing – erasing itself as he moved. This was the test that was like life: you went through it once and that was your only chance.

He was afraid that his muscles were going to go into spasm or to lock without warning but he couldn't turn the other way because there wasn't room. *Don't do something sudden out of desperation,* he thought. *Just keep going.*

He couldn't believe that he was going to make it to the top. He would have lost hope if he hadn't remembered that there were other people counting on him. Trying to remain calm, he forced himself to go on. For a while it seemed to him that he was gaining and losing, only to stay in the same place. Then he made some progress. The idea of stopping, and of looking down, began to pull at him. He wanted to look back even though he knew that that would be the end. He kept on.

As he reached for the top, he lunged ahead and up, getting his hand, his good arm and a leg over the edge of the stone shelf. He rolled forward, pressing himself to the security of free ground. Behind him another section of rock slipped downward and fell with a crash to the quarry floor.

This time he looked back, to see if the others were all right. They were both standing where he'd told them to. Maria was clapping her hands. He waved.

Everything was clear and dreamlike in the moonlight. He moved with a steady pace. If he hadn't felt strange, he would have liked to run. Anyone who saw him would have thought there was nothing wrong, but he knew that something peculiar was happening to him. Being knocked out, and then landing in the quarry, might have shaken up his head. Maybe he had a concussion. He'd have to worry about that later.

He had a strong sense of the unreality of everything he looked at. He was also uncannily aware of being protected. Later he'd imagine that there had been a giant hand above him. At the moment it was simply a presence.

This time, he thought, he wouldn't make the mistake of charging through the front door and on into the back room, if that was still where they were. If his wife had sent the children away for the afternoon, they'd be at home again now. And the man might have moved on; with the opportunities of a job like his, he probably had several women in the district. Or maybe not. Perhaps his wife's pregnancy was a sign that the man was committed to her.

As he neared the house he inspected all the overgrown fences, the broken-down walls, the disused paths. He was looking for the car. He had to wait until he was closer.

The car was parked outside the house. It had been positioned at the back, so that no passerby would be tempted to steal it, but it was right next to the door, to save its owner time and to keep him from getting wet if it rained.

He crept along the side of the house to the tool shed, pulled the loose plank away and reached in under the shelf where he kept an extra knife. It was still there, in its sheath. The ax was in its place, too, up under the slope of the shed roof over the woodpile. He stuck the knife down his boot and carried the ax in his hand.

Which part of the house would they be in? Not in the back room this time; the children would be in that bed. And not where the old woman's bed had stood; he could see the mattress sagging against one of the trees. They'd be upstairs, in his own bed.

He got in through a window, climbed the stairs stealthily, tiptoed beyond the other room where the children would be sleeping, and stopped outside the bedroom. He tried the door. It moved forward under his hand; they hadn't turned the key because they'd thought that he was safely disposed of.

He could hear them inside, breathing in sleep.

He pushed the door wide, snapped on the light with his elbow, stepped forward and swung the ax down on the back of the man's head. Then he pulled out the knife. The sight of the woman – her face partly covered by a white mask – brought him to a halt. He didn't know who she was. For an instant he wondered if he'd gone out of his mind, or if he'd entered the wrong house by mistake and just imagined all the rooms to be familiar in the half-dark and moonlight. Had a strange couple been invited over for the night?

She made a sound and opened her eyes. He realized that what she was wearing was a large bandage. He must have broken her nose when he'd hit her earlier in the evening.

He dropped the knife on the bed, pulled her by the hair and got her neck into the crook of his arm. He picked up the knife again. She hadn't even had time to scream. 'Where's the hook?' he demanded. She tried to speak. He released his grip slightly.

She said, 'It wasn't my idea. I didn't want to –'

'Where is it?' he repeated. 'Quick. Or I'll take one of your eyes out.' He pushed the knife forward at her.

'It's gone.'

'Where?'

'I threw it out. He said to.'

'Where?'

'In the garbage.'

'Outside?'

'No. Still in the bag. Under the sink.'

He said that they'd go there together and not to make any noise. She wanted to talk. He tightened his grip, pulled her out of the bed and forced her to walk in front of him. As he dragged her from under the covers he saw her eyes go to the man and the ax. She began to moan. He told her to shut up. She started to cry. 'Quiet,' he said. 'If you wake the kids, I'll kill you.'

'I won't do anything,' she whispered. She breathed fast, choking. He loosened his hold on her.

'I didn't want anything to happen to you,' she said. 'I did it for the food and cigarettes. I –'

'Move,' he hissed, shoving her forward.

When they arrived in the kitchen, he made her point out the bag that contained the hook. With the knife still in his hand he lifted the bag out of the pail and dumped it into the sink. 'Find it,' he told her.

That was the moment where he almost relented: when, pressing her forward and still gripping her neck in his arm, he saw her hands shake uncontrollably as they searched through the eggshells and the rotten ends of cabbage leaves. He felt such pity at the sight that he almost let her go. The next instant, she had the hook and she was trying to twist around, to reach up and stick it into his face, at the same time kicking backward at him. The trembling had been caused by hope, not fear.

He lifted her off her feet, threw the knife away and brought his hand forward to press more tightly into her neck. He squeezed as hard as he could until her body relaxed and – as far as he could tell – her breathing stopped, but she could be pretending. He waited. And afterwards, to make sure, he chopped the back of her neck with the side of his hand. He wasn't going to leave anyone half-dead. *No prisoners, no survivors, no ghosts:* that was what his friends used to say.

He moved her to a chair and ran some water over the hook, cleaned it with the towel by the sink and screwed it back into its socket.

From then on, he worked as if he had actually planned everything, knowing how much time he could save by doing which thing first. He went through the neatly folded clothes that had been placed on the bedroom chair. He found car keys, identification, a notebook and jewelry. He removed a watch, a heavy gold bracelet and neck chain, a large gold ring with an eagle stamped on it. He put the keys in his pocket. The shoes and knife were under the side of the bed.

He retrieved the ax from the body, wiped it on the man's trousers, looked at the shoes to determine whether or not they'd fit anyone he knew, and decided to sell them. He threw them – with the knife, the papers and notebook and jewelry – into the man's shirt, tied the arms to make a bundle and stuck it under the bed. Then he wrapped the trousers around the man's head and carried him out to the car. On the way back to the front of the house, he collected a hammer, saw, screwdriver, nails, screws and bolts and a lamp. He left them all on the front seat and returned to the house for two of the ropes and the ax, which he'd stood in a corner.

He pulled the nightdress off his wife, looked it over for bloodstains and dropped it into the laundry pile. He carried her outside and slung her into the back seat of the car, on top of the man. The ax and ropes went into the front with the rest of the tools. He wanted to stop but he didn't dare. As soon as the wish for sleep crossed his mind, he knew how close he was to complete exhaustion.

He looked around the kitchen to see if he'd forgotten anything that should be hidden or cleaned. His eye fell on the man's coat – an extremely beautiful and expensive-looking leather coat hanging on the back of the door. In an inside pocket there was a pistol. How had that gone unnoticed by the children?

He went through the other pockets quickly, pulling out an unused handkerchief, an open pack of cigarettes, a wad of money, a spare magazine for the gun, a map and an address book. He himself would never have gone to another room and left such treasures unguarded. A couple of empty bottles and two glasses on the table might have explained such carelessness. They'd been drunk. After what they'd been through earlier in the evening, they'd undoubtedly taken to the bottle, starting as they bandaged his wife's nose, continuing during the struggle to drag him and the old woman into the car and then pausing while they had to deal with the return of the children to the house. Perhaps they'd made the kids drunk too, to be sure that there would be no interruption, and no awakenings when they were away from the house. They'd both go, of course; each to see that the other did what should be done.

He kept the pistol on him. The rest of the things he put under the bed upstairs, except for the coat, which he took out to the car. He threw it over the two in the back seat. It was too dangerous to keep, no matter how much it was worth. To sell the car – and the shoes and jewelry – would be easy. A dead man's coat was another matter.

He released the brake and pushed the car away from the house. He didn't think a short distance would be much use in disguising the noise of the engine starting up, but after having made so many mistakes earlier, he didn't want to ruin everything now. He was already so tired that he was forgetting things: he was behind the wheel, the car moving, when he remembered that he'd meant to bring the two women another blanket and his wife's coat.

He drove to the quarry without seeing anyone and, he hoped, without being seen.

Before anything else, he heaved the two bodies over the side. He tore the bandage from his wife's face and threw the sticky ball of gauze and adhesive into the bushes before he let her drop down. The man went after that, with the trousers still knotted around his head.

He leaned over the edge. 'Are you down there?' he called softly.

Maria's voice came back: 'Is that you?'

'I've got a car and some ropes. The ladder's got to be a last resort. You're going to have to do most of the work.'

*

They washed, changed their clothes and sat down to a meal. The children were sleeping so soundly that he was sure his guess was right: they'd been given something to keep them quiet. In the morning he'd give them another kind of sedative: he'd tell them a story. This time the fiction would be about their mother and a strange, bad man and – unlike the tales of kings and princesses – no one would ask to hear it a second time.

Maria had a story, too. She said right at the beginning – that first night – that she was going to tell him all the information he'd ever want to know about her; he'd never have to question her again and he shouldn't try to interrupt, otherwise she wouldn't be able to get through to the end. In the half-dark before dawn she spoke in a hoarse whisper so hurried that he couldn't have stopped her anyway.

She was at school when the town she lived in had been caught in a daylight attack. Her first thought was to find her sister. Her sister was in one of the upper grades composed entirely of girls because the boys had been taken into combat.

She'd fled from her classroom only to encounter soldiers raising their guns at her. Grenades came through the windows. One of her friends, standing next to her, was shot in the face and fell to the floor without making a sound, the back of her head blown out against the wall. There was panic in all the corridors. Soon everyone was screaming and pushing. She ran into the gymnasium, where she climbed up an exercise rope that hung from one of the beams, then pulled the rope up after her and hid in the rafters. When the rest of the school took refuge in the gym, followed by the soldiers, she was perfectly placed to see the massacre that followed and, after she turned her head away, to hear it. That was what she said she kept remembering – not anything she'd seen, but what she'd heard: all the different sounds of fear and pain and the laughter: the sound of men laughing at suffering. Her position wasn't so safe a few hours later when the retreating troops set fire to the building. And when she got out alive – even without injury – and reached home, all her mother had had to say to her was, 'Where's your sister?' Much later, at the height of an argument about Maria's racketeer boyfriend, her mother had shouted, 'If only you'd been the one to die and not your sister. Why couldn't it have been you?' That was the reason, Maria said, why she'd left home.

He still thought that once they'd concocted a good story, he should have gone straight to the house where the two children lived: to install Anna there, drive the parents back to the quarry and throw them in. When the girl and boy woke in the morning, Anna could have told them that the fairies had come to take the parents away and that they'd left her in their place. But Anna had said no and anyway, by the time they'd managed to get her to the top of the rock face, all three of them were at the end of their strength.

He'd wanted to go after Maria's lover, too – the man who had seduced her, taken her out on wild sprees with his black-market friends, indirectly caused her family to disown her and – undoubtedly – had been planning to turn her into a whore: he'd driven her out to the quarry at night; she knew what it was but he'd told her that the place represented a part of their country's history that no one was ever going to record, so she ought to see it. It shouldn't upset her: the people down there deserved to be there; they had all transgressed in some way. Maria had found herself having to live up to her reputation – based on her looks – for being tempestuous as well as sensual. She'd said: sure, she wasn't scared. He'd parked the car near the edge, pulled her out, made her look over and had asked her if she could see the rats. And then he'd said: what the hell had she wanted to go and get herself pregnant for? What use was she going to be to him now, and anyway didn't she know he was married? Of course he had a wife; everybody did. You got married the first time so she'd say yes and all the other times afterwards, you just promised it. Why didn't she know that? Everybody else knew. And now he'd had all the trouble of breaking her in without getting his money's worth because she was just a dumb farm girl after all.

He'd slapped her. She'd taken a step back. He'd called her obscene names. He'd hit her again, this time on the other side of her face, and then advanced on her. As she took the next step back, she turned to see how close to the edge she was and while she was still trying to protect herself rather than thinking of attacking him, he made a rush at her and pushed her quickly several times, until she went over.

The moment when she realized that she was falling – she wouldn't describe it except to say that it was worse than the moment when she knew that she'd never get out. From above her he'd shouted, 'And you can stay there.'

It would have been simple to find the man. Maria could remain unseen and point him out; it would be easy to kill him.

'Let's see if he comes around saying it was all a joke,' she said. 'Then I'll kill him myself. But those people he runs around with are pretty rough. They'll probably take care of him.'

'Unless they come after me.'

'No. I don't think we'll have to worry about that. As far as they're concerned, there isn't any connection. And he'll probably think he was so drunk that he dreamt it.'

After a few days went by, it was too late: he no longer had the readiness, nor the high sense of righteousness, to take revenge. He wanted peace; and to begin life again, with Maria. She wasn't in love with him but that was something he didn't have to think about at the moment. He loved. And that was enough. As long as Anna stayed with them, Maria would probably be satisfied. Anna had replaced mother and sister; he was a substitute for the lover and possibly also the father.

As it turned out, they couldn't find anyone who had seen Maria's lover since the night he'd been out at the quarry with her. But they decided that if any questions came up, Anna would say she'd heard a rumor that the man had killed an aid worker and the married woman he was sleeping with: because the two men were in some kind of smuggling racket together and the woman was sleeping with them both and didn't know which one was the father of her unborn child.

Their other enemies were in plain view. One day Anna and Maria went shopping in town while the younger children were being looked after in a nursery group. The older ones were away at the first educational classes they'd seen since the evacuation: a kind of school that had just been started up by a group of mothers and grandmothers, one of whom – before her retirement – had been a teacher of mathematics.

Maria was rummaging through bins of patched and worn children's clothing when Anna saw one of her tormentors: the mother from the family with whom she'd been housed. The woman was reaching into a pile of clothes. 'Still grabbing,' Anna said. The woman didn't react at first, but after a moment she looked up.

Maria later perfected an imitation of the woman's horrified understanding and recoil. When she and Anna recounted the story of the meeting, Maria would act it out while Anna described it, declaring solemnly, 'She just stood there, as if turned to stone.'

Anna said to the woman, 'We'll call in to see the children in a few days. I'm still very fond of them. And I'll pick up my refugee rations, of course. I won't put you to the trouble of giving me a roof over my head, even if it is your duty. We'll speak to the authorities and see what we can do about having me transferred to the family I'm with now. I'm not vindictive.' The woman closed her eyes with relief and possibly from faintness. Anna continued in an ordinary tone of voice, saying, 'On the other hand, you're going to have to pay my medical bills. I've had quite a lot of trouble with my leg after the fall I had. You owe me that. And you know how long I'm going to have to wait to find a doctor. So maybe you'd better leave those clothes alone. You aren't going to be able to afford them.' The woman nodded slowly and moved away, putting out a hand to support herself against the wall as she left.

'It was wonderful,' Maria told him. But Anna said, 'As soon as they pay up for the doctor, that's the end. I don't want them to get so scared that they try it again. I think if they ever see the chance, they'll move.'

Maria disagreed. 'I don't see why. It's their word against yours. I wouldn't.' She turned to him and asked, 'Would you?'

'No,' he said. 'This is home.'

One night he went out into the orchard and dug a false grave and filled it in again. Every time he pushed the blade of the shovel into the ground he thought what bad luck it was that after climbing free from the quarry he'd been too used up to think straight; because, if he'd been fully alert, he'd have buried his wife instead of taking her in the car. That way, they'd have had a body. As it was, he'd have to pretend – if anyone wanted to investigate – that he couldn't remember exactly which spot he'd chosen, that he'd done the grave-digging at night in order to keep the children from being upset and he was as mystified as anyone else to find that what certainly looked like the place now turned out to be wrong. The authorities weren't going to start digging up the entire orchard. However, if by some extraordinary chance they did, he'd be forced to admit in the end that he'd lied. But that wasn't so serious. Anyone would understand that he'd want to tell a lie: to keep drawing the rations. He'd say that there wasn't any corpse – the old battle-ax had fooled them all: she'd risen from her bed and gone off with one of the aid workers who had claimed that he could house her someplace closer to where she used to live.

Nevertheless, he kept digging. And soon afterwards he went to town and reported the death of the old woman. No one did anything except put the information on paper. He was told that he was now eligible to receive another refugee.

'We buried her in the orchard,' he began to explain.

'Yes, yes,' the official said. 'No possessions?'

'I'm afraid we had to burn the nightdress. It was too –'

'Of course. They have her age down here as "from eighty-five to a hundred". It's a miracle that she lasted so long.'

'We already have a new refugee,' he said. 'She had some trouble with the family she was with. I can give you their name. They've agreed to let you transfer her. We've been taking care of her for a few weeks, but we need the extra rations.'

'I'll see what I can do,' the official told him.

*

The new school was a success. Within days everyone had heard about it. It attracted more pupils every week and, luckily, a few extra teachers too.

The next bit of good luck turned up when a huge shipment of flour, sugar and salt came through legally and was distributed by the authorities.

Some of the old occupations came back, even if not as they had been practiced before the fighting. So few professionals survived anywhere that amateurs were considered better than nothing: as long as they did the work, who cared? Two girls, whose father had been a plumber, set themselves up in business using the knowledge he'd passed on to them and the tools and material he'd left behind. Even children joined the scramble for employment. A boy who had inherited his uncle's optical equipment – and had discovered all of it, unbroken, behind a trick panel in the cellar – was now reading the medical books he'd been left. He planned to begin work as soon as he had some answers to the letters he'd sent out.

'But that's silly,' Anna commented. 'You need lenses and somebody's got to grind them. That's specialized work. They're made in factories, in dust-free conditions. That belongs to another world. That's all over now. I suppose you have to admire his initiative.'

'And his optimism,' Maria said. 'He'll probably be just the right age to be drafted when the next wave of fighting begins.'

'Don't even say it. Everybody's talking about it again.'

'They're always talking about it,' he said. 'You can't get a newspaper unless you know the right people and have the right stuff to trade, but if you do, you can read any publication you like from other countries. The only trouble is: what they print about us won't do you any good because they don't know what's going on here any more than we do.'

Local news traveled – as usual – by the grapevine, which was extremely effective, although the information relayed was occasionally completely unfounded. If you wanted customers, or were looking for a particular thing you needed for your work, the best way to get results was still to put out the word among friends, neighbors, acquaintances and strangers. A woman on the other side of town had done just that after she'd had a dream that she could cure her rheumatism by dancing. She'd talked an official into lending her a hall and some chairs and then she'd simply accosted people on the street to let them know that she was in business. One of the first men to turn up became her second-in-command by offering to bring his accordion and to supply the music. The woman rapidly collected a dedicated group of enthusiasts who were willing to pay. Her dream hadn't mentioned remuneration; that was a natural development and a pleasant surprise. Even more unexpected was the fact that after she'd molded her idea into a reality and had given it the name of 'The Tuesday and Thursday Tango Tea', she was besieged by racketeers' girlfriends who had time on their hands and wanted to pick up some refinement. Within a few weeks she'd become one of the luminaries of what – temporarily, at least – passed for society in their part of the world. It wasn't long before the root tea and watery soup grew to resemble real tea and alcohol. To the accordionist's dismay, the music also improved when the woman entered into a contract with a professional band that traveled from town to town all week long. They played on Thursdays, which became the popular day and helped to divide the clientele into rich and poor as well as dubious or respectable. Most dancers became Tuesday people or Thursday people. After a while no one went on both nights, except the woman who had thought the thing up and who, despite a life formerly marked by bouts of invalidism, managed to remain at the helm.

Before the school began, there had been a local mail service run as a cooperative effort by children. Each child had had to complete a certain number of hours stamping and sorting and out on the rounds. An exception had been made for one of the founder members who was born lame and another two who had been injured in infancy by enemy action. The school cut into the children's working time but added to the number of recruits. Since paper was scarce, their next project was going to be a paper factory and a shop where old paper could be exchanged for credits. That was for the future, as were most other similar ideas. But the town was getting organized, pulling the outlying regions into its returning life. A neighboring district had set up hospital facilities that were said to include emergency transportation to the nearest big city; no one had investigated the claim yet, as there was a strict list of conditions that had to be met by patients: all cases not considered critical were refused. However, the possibility was there and that meant hope for development: more medicine, equipment, doctors and nurses.

Some of the schemes people dreamt up were crazy, some illegal and some – often both crazy and illegal – worked, like the convoluted system of barter and banking started up by an old man who said he was ninety but was probably in his seventies and who, after a few days' trading, became known as Major Money.

It seemed for a while as if life might continue along its peaceful course: getting back to normal and also heading towards a future of unbroken peace. But just as things were improving, the winter brought hardship again. No matter how happy they were, it was impossible to forget the cold and hunger. A series of fevers and children's diseases ran through the entire sector. There were deaths as well as children who survived with damaged hearing, eyesight and lungs. Food was scarce and once more it was a long winter.

The next time the aid workers turned up, they brought two nine-year-old children: a twin brother and sister, who were almost completely silent for a few days. They didn't even trust the other children, preferring Anna's company. But they helped with any work that had to be done. After a while, slowly, they joined in the conversation. Soon they were enrolled in the school and sharing sentry duty on the first planting in the garden.

'They're nice kids,' Anna told him. 'I think they're going to be fine as long as nobody asks them any stupid questions, like, "Where are your parents?"'

The days were warmer, longer, lighter. It was nearly spring.

With the good weather came better food and more of it. One or two luxuries turned up as a result of haggling at the weekly market. It began to seem as if, for that year at least, they could be leaving the bad days behind. There was work and building material. He'd even been able to get hold of some cans of paint that hadn't dried out.

And then, after so many years, the fair came back to town. Everyone took its appearance as a sign that someone was sure about an eventual peaceful settlement to the hostilities. The traveling musicians had been the first professional entertainment to return to the region, but they hadn't been the real thing: they could pick up their instruments and run if they had to. A whole fairground was different; you needed tents and ladders, transport trucks and food for the animals.

Every day his children told him news of the marvels to be seen at the fair. He heard the same descriptions repeated by adults in town: that there was a big tent with a cage full of animals and even room for a trapeze act as well as tightrope walkers. The animals weren't the wonderful striped, spotted or maned big cats; they were the more ordinary bears and seals, but the bears at any rate were dangerous, so the children could derive some pleasure from them. One of the bears in particular was gigantic. It was the only one kept muzzled and chained. Word of its size and fierceness spread through the neighborhood before anyone had seen it.

Everybody wanted to go to the fair. It was traveling around the country, which meant that it would set down near them only for a short while. It would be the big treat of the year. Of course he'd have to take everyone in the house – the whole crowd of them.

He produced his wallet and counted out bills. A few of the children were so impatient that they danced up and down in front of him. He paid the money to the woman in the ticket booth. She handed him a long ribbon of paper, still unbroken. He passed it to Anna, who began to tear the single strip into separate pieces, giving a ticket to each child. 'Remember now,' she told them, 'don't get lost. Come back here just inside the gate when the whistle blows and don't speak to strangers, even if they tell you they're from school or the district hospital or the police.'

'Especially not if they tell you something like that,' he said. 'If they try to get you to go with them for any reason at all, you just run away. And if they grab you: kick, bite, and yell as loud as you can.'

The children nodded. They remembered what had happened to their mother: a man had come to their house and he'd made her say that their father had walked out on them, taking the old woman with him for the sake of the aid money. The real truth was that the man had killed the old woman and burned her in the stove. Then he'd beaten up their mother so badly that her face was covered with bandages; he'd said that their father had done it, but they didn't believe that. Their mother had given them a hot drink and put them to bed. She'd told them that everything would be all right in the morning. And that was true, because in the morning their father was back. The man had tried to kill him and then he'd taken their mother away as a prisoner, probably to a different country so that she could never return. But their father was going to bring them up himself, with the help of Anna and her daughter, Maria, so at least they'd have somebody to look after them: somebody who loved them. And they were never to tell anybody about that other man killing the old woman. They should say that she died of old age and they'd buried her in the orchard; because if they didn't, the aid people weren't going to give them their food allowance and the authorities might even accuse their father of getting rid of her himself.

Maria counted out the spending money for each child. 'If you buy any food,' she said, 'try not to eat it too fast. And be careful of that ride over there – the one that goes up and down and tilts while it spins. It makes you feel horrible. I remember that one from my first trip to the fair. You feel awful for days.'

Anna said, 'I'll take the little ones to see the baby animals.' The smaller children shouted: yes, baby animals.

'What are the baby animals?' he asked.

Anna shrugged. 'Lambs, piglets, baby chicks.'

'Yum-yum,' Maria whispered.

He laughed. Maybe that was what had happened to the tigers.

'Remember, everybody,' Anna repeated. 'When you hear the whistle.' The children ran, breaking into groups before they were out of sight.

'They'll all be sick this evening,' he predicted.

'Sick, but happy. And with nice memories. We'll see you later.' Anna moved away, the three smaller children clinging to her.

'Isn't she wonderful?' Maria said. 'If only my mother had been like that. God, it's strange. All the best things in my life happened within twenty-four hours of being shoved into the pit of hell. What a comedy.'

'Happy endings. That's what I like. To survive and to live well, knowing that you've deserved it.'

They set off hand in hand to investigate the shows. He looked around at the other parents and their children, all of them trying, and failing, to do simple tricks that had once been so easy for him:

throwing a hoop over a wooden stake, hitting a moving toy bird with a ball, shooting down a target. He still had a good eye, but that wasn't enough.

Maria said, 'I was always told those places were rigged: the stake is angled away from you and it's just a little too big for the hoop to fit it. And the ducks over there are on a supporting piece that never moves unless you complain, and then they flip a switch that releases the spring and they show you that you can knock the thing over easily: you're just missing it every time.'

'I guess so. They get away with what they can. On some of these things they probably have a way of letting a few people win, so the others can see it.'

'Their friends and relatives.'

'But if you don't win at one, you try the next. Or you can ride on one of the cars, or have your future told.'

'Oh. Do you want to do that?'

'Not for anything. It's hard enough dealing with the past and the present. Come on.'

They saw Anna a long way ahead. She was kneeling in the middle of her bevy of children and using a handkerchief to take a speck of dirt out of a child's eye.

He looked up at the big wheel and at the smaller, slower merry-go-round with its painted horses. 'How about that?' he suggested. 'It wouldn't be too fast.'

'No, thanks. I seem to remember that it starts slow and speeds up. And then it's too late to jump off.'

'All right. Where to?'

'How about the House of Horrors? That's pretty tame.'

'The House of Horrors. Definitely. Unless you don't think it's a good idea.'

She put a hand on her belly, and said, 'If this child can thrive on everything it's been through already, I don't think a haunted house or two is going to hurt it.'

They couldn't find the House of Horrors. They trailed around the stands and cages, wondering what they could do with their time until the whistle blew to mark the hour. They passed the seals and the bears, the table where there was a glass jar full of pebbles whose number could be guessed. Maria wanted to sit down. 'Here,' she said.

They entered a tent inscribed with the name *Professor Miracolo*. The show was about to begin. There wasn't time to bother with tickets; as soon as he'd paid at the desk, they were waved ahead into a small, semi-circular theater already crowded with other customers. They were barely in their seats when the side lights dimmed and the stage was flooded by a dazzling glare from above.

Two men stepped into the field of brightness. One told the members of the audience what they were going to see: 'The world's greatest . . . the most renowned . . . expert in the arts of contortion . . . the foremost practitioner of magic transformations learned through years of study in the fabled schools of the mystic East . . . The one and only Professor Miracolo will now perform his internationally celebrated repertoire of astounding magical acts, concluding with the incredible, supernatural finger-balancing exercise, a feat so hazardous that only the Professor himself has been able to master it.'

They watched the Professor – who was dressed in a top hat and tails – remove his hat and go through the colored ribbon trick, the flags and the rabbit. Further well-known mystifications called for audience participation: children were chosen from the crowd to cut a piece of paper with scissors that had been functioning perfectly well for the Professor but, as soon as he handed them over, wouldn't open for the child. Much laughter ensued at the expense of the young volunteers, who were utterly confounded by the business. 'That's so mean,' Maria murmured. 'It's just a knob he flicks to the side every time he takes the scissors back to look at them. It locks the blades, like a safety catch.' She applauded loudly as a child stepped back and rejoined its parents.

Professor Miracolo set up a display that included four candles. He was helped by a woman in her forties who was dressed in a spangled costume with a skirt like a dancer's tutu. Her hair was piled up in a glistening mound, her shoes were high-heeled gold sandals. As she retired behind the curtains with the announcer, the Professor lit the candles by pointing a wand at them, one by one.

Maria turned her face away at the sight of the flames. She looked for the way out. He pulled her closer and ran his hand over her hair.

Professor Miracolo waved his wand again. The row of lights sank from sight. He repeated the action and they all came back. He singled out the candle at the end, the one at the beginning. It was easy to see that the flames were live fire; how did he do it? The audience applauded, even Maria.

For the last, the culminating show of skill, the barker rolled a large, heavy-looking ball into the spotlight. He told everyone that this magical demonstration was the best of all, saved to the last, and only the Professor – the highest genius in the world of magic – could carry out this extraordinary proof of mind over matter.

Professor Miracolo emerged from between the dark curtains. He approached the ball, which reached above his knees. He bent over it, put his hands on it and then lifted himself up into a handstand. An outbreak of clapping stopped as he began to take one hand away. There was silence while everyone watched. He brought back the hand, placed it so that only one finger touched the ball and – in a move that looked both naturally easy and strangely untrue – put all his weight on that one finger and took away the other hand. He was balancing upside-down on top of a round rubber ball and using only a single finger of one hand. The audience was so astonished that for a while everyone simply sat and looked. Then people began to realize that no matter how impossible it seemed, the trick was worth a show of appreciation. They went wild.

At the height of the cheering and stamping, the lights blinked out and came back almost immediately. The ball had disappeared and the Professor was revealed standing between the announcer and the female assistant. All three of them bowed.

They came out into the sunlight and he repeated what he'd already said several times: 'It's impossible.'

'I don't understand it, either,' Maria said, 'but I had it explained to me once. Apparently you can give the illusion of practically anything if you cut off the real thing by a reflection from a mirror.'

'But he was right in front of us.'

'I know. It's amazing.'

'I really liked that,' he said. 'If I were ten years old, it would drive me crazy, but I think I've reached just the perfect age for magic.'

'Look,' she said. 'The House of Horrors. We were going in the wrong direction.'

'And some of our bunch coming out of it.' He whistled. The children turned their heads. He called to them. They came running to tell him about their adventures. Two of the girls admitted that they'd been scared in the House of Horrors but the two older boys said it was nothing – just kid stuff: not a single good thing; you could see the wires everywhere, like a puppet show.

One of the younger boys didn't say anything. He stayed behind when the others went on to the next entertainment.

'Did you see Professor Miracolo?' Maria asked him.

'Oh, that was the best.' He flushed with eagerness to talk about the magic. They walked together to the entrance of the House of Horrors. Another thing he'd liked, he told them, was the princess in the thimble, who could dance to the music of a guitar even though she was so tiny that you had to look at her through a magnifying glass.

'You didn't like the haunted house?' she said.

'Not as much. Everybody was screaming and it was dark.'

'Want to try it again?' he asked. 'You can come with us. If you've already been through once, you'll remember when things are going to jump out, so you'll know what to expect. And you can tell us about the really bad ones ahead of time. I don't want Maria to be upset.'

The boy nodded. It was impossible to tell whether he was reluctant or overjoyed, but the answer came a few minutes later, after they'd taken their seats in the open carriage – the boy behind and he and Maria in front. His son's voice filled with confidence as he began his commentary.

I've got a rival, he thought. *The boy's hardly more than a child and he's fallen in love with his father's woman.*

The track was full of curves, sudden twists and bumps. As they creaked around the corner, ghosts wavered into their faces from the sides of the tunnel. All around them people burst into shouts and laughter.

'There's a very noisy skeleton next,' the boy informed them.

He was glad of the warning. The sound took him back to the days when he was in uniform. With almost the same boom and crunch, followed by a loud crack, a skeleton shot towards them, seeming at the last moment to fly over their heads. Shortly afterwards a shoal of smaller skeletons danced in a moving archway, giggling and gibbering above and beside the train; one of them had part of a skeletal arm in its mouth, with blood dripping down the sides of its bony jaws and blood smeared across the captive hand.

He laughed, but his son didn't. *Out of consideration for me. Because of my lost hand. But one hand is like another once it's bare of flesh; one corpse is like the others when it's turned to bones.*

Every day he had to resist the urge to go out to the quarry. The temptation was almost unbearable, but he knew that that was the way people wrecked their lives: by picking at the details, over and over again, trying to cover their tracks and get everything right. It was better, even if you'd made mistakes, to leave it and not go back – to let the world move on. Time would overtake the past.

He had to keep repeating the good advice he'd decided to abide by: not to go back there for at least a year and not to admit anything, ever. He'd report the disappearance after it was too late to tell one person from another; and then they'd have the incident officially closed. His wife had run off with an aid worker: that was all, unless somebody went down there and started to identify people, in which case it would appear that the man had probably tried to kill her but in the act of pushing her into the quarry, he'd fallen in too. Or maybe her assailant had succeeded in killing her and somebody from his gang of crooks had pushed him over the side later; the state of his head could be attributed to that, or even to something done to him by other people down there in the pit. That was as much as anyone would be able to guess.

The train ran through cackling monsters, witches, cauldrons of boiling oil and bright, crawling things that appeared to be falling from the tunnel roof and landing all over the passengers: those were the most effective of all. Everyone tried frantically to brush the things off.

The boy crowed with delight. He said, 'There isn't anything there. It's like pictures. They don't stay there when you're in the light.'

Laughter overcame the sounds of distress. What had they been worried about? Maria too laughed heartily, secure against the arm he held around her. As the horrors came faster and with an ever greater excess of grotesque detail, the enjoyment increased. Everybody loved the ride, even the small children who had been brought in with parents. He remembered that his initial acquaintance with the place had been different, but it seemed to him that what made the difference was probably his own subsequent experience rather than any of the elaborate props and tricks of lighting added by the owners. Some of the dusty and faded monsters that worked on wheels or springs might have been the very same ones he'd met years ago. Yet they still had an effect on their audience. And on him. He was charmed. At the same time he was aware of how strange it was that – having lived through so many horrors – anyone should want to subject himself to this gallery of artificial terror. Was it a kind of protection, like a prophylactic medicine? The answer wasn't that no one knew the difference between the true and the false; they knew. But they still needed magic. The delights of illusion were similar to the pleasure of imagining a thing true when you knew that it couldn't be, or hoping for a marvelous event when you didn't really think it could happen. The workings of memory too, like the magician's sleight of hand, made you believe. You couldn't go on living if you didn't believe that through the power of heart and mind you could keep whatever you lost: that the part of you that was good could transform and outlast even the chaos of war – that there could still be love and that love didn't die.

They had to shade their eyes against the light when they came out. Maria said, 'That was fun. That was really nice.'

He caught sight of Anna up by the gates. 'See where Anna is?' he said to his son. 'Go tell her to stay there till we catch up.' The boy ran off. Maria called after him, 'Thanks for the guided tour.'

'That kid is wildly in love with you,' he said.

'I hope so. In my condition I can use all the encouragement I can get.'

He squeezed her to him and she turned up a smiling face. She breathed in deeply and then let the air out in a long sigh. 'This is what I'm going to tell my grandchildren about,' she said. 'Days like today.'

Acknowledgements

'Blessed Art Thou' was first published in Great Britain in *Three of a Kind* (Faber, 1985).

'Friends in the Country' and 'In the Act' were first published in Great Britain in *The End of Tragedy* (Faber, 1987).

'Something to Write Home About' was first published in Great Britain in *The Man Who Was Left Behind and Other Stories* (Faber, 1974).

'Theft' was first published in Great Britain by Faber in 1970.

'Inheritance' was first published in Great Britain in *The Pearlkillers* (Faber, 1986).

'I See a Long Journey' was first published in Great Britain in *Three of a Kind* (Faber, 1985).

'No Love Lost' was first published in Great Britain in *Days Like Today* (Faber, 2002).

Also by Rachel Ingalls

Mrs Caliban

With a new foreword by Irenosen Okojie in Faber Editions

Dorothy is a grieving housewife in the Californian suburbs. One day, she is doing chores when she hears strange voices on the radio announcing that a green-skinned sea monster has escaped from the Institute for Oceanographic Research – but little does she expect him to arrive in her kitchen. Vegetarian, sexually magnetic and excellent at housework, Larry the frogman is a revelation – and their passionate affair takes them on a journey beyond their wildest dreams . . .

'Still outpaces, out-weirds and out-romances anything today.' **Marlon James**

'Genius . . . A broadcast from a stranger and more dazzling dimension.' **Patricia Lockwood**

'So curiously right, so romantically obverse, that it creates its own terrible, brilliant reality.' **Sarah Hall**

'A feminist masterpiece: tender, erotic, singular.' **Carmen Maria Machado**

'Like *Revolutionary Road* written by Franz Kafka . . . Exquisite.' *The Times*

faber